15p

THE NINTH EARL

The Works of Jeffery Farnol:

THE NINTH EARL

by

JEFFERY FARNOL

SAMPSON LOW

25 Gilbert Street London W1

First published 1950

To

THE BEST AND TRUEST

OF FRIENDS

DAVID AND ANN

MADE AND PRINTED IN GREAT BRITAIN BY PURNELL AND SONS, LTD
PAULTON SOMERSET AND LONDON

CONTENTS

CONTENTS

The Ninth Earl

CHAPTER I

Concerning bones

" A SKELETON ? " said George, staring into the little lawyer's rubicund visage. " A skeleton—in a cupboard, sir ? "

Mr. John Jackman, plumpish, middle-aged, extremely precise as to person and demeanour, extracted a pinch of snuff from the large silver box on the desk before him, inhaled it with two discreet snorts, dusted himself daintily with snowy handkerchief and replied :

" Precisely ! In a cupboard ! A skeleton."

" Astounding ! " exclaimed George.

" Not at all, m' dear boy. For, as you are so very well aware, the family of Vane-Wynter is old as the Castle itself, and all old families have skeletons in cupboards, and this family is so extremely ancient there may be half a dozen other skeletons waiting to be found."

" Though not dry bones, surely, sir ! "

" Hum ! " quoth Mr. Jackman, and his rosy face assumed that expression of guileless innocence which divers human sharks had found so very deceptive ere now. " There are certain pages of the Vane-Wynter history reaching back to the bad old days that show unseemly blotches here and there."

" And when, sir, pray how was this gruesome discovery made ? "

" By act of God, in the late storm, George. A thunderbolt toppled down a chimney-stack which in its fall disclosed our skeleton-in-cupboard, which last, to be precise, was one of those secret hiding-places called a priest's-hole. But surely you and your aunt, living so near, must have heard and seen ? "

" We did both, sir, as did everyone in the village, though nobody heard tell of any skeleton."

" Naturally, for, as the Earl's steward, I forbade any mention of it until I had sent word to his lordship and notified the legal authorities."

" It's fortunate," said George, " that the family is never in residence at the Castle.

" Very ! " said Mr. Jackman " You have never yet seen the Earl, eh, George ? "

" Never, sir."

" Which is not surprising, since he is never at Raven-hurst these many years. So next time I visit him in London you will go with me, for meet his lordship you must."

" Must, sir ? "

" Must, George ! For—d'ye see, m' dear fellow—the years have proved my faith in you justified ; the hopes I had of you so completely realised that, though you are somewhat young, I have decided to take you into partner-ship. The firm henceforth shall be Jackman, Son, and Bell."

" Sir—sir——" gasped George, starting up from his chair. " You—I—indeed you—overwhelm me ! Sir—— Oh, Mr. Jackman, how can I thank you—what can I say——? "

" Not a word ! Deeds, George, deeds, not written but acted. My only regret is that your long-dead parents— grand folk as I remember them—are not alive to rejoice for their son's well-merited success."

" Yes—yes ! " said George, his grey eyes shining. " Would indeed they were ! "

" However," said Mr. Jackman, pausing in the act of snuffing, " if there is a heaven—mind, I say ' if ', George, there being not a jot or tittle of evidence sufficiently convincing to the legal mind that any such place truly exists—yet if it does, then they who so gloriously died are there alive in glory for evermore and will doubtless be aware of—Jackman, Son, and Bell."

" Sir," said George, his voice unwontedly gruff and shaken, " though they died too long ago for me to remember, I—thank God—have Aunt Isabel, and for her sake and my own I—I'm trying to thank you for your unfailing goodness to me, my schooling—college— university. Oh, sir, when I think of your kindness and measureless generosity I can only wonder——"

" George, as a boy I—loved your mother, and today I do not exactly hate Isabel, this noble aunt of yours ! Ah, well, well—sentiment is out of place in a lawyer's office, so pray sit down, partner, and let us to business. And egad, our present most pressing business is Jasper Shrig, chief of the Bow Street Office, who should be here shortly to report on this skeleton. You have met Shrig, I think ? "

" Once, sir."

" Well, let me tell you he's a tremendous fellow, not so much in size but in everything else ! Bold as a lion, guileful as a serpent, relentless as a bloodhound, though none would believe it from his looks. What did you think of him, for instance ? "

" Frankly, sir, he struck me as a dull, clumsy fellow."

" Aha ! " exclaimed Mr. Jackman, chuckling. " And by George, George, no one can seem more so ! Only wait until you see more of him, only wait—no, you won't have to, for I believe he is here ! Come in ! " he cried to a gentle tap upon the door, whereupon Mr. Beeby, the grey-haired head clerk, entered—to bow and announce :

" Mr. Jasper Shrig, of Bow Street, sir."

CHAPTER II

In which the ubiquitous Mr. Shrig reports

A SHORTISH, powerfully built man was this famous officer, very neat as to person, from snowy shirt-frill to the very soles of his top-boots. The eight buttons upon his trim, blue coat glittered, the six upon his red waistcoat twinkled, his well-polished boots gleamed ; and yet the brightest things about him were his eyes, that seemed to take in Mr. Jackman, George and the room in as many roving glances as he stood, hat in one fist, in the other a formidable knobbed stick with which he touched an eyebrow in salutation, saying :

" Your servant, gen'lemen ! "

Mr. Jackman, having set forth decanter and glasses, greeted him like an old friend :

" Glad to see you again, Shrig. How are you ? "

" Hearty, sir, I thankee."

" This is my young partner, Mr. Bell, whom I think you've met."

" Honoured, sir," quoth Mr. Shrig, bobbing that round head of his.

" Well now," said the little lawyer as they sat all three glass in hand, " wet your whistle, Shrig ; keep it moist, and let us hear your report concerning this ghastly discovery at Ravenhurst Castle."

Mr. Shrig tasted his wine, beamed at it, sipped it, sighed and spoke :

" Mr. Jackman, sir, and partner, fresh corpses, parties recently de-funct being wictims o' the Deed or Capital Act, should ought, and generally do, have summat to tell as to the how, when and—sometimes—the oo of it—if properly ob-served. But this here long-departed party being little more than rags and bones by reason o' rats,

4

mice and Old Father Time, is dumb as any eyester, or—werry nearly."

"Which," said Mr. Jackson, refilling the glasses, "which is only to be expected, under the circumstances."

"Ar!" sighed Mr. Shrig. "The party, de-funct, must ha' been laying there so werry patient, vaiting to be found, say thirty, say forty year and more. But, spite o' time and rats and mice aforesaid, this here relic o' poor humanity has found a woice, has spoke to me, werry faint and feeble, yet strong enough to tell me certain fax as I've dooly wrote into my little reader."

Here Mr. Shrig unbuttoned his trim coat and drew from its inner recesses a somewhat battered notebook, and, opening this at a certain page, continued:

"From obserwation personal—Fact number vun: long departed party a traveller nooly arrived. Evidence—boots and spurs. Fact number two: twelve silver coat-buttons. Dee-duckshon—long departed party a person o' condition. Fact number three: no money, no joolry, not so much as a signet ring. No papers, not a scrap. Dee-duckshon—same having been removed by party or parties unknown——"

"Good God!" exclaimed Mr. Jackman. "Are you suggesting murder, Shrig?"

"Sir, I am reporting fax and the dee-duckshons drawed therefrom."

"But this—this unfortunate individual may have been the victim of some accident, or have died by his own act, Shrig."

"Accident, sir—p'raps. By his own act—no, sir and partner, cer-tainly not!"

"Why so sure of this, Shrig?"

"Sir, on or near deceased was never a veapon, not so much as a penknife."

"Still, this is no proof he was murdered."

"Hows'ever, sir and partner, on ree-moving deceased, bit by bit, and using all doo care, I ob-served a stain werry large and therefore plain, as there could be no mistaking."

" Ah ! " sighed Mr. Jackman, almost whispering. " Blood ? "

" That i-denticle, sir. Deceased had bled werry copious indeed ! Hence I dee-dooced same as wictim of the Capital Act, Mr. Jackman, sir and partner."

" Now this," said the little lawyer in voice troubled as his look, " this is perfectly shocking, and horridly mysterious ! "

" Ar ! " nodded Mr. Shrig, and, glancing at George : " What says your respected partner ? "

" Well," answered George, speaking for the first time, " I would know who could possibly benefit by such crime."

" Eggs-actly ! " exclaimed Mr. Shrig, closing his note-book with a snap. " Know that, and this here mystery—ain't ! And here, sirs, for your inspection, are the silver buttons aforementioned." And from capacious side-pocket he produced a knotted bandanna handkerchief, which he untied, saying as he did so :

" They're werry black and tarnished, vich is only to be expected seeing as they've been bled on so copious. Take a peep at 'em, sirs."

Mr. Jackman did so, but very much askance.

" Yes," said he, shrinking back in his chair, " I perceive they are silver."

" And deeply engraved ! " said George, peering closer. " A monogram—I think. But they are in such a state that I cannot make out the letters——"

" Then, sir," said Mr. Shrig, " take a peep at this here ! " and from pocket of his red waistcoat he drew another button that gleamed and glittered in the afternoon sun-shine. " Now, sir, having cleaned same for your better in-spection, how about it, gen'lemen ? "

With this shining button on his open palm, George held it towards Mr. Jackman, and together they examined it.

" Yes, George, by George—you're right ! It is a monogram ! See, here is a ' P ' and two ' X's '—which don't make sense and can't be. Wait though—yes, by heaven! Look, George; I'll trace it with this pencil—watch now."

So, wondering, George looked, and what he saw was this:

But what Mr. Jackman's pencil traced was this:

"There! D'you see it, George, d'ye see it? P V W, Philip Vane-Wynter—the seventh Earl—who died in America! Shrig, in heaven's name—what is the meaning of this?"

"Mr. Jackman, sir, this you are agoing to tell me—I hope. F'instance, this seventh Earl, this here Philip Vane-Wynter, sir, I'll ax you to say all as you know concerning same."

"Which is very little, I'm afraid. I know that he died young, somewhere in America."

"Married or single, sir?"

"He married an American lady, but they both died young."

"Did you know him personal, sir, or ever see him."

"I may have done, for he was often here, in this very room, to consult with my father, who, besides being his lawyer and man of business, was also his valued friend, but I was a child then and too young to remember."

"Hows'ever," sighed Mr. Shrig, "can you inform me what year he died?"

"Certainly I can. George, pray bring me the Wynter deed-box, the one marked A. Thankee! Now, let's see and make sure."

So saying, Mr. Jackman, opening this box, took thence divers papers and packets neatly docketed and tied with red tape. Selecting one of these, he spread the sheet on the desk before him and read:

"'In re Philip, George, seventh Earl of Ravenhurst, et cetera, was born at the Castle of Ravenhurst January eleven, seventeen hundred and thirty-six. Inherited the title, et cetera, March nine, seventeen fifty-five. Sailed to America seventeen fifty-seven. Married Samantha, Dorothy Mallory, seventeen fifty-eight. Killed with his wife in an Indian Massacre, seventeen hundred and sixty. So ended young Philip, George, seventh Earl.'"

"Har!" murmured Mr. Shrig. "In America! Died and lays buried there. Con-sequently he could never have returned to England, to his own village of Ravenhurst, nor his werry own castle o' Ravenhurst. And yet, Mr. Jackman, sir and partner, these here buttons now tells us, werry loud and plain, as come back he surely did, and, seeing as how corpses ain't likely travellers as a rule, except properly and dooly boxed, aforesaid buttons are telling as Philip, seventh Earl, lived long enough to bring all twelve of 'em to England, to his willage of Ravenhurst, to his castle—to his death."

"Shrig, what are you suggesting?"

"Sir, these here buttons are saying as he came there so werry much alive, that he had to die for reasons unknown —as yet."

"Great good heavens!" exclaimed Mr. Jackman. "You voice terrible things, Shrig!"

"Sir, 'tis these here buttons as is so elo-quent. And if their testimony don't suffice, I have summat else here, ar—

summat as speaks louder, plainer and even more to the p'int, summat as I found——" He paused suddenly as once again came a gentle tapping on the door.

"Who is it?" cried Mr. Jackman in voice wholly unlike his usual jovial tone. "Who is it?" The door opened to show Mr. Beeby bowing even lower than usual as he said in accents of awe:

"Sir, my lord the Earl of Ravenhurst to see you." Uttering these words, he stood aside, and in this moment George instinctively rose to his feet, for now it was that he beheld the two people who were so to alter and trouble the hitherto even tenor of his life.

CHAPTER III

Introduces a noble person and—the Beautiful Unlovely

FROM earliest childhood George, like other village boys, had known of " my lord the Earl " who once had lived in " the Castle up yon 'pon the hill ", had heard vague though awesome tales of his vast power and wealth. So that, although never seen, the Earl had become as dominating in fancy as his great house with its grim old tower was in reality.

Thus George's grey eyes widened in amazement, bordering on disbelief, to behold this noble person, this most potent gentleman, for—a shambling creature whose silvery head was bowed between the one hand that clutched and bore so heavily upon ebony stick, and the other that clasped the round, silk-mittened arm of the most beautiful woman George had ever seen : a handsome face, though arrogant and unlovely (thought George), with something fierce and untamed in its expression ; a shapely body from plumed bonnet to sandalled foot, instinct with grace and a passionate vitality in which was something of the animal. George, thus intent, was thinking of panthers and tigers, when :

" Jackman, who is this—young man ? "

The voice uttering this demand, though soft to feebleness, was yet so compelling that George started and beheld the Earl regarding him, beneath pent of brow and droop of silvery hair, with eyes that were compelling as his tone, in so much that George flushed hotly, while Mr. Jackman, bowing, hastened to answer :

" My lord, permit me to introduce my new partner, Mr. Bell. Henceforth, my lord, the firm is Jackman, Son, and Bell and shall be as zealous to serve and protect your lordship's many interests as in the long past."

"I hope so, Jackman, I hope so!" sighed his lordship, sinking into the proffered armchair. "Yes, I trust so, Jackman, for all our sakes, though I detest change—and your Mr. Bell appears over young for position of such onerous responsibility; I repeat—over young, Jackman!"

"That, my lord," George retorted, stung more by the lady's glance of open disparagement than his lordship's tone, "that time will remedy, sir."

"Ah," sighed the Earl, sinking back in his chair, the better, as it seemed, to survey George from his close-cut auburn curls, that no amount of brushing would reduce, to the toes of his dusty boots, and up again—a keenly, searching glance that paused at last upon the crooked little finger of his left hand, noting which, George hid it in his pocket.

"Indeed, Mr. Bell," the Earl murmured, "time may remedy many things, but—it destroys all things, soon or late! Ah well, you may be seated, gentlemen—nay, first I take joy to present my beloved ward, the Lady Clytie Moor——"

"Oh, but dearest," said she, in softly rich, caressing voice, "I am acquainted with Mr. Jackman, of course. As for these other—gentlemen?" Again George flushed, while the Earl, with a gentle smile, glanced from him to Mr. Shrig, saying:

"Jackman, I presume this is the law officer mentioned in your letter?" And forthwith Mr. Shrig replied:

"That i-denticle, my lord, name of Shrig, baptismal, Jarsper, at your sarvice."

"Now," sighed the Earl, with feeble though commanding gesture, "pray be seated. You here beside me, Clytie." Gracefully she sank upon the chair indicated, leaning to slip her hand within his arm as he continued:

"You behold me here, Jackman, in answer to your letter informing me of this amazing and perfectly shocking discovery at the Castle."

"Shocking indeed, my lord," sighed the lawyer, "and I fear I must grieve and shock you even more deeply!

For, since my letter, Mr. Shrig has made such further discoveries that I—we, my partner and I, have grave reason to believe these sad remains are those of your lordship's cousin Philip, seventh——"

"Horrible!" exclaimed the Earl. "A horrible suggestion, Jackman, and quite impossible! My unfortunate cousin Philip died long ago in America, killed with many others in a battle or massacred by the Indians! But you should know all this, of course—as a matter of business."

"All this I did know, my lord, knew and believed until some half-hour ago. But now—I will ask your lordship to examine these silver buttons, particularly this one which Mr. Shrig has cleaned for our inspection, this and its fellows he found upon, or rather—with the—um—skeleton, and which, as you will see, bears the monogram of your cousin, Lord Philip, to wit, the letters P V W, if your lordship will trouble to look."

His lordship troubled himself so far as to examine this mute witness, with and without the large magnifying-glass Mr. Jackman proffered, turning this button this way and that in the long, white fingers of hands George thought looked remarkably powerful for a man so old and feeble. Having surveyed this button from all angles, the Earl passed it to Lady Clytie, saying tranquilly:

"A perfect work of art, Jackman, but no least use as evidence of Cousin Philip, for these three letters may be read in six or seven different ways. So, my good sir, your perspicacious law officer must afford better evidence ere I tolerate such very preposterous suggestion. Indeed I demand and must have proof absolute and incontrovertible!"

"In-contro——" Mr. Shrig sighed and shook his head, saying despondently, "Here, m'lud, is a vord as con-flummerates me complete! And proof is a ab-straction, a skittish article werry hard to come by at the best o' times. But since y'r ludship demands same so determinated, I'll do my best as in dooty bound. And so, my lord, gentlemen and lady, I must ax you to try to see all as I saw laying amidst the dust and cobwebs o' forty-odd years—rags and bones as had once been a man, and a man struck from life to death werry sudden-like ! Ar—but this were a man of natur' so powerful determined that—as he lays there helpless, bleeding his precious life out with every beat of his failing heart—or, as you might say, his dewoted throbber —he yet finds strength to take and—kiss a object as he thinks werry precious indeed. For, my lord, gentlemen and lady, among the bones of his right hand, laying close agin his lipless teeth, I found—a small, gold locket, same containing a picture, vich I now pro-dooce in evidence ! "

"Eh—a picture ? " exclaimed Mr. Jackman, starting forward in his chair.   "A miniature portrait, Shrig ? "

"That i-denticle, sir ! This here unfortu'ate gen'leman had died kissing the portrait of his lady vife, the mother of his child——"

"Child ? " The repetition was a whisper so hushed and vague that George could never be sure whence it came, more especially as just then all his attention was centred upon the gold locket or pendant Mr. Shrig had taken from that waistcoat pocket of his and now opened, saying as he did so :

"On the right side o' this is portrait o' lady, young and golden hair ; on the left—these here vords wrote werry plain though small." And in quite dispassionate, official voice he read aloud these expressive words penned so long ago :

"'To Philip, my ever beloved lord and husband on this the first birthday of our little son Philip George, someday eighth Earl of Ravenhurst.   New York, seventeen hundred and sixty.'"

"A—son ! " gasped the lawyer, starting afoot.   "An— heir ! "

"Vich," quoth Mr. Shrig, nodding at this mute though most eloquent witness, "vich is rayther inclined to upset the applecart ! "

"Give me—that thing ! said the Earl, reaching out an imperious hand, whereat Mr. Shrig merely beamed—and shook his head, saying :

"M'lud, though villing to o-bleege, can't be done ! This here locket being sich important evidence is therefor, and for the time being must remain, in possession of the law."

That so masterful hand drooped, suddenly feeble, and sank to die upon cushioned chair-arm, seeming thus so pitifully helpless that the Lady Clytie clasped and raised it to the cherishing comfort of her ruddy lips while her great dark eyes seemed to glare upon Mr. Shrig, who merely blinked, as she murmured, and very tenderly :

"Dearest, never trouble for this odious, top-booted wretch ; leave him to the Devil and damnation."

Mr. Shrig blinked again, the lawyer stared, George held his breath, the Earl smiled in gentle resignation as he murmured :

"Hush, Clytie my love, the poor man means very well, and the law, if an ass, is still the law and must be respected. And so "—here he raised silvery head to look up at Mr. Shrig like the very plaintive, ancient gentleman he now seemed, saying in tone of ironic humility—" most zealous of officers, a person stricken alike in years and health, even myself, begs you will permit him to glance at that so evidential trinket." Upon the table, even as the words were uttered, Mr. Shrig placed the open locket, above which silvery head and plumed bonnet were bowed together ; and now for a while was silence, an odd stillness, a hush so profound that George could hear the tick of Mr. Jackman's watch in its fob, and the rustle and twitter of birds nesting in the eaves above the open lattice. At last the Earl sighed and spoke :

"Alas, poor Cousin Philip ! I am convinced at last—or very nearly. I am also painfully confounded, not to say utterly dismayed ! For it would seen that I and my son, Viscount Hurst, are usurpers and are like to be out-casts—if—Cousin Philip's son is alive and can be found.

Look you at this, Jackman; study it and favour me with your legal opinion." And with elaboration of care he passed the locket to Mr. Jackman, who gazed at it in wide-eyed dismay, shook his head at it and answered :

"My lord, I am compelled to inform you that, if alive and if found, this young man, Philip George, being undoubted heir, must naturally succeed to the title and estates——"

"Precisely, Jackman, if he is alive and if found ! Here are two ' ifs '—small words and yet how infinitely potent ! Meantime I shall, of course, remain in possession, while you, I presume, will institute search for the—rightful heir ? "

"I can do no other, my lord."

"Certainly, my dear man, certainly ! Your natural probity and honourable profession demand that you leave no—eh—stone unturned."

"And," said the Lady Clytie with vicious snap of sharp, white teeth, "under stones one sometimes may find loathsome, slimy horrors ! "

"I opine, Jackman, you will employ this very zealous officer for this somewhat hopeless quest ? "

" 'Tis so I propose, my lord."

"Well, well," he sighed, reaching feebly for his ebony crutch-stick, " 'twould seem there is no more to say—except that I propose residing at Ravenhurst, though I detest the great place. However, we shall remain for the summer. Your letter informed me the damage was quite negligible. The house is fairly habitable, I trust ? "

"Oh, quite, my lord ; I have seen to that. And there have been caretakers, of course, worthy folk of my own choosing."

"Very well, Jackman. I trust also the—those mournful remains have been removed ? "

"Ar !" said Mr. Shrig. "They have, m'lud ; every westige, every rag and every bone."

"Very right ! Very proper ! " sighed the Earl. "They shall, in due season, be honourably interred in the family vault—if there is room. And now, gentlemen, I bid you good afternoon. Clytie, your arm, my love."

Gracefully, blooming Youth bent to help stricken Age; then, with large white hand once again clasping her round, mittened arm, the Earl struggled to his feet and, meeting George's glance, smiled up at him wistfully, saying:

"Ah, Mr. Bell, there was a time when I was tall and, I think, strong as yourself . . . but time and sickness have together made of me the poor wreck you see. Be grateful, sir, for youth and strength. Oh, be grateful!"

George bowed and opened the door, then, at gesture from Mr. Jackman, followed their visitors to the waiting carriage. With the aid of two stalwart footmen the Earl contrived to mount into this spacious vehicle; but scarcely was he seated than he leaned suddenly forward to say:

"Mr. Bell, your hand—that little finger—an old hurt, I presume? Ah, yes—I see! Jackman, when you favour me with your presence at the Castle—bring your young partner with you."

Then, signalling to bewigged footman, who signalled to stately coachman, the great carriage rolled away, leaving George once again flushed of cheek and wide of eye, staring after it, and Mr. Jackman staring at him.

"A-mazing!" exclaimed the lawyer.

"What is, sir?"

"That the Earl should have observed that odd little finger of yours, George."

"Ar—but," quoth Mr. Shrig, as they re-entered the house, "our lord is a werry sharp lord indeed; gimblets, swords, stilletters nor yet razors and needles can't be no sharper! Vich makes me o-pine as somebody someday is like to get cut or stabbed——"

"Eh?" demanded Mr. Jackman, pinch of snuff suddenly arrested beneath his short, pugnacious nose. "Cut? Stabbed? Shrig, what on earth d'ye mean?"

But, shaking his head, Mr. Shrig replied:

"Mr. Jackman, sir and partner, ekker alone responds."

CHAPTER IV

Introduces Mistress Isabel Standish, a beauty though an aunt

MISTRESS ISABEL STANDISH, tall, dignified and handsome despite crumpled sun-bonnet and the dab of earth upon her shapely, high-bridged nose, was busied in the spacious garden of her cottage, known from time immemorial as Sparklebrook because of the rill that ran sparkling through a bowery corner of the garden.

A place of beauty this—with its three gables, steep-thatched eaves, bright lattices and massive walls mellowed by the gentle hand of time. Too large for an ordinary cottage, too small for a farmstead, it was cosy as the one, roomy as the other (or almost), and, besides, was blest by that Magic Feminine which can transmute brick and mortar, wood and stone into that best and loveliest of all earthly places—home.

Just at present this Essential Feminine, this Presiding Genius, was kneeling (in stately fashion), performing with a trowel where flowers bloomed in fragrant riot, while in the herb-and-vegetable garden nearby an aged man laboured, more or less diligently, with a hoe—that is to say, whenever the trowel was at work the hoe was idle, serving its user as a prop, but the instant busy trowel paused or stately head turned hoe-wards that implement was as instantly at work.

" Jabez ! " said Mistress Isabel, sitting back on her heels (though with dignity). " Jabez ! "

" Ay, marm ? " replied the sturdy aged one, dabbing at perfectly cool brow with vivid bandanna handkerchief. " Ay ay, Miss Belle ? "

" Saint Mark, Jabez, has just struck the half after four. So you in and bid Betty set on the kettle for tea."

"Ay ay, Miss Belle!" said he, saluting with the hoe as if it had been a boarding-pike, like the old man-o'-war's man he was, then, taking three paces cottagewards, he set hand to mouth and bellowed:

"Oho, Bet—Betty ahoy! Set on kettle f' tay. Miss Belle's orders, so jump to it, lass."

"Drat the man!" exclaimed Miss Isabel, rising (with grace) to shake her trowel at him (with superb gesture). "I could have done that myself."

"Done wot, marm?"

"Shouted, man, shouted."

"No, marm, not you, Miss Belle; being only a lady-ooman ee could ha' done no more than squeal like——"

"Squeal?" she repeated indignantly. "I couldn't, I shouldn't, and wouldn't."

"Ay, but ee would, I tell ee, accordin to natur, marm, you bein' only femmy-nine, Miss Belle. And sich bein' so, so it be and——"

"Oh, get back to your hoeing! And finish that patch or no tea, not a drop!"

"Lordy, Miss Belle, and me that old, and oncommon dry, a' the day so perishin' 'ot——"

"And yourself so comfortably cool, Jabez! So put away that dreadful bandanna thing and hoe, Jabez, hoe!"

"With a-yo-heave-ho and a rumbelow and a heave, my mariners all O!" cried a joyful voice, and over the wicket-gate leapt George. He tossed his hat at old Jabez (who caught it with a sailorman's dexterity), and, clasping Miss Isabel in those powerful arms of his, whirled her lightly aloft—transforming this stately and somewhat formidable lady into mere feminine creature, pleading for release. So, as lightly, George set her down, saying to old Jabez:

"Toss me my dicer, old Heartofoak!" The chuckling aged one obeyed. George caught the hat, put it on that he might take it off with prodigious flourish to salute his aunt with ceremonious bow and the words:

"Dear Aunt Isabel, who so truly is a belle, you behold in me a youngish gent whose foot is now firmly planted on the metaphorical ladder! For, madam, Mr. George Bell of the very old and greatly respected firm of Attorneys at Law, namely and to wit, Messrs. Jackman, Son, and Bell, humbly and gratefully makes you his acknowledgments of all your past care and inspiring faith in him and——"

"George!" she cried, forgetting (almost) to be dignified. "Oh, George . . . my dear . . . do you mean . . . can it be . . . what do you mean?"

"That Mr. Jackman, bless his heart, has this very day made me his partner and, as such, has introduced me to one of our wealthiest and most important clients, the Earl of Ravenhurst, no less! And all this I owe to you and your constant faith in me and belief in my success. So, Aunt Isabel . . . you are my mother, father, sister and brother, my one and only family—come and be kissed!" And kissed she was until her sun-bonnet, more rumpled than ever, fell back and her handsome, usually austere features aglow and gentled by love and radiant happiness. And now out from kitchen window came Betty's mob-capped head to enquire:

"Will ee have tea inside or out, Miss Belle?"

"Inside, of course!" laughed George. "But outside and here, Bet, under old Tom," and he gestured towards a certain gnarled old pear tree whose wide branches made a pleasant shade. "Hold hard, Bet, and I'll bear a hand with the tray and out through the casement with it. Aha, plenty of bread and butter, I see—good!"

Thus presently down they sat, aunt and nephew, at rustic table and on rustic chairs made by George's capable hands. And, now performing with the teapot, aunt demanded of nephew:

"Now, George, tell me about everything—especially the Earl."

"The Earl?" repeated George, forgetting to eat. "The Earl is an anomaly, Aunt, an absolute self-contradiction . . . all outward feebleness and inward strength! Hair white as snow but an eye of fire! Face unnaturally pale, smooth and unwrinkled and of serenity that is rather awful because it never seems to change except when he smiles—faintly and when least expected! A tottery form bowed and feeble—yet with the shoulders, arms and hands of a Hercules! A voice pitiably weak to sue or plead or softly deep to suddenly command. Ay, by Jupiter, he is the most powerfully feeble, compellingly young-old man imaginable! And, Aunt—he does not like me."

"Oh, and why not, pray?"

"Probably because he sensed my instant dislike of him; he's so confoundingly quick and sharp."

"And why did you dislike him so instantly?"

"Yes, I'm wondering at this myself, for I have no idea. Ah, and this reminds me—the last thing he did was to peer up at me with those surprisingly keen eyes of his and remark upon this crooked finger of mine. Then, and before I could reply, he nodded, smiled, and said: 'Ah yes, I see.'"

"Now that," said Miss Isabel, setting down her cup with unwonted clatter, "that was—extremely odd."

"So I thought, Aunt, but then, as I tell you, he is an extremely odd person. . . . And now I must tell you about the skeleton!" This George did so vividly and with such detail that his aunt quite forgot to drink her tea.

"A dreadful story!" she sighed, when the relation was ended. "Very harrowing and quite heart-breaking. . . . To think of that poor, dying man kissing his young wife's portrait with his last strength! Ah well, his agony ended long since and he is reunited with his beloved these many years, I pray God!"

"Amen!" said George reverently.

After this they were silent some while until, as Miss Isabel refilled his cup, George said:

"By the way, the Earl informed us that he intends residing at Ravenhurst at least for the summer though he also said he detested the place. I wonder why?"

"Perhaps because our village is such a very quiet, drowsy place."

" And that's why I love it, my dear."

" So do I, George, and always shall."

" I have always thought the house such a splendid place, especially the old part with its battlements and tower, though pretty grim, of course."

" Yes, George, that is the horrid part ; a frightful place, a—perfect nightmare—full of dark corners and grim passages that echo, and dungeons ! Yes, and one dreadful place called an oubliette with neither door nor window— only a hole above through which miserable prisoners were dropped to die in the dark and be forgotten ; that's why those nasty French name such horrors oubliettes ! I was shown over the place when I was a girl and dreamed of it for weeks after."

" Oubliette !" George repeated. " Oublier—to forget, out of mind and recollection . . . a place of darkness to die in and be forgotten. It sounds most infernally unpleasant."

" Yes, George, ghastly. But that sort of fiendish cruelty ended long ago, thank God ! "

" And yet there are fools who talk of the ' good old times ' ! Well, they can have 'em ! These are the times for me—to sit and drink tea in such lovely garden with an aunt lovely as her flowers—and, 'pon my life, you are uncommon handsome, Aunt Belle ! "

" George, don't be silly ! "

" The wonder is you have never married. I know you refused my good old Jackman, and there were others, the Reverend Aeneas, and——"

" George, do not be a fool ! Pray hold your tongue or change the subject."

" Handsomest of aunts, I hear and obey, thus. At about three o'clock this very afternoon I beheld the most beautiful and most unlovely creature I have ever seen ! "

" Ho ! " exclaimed Miss Isabel, cup arrested at shapely mouth. " That of course, means a lady."

" Who scowls like a thundercloud and curses like any tarry sailor man or pipeclayed dragoon ! "

" Then, just as ' of course ' she is no lady ! "

" And her ridiculous name is Clytie Moor."

" I consider that a pretty name, George."

" And she looked down her beautiful nose at me quite frequently with the utmost scorn, not to say contempt ! "

" And you at her with the eyes of an adoring sheep, eh, George ? "

" No how ! " he answered in the Sussex idiom. " No wise nor no when, m'dear. Mislikes she I did, dracky-minute and no question. 'Er be no wench for the loikes of I, none whatever, no ! In a word, Aunt Belle, she revolted me."

" And no wonder—if she really swears."

" And curse, quite trippingly, Aunt, as to the manner born, though in accents soft and lusciously sweet ! " said George, frowning at the tea in his cup.

" Moor ? " his aunt repeated, pondering the name. " I have no recollection of the name."

" But you knew the Earl quite well, didn't you, Aunt ? "

" Years and years ago when I was a child."

" Dear Aunt Methuselah ! " laughed George. " What was he like in those dim, distant times ? "

" Very different from the poor invalid you describe, my dear ! "

" How so, Aunt Belle ? "

" He was very handsome, black-haired, immensely strong and the gayest of companions. Your grandfather and he were intimate friends—they used to ride and hunt together, and what horsemen they were ! "

" He sounds a grand sort of fellow, Aunt ! "

" And he was indeed ; a splendid man, George. Your dear mother and I simply adored him for the truly noble man he was, by nature as by birth."

" Yes," George nodded, " he must have been the right sort or Grandfather Standish would never have suffered his friendship."

" But today," sighed Miss Isabel, " according to your description, the years have sadly changed him ! "

"They have indeed, Aunt."

"I suppose, since the Earl intends to reside here, you will renew your friendship with his son, the young Viscount. You knew each other at Cambridge, didn't you?"

"More or less, my dear, but he, being progeny of an earl, blue blood and what not, moved in a sphere remote from mine, coaching and wine parties, hunting, cards, and so on. Besides, I was usually pretty hard at work—like the almost too virtuous soul I am. And so I——"

"Contrived to find time to have your nice Greek nose broken; such a very nice, straight nose, George."

"However," said he, feeling this feature thoughtfully, "now, instead of Greek it's slightly Roman, thanks to Jessamy Todd——"

"The brutal wretch! Who is he?"

"Aunt!" exclaimed George, in shocked accents. "Jessamy is the champion of all England and never beaten!"

"Then he ought to be—soundly, of course!"

"And, my dear, Jessamy is my friend."

"And as a mark of friendship—spoils your nose!"

"My own fault entirely. I had just stopped and, yes, by Jupiter—staggered him beautifully with a perfectly lovely left, so in I went for a finisher and, e'gad, I got it—took his right counter fair and square on the trumpet!"

"Trumpet, George?"

"Nose, my blessed innocent, my beak, breezer or claret-jug! Those are some of the synonyms, but also we have snitch——"

"Cease, George! You become odiously vulgar! Tell me, instead, what the highly respected firm of Jackman, Son—and Bell propose doing in the interests of the unknown legal heir."

"Writing instructions to our agents in America, New York and Boston, to search all church registers—births, marriages and deaths——" Here Miss Isabel shivered so violently that George exclaimed in sudden anxiety: "Good lord! Aunt, and what's the matter? My dear, are you cold—and chill? And the sun so warm! Have you a chill?"

"No—yes!" she answered, glancing, almost fearfully, over her shoulder. "It was as though . . . a ghostly hand . . . touched my heart! I . . . I am haunted by the thought of . . . poor, young Earl Philip . . . dying . . . with his lips upon his wife's portrait! And . . . that poor wife, the mother with her baby, her little son and heir! What of them, I wonder?"

"Ay, what indeed?" repeated George gloomily. "This is for us to discover, though I doubt if we ever shall. Mr. Jackman has engaged the man Shrig, but what can he do—after this lapse of time? Little enough. And I am deputed to act with him, but what can I do? Even less. Oh, a confoundingly confounded, hopeless task it will be!"

"However, George, I shall pray God's blessing on your efforts for the sake of that little helpless baby."

"Who by this time, Aunt, will be a man of thirty years old, or thereabout—if he is yet alive. But enough of this!" said he, rising to proffer his arm with elaborate bow. "Come, madam, my Belle Aunt, pray take a stroll with Mr. Bell of Jackman, Son—and—Bell! Let us ramble amid the onions, yes, and see if perchance the beans we planted are showing ever a bean yet."

Smiling, Miss Isabel rose, and, slipping that very capable hand of hers within his arm, away they paced together through this sunny, fragrant garden, talking and laughing now, as was their happy wont; for how should they know of those strange and terrible events that were to beset them ere the year was out, troubles and perils engendered —of rags and bones and a small, gold locket?

Surely it is a wise and gentle Providence whose beneficent fiat is: "sufficient unto the day . . ." O children of Earth, be happy while ye may; make faith and hope your companions upon life's toilsome journey, for these are the Angels of God.

CHAPTER V

Concerning Old Hagah, called a witch

BOYS were hooting while dogs barked and leapt fiercely about a wretched old creature who, back to a tree, was striving to defend herself with feeble blows of a quite inadequate staff. For already her poor gown was torn and one bony arm ran blood; over a nearby stile a burly, young fellow lounged to watch and grin as one dog, bigger and fiercer than the others, leapt and seized the thin shawl about the old creature's age-bowed shoulders—then this worrying ferocity was smitten away by a stick plied with such strength and accuracy that savage dogs and crueller boys fled howling and yelping in unison.

"Young—devils!" panted George who had been running, then espying the man who lounged and grinned, he turned on this fellow in scowling fury:

"Shame on you Tom Ferris, damn you—to see any woman—so misused, especially one so old as Hagah!"

"Eh, a woman, Mast' Jarge? She be naun but a black witch as ee do know well, same as I do! A brimstone witch she be, as should to the fire or water, ah and 'er would 'ave none s'long ago—as 'tis, I spits at 'er."

"Do!" snarled George. "Do so and I'll thrash you!" Tom Ferris spat and reeled sideways from the resounding slap of George's open hand.

"That's to start!" he nodded, dropping stick and clenching eager fists. "Now come over that stile—no, I'll come to you." So saying George vaulted the stile, steadied himself to meet Tom's rushing onslaught, avoided Tom's left, ducked swinging right and countered so heavily on Tom's bristly chin that down he went headlong.

"Come, get up!" cried George; Tom merely blinked. "Up with you and fight—d'ye hear?"

" Ay, I hears ! " answered Tom, composing himself comfortably at ease. " But lookee, Mast' Jarge, I beant agoin' to stand up for to be knocked back'ards again b' the likes o' you, sir, none whatever."

" So you won't fight ? "

" Ay, right j'yful, but not wi' the likes of ee, Mast' Jarge. You fights for the sport of it, me only when I has to."

" You're a poor sort of animal, Tom."

" Mebbe so, sir, but there's them as thinks different, 'specially some as goes in petticuts ! "

" Petticoats ! " snarled George. " However, there's one over yonder now and in it a poor, helpless old soul you watched being savaged. So if you won't fight you shall beg her pardon instead, ay, and make good her damage out of your pocket, curse you ! "

" Not me, Mast' Jarge ! "

" You will, Tom. Ha yes, by Jupiter you shall if I have to kick you to her over the stile. So what about it, do you walk or do I kick ?"

Tom looked up at the scowling face above him, down at the powerful foot back-drawn to kick, and rising—walked.

The little, old woman, sharp of nose and peaked of chin crouched thus beneath the tree, seemed indeed the veriest witch at first glance, but her deep-sunken eyes were misted with grief, her thin cheeks streaked with tears, yet she rose to front them, staff upraised to smite, desperate in her weakness, and glaring fiercely to mask her fear, showed thus more witchlike than ever. But George had seen those tears and for these and many other reasons, bared his head to her aged womanhood greeting her like the friend she was :

" Dear old Hagah, here comes Tom to beg your pardon and hope you are not hurt ! " And then whispering aside to Ferris : " Speak up, damn you ! " And forthwith Tom spoke :

" Gammer Hagah, witch or no, I wishes ee well and axes pardin' for settin' they raskell lads and dogs onto ee. And for your tore gownd marm, this yere shillin'——"

" Not enough ! " hissed George.

" This yere 'arf a crown——"

" Double it ! " growled George.

" This yere five shillin', marm——"

The frail, old body straightened, the sunken eyes flashed, the pale, shrivelled lips curled bitterly scornful as she replied :

" Keep your money, Tom Ferris ; I'll naun of 't—you as I helped into the world, same as I did your feyther and his'n afore him ! Ah, they didna call me ' witch ' when trouble or sickness grieved 'em ; no, they come pleading help and comfort of Hagah the Wise Woman ! Old, very, very old I be, and long past troubling for fools the like of ee or them as do plague me and cry ' witch ' these days. So go thy ways, Tom, and learn thyself to be a man, ah—and the good Lord above bless ee, my poor child ! "

Slowly Tom Ferris turned and took three slow strides away, turned again and made three quick strides back, then, stooping he laid the five shillings at her feet, saying and with look and tone very humble :

" Tak' 'em or leave 'em. "   Having said which he knuckled an eyebrow, vaulted the style and strode away with, for him, uncommon haste.

" I dunnot want the lad's money ! " muttered the old creature, frowning at the coins.

" Yet he meant well," said George, taking them up, " so here they are ! "   And he placed them in her unwilling hand.   " Also I believe he was sincere, Hagah."

" Ay, there be good in Tom," she nodded, " same as in most of us if us do but trouble to find it ! Ay, good," she repeated, " good in all God's creatures except—the Black Wynters.   And now, Master George, I thankee for taking my part so powerful and timely."

" But your arm bleeds——"

" Lord bless ee 'tes naun but bit of a scrat."

" However, I'll bind it up for you."

" Nay, now never trouble for me, sir——"

B

" This handkerchief is quite clean—and don't you ' sir ' me, my dear, as if we were strangers ! Didn't you save my life when I was no more than a puling infant—ay, by Jupiter, and after the doctors had given me up, eh, my dear old Hagah ?

" Ay, maybe I did ! And seems but yesterday these hands o' yours a baby's, small and pink and now so big and strong and—gentle——"

" What was my ailment—chickenpox or measles ? "

" Neether ; 'twere a fever as I cured by a herbal potion, though folks said 'twere black witchcraft, all 'cept Miss Belle. Ah, she were a lovely lady then."

" So she is now."

" Ay, so she be, sure-ly ! "

" Then why do you never visit us at Sparklebrook these days, Hagah ? You know there is always a hearty welcome for you there."

" So I do, Master Georgie, but I be too very old ; my visiting days be over."

" Nonsense ; you're spry as ever you were, or as long as I remember you, which is all my life."

" Ay, nature and our Good Lord has given me wonderful health——"

" And wisdom, Hagah. There, so much for your hurt arm ! And now what ? "

" I'll be getting along home."

" Yes," said George, as they went on together, " you're a wonderful person, Hagah, for you never seem to change or get any older ! Today you are as I remember you twenty-odd years ago. I have often wondered exactly how old you are. And, egad, Aunt Isabel says the same—that today you seem just as she remembers you, as long as she can remember ! So, dear old Hagah, tell me just how old you really are."

" Ah, Master Georgie," she answered mournfully and speaking now like an educated person, " I am too old, so old indeed, that those I most loved are all dead long and long ago ! Yes, my world died around me and today I am a very lonely wretch waiting to die, too, and by God's sweet mercy find my world again . . . faces of those I so loved and have never forgotten, hear their dear voices glad again—ah, but with a better life . . . faces and voices that come to me only in dreams nowadays. . . ." Old Hagah's breath began to labour, for the road now led up-hill; and George, heeding this and how her steps faltered, drew her hand within his arm, and, thus linked, they achieved the ascent, and here he insisted she must rest a while. So down they sat together like the age-old friends they were.

Below them lay the village bowered in trees and sheltered by the green slope of the gentle downs, beyond which they could glimpse the open sea. But George's musing gaze was fixed upon the tall, grim tower of Ravenhurst Castle that, even from this eminence, seemed to dominate all. And thus intent, he enquired suddenly:

"Being so very old, Hagah, you must remember Philip, the seventh Earl—you do, don't you?"

And after brief silence she answered and in the country idiom:

"Ay, sure-ly!"

"Well, what was he like?"

"A right lovesome babby!"

"I mean—as a man."

"A right noble and kindly young gentleman, him being one of the good Vane-Wynters, them as be born to suffer."

"And did he suffer?"

"Ay, he did so, right bitterly, no question!"

"Well now, Hagah, I want you to tell me all you remember concerning him—everything!"

"That'll be nothing!" she replied, shaking that indomitable old head of hers. "Least said soonest mended, Mast' Jarge."

"My dear," said he, patting the thin old arm that was still linked with his own, "why talk so, when you can speak as good or better English than I?"

"Happen because when I be along o' them as I do love

I forget as I be only poor old Hagah as they names
' witch '."

"Then, if you love me, forget it now, and pray tell me
what you mean by saying he was ' born to suffer ' ? "

"Because he was of the red, good Vane-Wynters, and,
according to the old legend, ' red must suffer that black
may triumph ? ' Ah, but—beyond the grave, suffering
shall be changed to abiding joy, and triumph to everlasting
shame and grief.   There's a verse that says so, graven deep
in the stone of the old tower yonder ! "   And scowling, she
pointed thither with bony finger.   "So today he's back
there again ! "

"If you mean the Earl, he certainly is, and with a host
of servants—all Londoners ! "

"Ah well," sighed she, rising suddenly, though with an
effort, "I'll be on my way."

"But, Hagah, you haven't told me how Earl Philip
suffered so long ago."

"Master Georgie, ' a wise head keeps a still tongue '.
So all I'll tell is this—his poor, young heart broke when
the lady he would have wed ran away with another man."

"Who was this man ? "

Old Hagah merely frowned, shook her head, then,
turning to be gone, paused and demanded sharply :

"What for are ye so curious about him ? "

"Because," answered George, glancing at the distant
tower again, "in the Castle yonder, not long ago, were
found the remains of a man long dead and . . . we believe
this unfortunate man was Philip, seven—— Good lord !
What is it ? " cried George, reaching out supporting arms,
for old Hagah seemed convulsed by some dreadful spasm,
her eyes glared wildly, her pallid lips rounded to a black O
of horror, and yet she was dumb.

"Hagah . . . my dear soul, what ails you——? "

With sudden and unexpected strength, she broke from
him, gasping :

"Lemme go !   Don't ee tech me . . . I must think !
Oh, dear God, help me . . . to think !   Oh, merciful

Lord, show me what I must do . . . the black and the red . . . ah, no more blood, not again . . . ah, not again—— " With such wildly uttered, wholly unintelligible words, she turned and began to hobble downhill towards the peaceful village, and when he would have followed she wailed and smote at him with her staff.

So George, startled and amazed, stood to watch her go ; thus when at last he took his way townwards, the fearful horror he had seen in old Hagah's wide eyes haunted and troubled him with a strange dread, a vague premonition of coming evil.

CHAPTER VI

*Which, among other things, tells of the ghost of a baby
on a tombstone*

WITHIN that very pleasant, slumberous though dignified
town of Horsham, in a grassy, tree-shaded thoroughfare
that was (and is) neither street, road, alley nor lane, and
called, for some reason not apparent, the Causeway,
Mr. Jackman had his abode and place of business.

Here in one of the stately old houses generations of
Jackmans had lived and transacted business, which fact was
duly set forth upon a small brass plate, with dignified
simplicity, and had been wont to bear the legend :

JACKMAN AND SON,
Attorneys at Law.

But upon this particular summer morning George stood
gazing at this plate, with his grey eyes bright as the day
because this inscription now informed the world that here
were to be found

JACKMAN, SON, AND BELL,
Attorneys at Law,
etc.

So George gazed until, becoming aware of a presence,
he started, turned—and beheld Mr. Jasper Shrig of Bow
Street, who also gazed and beamed at this newly engraved
lettering.

" Bell ! " he murmured, caressing his smooth, shaven
chin with knob of the formidable, knobbed stick he bore.
" Bell ! " he repeated, as if testing the sound of it.   " And
a werry good name, too, being easy to be took down,

easier to pro-nounce, and sounding like a knell—as calls to
mind old church towers and nice, green graveyards——"

"Which," George retorted, "is a devilish unpleasant
suggestion!"

"Ay, p'r'aps 'tis, Mr. Bell sir, so I dooly axes pardon
therefor, for, d'ye see, sir, my mind nat'rally runs to
graveyards, bones and sich just at present. And talking o'
Mr. Jackman——"

"Eh, Mr. Jackman?"

"That i-denticle, sir, said gen'leman has went to London."

"Did he, by Jupiter——"

"No, sir, by the night mail. But afore so doing, wrote
you this here!" And from the cavernous interior of his
hat Mr. Shrig extracted a letter which he handed to George
with a little bow, who broke the seal forthwith, and read:

> "Thursday night.   In haste.
> *12th July*, 1816.

"MY DEAR GEORGE,

"Thanks to discovery of letter writ by my respected
father forty-five years ago, to his friend Richard Spenlow
of Spenlow and Hicks, Lincoln's Inn, re Earl Philip's
departure for America, 10th May, 1763, per ship *Swiftsure*
of London, thither I go hoping (against hope) to discover
other facts. Meanwhile do you accompany and aid
Shrig in his researches, you will find him a lively companion and his methods highly original. Though as
to finding this long missing heir my hope (as I say) is
exceeding small. However, pray know me for

> "Your friend and (I trust) longtime
> partner,
>
> "JOHN JACKMAN."

Refolding this letter, George beheld Mr. Shrig beaming
at him, though with eyes remarkably keen, a quick, bright
glance that, having taken him in as it were, from hat to
boots, roved hither and yon as if finding great interest in
all about them.

" Well," said George. " Mr. Jackman suggests I accompany you in your enquiries. How say you ? "

" Sir, I says ar, and heartily ! For, Mr. Bell sir, you look, if I may say so, a cove dependable, 'specially in tight corners ! And, sir, tight corners seem made especial for me, ar—and never a corner as ain't chockful o' windictiveness in shape o' boots, bludgeons, knives—and—a occasional chimbley-pot ! In vich circumstances, sir, I'm pretty sure you'd be the true-blue article."

" I'm glad you think so," laughed George. " But why are you so sure of me ? "

" Because, sir, you reminds me of another young gen'leman as is a reg'lar two-fisted terror, a Mr. Robin Dale—— "

" Oho ! " cried George. " Lord love you, Shrig, do you know Robin ? "

" Ar—from his boyhood hour, sir ! And I can tell you as how Mr. Robin is about the only man I ever heard tell on as knocked Jessamy Todd off his pins ! "

" Did he, though—did he ? And Jessamy Todd ! Don't tell me," said George, in a tone very like awe, " that you know Jessamy also ? "

" That I do, sir, and his partner Jerry Jarvis the Tinker as wrote werses—pomes as rhymes, as a gen'leman had printed into a book ! "

" Jessamy Todd, Robin Dale . . . and you know 'em both ! Shrig, this is perfectly marvellous ! Robin and I were at the university together, we used to spar regularly, and I know how mighty good he is, but, by Jove, I never knew he had floored Jessamy. Did you see ? "

" No, sir, vorse luck ! But Jessamy told me of it—so did Jerry Jarvis. And talking o' this here wanished heir, Mr. Bell, sir—— "

" Eh—who ? " exclaimed George, jerked thus abruptly from past to present. " Oh—ah, yes—yes, to be sure. What do you suggest ? "

" First, the King's Head, sir ; second, The Black Hoss ; and third, any other inn, tavern or ale-houses as you knows.

For this being market-day they'll be busy and full o' talk."

"Certainly, Shrig, but nothing to help us, merely talk of crops, cattle and so on."

"Hows'ever, sir, today, folk may talk o' summat else and werry different."

"How so, and of what, pray?"

"Rags and bones, p'r'aps, and the seventh Earl."

"But how on earth can they? We only knew of this ourselves a few days ago."

"Sir, I'm lodging at the King's Head—and, Mr. Bell sir, besides eyes and ears I've got a tongue, or, as you might say, a chaffer, and on occasion I uses 'em all——"

"Meaning you've told, made this quite horrible affair public?"

"Ar, as public, sir, and as horrible as in me lay to do! Mr. Bell, sir, I made them poor bones rattle thereselves into a skellington as jigged! I made that fatherless infant veep for his wanished dad! Sir, I told them as listened sech a tale o' blood and grief that, arter I'd done, they was so dumb-struck that as I drank my ale I could hear myself swaller!"

It was now that, leaving the dignified hush of the Causeway, they emerged into the busy street and riot of voices, for all about them were folk, men and women of all sorts and conditions—sturdy, red-faced farmers with their buxom wives and daughters, redder-faced squires with their ladies, drovers and yeomen in their best smock-frocks, and a joyous bustle everywhere, more especially about, and within, that ancient, spacious hostelry of the King's Head. Hither, by means of cheery word and powerful shoulder, Mr. Shrig won his way, with George at his heels, until they reached the long coffee-room thronged, it seemed, with folk of the better sort. Here, in remote corner, Mr. Shrig halted and, beckoning George near, uttered the one word:

"Hark!"

So George listened to this entirely masculine babblement (for in these coarser days no woman would enter such places) ; so male voices only talked, laughed or shouted greetings ; and thus for some while, George listened to no purpose. But, little by little, among this confused babel, he began to distinguish individual voices, then words, and at last :

" Devy'lish queer tale, doncheknow ! "

" Queer ? M'dear f'ler, I'd call it more than queer. . . ."

And now, from different quarter :

" Ah, a skeleton ! Didn't ye hear about it . . . ghastly . . . rags and bones. . . . Yes, so I hear . . . believed to be remains . . . seventh Earl. . . ."

And then, from yet another direction :

" Murder . . . suicide . . . who knows ?   Who can say . . . best say nothing . . . dangerous. . . ."

" Pack o' damn nonsense ! " piped a voice, shrill with age, and dominating. " Philip died abroad, slaughtered by damn Indians . . . saw his name posted in the *Gazette* . . . fifty odd years ago . . . knew him well . . . rode with him in the hunting field . . . regular dare-devil, so was I.   Challenged his cousin to a duel ; some woman, a course. I was his second, but it didn't come off, pity ! Got himself killed abroad instead, great pity.   So no more tattle o' suicide or murder—damn nonsense ! " The fiercely indignant old voice snorted, coughed and was lost in the general hubbub, whereupon Mr. Shrig, motioning George to bide still, edged himself into the crowd and vanished.

Thus alone, George listened the more intently and several times caught the grim words, uttered here and there : " Skeleton. . . ."   " Rags and bones ? . . ." " Murder. . . ."

" The old gent," said Mr. Shrig, appearing suddenly at his elbow, " is Sir John Trent, a regular old cock o' the roost as I've heered tell on afore now, a fighter years ago, steel and ball, a dooelist, and what he don't know o' life— and death—ain't ! So tomorrow, sir, I suggest us goes a-wisiting."

" You mean we call on Sir John ? "

" Ah ! D'ye happen to know him, Mr. Bell ? "

" Oh yes, he is one of our clients, always has been, and is sometimes pretty troublesome—a fiery old boy."

" And now, sir, talking o' vitches——"

" Of what ? " George enquired.

" A vitch, sir, spelt vith a wee, W I T C H. There is a werry old, ex-tremely aged fee-male party name of Hagah as they calls a vitch and——"

" Ay, so they do, the fools—and the dear old soul so perfectly harmless and——"

" Sure o' that, sir, are you ? "

" Of course I am, dammit ! "

" Hows'ever, Mr. Bell, I never see a vitch as looked more so—that nose and chin and they eyes sharp as needles and a desp'rate fierce——"

" And no wonder ! Hardship and ill-usage are apt to make anyone fierce, and in her long life poor old Hagah has suffered very much by reason of ignorance and foolish superstition ! "

" And that great, black tomcat o' hern, eyes big and yeller as guineas and never a blink."

" And her only companion, Shrig. Loneliness now as ever. Long ago they threatened to burn her, damn them ! And once they would have drowned her but that my grandfather, Squire Standish, happened along on his horse and scattered the mob with hoofs and whip, bless him ! Since when, Hagah has been devoted to us—ay, and saved my baby life ! "

" Vitch, sir, nothing could be fairer."

" So you've seen her already, have you, Shrig ? "

" Ar, from a distance, sir."

" Well, where do we go now, pray ? "

" Sir, in my comings and goings I have found me a little inn, werry cosy and peaceful, with a signboard and summat painted thereon as looks werry like a sack o' po-taters but says as it's a bear."

" Precisely ! " laughed George. " And the Bear lies just beyond our village."

" Ar, and not so werry fur from your resi-dence."

" Sparklebrook, my aunt's cottage."

" And, if I may say so, a werry handsome upstanding figure of a lady she is, sir, and no error ! "

" Don't tell me you know her, too ? "

" Not yet, sir, but I live in hopes. And talking o' Bears, I'm hoping as you'll honour me in a pint, sir, or say a couple ? "

" Gladly, if you'll honour me in another."

" Ditter, sir ! Ale and England goes nat'rally together and can't be beat, as old Boney found out t'other day at Vaterloo."

" Ay, thank God——"

" Heartily ! " quoth Mr. Shrig, his bright glance following a lark that soared above them as if upborne upon its own melody. " And talking of the Lady Clytie Moor——"

" Eh ? Well, what of her ? "

" A bee-u-tiful creatur', and, though a lady, a reg'lar femmy-nine rasper——"

" Then let's talk of something better—the Bear, for instance, for there it is, ay, and landlord Ben waiting to greet us."

So to this small, though very cosy inn, set about by a garden abloom with flowers, they hastened to be welcomed by sturdy Ben with friendly grin and two pewter pots abrim with creamy foam, saying :

" Master Jarge, I see ee a-coming——"

" And p'r'aps," suggested Mr. Shrig, tendering a coin, " you'll j'ine us, landlord, and tell us more con-carning this ghost or apparition ? "

" Eh, ghost ? " enquired George, tankard at lip. " What ghost, Ben ? "

" Why, Must' Jarge, I don't prezackly know. I nowise never heard o' no ghost till this yere gen'leman takin' his pint along o' us last night axed if any o' we had seen aught o' the ghost o' this poor gen'leman as was found up yon at the Castle, laying in his bones."

" Oh ? " murmured George, glancing at Mr. Shrig, who chanced to be gazing dreamily out of the open lattice along the winding, tree-shaded road as he answered :

" Ar ! Talking o' speckilators, goblings and sich like, there's some folk as can't see and some as can—like that werry old person as I heered tell of here last night, a Mr. Terris or Ferris."

" Oh, him ! " laughed Ben. " Old Gaffer Ferris be a bit doddlish, 'specially arter a pint or so o' my ale."

" Like enough ! " nodded Mr. Shrig, his glance still questing the road. " Though last evening somebody said as how old Mr. Ferris see a ghost once, though mebbe I'm mistook——"

" No, sir, youm right, for 'twere Tom Finch last night as says, along o' your talk o' ghosts, as how old Jabez Ferris did see one once years and years ago. Though 'tweren't no ghost, for what old Jabez see, or says 'e see, was, properly speakin', no more than a babby on a tumbstone."

" Only that ? " exclaimed Mr. Shrig like one vastly disappointed. " Only a—baby on a tombstone ? " Here he shook his head with such very evident disparagement that Ben actually flushed and retorted :

" Mister, lemme tell ee as how babbies on tumbstones ain't to be found in every village, specially at midnight ! "

" Eh ? Midnight ? " repeated Mr. Shrig, as with sudden respectful interest. " Midnight, says you ? Come, that's better, says I. Ar, that's oceans better, that is ! And—how long ago ? "

" 'Twere long afore I were born ! So long ago as old Jabez were then a young sailorman off fighting they French as sent him limpin' 'ome w' a ball in his leg as old Hagah, being a witch, cured by spells and 'chantments——"

" Ben, don't be a fool ! " said George. " It was by her skill in medicine and surgery."

" Asking y'r pardon, Master Jarge, but everyone said as how she witched that old bullet out o' Jabez's leg by sayin' the Lord's prayer backards—or some sich as 'e'll tell ee, for old gaffer'll be here along drackly-minute for his morning pint—ay, and yonder 'e comes.

" So I see," nodded Mr. Shrig, " and a hearty old Meethoosalem he looks—at this distance."

" Sure-ly, sir, 'e do look even heartier near-to. I'll go draw his ale."

" So," said George, soon as they were alone, " you were watching for him, eh, Shrig ? "

" Sir, since you ax so p'inted, I answers open and free— that's so."

" But surely you don't swallow this ridiculous tale ? "

" Mr. Bell, sir, there's time I can swaller so werry much as is ass-tounding ! "

Old Jabez, being athirst (as usual), used his aged legs with surprising vigour and voice also, for, as he drew near, he hailed lustily, sailor fashion :

" Oho, Ben, stand by ! Ale, m'lad, ale ! I be comin' abord, so ale, Ben, ale ! " With the word upon his clean-shaven lips, he stumped in—then checked stride and speech to stare at George and shake his old head reprovingly.

" Eh—Master Jarge," he exclaimed in tone of virtuous rebuke, " arl 'mazed and 'sprised I be for to see ee settin' yere a-gulpin' ale 'stead o' bein' 'ard at work wi' y'r laws— like I been wi' spade and 'oe, ar, and rake, fork and barrer likewise ! Me so old and a weel-barrer, and you s' young and a pint pot ! Ef I was to tell on ee t' y'r leddy aunt wot would Miss Belle say to ee ! Lordy-lord, I shivers to think ! And, Master Jarge, she've been an' gone an' give me notice again, she 'ave ! "

" Oho, and what was it this time, old Heartofoak ? "

" The 'o' Master Jarge, the danged 'o'! I apped to ketch it agin one of 'er noo rose bushes—and she turned me adrift—on the spot, though I didn't tak' no 'eed. But one o' these times I'll tak' 'er at 'er word and bear away and never nowise come back no more—nohow ! No, not ef 'er goos down t' me on 'er bended marrer-bones ! And wot'll 'er do then ? "

"Lord knows, old hearty! But I know the place would never be the same without you."

"You'm right, Master Jarge, no more it would—woeful sad-like 'twould be. And wot of 'er cabbages and sich? Her bean't no 'and wi' spade or fork, being only a lady——"

Here Ben reappeared, bearing a fourth cream-topped tankard and saying:

"Gaffer, this yere gen'leman be wishful for to 'ear your tale o' the babby on the tumbstone."

"Oh, du 'e so?" quoth Mr. Ferris, baring his old bald head to mop it, quite needlessly, with the vast red bandanna. "Then so 'e shall—on condition as 'e won't lemme pine nor yet perish wi' thirst, and the day so 'ot——"

"Friend," said Mr. Shrig heartily, "the vord is—ale for a tale! So let's hear."

"So ee shall, master, only gimme time for to empty my pot and I'll thankee kindly when 'tis full again!" So saying, he nodded to the company, puffed the foam from his tankard, emptied it at a draught, handed it to Ben and sighed ecstatically:

"Ah, thirst be a noble gift o' natur' ef a man may squench it praper wi' such ale as Ben du brew, no question! And lookee now, theer bean't no man as ever I heered on as ever see the ghost of a babby—on a tumb-stone—as changed and growed itself into old Nick—in the blink of an eye! Not many folk ever see the like o' that, eh?"

"Now let me think!" said Mr. Shrig, seeming to ponder this question. "No, I don't believe I ever did—leastways not vun as changed so rapid——"

"No!" cried old Jabez rather truculently. "Nor you never nowise will, nowhen and nohow, nor nobody else in this here world won't neither!"

Mr. Shrig's agreement was so instant and hearty that the aged one, thus mollified, nodded, sipped his ale and began:

"Ages ago, when I were a praper upstanding young man, being cap'n o' the fore-top o' the old *Bully Sawyer*, seventy-four, I takes a Frenchee musket ball into my larboard leg and comes 'ome limpin' an' thinkin' as how I'm crippled, a sheer hulk for the rest o' my days, but old Hagah, being a witch——"

"A woman," said George, "so good and wise she did more for you than all the surgeons!"

"Ay, ay, Mast' Jarge, cured me she did by her spells and 'chantments, no question! Ay, 'er magicked that old ball out o' my leg, sure-ly, and made me shipshape again and arl a-taunto! And 'twere then as it—'appened——"

Here, like true artist, old Jabez paused to sip his ale.

"Well, get on, old 'un!" said Ben, with ever-renewed interest for this tale he had listened to so often. "Get on, Gaffer, will ee!"

"Be ee a-harkin', Ben, wi' both they ears o' yours, eh?"

"Ay, wi' both on 'em, sure-ly!"

"Then stand by, for 'ere we go. In them days I were courtin' my Susan, and the shortest course to 'er feyther's cottage lay athwart the churchyard, so theer I goes. 'Twere a fine summer night, the moon full and bearin' about two p'ints to starboard o' the Pole Star and arl things plain and clear, and I'm 'bout 'arfway 'cross the churchyard when I brings up mighty short and sudden—for there—right afore me—layin' atop o' Gammer Grigg's 'eadstone as had fell flat—lays a babby, starin' up at me wi' eyes bright as di'monds and never a wink nor so much as a blink and nary a guggle nor croak!"

"So?" exclaimed Mr. Shrig, for the aged one had paused for another sip of ale. "And how then?" From his hat old Jabez drew the red bandanna handkerchief, wiped his lips and polished his scalp therewith, set it carefully back again, glanced eagle-eyed at his hearers and continued:

"Never a guggle nor croak! So then I hauls my wind to go 'bout, looks again—and—that theer babby had been witched into a gurt tall man—in a black cloak—and—glarin' 'pon me from the shadder of 'is 'at as being un-cocked, flopped and flapped arl 'bout his face—ah, but I

see two fiery, flamin' eyes in a face as were no more nor
a glimmerin' gleam! 'Twere old Nick hisself, no question!
So I braced about and bore away afore 'e could witch me
likewise, and were nigh choked wi' the reek o' brimstone
as I went! And ef you ax me, I du b'leeve 'twere arl
along-on-account-on that theer old Hagah——"

"Nonsense! exclaimed George.

"Eggs-ackly!" quoth Mr. Shrig, setting down his
empty tankard with a bang. "Your tale, old friend, is
ass-tounding! Ar, so werry much so I'm wishful to know
just when you see this miracklous event. Can you
remember how long ago . . . the year?"

"Ay, sure-ly! 'Twere about the time as Farmer Denby's
old sow farrered twenty-two and they arl died 'cept two as
never done no good till they died, too, so the old sow has
arl that trouble for nowt. Ay, I reckon 'twould be over
fifty year ago."

"And that," said Mr. Shrig, leaning forward, "that
would be about the year seventeen hundred and sixty,
eh, old friend?" And now George also leaned forward
with suddenly awakened interest while old Jabez pondered
the question, saying at last:

"Ay, 'twould be about then, for I mind that same week
the weathercock o' St. Mark carried away and was blowed
into the stableyard o' the Raven, and 'twere I as mended
it and set it up again good as noo, and theer it's been ever
since. Parson Netherby give me ten shillings extra and
mentioned me in his sarmon, that 'e did."

"And here," said Mr. Shrig, diving hand into breeches
pocket, "here is another o' the same, old friend, and my
thanks along of it. And so, a werry good day till us meets
again."

CHAPTER VII

In which Mr. Shrig asks questions

"WELL," enquired George, as they stepped out upon the sunny road, "what do you think of old Jabez's ridiculous tale?"

"Oceans, sir!"

"D'you mean you actually believe it?"

"Every vord, sir, or—pretty near. So my vord now and therefore is—weathercock?"

"Eh—weathercock?"

"That werry i-dentical, sir! There should be some mention o' same in the church register as'll give us the year."

"Good lord!" exclaimed George, halting in amazement, "Then you must think that baby was—or is—the——" He leapt, seized Mr. Shrig in powerful arm and hurled him into the ditch as over the hedge directly above them leaped a great black horse to land in cloud of dust and therein rear, plunge, caper and dance until his rider, checking him at last, turned that she might frown upon George, who scowled up at her.

"Fool! Oaf!" she panted. "Why did you—frighten my horse?"

"Marm," George retorted, "why did you try to kill us?"

"How dare you—say such a vile thing?"

"Or," George added, scornfully, "since you can't ride, why make the attempt?"

"I knew," she cried, "you were detestable—a perfectly odious wretch—the first moment I saw you!"

"And I," said George, "felt precisely the same regarding you, my lady Clytie! You revolted me then, you are abhorrent to me now and always will——"

44

She struck at him with the light riding-switch she carried, but, warding the blow, George twisted it from her grasp, snapped it asunder and, tossing the pieces along the road, gestured towards them, saying :

" Follow your whip, gracious lady, and I hope to God we don't meet often."

For a moment she looked down at him through the long lashes of eyes half closed, her ruddy lips back-drawn from white teeth tight-clenched ; and, meeting this look, George thought again how beautifully evil was this face. Thus for a breathless moment they glared upon each other, then her shapely body relaxed, she sighed deeply, nodded slowly and said murmurously :

" We shall see ! " Then, crying to her eager horse, away she went at furious gallop in swirl of dust. For a moment George stared after her, then, turning beheld Mr. Shrig seated comfortably on the side of his ditch, that chanced to be dry, also watching Lady Clytie's wild career.

" By goles ! " he sighed, rising with surprising nimbleness. " She is a reg'lar ama-zeen—like them ladies as used to hunt their husbands vith bows and arrers, not to mention spears and battleaxes. She's a parfect out-and-outer and a werry bee-oo-tiful young party, too, a lovelly fee-male and no error ! "

" Beautiful—yes ! " nodded George. " But lovely—no ! Certainly not ! Anything but."

" Vich you told her werry plain and p'inted ! "

" Ay, I did ! And wish I'd said more, for b'gad she's a feminine devil, a female demon and——"

" Ree-markable handsome."

" Why harp on it, Shrig ? She's handsome enough, I suppose—in a horrible, dark sort of way. . . . And," he continued indignantly, after three or four strides, " she might have killed us."

Two or three more strides and :

" Do you think—she meant to ? "

Having duly considered the question, Mr. Shrig replied :

" Sir, and friend, all as I can tell you is—ekker alone responds ! "

" Yes, yes," said George impatiently, " but how does echo respond—what does it say ? "

" No more, Mr. Bell sir, than natur' allows to sich. And there's another on 'em ! "

" Another of what ? "

" Lovelly and handsome vomen—yonder ! " Now glancing whither directed.

" Yes, old fellow," said George, his black scowl vanishing, " by Jove and Jupiter, you're right this time ; she is handsome, and lovely, too ! Come and meet her."

Mistress Isabel, who was busied (of course, with gracious dignity) using that same hoe old Jabez had so mismanaged, glanced up at click of the opening wicket-gate and her rather austere features were softened by the smile of welcome that made her so truly beautiful.

" Aunt," said George, as she turned to greet them, " here is Mr. Jasper Shrig of Bow Street ; sir, my aunt, Mistress Isabel Standish."

" Honoured, ma'm ! " said he, hat in hand. " Honour is the only vord for it."

" Mr. Shrig," she replied with gracious curtsy, " you are welcome. My nephew has spoken of you. . . . Sherry, George, and bid Betty set another cover, for of course you will dine with me." Mr. Shrig removed his hat again, saying :

" My lady, the vord now is ' gratitood '."

" You are a law officer, I understand, from London."

" That i-denticle, my lady."

" And very famous, my nephew informs me."

" He does me proud, ma'm."

" Shall you remain long in the country, sir ? "

" As possible, ma'm, for the longer I live in London the better I like the country, 'specially the downland country, and most especially this here garden wi' all these bee-oo-tiful flowers, but none on 'em so much so as their mistress, no, neether bud nor blossom ! "

"Goodness!" she exclaimed, opening those splendid eyes of hers wider than usual. "You are a most surprising law officer, Mr. Shrig!"

"Werry true, my lady; there's others has thought the same."

"Oh, but, Mr. Shrig, I am no titled lady, merely plain Isabel Standish."

"Ar, but—there's ladies by fortun' and ladies by natur, and my eyes, or as you might say ogles, tells me as you might be both, and there y'are, my lady!" She laughed so gaily that George set down well-laden tray to peer from the cottage window and thus beheld his stately aunt and Mr. Shrig seated side by side in animated conversation.

"Mr. Shrig," she was saying, "I should like to ask you a few questions, if I may?"

"Vich, my lady, I'll answer full and free on condition as you answer a few o' mine."

"Agreed, sir. First then, are you quite convinced those sad and very dreadful remains are those of Philip, the seventh Earl?"

"According to the evidence, my lady, nobody could be more so. Con-sequently my first question is: did you ever hear tell of a baby on a tombstone?" Again Miss Isabel laughed ere she replied:

"Yes, indeed! So has everyone in the village and for miles around. Old Jabez has been telling his ghost story ever since I can remember."

"Second question: can you mind the present Earl, being now the eighth, years ago, how he looked and how he did?"

"Oh yes. He was tall, handsome and immensely strong. I remember seeing him bend a poker in those big, white hands of his . . . he lived here at the Castle in those days."

"Third question: married or single, marm?"

"Single. He did not marry until years later; in London, I believe. I never met his Countess."

At this moment back came George to set down a well-laden tray, saying as he did so :

" By the way, Aunt, I can tell you, if Shrig hasn't, that a certain Lady Clytie Moor did her best to kill us on our way here ! " And he related the incident with such fury of word and gesture that Miss Isabel looked and listened in ever-growing surprise.

" But, my dear George," she demurred, " it was an accident, of course, though one might imagine from your manner that you deemed it intentional——"

" I wonder ! " said he, filling the glasses.

" Nonsense, George ! An attempt at murder—how utterly preposterous ! "

" However," said he, frowning at the recollection, " her horse's fore-hoofs for the moment looked like braining Mr. Shrig."

" But, my lady, your nevvy acted that prompt I was in the ditch, flat as any flounder in the twinkle of a bedpost ! "

" In the ditch ? Do you mean he actually threw you there ? "

" Lady, he tossed me there like as I'd been a feather—otherwise 'stead o' setting here so j'yful wi' life along o' you, I should be stiffening ready for a vooden overcoat. Vich being so, friend George sir, my name to you is Jarsper as I'm hoping you'll use henceforth."

" Agreed, Jasper, if you'll remember I'm George." At this moment Saint Mark chimed one o'clock, and Betty, abloom in mobcap and apron, appeared to announce :

" Dinner be ready, Miss Belle, ma'm."

So they went to eat and drink, talk and laugh together in ever-growing good fellowship. Thus when, some while later, Mr. Shrig took his leave, Mistress Isabel grasped his hand with clasp warm and hearty as his own, saying as heartily :

" Jasper Shrig, you will always be welcome here at Sparklebrook Cottage ! " Whereto he replied, hat in hand :

" Mistress Isabel, you'll never velcome any guest oo's gratitood is truer, my lady, than yours most trooly J. S."

And when the wicket-gate had clicked behind him, Mr. Shrig went at leisured pace, his lips pursed in soundless whistle as was his wont when busied on some problem or, for the time being Crime and Vindictiveness were forgotten—or very nearly.

"George," said Miss Isabel in her downright manner, "I like your Jasper Shrig."

"Good," he nodded. "Though I'm surprised you should do so."

"Oh why, pray?"

"Well, he's such a queer sort of customer and generally up to his ears in crime, principally murder. Mr. Jackman says he's a terrible fellow and likens him to a lion, a serpent and a bloodhound! Jasper Shrig has discovered and captured no end of criminals and sent many of them to the gallows."

"And the right place for them, George; but for you now—the kitchen garden and a spade, for I confess that as a digger I am my own disappointment, so, my dear, come and do it for me."

"Ay, ay, commander!" he answered, knuckling an eyebrow and making a leg, sailor fashion.

"Well, off with your coat; remember it is your second best——"

"Ay, ay again, cap'n, off it is!"

But in the kitchen garden they found the aged one so extremely hard at work that he had not time for speech or even a glance until Miss Isabel exclaimed:

"Why, Jabez—I thought we'd given one another notice and discharged each other!"

The old fellow drove his spade deep, leaned on it and nodded, saying:

"So did I, Miss Belle; but seeing as 'ow you's you, me's I, and us is ourselves, it can't be nohow, nowise nowhen, never—no! Us and this yere gardin' b'longs together till death do us part, amen! Now goo away, both on ee, and leave I to me work—like as only I can work."

" Good for you, old Heartofoak ! " laughed George.
" Commander, you are commanded, the vord now is—go ! "
And, laughing, back they went together, leaving the aged
one to his labour. . . .

Meantime, perched upon shady stile afar, Mr. Shrig was
inscribing on a particular page of his " little reader " a
certain name with divers curls and flourishes, which done,
he beamed and nodded at it, winked and whistled sound-
lessly at it ; then, closing the notebook, thrust it carefully
into the breast of his trim coat, took up his knobbed stick
that was so very like a bludgeon, and strode away townwards.

CHAPTER VIII

Concerning two letters

WITH only the briefest of side glances at that shining brass plate which proclaimed these the business premises of Messrs. Jackman, Son, and Bell, George mounted the three steps leading up to the gracious doorway and entered the spacious outer office, there to be greeted most deferentially by Mr. Beeby, the head clerk, and bowed to by the four juniors, which salutations he returned as politely; then, entering Mr. Jackman's sanctum, his own during that gentleman's absence, he laid by hat and stick and was about to ring for the morning letters, when with gentle tap Mr. Beeby entered to bow again and say:

" Excuse me, Mr. Bell, sir, but——"

" Hold hard ! " exclaimed George. " What the deuce ? Why all this confounded bowing and scraping, Ned ? "

" Well, sir, now that you are a partner——"

" I'm still George, especially to you, old fellow ! You and I have been ' George ' and ' Ned ' too long for any such nonsensical change. So ' Ned ' and ' George ' we shall remain. Is this understood ? "

" Yes, yes, indeed ! " sighed Mr. Beeby, smoothing his grey hair with thin, nervous hand. " It is very, very gracious and—and George-like, Mr. George, but indeed ——"

" Then drop the formality, Ned ; do not bow and scrape or ' sir ' and ' mister' me."

" Very well . . . and thank you, George, there shall be no formality between us—except on formal occasions," said Mr. Beeby warmly and with one of his too-infrequent smiles. " And now—this letter ! It was brought by a mounted servant in the Ravenhurst livery, about twenty minutes before your arrival, and I was directed to hand it personally to none but yourself——"

Mr. Beeby did so, then, checking a bow, went out, closing the door softly behind him.

Now glancing at this letter George saw it was sealed by a great smear of wax and bore the one carelessly scrawled word :

" Bell."

Breaking the seal, he read these words, written with the same contemptuous lack of care :

" Lady Clytie Moor takes pleasure to inform and warn the Bell person she has procured a larger and much stronger whip. Let Insolent Vulgarity beware."

George read this once and laughed, read it twice and scowled, perused it a third time and, acting on hotly youthful impulse, seized the nearest quill and scribbled this answer :

" The Bell person has the insolence to present his vulgar compliments to Lady Clytie Moor and suggests she take lessons in the proper manage of horses and herself. He also hopes she will not annoy him again by the infliction of her presence with or without a whip."

Having folded, sealed and addressed this missive, he summoned one of the junior clerks, a round-eyed, shock-headed, sharp-nosed young gentleman, to whom he gave the letter, saying :

" Wilks—Tom, old fellow, pray bear this letter to Lady Clytie Moor at the Castle—to her personally, mind ! If possible watch her read it, and, anyhow, wait an answer. Use your eyes and ears and report to me here as soon as possible. Off with you ! "

So away sped Tom, glad to be free of the office, while George sat to read the morning's correspondence, write or dictate answers, and thereafter dispatch such other business as required attention ; thus the morning was well advanced

when he bade " come in " to one who knocked, whereupon
Mr. Wilks reappeared, and his eyes seemed rounder and
hair rather more on end than usual as, closing the door,
he exclaimed :

"George, I say you know, b'gad she—— No, beg
pardon, sir, I was forgetting ! What I mean to say is——"

"Take a deep breath, Tom, and a chair ! Now sit back
and let's hear.   You saw the lady and gave her my letter ? "

"I did, sir, and she was—annoyed ! "

"Merely annoyed, no more ? "

"B'gad, yes, George—sir, she was most shocking
angry ! "

"Good ! " murmured George.

"Sir, she was so furious she raged at me as if I was to
blame ! "

"Better and better ! " sighed George.

"Then she—she actually hurled your letter on the
carpet and stamped on it ! "

"Excellent, Tom ! Stamped on it, did she ? "

"With both feet, sir, and mighty pretty ones they are !
Then she snatched it up, tore it to pieces and threw the
bits at me ! "

"Splendid ! " said George.   "Poor old Tom, the
wonder is she didn't tear and trample you as well ! "

"By heavens, Geor'—sir, for a moment I was afraid she
would—the way she flamed and glared at me, and then she
—actually and positively—swore ! "

"Mag-nificent ! " sighed George in a kind of ecstasy.
"What said she, Tom ; her very words—what ? "

"Well, sir, what she said and how she said it was very
strange and mighty queer . . . for in the very midst of
her fury—she smiled at me very kindly and said in voice
like cooing dove : ' Pray tell your '—these are her actual
words—' your damned Bell, I'll ring him till he cracks—
or I do ! Tell him I'll crush his very heart—like this ! '
and she pressed that pretty foot of hers into the carpet.
' Just like this ! ' says she, smiling.   ' Or he shall crush
mine ! Say that to your Mr. Accursed Bell and let him be

warned ! ' Then she left me and—well, here I am, and mighty glad to be. For 'twixt you and me, old fell—sir, though I adore the sex—to stamp and trample on a fellow's heart is coming it a bit too strong, eh, sir ? "

"Undoubtedly, Tom, so—be warned and beware ! "

"No no—not me ; the warning was for you."

"Ah, but," laughed George, "I was already warned ! Now pray tell Mr. Beeby I will see him about that probate —oh, here he is."

CHAPTER IX

Introduces Charles Mallory, Esquire

IT WAS evening and George on his homeward way, when he beheld a fine horse approaching, led by a hatless man, dusty and bedraggled, who limped ; he also bore one arm in a sling.

As George came up, this person saluted him, saying in matter-of-fact tone :

" Sir, do you happen to want a horse ? If so, this four-legged demon is yours at a price or no price at all. Though it is but fair to warn you the brute has bolted with me twice, thrown me once, looks gentle as a lamb, is fierce as a tiger and guileful as the very devil. Consequently, sir, the horse, though a noble animal, is my present abomination, especially this one ! So, if you desire such a horse—say the word."

During this speech George's quick glance had noted these several particulars : a face deeply bronzed, lit by well-opened brown eyes, and made the more attractive by a shapely, sensitive mouth that just now had a humorous twist ; a person this whose dusty garments were of expensive material and very excellent cut, who bore himself like a soldier and spoke like a man of breeding and refinement. Therefore George saluted him as such, saying with a laugh :

" Tomorrow, sir, your horse may prove more tractable and yourself of different mind."

" Sir, my offer stands—this lamb-like devil is yours now or when you will. And in justice to him I must inform you my injured arm is none of his doing ; 'tis small hurt I received at sea on my way here from America—or rather those United States, alas—which by a little statesmanlike concession would most surely have been preserved to us! But—no more of this depressing topic! My present need is a good inn; if you can direct me I shall be grateful."

"I can with pleasure!" replied George. "In the village yonder is the Raven, kept by Ned Marples, and no better inn or man anywhere. I can introduce you to both, for my way lies beyond."

"Pray do, sir, and make me doubly grateful. And my name is Mallory, sir—Charles Mallory at your service."

"And I am George Bell, sir, happy to be of service," said George as they went on together. "Pray, Mr. Mallory, have you been long in America? I mean—do you know it well?"

"I have and I do, sir. It is a grand and noble country, rich in all that pertains to man's innumerable wants, its resources and natural wealth equalled only by its vast size! Ha—devil take it, but for our cross, bungling government, England and America together might have ruled the whole world!"

"A glorious thought, Mr. Mallory! But—I am no politician—but is it not the fact that this late rebellion was caused by the irreconcilable Irish element?"

"Partly, sir; but it was we, or rather our damned government, gave the opportunity by using force instead of suasion."

"The tea-tax, sir?"

"Mr. Bell, this was but a side issue; there were many worse oppressions."

"But, sir, did not England spend much money, ay, and blood, in driving out the Dutch and French and later in warring against those savage Indians to protect the colony?"

"We did, sir, and the colonists were grateful and loyal until we began interfering with their internal economy, their trade and shipping, laying an embargo on their ports and heaping tax on tax! And no gentleman more loyal than George Washington himself! He was a captain in my regiment and as English as you or I! But alas, our worse than stupidity made him an American, our enemy and their first President."

" Did you know him ? "

" My father did. During one campaign against the French they shared the same tent."

" Did he then show sign of his later greatness ? "

" Yes and no. He was a very thoughtful man and so reticent that by many he was deemed unsociable—but deep down he was extremely sensitive, and thus, though warm-hearted and kindly, his friends were few, and thus fewer ever knew the best of him."

" And pray, sir, what of those wild Indians, those ferocious savages—— ? " Mr. Mallory frowned and shook his hatless, dark head, saying :

" They are a much maligned and ill-used people. I, like my late father, knew them well, travelled with and lived among many of the tribes—Huron, Iroquois and Delaware especially—and found them courteous, hospitable and scorners of lying and duplicity ; in fine, sir, gentlemen."

" Yet, sir, in England are frequent reports of their treachery, tales of brutal murders of lonely settlers, the massacre of solitary townships——"

" And, Mr. Bell, such reports are nearly always greatly exaggerated ! Indeed such evils usually tend the other way ! Indian lances and bows and arrows are small avail against musket, rifle and bayonet. I have seen the ghastly work of such weapons in Indian villages, squaws and papooses, yes, sir. Indian women and children slaughtered like cattle ! The white man is forever stealing more and more of their country—driving them farther into the badlands ! So, with arrow, spear and tomahawk the Red man leaps to its defence—only to go down before musket and bayonet, as he always will."

" So, Mr. Mallory, you side with the Indians ? "

" Say rather I grieve with them for the wrongs and injustices inflicted upon them. . . ."

Thus talking, they reached the village and the spacious yard of this goodly inn of the Raven. Here the horse that was a lamb, tiger, serpent, demon, having been duly tended, George led the way indoors, where Ned Marples hastened to welcome them. Mr. Mallory glanced at Ned's honest face, at the solid comfort around them, and nodded, saying :

" Landlord, Mr. Bell assures me there is no better inn or landlord than here, and my eyes confirm his judgment. Consequently my first need is a hot bath, my second and third a sitting-room with a fire, then dinner with a bottle of your best."

" Sir," answered Ned, bowing, " at your service and— with pleasure." And away he went.

" I am hoping you will dine with me, Mr. Bell."

" Thank you, but I am expected, sir, and already rather late."

" Some other time then. And by the way," said he as they shook hands, " what about your horse ? "

" My horse, sir ? "

" Certainly—down in the stables yonder."

" Oh, but, Mr. Mallory, I say, you know I—I couldn't accept such a splendid animal—as a gift. And I'm pretty sure I can't afford——"

" However, he will be there waiting for you to claim him whenever you will. Meanwhile I'm hoping we may meet again soon."

" Why then," replied George, heartily, " I'll take care we do ! And so for the present, goodbye, sir."

Reaching home, George found his aunt snipping roses and doing it as if she loved them (which indeed she did).

" My dear," said he, slipping his long arm about her, " I want my family's close attention ; is she listening with both auriculars ? "

" George, what on earth——"

" Family, be hushed and hearken ! I have just met a gentleman from—America ! "

" Not," she exclaimed with sudden interest, " not the wanted heir ? "

" No, that would be too much to expect—and yet—by

Jupiter, he might be! Such odd chances do happen—and he looked about the right age!"

"How old would that be, George?"

"About forty-five."

"Two years my senior. Is he one of those nasty American rebels?"

"Oh, no, he is English as you or I. He is also a soldier, or has been, and knew and greatly esteemed George Washington——"

"Then of course he is a rebel!"

"No again, my dear, for it seems Washington was loyal once and actually wore the King's uniform."

"And was a hateful wretch—with his Bunker Hills and Yorktowns!"

"However, I liked this Mr. Mallory so much that I felt greatly inclined to ask if he had ever heard tell of our Earl Philip."

"Why didn't you?"

"Well, the possibility that he had seemed so absurdly remote."

"No matter, you should have asked the question! Suppose he himself is the heir! Good gracious me! Describe him; what is he like, tall or short, dark or fair?"

"Tall and dark——"

"Ha! Then if he is a Wynter he is a bad Wynter! There used to be a foolish saying: 'As cruel as a "black winter",' Now his face—is he handsome?"

"Yes, in a hawkish sort of way."

"Ah well, Wynter or no, hawks are cruel birds, and I dislike hooked noses."

"But," said George, copying Mr. Shrig, "his nose, or as you might say beezer, snout or conk, m'lady, ain't hooked. No, it's quite a goodish beak, Aunt, better than mine though nothing like so beautiful as that which adorns the phiz of Mistress Isabel Standish, of course. Anyhow, I like him so well that I intend seeing him again, and should he prove up to expectation I shall, with your permission, ask him to tea here soon or late."

"Yes, do, George. For, judging by your very inadequate description, he might possibly be a Wynter . . . and besides, what should bring him to our quiet little village ; what, George, what ? "

"My dear," said he, leading her slowly cottage-wards, "this is a question to which Jasper Shrig would certainly reply : ' M'lady, " Echo alone responds ! " ' " And now, dear family, let us to supper."

CHAPTER X

Of Farmer Tulliver, his trouble, and the philosophy of Parson Aeneas Tomlyn

A SLUMBEROUS, lovely place was this little village of Ravenhurst, whose calm was seldom troubled by any harsher sound than murmur of soft-voiced Rusticity, clank of well-chain or drowsy rumble of leisured wagon-wheel ; here Tranquillity brooded—an all-pervading peace won so lately amid the smoke and bloody mire of Waterloo and upon the shot-riven decks of Nelson's ships at Trafalgar ; thus, for a while, the " Pax Brittanica " was to bless humanity.

So thought George as, having topped the hill, he paused to look down upon this small part of his so loved England, until, roused by the slow plodding of horse-hoofs, he glanced round and thus beheld sturdy, red-faced farmer Tulliver approaching astride a stout and glossy cob.

" Good evening, Abel," said he, as Mr. Tulliver reined up to shake hands. " How are things with you, old friend ? "

" Naun so well as they should ought for to be, Master George."

" Nothing wrong with the farm or stock, I hope, Abel ? "

" Nay, farm and all be well enough and so will be ever-so long as our men take pride in their labour, pitchfork and scythe, thatching a rick, laying a hedge, driving a straight furrow—ah, so long as we do love the good land and treat it kindly, we can snap fingers at they French and dangall foreigners ! No, my trouble be my darter Joan. Arl my days I've been Abel b' name and thought I were ' able' b' natur' ; but today I be nowise able to cope wi' our lass Joan ! And what d'ye say to that, Mr. George ? "

" I say, and beg you to remember, she is no longer a child but a fine and very lovely girl——"

" That she be—ah, and too well her do know it! Ye see, Mr. George, her mother, being re-fined b' natur', were ever wishful as our maid should grow up even more so, and sends her to a re-fining school in Brighthelmston, as they calls a ' ladies' semi-nary ', which were no place for daughter o' we! And now, ecod, they've edu-cated so much re-finement into her that, damme, she's rose above cows and is too fine for dairy-work! Reads books instead, which is bad enough, but po'try besides, wrote by some chap called Byron, which is worse! I read some on it t'other day—all about a maid in Athens as had stole his heart—such damn nonsense! "

" Easy now! " said George, laying white, though powerful hand on the farmer's brawny knee. " Don't be hard with her, Abel ; let her read, ay—give her money to buy all the books she wants, and you'll soon find she——"

" Not me, Mr. George—no ! There's her mother aiding and abetting her even now—and both agin me—such a dish o' tongues as has never happed afore wi' us."

" All the more reason for gentleness, Abel—a light hand on the reins, no curb, and for God's sake, man, no spurs ! "

" Thankee, Mr. George, friend ! I'm a patient man, as ee do know, but our maid being darter o' mine, is no fine lady nor ever can be, and the sooner her knows it the better for all on us at Burnt Ash Farm ! And as for spurs, Mr. George, I know just how and when to use 'em ! " So saying, he spurred his cob to snorting astonishment and galloped away and downhill in a cloud of dust. Leaning against a convenient stile to wait until this dust had subsided, George nodded his head, thinking of Farmer Tulliver's so beautiful and troublesome daughter whom he had seen grow from child to splendid womanhood ; and, because he had a sincere affection for her parents, he was not a little troubled by his old friend Abel's unwonted show of anger and wondering if he might possibly do anything to smooth and ease the situation, when he was roused by a loud hail:

" Aha, George ; well met, my son, well met ! "

Glancing up, he beheld Parson Aeneas Tomlyn striding towards him across the meadow, this famous scholar and truly reverend though extraordinary cleric who seemed two in one, for he showed as lean and unutterably sad gentleman by reason of haggard brow, long, melancholy nose and mournful-drooping lips—yet beneath this care-wrung brow the merriest, kindliest eyes danced and sparkled, while from these woeful-seeming lips issued the blithest of voices:

" What ho there, thou poor, pensively procrastinating pilgrim ! Why droopest thou, wherefore despond ? And this glory of God's sunshine all about thee ? " And forth-with George answered:

" Most reverend sir and my dear Aeneas, you come at the precisely right moment, for I must tell you there are certain of your large flock need their shepherd's care and guidance. Abel Tulliver has just galloped off in a fury because of his daughter Joan. . . . " And forthwith George recounted the farmer's trouble . . . " which," he ended, " makes me wonder and question if education is a blessing or curse ! "

" Here's fool of a question, George ! Education will be humanity's ultimate salvation."

" Ultimate—maybe, reverend sir. But today Joan is educated above her station—as Abel said : ' She's rose above cows and dairy work '."

" Because her education is not yet complete ! However, let us be rid of Ignorance at all costs, for with it will go most of the harms and evils of this troublous world. Meanwhile, if you are going my way, villagewards, let us go ! "

So down the hill they went, arm in arm, like the life-long friends they were. And presently the reverend gentleman, looking as though about to weep, began to whistle, " Come

lasses and lads ", merrily as any lark ; but after only a
bar or so paused to remark :

" By the way, George, this morning I had a visit from
your acquaintance, Mr. Shrig of Bow Street, who desired
to consult the church register."

" And what did you think of him, sir ? "

" As an extremely well-informed and most unexpected
person.   For instance, he knew I had been your tutor and
congratulated me on making ' sich a werry good job ' of
you."

" But how on earth did he know that ? "

" He said it was ' from information received '.   He also
told me Jackman had taken you into partnership, my son,
wherefore I congratulate you right heartily."

" Thanks, Aeneas.   But any success I may achieve
I owe, first to Aunt Isabel, bless her—and then to you, of
course ! "

" Indeed," sighed the reverend gentleman, " she is a
grand and truly noble woman ! "

" She is," nodded George.   " She was and always will
be !   And considering her looks, my wonder is no one
ever married her."

" Yes—it is—a great wonder ! " said the Reverend
Aeneas with another sigh.   " But talking of your Mr.
Shrig, he was quite horribly informative concerning that
skeleton, which he protests to be that of the seventh
Earl, poor young Philip who died so cruelly with his
lips upon the portrait of his young wife !   And this
reminds me that yesterday I paid my first visit to the
present Earl."

" Aha ! " exclaimed George.   " And pray how did he
impress you ? "

" Oddly, George, oddly !   Though to be sure he was
extremely courteous and very kindly promised a handsome
sum for the much needed repair of the church-tower."

" But did you like him, sir, personally ? "

" My son, I like and try to love all God's creatures."

" Did you manage to love the Earl, Aeneas ? "

"As a shepherd of souls, yes ; as a mere man, hardly."

"And the Lady Clytie Moor, did you meet her also?"

"I did ! She made me gracious welcome, she waited on me hand and foot, kept my cup abrim to overflowing—even the Earl drinks tea——"

"Then, Aeneas, you liked this lady?"

"Indeed ! And who would not? So very beautiful of form and feature, so gentle of look, so sweetly soft of voice, George, there is angelic music in it, as you will agree if you are so blest as to hear it."

"Sir, I have on two occasions and—well—I did not think of—angels."

"My son, you are young, and this lady so amazingly beautiful she may sweep any man off his feet——"

"Aeneas . . . ha, sir," laughed George, "you've hit it, for . . . she very nearly did ! " And he continued to laugh so infectiously that the Reverend Aeneas smiled, saying :

"George, you relieve me vastly, for no young man in love could laugh so gaily ! "

"And you're right again, sir ! For I'm not in love, not I, or ever possibly could be with this, let's say, proud young beauty—quite the reverse, in fact, quite ! " Here the Reverend Aeneas, rubbing his melancholy nose, viewed George so dubiously that he laughed again, saying :

"Now, Aeneas, d'you doubt me, sir?"

"No, my son, I never have and hope I never shall—though, as Mr. Pope has it, ' Beauty draws us with a single hair '—and methinks my young man doth protest over much?"

"Ay, I do ! " replied George, with a fervour almost fierce. "I do protest with all my strength."

"Dear me ! Why this passion of denial, my son?"

"Frankly, I don't know. I can only tell you it is absolutely sincere."

"Ah, well—now tell me why you gave Tom Ferris a black eye the other day."

"How d'you know I did, sir?"

" My son, there are few happenings in my parish that I don't hear about sooner or later. So, George, why ? "

" Well, passon," answered George, in the vernacular, " 'twere arl along-on-account-on Mistress Hagah as were bein' 'ard done by . . . no question. Boys and dogs and that theer Tom Ferris."

" The poor old soul ! And I understand you stopped him with a straight left and grassed him, very properly, with your right, my son ? "

" As you first taught me, Aeneas and dear sir, in between woeful spells at mathematics and furious bouts with Caesar or Virgil : ' Arma et vir, canbat.' Lord, what a grand tutor you were, Aeneas ! Dactyl and spondee, fist and footwork ! You taught me the true value of a straight left and how and when to use my right—— "

" Ah, but, George, my dear boy," sighed the reverend gentleman somewhat reproachfully, " I taught you far better things than sparring or even the classics, I hope ? "

" Aeneas, dear old sir, all that I am and hope to be I owe to Aunt Isabel and you, and—to both my gratitude is beyond expressing."

" Your Aunt Isabel, yes indeed ! Present my humble regards to her and say I shall come begging tea one afternoon."

" Why not now, sir ? "

" Son, tempt me not, for I must to divers of my flock, and first of all the Tullivers. So, fare thee well, George ! " And away strode this zealous shepherd of souls, vigorous and jaunty of bearing, yet doleful of visage as ever. Then home went George, to find his aunt and her Betty making strawberry jam and the cottage full of its sweet savour ; wherefore he stripped off coat and, armed with necessary tools, set about the construction of a rustical bower wherein Mistress Isabel might sit and read or sew or, with him, drink her beloved tea.

CHAPTER XI

Gives a too brief account of a short though momentous occasion

THE SUN, newly up, was giving the world, and all therein, glad promise of another glorious day, while Mistress Isabel, with Betty washing up the breakfast things, was singing " Sweet lass of Richmond Hill " ; thus, as George closed the wicket-gate and set off townwards, he whistled this merry, tuneful air, softly and in time with his step, when :

" Good morning ! " said a richly sweet voice. Whistle, step and breath also, it seemed, were checked together, for this (of course) was the voice of Lady Clytie Moor, and she was leaning gracefully across a stile, looking at him with expression as unexpectedly gentle as her tone. So George, suddenly mute and still, took off his hat and forgot to put in on again.

" What a radiantly beautiful morning, Mr. Bell ! "

" It—was ! "

" You mean until you met—poor me ! And yet O marvellous me to have such power—even upon the weather ! I am indeed a very potent personage, Mr. Bell ! "

" So I believe ! " he answered, gazing deep into those dark eyes that looked as keenly into his.

" Why then," said she, her ruddy lips upcurving with a smile he thought hatefully derisive, " you may put on your hat, for I detest red hair."

" So do I ! " he retorted, hiding the offensive curls obligingly.

" And now," she demanded, reaching white hand towards him imperiously, " will you have the kindness—no, the common courtesy—to help me over this stile ? "

" No ! " answered George, folding his arms.

"Did you . . . say . . . 'no'?" she enquired, as though amazed beyond belief. "Did you?"

"I did indeed!" he nodded. "You are much better there than here."

Her black brows knit in quick frown, her violet eyes widened to glare at him, her delicate nostrils showed suddenly dilated; then, as suddenly, she laughed.

"What an oafish peasant you are, Mr. Bell! What a perfectly graceless yokel!"

Here it was George who laughed and so unfeignedly that the white hand became a dimpled fist to threaten him.

"Yes!" he chuckled. "Oh yes, I am all that and a rustical hobbledehoy as well, and no fit company for your most gracious ladyship, so I bid you good morning."

"Then you still refuse to help me?"

"Madam, I do."

"I am wondering why, Mr. Bell?"

"Because your touch would be my affliction!"

"Oh," she sighed, as if in ecstasy of triumph. "Oh, Mr. Bell, how profoundly I must affect you? However, devil take you and your help, Mr. Bell; I'll manage alone!"

It was, to be sure, an awkward stile—high and narrow. George bowed and turned to be gone, but in that moment, despite her deft manage of belaced petticoats, he became suddenly aware of slender feet in dainty buckled shoes, of slim ankles silksheathed, of shapely. . . .

"Mr. Oafish Bell, what do you glare at?" she demanded, perched now and very precariously half-way across the stile. "If you will not help me, have the grace to look somewhere else or to go and be——" She uttered a gasping cry . . . she tottered . . . she slipped. Instinctively George leapt, and next moment she was in his arms, all fragrant, softly-yielding, perfectly helpless and supremely feminine. . . . So George stood notionless, speechless; and she lying thus upon his breast, neither looked at him nor uttered a word. When at last she spoke it was to enquire and very gently:

"Don't you think you ought to put down and be rid of—your affliction, Mr. Hobbledehoy?"

George released her so suddenly that she staggered and clutched his arm, saying plaintively:

"Are all strong men as rough and clumsy as you, Mr. Bell?"

Speechless, still, he gazed upon her, sensing now the power of her beauty, until:

"Oh," she murmured, brokenly, "why do you—look at me—so? Is it—hate, or——"

The question was never uttered, for George, still dumb-struck, loosed her fingers from his arm, gently as he might, and, turning from her, strode away as in very fury of haste. Hushed now was his cheery whistling, and he kept his frowning gaze bent earthwards, nor did he check or moderate his pace until he was within the portals of that stately house sacred to the business of

Messrs. Jackman, Son, and Bell.

CHAPTER XII

Chiefly concerning three letters

IT WAS towards the late afternoon when, rosily cherubic as usual, Mr. Jackman came bustling in to nod a greeting to his young partner, saying :

" Well, here I am—and sit down, George, for I regret to say my journey to London was wholly vain, or very nearly. Here "—he gestured to the papers, before him—" is the meagre result of all my trouble—a letter writ to my father at his then London address by Earl Philip fifty-nine years ago and of no practical use to us. Read it, partner, and give me your opinion ; pray read it aloud and let us comment upon it together." So George took this letter, yellowed by age, handling it with a care almost reverent, and read :

> " ' Ravenhurst House,
> St. James's Square.
> 1st September, 1757.

" ' MY DEAR JACKMAN,

" ' Acting upon your advice I shall, albeit unwillingly, take no further action against my damned cousin either by law or personal encounter. That he is a liar you have proved him, that he is a villain I have told him—and there, so far as he is concerned, the matter shall rest. As regards Lady Cecily, though shocked at her folly in trusting such a patent villain, and well-nigh heart-broke by her heartless usage of myself, yet mindful of her present unhappy situation thus deserted, disgraced and outcast, I herewith authorise and desire you to place five hundred guineas to her credit at once, with an assured annual income to her of two hundred and fifty guineas, paid quarterly. And now, my dear Jackman and trusted friend, I find myself, thus desolate, unable to endure London or even the peace and seclusion of Ravenhurst, both painful reminders of past happiness. I shall therefore leave England and for some considerable time, and journey to America, that wild and almost unknown country, and in this New World seek the solace of action and change of scene. To this end you will therefore secure me passage in some ship or, expense being no object, charter a vessel of my own. So, my dear Jackman, pray know me for your most grateful client, sorrowful friend and constant well wisher.

" ' RAVENHURST.

" ' I shall travel under and be known henceforth as George Philip Vane. For God knoweth my life has proved vain hitherto.' "

" And there," said Mr. Jackman, as George laid down this letter with hands more reverent than before, " there, I submit, is a beam, a feeble ray to lighten our darkness somewhat——"

" Yes," said George fiercely, " and to blacken the——"

" Hush, partner ! Let us with legal mind, that is to say dispassionately, consider precisely what this letter shows us."

" A heartless villain and a noble gentleman ! " said George.

" Calmly, my dear fellow, calmly ! We are here afforded a glimpse of two young gentlemen with cause for such bitter animosity that but for my father's influence they would have fought, shed each other's blood, and most probably to fatal effect——"

" And later on, sir, one of them certainly did, it seems, shed his blood ' copiously ' according to Jasper Shrig, yonder at the castle, and most probably by the act or will of——"

" Caution, George, caution ! Do not jump to any such conclusion. Keep all and every suspicion unspoken and deal only with known facts and such poor evidence as we have."

" Poor indeed ! " sighed George.

" However," said Mr. Jackman, turning over the papers before him, " here is one other letter dated some thirteen months later which broadens our ray of light though little to our purpose.   But take and read it out, George, and see what we can make of it."   So taking this second letter, George read aloud therefrom :

" ' Mount Engle,
New York.
3rd October, 1758.

" ' MY DEAR JACKMAN,

" ' This heart, methought broke, is sound again, its wounds healed and my grief banished by touch of a hand, a woman's, be sure, and she the holiest, loveliest, noblest in all this world.   She is Samantha, Dorothy Mallory, very young and most beautiful, of a once noble English family from Dene-Mallory, in Kent.   We were married two months ago, and the world for us a glory. Being now a Benedict, I shall draw more largely on my estates, etc.   Pray arrange accordingly and know me ever your obliged and sincere friend,

" ' RAVENHURST.

" ' Post scriptum :   Your letter just received has greatly troubled my present happiness by your news of Lady Cecily's flight with her nameless child, poor distracted creature.   Pray do your utmost to discover her whereabouts and make such further provision for her own and her child's present and future welfare as you deem needful.   This I charge you by our past, present and future friendship.   R.' "

Very gently George laid down this letter and sat gazing at it speechlessly ; and then before he could voice the thought that had rendered him thus speechless Mr. Jackman passed certain other papers, saying :

" Here you shall read of his death, the bald, official account of the massacre which tells little, and this one other

letter that tells us very little more.   But take it, George,
and let us hear."

So George forthwith read aloud :

"' High Mallory,
New York County.
15th November, 1760.

"' SIR,
"' It is with inexpressible grief that I write to inform
you of the deaths of Philip Vane-Wynter, Earl of
Ravenhurst, and Dorothy, his countess and my only
beloved daughter, with their infant son.   They suffered
with many others in the late massacre by the Iroquois
at Bear Creek—but these, my beloved ones, were over
young to die and so cruelly.   Sir, I can write no more,
and therefore beg to remain,
"' Your obedient servant,
"' EDMUND MALLORY.' "

"And there," sighed Mr. Jackman, as George refolded
this letter, "there was the tragic end of poor young Lord
Philip and his wife and heir!   But now, according to
Shrig, those confounded silver buttons and the miniature,
we are faced with the new and very awkward possibility
that his lordship escaped the massacre.   The question
being—did he return alone or with his wife and child?
Our concern being, of course, the child, his heir, of whose
existence we have no tittle of evidence."

"Except," said George thoughtfully, "old Jabez
Ferris's story of the baby on the tombstone."   Forthwith
George briefly recounted this oft-told story, adding:
"That, sir, is the famous ghost story old Jabez tells, which
I have always thought too ridiculous for belief—but now,
well, what think you of it?"

"So much, George, that I must see the old man and hear
this from his own lips, with every possible detail."

"One other thing, sir!   The name Mallory is not very
common, and yet the other day I met a gentleman of that

name, and, what's more, he had lately returned from America, which, I submit, is a somewhat odd coincidence."

" Yes, yes—indeed ! " exclaimed Mr. Jackman, pinch of snuff arrested at nose.   " So extremely odd that I suggest you get in touch with this gentleman as soon as possible if you know his present whereabouts."

" He should be at the Raven Inn, sir."

" Then to the Raven you go, George.   Show the gentleman this letter, and should he be any relation to the Mallory in question induce him to return with you if possible.   Off with you, my boy."

CHAPTER XIII

Concerns yet another and more fateful letter

STRIDING rapidly towards the village, George must needs pause to frown at a certain high and narrow stile, but at sound of approaching hoofs and wheels glanced up and was surprised to see Mr. Mallory seated in a curricle mounted on extremely high wheels, drawn by a speedy-looking horse driven by Jasper Shrig, who, flourishing whip in salutation, reined up dexterously to say :

"Sir, and George, good arternoon ! You behold us, friend, Mr. Mallory and self, on our road to yourself and partner."

"And, Jasper, you behold me on my way to Mr. Mallory ! "

"Good ! " said he, reaching down to shake hands. "Were you coming to claim that horse of yours at last ? "

"No, sir, 'twas to beg your help in quite another matter."

"Then, friend and sir," said Mr. Shrig, "the rumble is waiting and at your sarvice."

Forthwith George swung himself up to the lofty hind seat, and away they bowled, talking all thereon this wise :

MR. MALLORY (*turning to ask the question*) : Pray how can I help you, Mr. Bell ?

GEORGE : Sir, have you ever known or heard of a gentleman named Edmund Mallory ?

MR. MALLORY (*vastly surprised*) : Sir, he was my grandfather !

MR. SHRIG (*flourishing whip triumphantly*) : Blow my dicky, a bull's-eye !

GEORGE (*quite mystified*) : Jasper, what on earth ?

MR. SHRIG (*reining to a walk the better to explain*) : Friend

75

and sir, I draw my bow at a venture and brought down Mr. Mallory's grandfeyther——

GEORGE (*more mystified*): Eh? Grandfather? Good lord.

MR. MALLORY: Pray explain.

MR. SHRIG: Sirs, in my comings and goings I hears of a gen'leman at the Raven, name o' Mallory, lately from America. So I takes particular care to meet said gen'leman b' means of his hoss as has been and was being savaged by windictiveness in the shape o' the head ostler Timms, to make said hoss unrideable vith the idea of buying him cheap——

MR. MALLORY (*surprised and angry*): So this is the explanation of the poor brute's behaviour? Well, the damned rascal shall suffer for it himself——

MR. SHRIG: Sir, he has! Ar and b' means o' my old nobbler here. (Directs attention to the bludgeon-like stick lying at his feet.) Having, sirs, thus dooly performed on this raskell Timms, I comforts your hoss, and a werry fancy bit o' blood he is, and so doing—you finds me and presently honours me in a glass or so and mentions as how you're minded to show the Earl o' Ravenhurst a letter. Therefore, sirs, I drawed my bow as aforesaid and—there y'are!

By this time they had reached the town, and thus presently turned into the austere quiet and dignified seclusion of the Causeway.

It was as Mr. Shrig reined to a standstill that a man appeared, seemingly from nowhere, a meek-seeming person whose hay-like whiskers drooped dejectedly but who grasped the bridle of this spirited horse with a hand of mastery.

" Anything, Dan'l? " enquired Mr. Shrig when they had descended from this lofty vehicle.

" Nary a thing, Jarsper."

" Then let's say—thirty minutes, say—an hour."

" Very good, Jarsper," sighed the man Dan'l despondently, and then with sudden nimbleness had mounted to the lofty driving seat, wheeled the fiery animal and was gone.

So George ushered their visitor indoors, there to be greeted by Mr. Jackman, who, having bowed him to a chair, broached the subject forthwith, saying :

" Sir, we beg your consideration for this letter written from High Mallory, New York, dated November the fifteenth, seventeen hundred and sixty, and subscribed Edmund Mallory."

" Mr. Jackman, High Mallory was my home, Edmund Mallory my grandfather, and this letter written before I was born."

" Then, sir, pray read it and know we shall be immensely grateful for any further news you may be able to give us, any single particular concerning Philip, seventh Earl of Ravenhurst."

" Indeed," said Charles Mallory when he had perused his grandfather's faded script, " it was a sad and most tragic story ! But now, from what Mr. Shrig has told me, it becomes even darker and strangely terrible. Consequently I am here to afford you such help as I may by showing another letter written by this most unhappy Earl Philip to his brother-in-law—my father Charles, then a young man of twenty-two—though first I should explain how I came by it. When my father died I was far away in the Indian country among the Tuscaroras and, travel in that wilderness so very difficult, it was months before I reached High Mallory. Being the last of my name, I resolved to sell my estates and, here in the England I had never seen, end my days at our ancestral home of High Mallory in Kent. It was then, on going through my father's effects, that I found at the back of a drawer where it had lain hidden so long this letter, which, as it seems to me, written with a noble gentleman's blood and tears—hear it, sirs, and judge for yourselves."

From the breast of his very elegant coat Mr. Mallory drew a leather case, whence he took a folded paper which he spread out very tenderly.

"Gentlemen, this bears no address but is dated January the second, seventeen hundred and sixty, its message this :

"'She is dead. Oh, Charles, she is dead. My beloved wife and your sweet sister is dead. Three days ago I buried her here in the forest and with her my broken heart. Five days after you left us we were surprised by a strong war party of the Iroquois and myself struck down early in the battle. I awoke to find our Sachem Martocheegah bending above me, who presently showed me the dead body of my beloved. She had been killed by an arrow and instantly. I hope and pray God, though her long beautiful hair—— I cannot write it. But, oh, Charles, beneath her, safe and all unharmed, lay our little Philip, asleep. It seemed she had died shielding him with her own most precious body. Tomorrow, with Martocheegah and such of his warriors as remain, I, the most grievous of men, march for the sea with intent to sail for England with our child, and this despite my wound, though what is bodily pain compared to agony of mind for my irreparable loss. Gladly would I welcome any death that should reunite me with my ever beloved dead— yet needs must I live for our child, the little son she died to preserve. For him, therefore, I endure life, though all the best of me lies with my ever beloved in her lonely, unmarked grave. Now farewell to thee, Charles, dear friend and brother, should we meet no more ; forget not thy once happy Philip, Vane-Wynter.

"'RAVENHURST.'"

"The poor fellow!" exclaimed George impulsively, as Charles Mallory tendered this letter for their inspection. "He certainly was the most unfortunate gentleman!"

"Vich," quoth Mr. Shrig, "nobody can't deny!"

"Sir," said Mr. Jackman, returning the letter with a bow, "we beg to thank you. Thus we must presume Philip's son and heir to be alive—the ninth Earl—and therefore it becomes our duty to attempt his discovery which, all things considered, would seem a perfectly hopeless task. Meanwhile you, Mr. Mallory, will naturally desire to exhibit this most important missive to Lord Roland, the present Earl ? "

" At once, sir ! And I should esteem it a favour if your partner Mr. Bell would accompany me."

" Certainly, certainly ! " answered Mr. Jackman.

" With pleasure, sir ! " said George.

" Vich therefore," quoth Mr. Shrig, rising, " my gig is at your sarvice, sir."

CHAPTER XIV

Which is suggestively ghostly

RAVENHURST CASTLE, though a familiar object to George since he could remember, had been to his boyish mind a place of dread by reason of vague tales of its frightful dungeons and evil past; thus today, as they approached, he gazed at it with something of that same childish awe tempered with growing interest and speculation.

Throned majestically upon green upland above the bowery village, it dominated this fair countryside and therefore must forever be looked up to by all folk—the high, the middle and the low.

A place of strength, of fearful doom and of lawless revelry, it had been in the bad old times when might was right, but succeeding ages had mellowed and gentled it, the magic of time had transformed grimly massive walls into glowing brick and carven oak, its scowling battlements into graceful chimney-stacks and gables, thus today all that remained of its evil past was the great, old tower, ominous and grimly threatening as ever. . . . So thought George, for it was up at this tower he was staring, this, the last relic of the Vane-Wynters' mighty stronghold, as Mr. Shrig pulled up before the great house.

The stalwart footman who answered their summons was a stranger to George, for, being of the Earl's London household and himself a Londoner, this powdered and ornate lackey was therefore superior to all country folk and things in general, which fact he contrived to make slyly obvious.

" Neems—hif you please, gentlemen."

George mentioned them.

" H-and your pleesyah, sirs ? "

" To see the Earl on important business," answered Mr. Mallory.

" His ludship, gentlemen, h-is in repose."

" The matter is urgent ! " said Mr. Mallory.

" Sir, his ludship h-admits of none such of an after-noon——"

" However," said George, becoming impatient, " you will give the Earl my card—this ! Take it and stir your confounded stumps ! "

" S-stumps ? " repeated the footman with look and tone of lofty disapprobation.

" Legs ! " said George. " Those two, too-chubby pins of yours—off with you or by Jupiter——"

" What is it, Martin ? " said a richly sweet voice, and before them was Beauty Feminine, all luscious allurement from crown of raven hair to proudly arched foot. " What is the trouble, Martin ? " she enquired.

" These—this gentleman, m'lady actu-ally threatened me and——"

" No, no, Martin," said she in tone of gentle mockery, " it is only Mr. Bell's very unfortunate manner ! Though indeed he is a most important personage. Pray, Mr. Bell, why do you so—honour us ? "

" Not you, madam ! " George retorted with grandiloquent bow. " I would merely see the Earl to introduce this gentleman. Mr. Mallory, sir—Lady Clytie Moor."

A stately bow, a gracious curtsy ; then :

" Martin," said she, her mocking gaze still on stolid George, " haste you to the Tower Garden and warn his lordship that Mr. Bell approaches with a friend on most important business."

" And yet," said Mr. Mallory as the footman stalked away, " my business can wait. I would not disturb his lordship."

" Oh, but, sir," said she, glancing again at George's averted face, " you are with—Mr. Bell—and the Earl will always trouble himself to see—Mr. Bell ! So, pray, go with me."

She led them along the wide terrace, across spacious gardens, past trim stableyard, where stood Mr. Shrig's high-wheeled vehicle, and so at last to a grim enclosure screened forever from those fierce blusterers, the north and east winds, shut in by wings of the great house and backed by the mighty keep ; this grim old tower whose battlements scowled down upon him, malevolent and threatening as ever—or so it seemed to George. . . . And here beside a small table, seated in deeply cushioned armchair, they found the Earl.

" Dearest," said Lady Clytie, laying gentle hand upon bowed shoulder, " here is a Mr. Mallory and—Mr. Bell ! "

My lord glanced up from the book he had been reading with those strangely youthful eyes of his, saying plaintively :

" Gentlemen, pardon my not rising, but I am old and stricken. Ah, Mr. Bell, do you come to warn me your quest has been successful ? "

" Not yet, my lord."

" Ah—not—yet ! " repeated the Earl slowly. And now his keen gaze was upon George's left hand with its malformed little finger ; and George, instantly aware of this, hid it in his pocket. " Not—yet ? " said the Earl again. " Am I thus to understand you expect this search to succeed ? "

" The vague possibility, sir, becomes almost probable, thanks to the information supplied by this gentleman, Mr. Mallory."

" Indeed ? Then, sir, I am all attention—nay, first be at your ease, gentlemen," and he motioned feebly to a rustic bench nearby. Here seated, Mr. Mallory drew forth the letter, described briefly its discovery, and tendered it to the Earl, who took it in that large white hand that looked so powerful yet shook as with such pitiful weakness, saying as he did so :

" My glasses, Clytie."

" Here, dearest ! " So upon his high-bridged nose my lord perched these spectacles, while George, glancing at the book he had been reading without aid, pondered.

Very slowly the Earl perused this letter with its tale of death and disaster ; then, bowing his silvery head, remained still and speechless, until :

" Oh, my dearest," cried Lady Clytie, touching that bowed head caressingly, " is it a horrid letter ? Is it trouble . . . about Raymond again ? " And in voice suggesting tears the Earl replied :

" Dear child—read ! Take it and read . . . ! "

With eager gesture that was almost a snatch, she took the letter, bowing her head above it so that George saw only the sheen of her night-black hair ; but as he watched her read, he was suddenly astonished to behold something bright and sparkling fall to splash upon the so woeful screed. When at last she looked up, her cheeks were wet and eyes abrim with compassionate tears—and in this moment to beauty was added a perfect loveliness.

" Oh ! " she murmured brokenly. " That poor, brave mother ! Yet . . . how splendid . . . so to die ! But . . . her baby . . . her little . . . lonely babe with only . . . men to care for it ! Oh, my dearest, what of that poor . . . little motherless child ? "

" My dear," sighed the Earl, " if he yet lives—of which there is no proof whatsoever—he is now a grown man." Here he glanced at George. " Older than you, Mr. Bell."

" Oh no, dearest, no ! " cried she, drying her tears as if they offended her and looking at George. " No, nothing like so aged or grim as Mr. Bell ! "

" Gentlemen," sighed my lord, returning the letter, " this terse though grievous story not only touches me most sensibly but lends force to the presumption that my unfortunate cousin Philip died unhappily as he lived."

" And," said George, leaning forward, " the presumption is that he died here, my lord, at the Castle—and by violence."

" Violence ? " repeated the Earl softly. " Meaning of course, suicide or murder ? "

" Can your lordship suggest any other cause for Lord Philip's sudden death ? "

"Certainly, sir. He might have died by accident, or, having regard to his state of mind, by his own act."

"Your lordship was in residence here at the time, I believe?"

"I was, sir. But, oh, Mr. Bell," sighed the Earl with gesture of ineffable weariness, "had I been aware of my poor cousin's return and death should I not have published the fact long ago? As it is, I can only presume Lord Philip, for reasons known only to himself, stole here secretly and, being sick of mind and body, ended himself and his sorrows wilfully or by some mischance reopened his wounds, mentioned in that woeful letter, and so died. Such is my theory, Mr. Bell. There remains for you and Jackman merely to prosecute your search for Earl Philip's son and heir. And now," said he, turning to Mr. Mallory, "since it seems, sir, you are a connection of mine, pray tell me other news you may have concerning my unhappy cousin and your uncle."

"Then, my lord," said George, rising, "by your leave I will take a nearer view of the tower yonder."

"Certainly. Lady Clytie will be glad to act as your guide." Sighing, but obedient, she rose, to sink before George in profound curtsy and say:

"Mr. Bell, sir, by my lord's desire, you behold me very humbly at your service. Pray follow me." Mutely he did so until, being within the tower's looming shadow, he paused to say:

"Madam, pray believe I do not desire your service or your presence now or at any other time. I hope you can believe this?"

"Oh, I do!" she laughed. "This makes your presence less of an ordeal to me. . . . Though I wonder why we hate, loathe and abominate each other so perfectly. We do—do we not?"

"Extremely!" he answered, with fervour.

"We detested one another the first moment we met—did we not, Mr. Bell?"

"We did—and instantly!" he nodded.

" Well, I'm wondering why—for what reason ? "

" Natural antipathy ! " he answered. " We dislike each other by instinct, which is generally a surer guide than reason."

" But I have a great many excellent reasons for detesting Mr. Bell—his horrid red hair, his odious manners, his looks, voice, walk and general gracelessness."

" Good ! " exclaimed George, so heartily that she turned to stare and demand :

" Oh, indeed, sir ! Why so, if you please ? "

" Because, madam, disliking you as I do and always must, I should find it so extremely awkward and tiresome if you happened to love me."

" Love . . . you . . . ? " she gasped. " Oh, what . . . abomination ! "

" Exactly ! " he nodded. " It doesn't bear thinking upon. So let us talk of something less horrible—murder, for instance. This frightful old tower reeks of it ! Here in the past has been much evil—yes, of this I'm certain."

" How can you be so sure ? "

" I don't know, but sure I am. Besides, it has a black history. Look at it—those frowning battlements and narrow loop-holes ! It stands like Cruelty manifest threatening all and sundry now—as it always has done."

" Goodness gracious, Mr. Bell ! " she mocked. " What a ridiculously fanciful personage Mr. Bell is, to be sure ! "

" Yes," he answered, gazing up at this huge and forbidding structure, " yes I am ! As a child I used to fancy this dreadful thing was threatening me with terror of its great, gloomy dungeons, its hidden torture chambers and great gallows set high that all folk must see my lord's victims die. The jibbet-post stands there yet—beyond the battlements above us."

" Oh, Mr. Bell, how absurdly mistaken you are ! That pole, which we cannot see from here, is simply a flagstaff."

" Today—yes, madam ! But once upon a time it quivered to the struggling agony of poor, dying wretches !

No wonder our country folk believe this ghastly tower to be haunted."

" Does Mr. Bell actually so believe ? "

" Has Lady Clytie Moor the least interest in Mr. Bell ? "

" None whatever, sir."

" Then Mr. Bell suggests she leave Mr. Bell to explore this wicked old tower alone with Mr. Bell."

" On the contrary, sir, she will accompany Mr. Inquisitive Bell as my lord, its owner, desired her to do, though much against her will, of course."

George bowed ironically, she curtsied mockingly, and together they stepped from the fragrant, sunny air into the dank gloom of this age-old tower, a spacious echoing dimness breathing of decay.

" A horrid place ! " she exclaimed, halting to peer up and around them in the all-pervading dimness.

" Yes ! " said George.

" Then why come here ? "

" Curiosity," said George.

" And it smells like—like a tomb !'"

" It probably is ! " said George.

" How . . . what do you mean ? "

" That there are dungeons beneath us and below them again—a horrible death-trap called an oubliette."

" You seem to know all about it."

" Not all . . . God forbid ! But when a boy I ventured here more than once, and, though a pretty daring urchin— the place terrified me—yes, even then ! "

" Does it terrify you now ? "

" Yes, yes indeed, though in a different way."

" How ? In what way ? Tell me."

" By the sure knowledge that these old walls have shut in so much of hopeless misery, have rung with the wailing cries of tortured flesh, have known so much of cruel dying. . . . I say again, if ever a place could possibly be haunted, then surely this——" He was suddenly dumbstruck and motionless as from somewhere in the dimness around them stole a rustle of stealthy movement—

then from a corner, darkly remote, rose a vague glow, a pallid, unearthly light that glimmered, brightened and vanished, leaving the darkness more profound.

" What . . . oh what . . . is it ? " she whispered brokenly.

" Hush—listen ! " said George between clenched teeth. And now her hands were upon his arm, hands that clasped and clung, terror-shaken.

" Oh God . . . it's there ! There . . . in the corner . . . look ! " And now indeed George descried a shapeless something that rose slowly above the flagstones . . . up . . . and up . . . and then, to his inexpressible relief, from the same shadowy corner, a familiar voice said:

" Talking o' ghosts, or, as you might say, phanitums, lady——"

" Who is it . . . who are you ? " she cried breathlessly, her terror banished by fury of anger. " What are you doing ?   Who—who are you ? "

" Shrig's the monnicker, lady.   Shrig o' Bow Street——"

" Vile . . . cursed . . . wretch ! " she panted.   " How dare you trespass, damn you ?   Visitors are no longer permitted at the Castle ! "

" Conse-quently I'm no wisitor, lady."

" Then what are you ? "

" A limb, lady—a limb o' the law, werry much at your sarvice.   And talking o' ghosts," said Mr. Shrig, emerging from the deeper shadows, " this here old place is full o' same, for summat o' the sort has been persooing me, high, lady, and low, vich I have therefore been a-seeking by means o' this here—look at it ! " And he showed them a misshapen candle-end at which he gazed in a sort of rapture ; then, removing his hat, he placed it carefully therein as though it had been something extremely rare and precious.

" A candle-end ! " he murmured, in tone of awed wonder. " Two inches or so o' taller candle—ar, but it has showed me so much—so ass-tonishing much that I am dooly ass-tounded ! "

" What in the world ? " George inquired. " You can't mean ghosts, Jasper ? "

" Ar, but I do, George and sir, plenty on 'em—and all in the form of—a rat ! Ar, all except vun—the vun as met me face to face and stared at me . . . eye to eye . . . a ghost o' the past, same being a ghost o' the fourth Earl o' Ravenhurst in armour and a vig and told me so much that now I can clasp my daddle, my famble, or, as you might say, my hand upon the ninth Earl—sooner than expected ——"

" Eh, the ninth Earl ? " George repeated. " Then by Jupiter, you must mean—good heavens, Jasper, do you mean—the missing heir ? "

" That i-denticle ! "

" But how, Jasper, how ? And this ghost you mention . . . I don't understand——"

" Sir and friend, I didn't expect as how you could or can——"

" Then let me hear. In heaven's name, Jasper, explain ? "

" Not afore a young fee-male, sir, and her sech a werry fine lady."

" Oh indeed ? " she exclaimed. " Well now, I'll leave you to your horrid selves, gladly—very, very gladly ! "

" Then, madam," George retorted, bowing with wide-armed flourish of hat, " I as gladly bid you goodbye——"

" Oh, Mr. Bell," she sighed, " what a perfectly oafish booby you are ! " Crossing to the narrow, old doorway, she paused there to smile back at him and say in her sweetest tone, " The sooner Mr. Odious Bell is a ghost the better, and then—may the devil take him ! " Smiling still and with gracious gesture of farewell, she stepped into the golden sunshine and was gone.

" Burn my neck ! " murmured Mr. Shrig. " Ar, dog bite me if ever I heard a young fee-male party vith such gift o' speech or tongue so hell-oh-quent——"

" Ay, by Jupiter," laughed George, " a most shrewish fine lady with a rare gift of vituperation : But——"

" Hold hard, friend George. That's a noo un to me—

wi-tooper-ation!" And out came notebook and pencil. "Do you spell same by a wee or a double-you?"

"Now," said George, when this word had been written with painful care, "now, for heaven's sake, Jasper, let me hear—tell me precisely what you have discovered."

"Not afore my fax is so proved, sir and George——"

"But—confound you, Jasper—what about this ghost the fourth Earl, and so on—what?"

"Sir, all as I can tell you or anyone for the present is as ekker alone can say. And so," quoth Mr. Shrig, putting on his hat with due care for that so precious candle-end, "the vord now is action, sir, vich so being, us'll cut short our wisit here and—set about it. So, sir and George, let's go."

CHAPTER XV

Being chiefly a relation of relations

" A GRAND old place ! " said Mr. Mallory, glancing back at the Castle, as Jasper Shrig chirruped to his horse. " Indeed, I like Ravenhurst and its neighbourhood so much that I am half minded to remain here for the rest of my days could I find a residence suitable to such solitary person as myself."

" Good ! " said George heartily. " And I know of several likely properties."

" Then, my dear Bell, since we may possibly become neighbours, I suggest we take old Father Time by the forelock and drop formality. My name, to a friend, is Charles. How say you ? "

" That mine is George—and here's my hand, Charles."

" And now," quoth Mr. Shrig, touching his spirited animal with the whip, " talking of hair——"

" Yes, by Jupiter ! Smell it, Jasper ; it's a sea-wind sweet with brine—makes me wish I were a sailorman ! "

" Sir and friend, in that there hair was a h-aitch ! And besides, the hair as I mean is red."

" If you allude to mine, Jasper, you needn't, for, d'ye see, Lady Clytie reminded me of it again today, as you may remember."

" Ar ! Said as how she dee-tested it."

" Well, so do I ! And yet, damme, but I'm proud of it, too, for my father's sake ! "

" So ? " nodded Mr. Shrig, reining his horse to slower pace. " Your pa's hair was ditto, eh ? "

" Yes, though his face was better than this phiz of mine, handsomer, and so on. Judging by his portrait he was a fine-looking fellow in spite of his red hair—which he wore tied in a queue."

" Cap'n George Edward Bell o' Shoreham ! "

" Yes, he hailed from Sussex. But, Jasper, how should you know ? "

" St. Mark told me as how Cap'n George Edward Bell o' Shoreham, batchelor, married Helen Araminta Standish, eldest daughter o' Robert Standish, Knight o' this parish."

" Yes, Sir Robert was my grandfather, and a truly grand old fellow as I remember him until he died—of a broken heart, they said."

" Pray, George, may we hear why ? "

" If you wish, Charles, though 'tis a fairly long story."

" So much the better ! " said Mr. Shrig, reining to a walk. " 'Twill make our road shorter."

" Ay ay, Jasper. However, I'll be brief as possible. Know, then, Grandfather Standish owned a fleet of ships trading across the world, and George Bell was his youngest and boldest captain. According to Aunt Isabel he was a right gallant sailorman, had fought the French repeatedly and captured several prizes, and once by daring seamanship had sailed right through an enemy squadron. It was after this exploit that my wilful mother married him, and when I was born she gave me his name and ever since I've done my best to be worthy of it. Well, I was just one year old, weaned and so forth you'll understand, when my mother decided she and I would sail with my father to the Indies in one of Grandfather's newest and finest ships which he himself had christened the *Wilful Helen* after her. The ship, as I say, was new, speedy, heavily armed, and manned by a crew chosen by my father, and, because of his prowess, Grandfather decided that instead of joining the lumbering convoy the *Wilful Helen* should sail alone. Ah—but—the day before my mother and I went aboard, Aunt Isabel, who could be wilful also and even more determined than her twin sister, absolutely refused to part with me. My mother stormed and wept, Aunt Isabel outwept and stormed her, Grandfather threw up his hands and left them to it, and in the end, of course, Aunt Isabel had her way and I remained safe in her charge. Thus,

D

thanks to her, I am alive and now speaking. For hardly was the *Wilful Helen* clear of the Channel than she was attacked by two French cruisers, with a third in the offing. Seeing the odds against him, my poor father, for his young wife's sake, would have struck and surrendered without firing a shot, and very properly. Ah, but his wilful Helen, my valiant mother, would none of it—but—according to the survivors, she leapt to the nearest quarter-deck gun, snatched the linstock and fired it herself."

" By God, you should be proud of such a mother, George ! "

" By God, Charles, I am ! And of my father, for he fought those ships till they were battered and ablaze, his own vessel sinking and himself dying in his wife's arms. And when the survivors begged her to join them in the only boat remaining, she merely smiled and shook her head at them above her young husband's body . . . and stayed with her beloved dead . . . and went down with him and his gallant ship. . . . So there was the end of the *Wilful Helen*, of Helen the wilful and of her beloved Captain George, this father and mother I was never so blest as to know."

Now when George had ended his tale, they drove some distance in silence except for the muffled rumble of the gig's tall wheels. At last Charles said :

" My dear fellow, with such heroic mother and gallant father you have much to live up to ! "

" Yes ! " sighed George. " Yes, I have indeed ! They were sublime, and I am—so damnably human. Ah, but thank the Lord I have Aunt Isabel ! "

" And," quoth Mr. Shrig, " your grandfeyther."

" No, he died years ago, as I told you."

" Sir and friend, I mean t'other one, your grandfeyther Bell."

" Well now . . . 'pon my word," exclaimed George in sudden perplexity, " now you mention it, I don't remember that I ever heard mention of him . . . which is rather odd."

"Ar!" replied Mr. Shrig, touching his horse to a fast trot. "Nothing could be no odder . . . P'r'aps, if you axed your lady aunt——?"

"Aunt Isabel, of course! I wonder why she has never spoken of my father's people—at least, not that I can recollect. However, I'll enquire."

"Then now," quoth Mr. Shrig, "talking o' dungeons—therein, besides ghosts, mostly in the form o' rats, as aforesaid, mouldy bones, rusty chains and sich-like odds and ends, I dis-covered a message, vords deep—scratted into the stone, vich I dooly took down ex-act into my leetle reader, though, except for a vord here and there, I can't make heads nor yet tails on it but am hoping as p'r'aps you can." Reining to a standstill, Mr. Shrig drew forth that bulbous notebook of his, and, opening it at a certain page, passed it to George, who saw these words printed boldly and with painful care:

> " Vane Wynter tyl ther lyn bee spedde
> Ben eder blakke as nytt or redde
> Redde of sorwe shal ne lakke
> yn joyance al shal lyv ye blakke
> Yet better redde in griev & paine
> Yf redde to paradys attain
> Thanne blakke in earthly weal to dwell
> Dying shal bren in hotest hel.
> Writ b mee Gefroi Vane Wynter, yt be God hys
> grace am redde, Laus Deo. Here pent be myne
> couzen Raimond yt is blakke to myne deth.
>   In manas tuas Domine. Amen."

And having conned this over, George read aloud thus:

> " ' Vane-Wynter, till their line is sped,
> Shall be either black or red.
> The red of sorrow shall not lack,
> In happiness shall live the black.
> But, better be red in grief and pain
> If red to Paradise attain

Than black in earthly joys to dwell,
And dying, burn in hottest hell.
Written by me, Geoffrey Vane-Wynter, that, by
God's grace, am red.   Glory be to God . . . I
am prisoned here to my death by my cousin
Raymond, who is black.
            Into thy hands, O Lord.   Amen.' "

" And here," said George, closing and returning the
book, " here is a voice crying iniquity out of the black
past—poor fellow ! "

" Ar," nodded Mr. Shrig, stowing away his little reader.
" And also this here onfortu'ate gen'leman had red hair !
Vich don't hardly seem a healthy colour for this here
noble family."

" Yes indeed, Jasper, considering the seventh Earl,
Lord Philip was also red-haired. Consequently I'm glad to
be the merest commoner in spite of my ginger nob.   But
now, Jasper, heave ahead, old fellow, for, bearing south
not half a mile, is Sparklebrook and Aunt Isabel—while
Old Sol yonder, trending westerly, suggests—tea ! So,
friends, how say you ? "

" I shall be honoured ! " Charles replied.

" And myself, ditto—but," sighed Mr. Shrig, " Dooty,
vith a werry large D, forbids ! Therefore, George and
sir, present my humbel respex to your lady aunt and say
as how 'tis a pleasure yet to be—I hope ! "

CHAPTER XVI

Concerning tea and grandfathers

MISTRESS ISABEL, having discharged old Jabez again for some sin of omission, was doing her best with a spade, when she heard the wicket-gate's familiar click, and, glancing thitherward expectantly, her smile of welcome for George was banished by a frown to see him accompanied by a stranger whose distinguished air and easy bearing proclaimed him one of the Quality; thus her annoyance deepened because she knew that her hair, damp with labour, was all " rats'-tails ", her sun-bonnet awry, and her gown (kept for such rough work) old and shapeless. . . . Nevertheless, being her indomitable self, she relinquished toppling spade (though with superb gesture), and advanced to greet this most unwelcome visitor, noted firstly his rich though sombre attire, then his shapely mouth and longlashed eyes that made his lean, bronzed face better than handsome . . . while he beheld a woman in the lovely, glowing autumn of her days, shaped like a Juno and as stately, and instinctively he bared his head.

" Aunt," said George, glancing from one intent face to the other, " allow me to present Mr. Mallory! Sir, my one and only family and presiding genius, Mistress Standish."

" Madam," said Charles, bowing deeply, " your most humble, obedient servant! "

" Sir," she replied, with gracious inclination of head, " you would be the more welcome were I less dreadfully bedraggled."

" Mistress Standish," he murmured, " eyes never beheld bedragglement so beautified! " He said this with such deep sincerity that she flushed so youthfully that George grinned, saying:

"Aunt Belle, you behold us languishing for tea!"

"Then, my dear, you shall drink it out here among my roses, so soon as I am rid of my—beautiful bedragglement, Mr. Mallory." She laughed. "Meanwhile George shall guide you round our domain—one acre, two rods, poles or perches, sir, and not an inch wasted." So saying, she left them to pace this fragrant sunny garden side by side, and both alike profoundly thoughtful; yet when at last George spoke it was on impulse:

"Tell me, Charles, what did you think of her?"

And, as impulsively, Charles answered:

"Most beautiful!" and glanced cottagewards.

"Yes," George admitted reluctantly, "yes I suppose she is—yes, in spite of her ferocious, gipsy-like devilry and horrid black hair——"

"Ah," sighed Charles, "you allude to Lady Clytie?"

"Of course! Old fellow, I abominate her and, thank heaven, she loathes the very sight and sound of me! And yet—by Jupiter—here am I thinking and talking of her, which is dev'lish odd. Let's talk of something less infernally repulsive."

"Very well, George! When are you claiming that horse of yours at the Raven?"

"Never, Charles! Since I can't afford to buy such a splendid animal, how can I accept him as a gift? I am no end grateful for your generous offer, but—no."

"My dear George, pride is admirable between strangers but damnably out of place among friends, as I hope we are—or going to be?"

"Ar, no question o' that, maister," replied George in the vernacular. "I tuk to ee drackly minute as I sot eyes on ee, I did, and right amazin 'twere sure-ly! And yet, Charles, talking as one friend to another, I am at present too damnably slender of purse to accept such a present."

"Then, George, we will refer the matter to your family and let your presiding genius decide, for she is wise as Pallas Athene, and——" He checked suddenly and glanced up at the cottage more wistfully than ever.

" Well," George demanded, " pray what more of my family, old fellow ? " Charles turned and looked at him as he replied :

" Beautiful . . . beautiful as Juno ! "

" By Jove and Jupiter, yes ! " said George fervently. " And lovely as herself ! And, Charles, what's more——"
Out from the wide lattice above them came Miss Isabel's head to say :

" Hush ! If you must deal in such barefaced—not to say—fulsome personalities, for mercy's sake go farther away because Pallas Athene is dressing Juno's tresses, and your talk distracts both, and rats'-tails demand the strictest care and attention of each. . . ."

Thus presently, when Miss Isabel stepped into the sunny garden, never had her abundant hair seemed more glossy or artfully artlessly ordered, though here and there amid these shining braids was gleam of silver. . . . And now tea appeared, with Betty's smiling aid, tea in the best silver pot and delicate, most precious china—with cakes, buns and bread and butter cut thin and rolled.

So beneath the old pear tree down they sat to the proper enjoyment of this delectable, truly English meal.

" Aunt," said George, as he watched her deftly filling the cups, " we have just been paying a visit to the Castle——"

" Oh ? " she enquired, with quick side glance. " You mean—to Lady Clytie, I suppose ? Milk and sugar, Mr. Mallory ? "

" Thank you ! " he murmured.

" Well, George, and how did you find the lady ? "

" Scornful as ever, Aunt, and swore at me as usual. But our visit was for another purpose—eh, Charles ? "

" It was ! " he answered, and, turning to Miss Isabel, he described their visit, told of the letter, and ended by giving it for her perusal. . . . And once again this age-old woeful screed was hallowed by a woman's pitiful tears ; seeing which, George instantly hugged her, saying :

" Dear Aunt Belle, even Lady Clytie wept over it, which astonished me no end ! But this letter, we think

proves Lord Philip returned and—with his son and heir.
The question is, how did he die and—what became of his
baby son——"

"To vich—ekker alone responds—as yet!"

They started, all three, and thus beheld Mr. Shrig
surprisingly near, for it seemed the wicket-gate had failed
somehow to click its customary warning. Hat in one
hand, knobbed stick in the other, he stood, hesitant and
wistful, as he enquired:

"My lady, your werry humble servant J. S. hopes as
he don't in-trood?"

"Why, of course not!" she answered, smiling. "You
are very welcome Mr. Jasper. Come and sit here—here
beside me."

"Ah, my lady," said he, with his bobbing jerky bow,
"I am dooly honoured!" So down sat he, while away
strode George for another cup and saucer.

"Were you also at the Castle today, Mr. Jasper?"

"Ay, my lady, and a werry in-formative castle I found
it! And," he continued, as George came striding back,
"talking o' grandfeythers, my own grandfeyther on my
mother's side earned his bread with a spade, him being a
gardiner, and a werry good 'un, too! But he never set
foot to spade in such gardin as this, nor yet growed sech
bee-ootiful roses as now blooms around us—vich couldn't
be expected, seeing as how my grandfeyther's gardin was
never blessed by wision so fair as the lady as here and now
is blessing us by her lovely presence. George, friend and
sir, my grandfeyther never set eyes on lady the like o' your
gracious aunt, never!"

"Oh, Mr. Jasper!" she laughed, passing his cup.
"I protest you will make me quite vain." Here, chancing
to meet Charles Mallory's intent gaze, she flushed again
and more youthfully than ever, while, for that matter, so
did he, as averting his eyes with diffidence as youthful, he
plied Mr. Shrig with cake and bread and butter.

"Aha!" exclaimed George, eyeing Shrig's placid
countenance with covert smile.

"Talking of grandfathers! Aunt, pray what of my grandfather Bell? Why have I never heard anything about my grandfather's people, his family, and so on."

"Because," she answered, cup arrested at shapely mouth, "I never heard of them, either, my dear. Your father was an orphan reared by strangers."

"Well, who were these strangers?"

"I believe the name was Benson or Mason . . . living either at Rye or Winchelsea. . . . Anyhow, they must have been quite horrid people, for I remember your poor father told us once how they used him so cruelly that he ran away to sea."

"But, Aunt, didn't my father ever speak of his own folk, the Bells?"

"Yes, to say he knew nothing whatever concerning them and to wonder about them, as you are doing now; and why, George—why the sudden interest? My good gracious!" she exclaimed, turning swiftly as the wicket-gate clicked so violently open to the hasty entrance of a young, country fellow, who, thus suddenly aware to the company, halted and stood gasping and speechless.

"Dear me—what now?" demanded Miss Isabel. "Henry Jevons, whatever is the matter? Speak, Henry, speak!"

"Oh, Miss Isabel," he gasped, "an accident, ma'm . . . on the hill . . . a gentleman——"

Up leapt George, saying:

"We're with you, Harry—lead the way—is he badly hurt?"

"'Fraid so, sir."

"Oh, that dreadful hill!" sighed Miss Isabel, rising. "George, if the poor gentleman is still alive you will bring him to me, of course. Now hurry, while Betty and I prepare. . . ."

CHAPTER XVII

Introduces Raymond, Viscount Hurst—and one other

AT THE foot of this steep, winding hill they beheld, firstly, the wreck of a smart curricle, and, secondly, a pair of legs out-thrust towards them from broken hedge, slim legs ominously motionless and splendidly encased in gleaming, gold-tasselled Hessian boots ; now even as they extricated the owner of these legs, George exclaimed :

" Good—great heavens ! It's Corks of Trinity ! It's Viscount Hurst, the Earl of Ravenhurst's son ! And—he looks uncommonly dead, poor fellow ! "

" Ar ! " quoth Mr. Shrig. " But he ain't—yet ! "

" No—he still breathes ! " said Charles, loosening the injured man's stock and neckerchief. " Now—let him lie flat—so."

" He shows pretty bloody, Charles ! "

" Merely scratches ! " said Charles, his quick, deft hands still busied upon this slender, inanimate form. " And there are no bones broken, thanks to the hedge."

" Good lord ! " exclaimed George, in awed tone. " Are you surgeon as well as soldier, Charles ? "

" No, merely a soldier with too much experience of wounds and sickness, George. . . . The sooner we get him to the care of your noble aunt the better. What we need is a gate or hurdle."

" Ay, sir," said Jevons, " there be a hurdle in meddow yonder ! " and away he sped, while nearby Mr. Shrig seemed lost in contemplation of the wrecked vehicle, more particularly the off-side axle which had lost its wheel. Having studied this axle with peculiar interest, he went where the errant wheel had bowled itself into the opposite ditch. He tested the ornate hub-cap, and, finding it turn easily, he beamed and nodded at it ; then, lips pursed in soundless whistle, turned to help bear the still unconscious young Viscount to the ministering care of Mistress Isabel.

They found her, with Betty in support, armed with sponges, towels and bandages, with bowl and basin of water hot and cold, besides divers oft-tried, homely remedies in pots and bottles.

"How young he looks! Poor boy!" sighed Miss Isabel, stooping over her unconscious patient, whose face, topped by pale-gold hair, showed indeed very youthful and somehow oddly plaintive. "Poor boy!" she repeated. "Lay him here. Now, Betty, be ready with the towel when I say."

"And, Aunt Belle, here's Charles to help you, for, besides being a soldier, he's no end of a surgeon."

"Then, Mr. Charles," said she, with swift, bright up-glance, "I shall be very glad of you, and grateful."

So the Viscount's injuries were tended with such assured skill that Miss Isabel, watching Charles Mallory's intent face and quick, deft hands, was content for once in her life to merely look on, and, being thus content—wondered . . . until. . . .

The Viscount sighed deeply, his long lashes fluttered. . . . Miss Isabel leaned above him . . . the lashes parted to show eyes vividly blue that gazed up into her own . . . then the shapely pallid lips curved to joyous, smiling whisper:

"Dooce take me . . . an angel! So . . . old Death's got me at last and . . . I'm in heaven . . . more than I dared hope. . . ."

"No, no!" said George heartily. "You're very much alive, Corks old fellow."

"Eh?" gasped the Viscount. "Who the . . . devil are you? Go away, you . . . spoil it all! B'lieve I know you. . . . Cert'nly . . . Bell of Peterhouse, eh?"

"Yes, old fellow, and this angel is my aunt, Mistress Standish; Aunt, Viscount Hurst."

"Madam," said he in stronger voice, "soon as possible I'll get up and bow, meanwhile I do it in spirit. . . . And

I say, Bell old f'lo', seeing I am so truly a ' friend in need,'
pray introduce me to these my ' friends in deed '."

This done, he contrived, with Charles Mallory's assistance,
to sit up and shake hands, lifting Miss Isabel's to his pale
lips. "Now please," said he, leaning back to the cushions
for his comfort, "tell me how it happened, for, d'ye see,
all I can remember is that I was half-way down a hill,
dooced steep, though well in hand, then a jolting toss and—
nothing more. So, y'know, I'm rather curious to know
why and how ? "

" M'lud," answered Mr. Shrig, promptly, "your off-side
veel took French leave and rolled itself into a ditch, and—
there y'are ! "

" Yes," sighed the young Viscount, glancing up and
around with a smile Miss Isabel thought strangely pathetic,
"yes, here I am and greatly obliged to you all. . . . By
your kindness I am alive and so much so that now——"
Here he contrived to get to his feet and salute them with a
profound though somewhat tottery bow.

" Oh, take care ! " said Miss Isabel, settling him back
among the cushions. "Though you are wonderfully
recovered, indeed you have had a miraculous escape, my
lord."

" Oh, I say, so you know ! " he moaned. "Considering
you have saved my confounded life and that I thought you
were an angel, and no wonder, please know me for your
most humble grateful servant to command. So do pray
call me Raymond—it's a fool of a name, I know, and I'll
answer just as well, or better, to Tom, Dick, Harry or
Corko, so, Miss Isabel, pray take your choice."

" Then, Raymond," she laughed, "since you are so
wonderfully better, you shall have tea with us, for we had
scarcely begun. . . . So, George, help me indoors with all
these things."

" Pray suffer me ! " said Charles, gentle of voice though
masterful of hand as he relieved her of the heavy bowl she
had taken up. "Now that basin," said he, "and all the
other oddments into this bowl; I can carry them all."

Mutely and instinctively she obeyed, and now once again she wondered, as side by side they crossed the garden, cottagewards; while the young Viscount, gazing after them murmured:

"Bell, I'm no end glad of that toss I took on the hill——"

"Eh? Glad? Are you, by Jupiter! Let me tell you, my Lord Viscount, you'd now be dead as mutton but for that hedge and Charles's skill!"

"However, you don't have to go on calling me 'viscount', demmit!"

"However, my lord, I shall, so long as your confounded lordship continues to call me 'Bell'. Either 'George' me or 'Mister' me, Viscount."

"Agreed, George!"

"Very good, Raymond!"

"Hold hard, George! When alone, let it be 'Corks'. And I'm glad of my toss because it has landed me—here among you all—and, George, old f'lo', 'pon my honour I really did think she was an angel——"

"Naturally, Corks old man, for so she is, or very nearly."

"So now," said Mr. Shrig, his roving gaze upturned to the foliage of the ancient pear tree above them, "talking of veels, m'lud, had you travelled far on them same?"

"From London with only four changes, and in pretty good time!"

"And, m'lud, where did you change hosses last?"

"Place is called Hailsham—which reminds me—what became of the poor brute——"

"Bolted!" answered George. "There was no sign of any horse——"

"Hailsham!" repeated Mr. Shrig. "But you stopped again, eh, m'lud? Here in Ravenhurst willage p'r'aps, let's say—at the Raven."

"Yes, yes I did—but how the dooce should you know?"

" Dee-duckshon, sir. Did you meet or see any person beknown to you ? "

" Not a soul."

" Have you been the wictim of accidents afore today, m'lud ? "

" Well now, demme, but it's queer you should ask because, as a matter of fact, I have—yes, b'gad, I've always been such a dev'lish unlucky f'lo'."

" Could you describe said accidents, sir ? "

" Hardly, for d'ye see, they were—just accidents, odd happenings."

" As f'rinstance, m'lud ? "

" Oh well—unloaded guns go off at me, boats sink under me, stirrup-leathers break. I was stolen when a puling infant, nearly broke my neck as a boy. As I told you, I was always unlucky till today—for yonder she comes, and with the tea ! "

Thus presently Miss Isabel, seated now between Charles Mallory and the Viscount, performed again with the teapot, once more was the pleasant tinkle of delicate china and murmurous conversation, until George, at mute signal from Mr. Shrig, glanced whither thus directed and beheld one who leaned across the wicket-gate, gazing in at them with a still and almost terrible fixity of gaze. George frowned and made to rise, but ere he might do so the Viscount had spied this silent intruder and exclaimed in tone of astonishment :

" Humphrey ! You—of all people ! "

The stranger clicked open the gate, his dark gaze still intent, himself a figure supremely elegant from gilded spurs to modish hat which shadowed a face classically handsome but so pale and set that it might have been chiselled from ivory or marble, a seemingly ageless face and therefore difficult to estimate.

" Again Raymond ! " said he in voice deep, soft and reproachful. " Reckless as ever ! Rash, rash fellow ! "

" Listen to him ! " cried the Viscount indignantly. " Here stands Mentor in the form of my cousin Sir

Humphrey Carr, and as usual blaming me for my confounded ill luck ! "

Here, with a leisured grace, Sir Humphrey advanced, hat in one hand, gold-handled riding crop in the other, to bow ceremoniously, saying :

" Madam and gentlemen, if this be an intrusion pray let a natural anxiety excuse it, for in the village I heard a gentleman had been killed, and a young fellow actually told me the dead man was Viscount Hurst and directed me to him here. So hither I hastened, Raymond, to find you——"

" Drinking tea, Humphrey, and—most surprisingly alive."

" And, cousin, I rejoice to know it."

" Then, Humphrey, come and know these my good friends also, to whom I certainly owe my very confounded life."

The introductions spoken and duly acknowledged, Miss Isabel enquired :

" Would you care to join us at tea, Sir Humphrey ? "

" Extremely ! " he answered. " But, alas, it is a pleasure I must deny myself ! For, remembering the wildly exaggerated reports of Raymond's accident—reckless fellow—I must ride at once to inform the Earl his dearly beloved son is—so surprisingly alive—thank God ! "

" And these good friends, Humphrey ! "

" To these also my gratitude ! "

" And, Humphrey, I was not reckless——"

" My dear Ray, you have never been anything else ! You are rash by nature and for ever risking your precious life—seeking always the most perilous way and joying in it. Really you should curb this mischievous propensity, if only for the sake of your—doting sire, my dear Raymond."

" Humphrey, I tell you these accidents happen to me simply because I was born under some doocedly unlucky star and consequently fated for accidents. Today, for instance, my wheel came off—yet I'm alive. Though I'm beginning to wonder how long my good luck will hold, for more than once lately, old Death's dooced scythe has missed me only by a hair."

" M'lud," enquired Mr. Shrig in the act of sipping tea, " did you say ' hair ? ' "

" Yes, and I say it again."

" B'reason o' that gun as missed you by sich a narrer squeak and the boat as left you to swim for your life, and sich like inci-dents ? "

" Yes."

" Has this gen'leman, your dewoted cousin, heard o' same ? "

" No, how should he ? "

" How indeed, m'lud !   Vich is the reason as he should ought to know.   How say you yourself, Sir Humphrey, sir ? "

" I say yes, most certainly ! " replied Humphrey.   " Pray let us all hear of your misadventures, Ray ; your audience is agog and none more so than myself."

" Oh, but I say, you know," said the Viscount self-consciously, " when it comes to telling there's precious little to tell."

" That there gun ! " murmured Mr. Shrig.

" Well, as you know, Humphrey, I'm always dooced careful to unload my guns, yet not long ago my favourite Manton went off and blew a hole in the ceiling, which was a trifle odd, considering ! "

" But my dear Ray, are you sure—quite sure you un-loaded it——? "

" Yes, of course I'm sure."

" That there boat ! " murmured Mr. Shrig.

" Yes, what of the boat, Raymond ; do pray tell us."

" The confounded thing merely gave me a ducking, that's all ! "

" I didn't know you could swim, Ray."

" I can't, but my groom Tim O'Brian can."

" Have you experienced any other mischances ? "

" Lots—fool riders cannon into me, drunken wagoners

all but run me down—so on and so forth. But," sighed the Viscount wearily, "I think that'll do for the present."

"Then I will spur and speed for the Castle to reassure your devoted father with the glad news that his only son and heir still lives. I will also send a carriage for you. And, my dear Raymond, accept my heartfelt congratulations—for indeed it seems some angel has you in his particular and most especial care."

"Ar!" nodded Mr. Shrig. "Or, contrarvise, a demon o' wiciousness is a dogging of you werry determinated, m'lud."

Sir Humphrey, in the act of bowing, turned and looked at Mr. Shrig; he also smiled, saying lightly:

"Were I a betting man, I would back my bright angel against your black demon, heavily at any odds! So, gentlemen," said he, with gracious flourish of whip, "I bid you good day!" Then, baring his dark head, he bowed to Miss Isabel, murmuring:

"Gracious lady, accept my thanks on poor, dear Raymond's behalf—rash and random fellow—and, believe me, your very humble servant." Then, donning his hat as if it had been a royal diadem, he departed with leisured, graceful stride, leaving a shadow behind, or so it seemed to George, though, to be sure, old Sol, now sinking westward, had veiled his jovial visage in cloud, threatening rain. . . . So indoors they went, bearing the tea-things with them; and here, presently, by Mr. Shrig's humbly, preferred request, Miss Isabel, seated at the piano, played and sang to them until, as evening fell, a smart young groom presented himself to say the carriage awaited his lordship.

It was with very evident reluctance that the Viscount rose to take leave, sighing:

"I say you know there's so much I want to say to you, all I can say is nothing at all except just—thanks. Because, Miss Isabel, you've shown me what a home might be, and this is so new in my experience that I regard my accident as the best and luckiest thing that ever happened to me; so, because I can't say all I want to say because it's too deep for expression, I'm hoping you will understand. Do you?"

"So well," she answered and in her gentlest voice, "that you will always be dearly welcome here at Sparkle-brook. Remember this."

"Thanks!" he murmured. "I shall never forget." Here, turning to be gone, he staggered, then laughed, saying apologetically, "My pins are still a . . . trifle wobbly."

So, arm in arm with George and Mr. Shrig, away he went through the gathering shadows to where stood the waiting carriage into which they aided him and whence he instantly leaned forth to grasp their hands with a fervour oddly pathetic, or so thought George.

"Mr. Shrig and George, old f'lo'," said he, "if my accident has made us friends, as I hope, then I count myself most dooced lucky. So hurrah for our next meeting!"

"Hurrah it is!" replied George heartily, as, with cheery wave of hand, Raymond Viscount Hurst was borne away through these ever-deepening shadows.

"You knowed him at your university, eh, friend George?" enquired Mr. Shrig, gazing pensively after the smooth-running carriage.

"I did and I didn't, Jasper, for, being myself a commoner and he the son of an earl, we seldom met—probably my fault. But now, 'pon my life, he improves on acquaintance—a very likable fellow, eh, Jasper?"

"Ar," murmured Mr. Shrig, his gaze still intent though the carriage was now out of sight. "So werry likable that I—I don't like it!"

"What don't you like, pray?"

"His hair."

"Hair?" repeated George in sudden bewilderment. "What on earth's the matter with it?"

But, instead of answering, Mr. Shrig emitted a clear, flutelike whistle that seemed to find an echo followed by sound of hoofs and wheels.

" Who—what now, Jasper ? "

" Only Dan'l."

And presently, there beside them in the dusk, was the speedy-looking horse, the high-wheeled gig and the man Dan'l of the woebegone whiskers.

" You got it, Dan'l ? "

" Safe and sound, Jarsper, rolled up—in the rumble."

" You noticed the famble and general likeness, Dan ? "

" Ay—to the life, Jarsper ! "

With effortless ease Mr. Shrig mounted to the lofty driving-seat and took the reins.

" Hold hard ! " cried George. " What's your hurry ? "

" Dooty ! " answered Mr. Shrig. " Dooty friend, and wrote in capitals ! Vich being so, conway my respex and thanks to your lady aunt——"

" Very well. But, Jasper, why don't you like the Viscount's hair ? What's wrong with it ? "

" The colour ! "

" Eh ? The colour ? "

" Ar ! It should ought to be dark, the blacker the better ? "

" So ! " exclaimed George, intone suddenly hushed. " My God . . . this can only mean—— ? "

" Wiciousness ! " said Mr. Shrig, leaning across the silent Dan'l to whisper. " Wiciousness as crawls and creeps ! Windictiveness is up and doing—but so is J. S., not to mention Dan'l here and yourself, eh, sir and friend ? "

" Yes, Jasper—yes, of course ! You can count on me through thick and thin, to the last extremity, now or at any time ! Only tell me what I'm to do."

" Not a thing—until I give you the office. And not a vord o' this to any living soul ; be dumb as any eyester."

" Right, Jasper ! Now tell me just what you mean by ' vindictiveness ' ? Is it ' what ' or is it—' who ' ? "

" Friend George," sighed Mr. Shrig, taking up the reins, " all as I can say is as how ekker alone responds."

" Oh damn it, Jasper, that's no answer ! "

"No more it is and more's the pity!" sighed Mr. Shrig more dismally than ever. "But so being, so it must be, and so—if I might make a suggestion—keep a ogle on a certain noble young female party and, if possible, get her to talk o' past ewents. And so good night!" Whip cracked, hoofs stamped and, clattering away, were lost in the mournful rustle of leafage near and far where a fugitive wind was sighing dismally; but George stood there amid the gathering shadows gazing wide-eyed on newly imagined horrors while inexorable night deepened about him; and presently in this gloom was a thin, chill rain—yet it was not because of this that he shivered as, opening the wicket-gate, he sped across the now dark and rainswept garden to light and warmth and sweet sanity where his aunt and Betty were singing together as they prepared the evening meal.

CHAPTER XVIII

Which is a chapter of mystery and midnight

AT FIRST George thought it was the moon that had waked him as, yawning sleepily, he blinked dazzled eyes at the glory flooding in at the open lattice ; then he was aware of something that hopped in at him to fall upon the bed, and saw this for a small pebble. So up he leapt, and, peering from the window, was amazed to behold the small, shrouded form of old Hagah, her upturned face pallid and ghost-like in the vivid moonlight.

" Hush ! " she whispered. " Hush—I want ee ! Get dressed—boots and a spade, and—hush ! "

Thus presently, boots in hand, George crept down the stairs, as silently opened the door and whispered :

" Hagah, my dear, what is it ? "

" Boots and a spade ! " she hissed. " And, oh, be quick ! Get into your boots ! " Wondering, he obeyed, then, taking her little bony hand, led her across the garden where stood the roomy toolshed he had built for his carpentry.

" Well, here we are ! " said he. " But dear old Hagah, why the mystery and wherefore a spade ? "

" For to dig a hole," she whispered, " deep—deep enough to bury—this ! " And, pulling back her cloak, she discovered a small, black box, padlocked and clamped with iron.

" Oho ! " he exclaimed lightly. " What have we here ? "

" Danger ! " she whispered breathlessly, glancing fearfully around them. " Death and bloody murder ! " Even as she uttered the word, and plain to hear upon the stilly air, Saint Mark began to tell the hour.

" Aha ! " chuckled George. " Midnight. A black box ! A secret burial ! By Jove and Jupiter. Hagah, you are delightfully mysterious, my dear, but——" Here, clutching his arm, she tossed back her hood and looked up at him, her face thus plain to see in the pallid radiance of the moon, and, meeting this look, George laughed no more ; instead, he whispered :

"Hagah . . . you mean . . . Good lord, what do you mean ? " And as softly she repeated :

"Danger ! Death ! Murder—all in this box ! So come and bury it ! Hide it ! Come ! Whoso has killed once may kill again ! "

So, taking spade, George followed her until she halted in the shadow of the great old pear tree ; here to listen, peering fearfully round about ; then coming where a beam of moonlight made a small pool of radiance amid the gloom, she pointed, whispering :

"Here ! "

Deftly George cut and lifted a square of turf and, laying this by, fell to work silently as possible, plying spade vigorously until old Hagah whispered :

"Enough, Master George ; 'twill do ! " And now, sinking upon her knees, she lowered the box into this excavation and, folding her hands above it, remained thus a while as if in prayer, then, rising, whispered fiercely :

"Now bury the hateful, perilous thing ! Ah, bury and hide it, George ; hide it and leave no mark to show where it lies ! " And so, when he had filled the hole, trodden it down and scattered such of the soil as remained, he fitted the turf back in place, patted it level with flat of the spade and, setting his arm about the little old woman's frail shoulders, said complacently :

"There, Hagah my dear, your terror is buried, so forget it ! In a day or so there will be nothing to show . . . but, by Jove and Jupiter, I should like to know precisely what fearsome thing it is I've buried here for you.

"God love ee, my dearie Master Jarge ! " she murmured, clasping his hand in both her own. "Mebbe ee shall know someday, for then—ah—'stead o' fearsome evil it shall be a gurt joy and blessing. So there let it bide and be forgot till I come to claim it or you hear as the good Lord in His mercy has give me peace and rest at last and raised me to His blessedness everlasting."

"But, Hagah—my dear, can't you, won't you give me some hint——?"

"No!" she answered, sinking her voice again to fearful whisper. "No, only this—beware o' the black winter! And now I'll go——"

"Not yet, Hagah. Come indoors and we'll brew tea, cut bread and butter; aha, a goblin feast—come on."

"Thank you, dear George," she murmured very tenderly, "but indeed I must go."

"Why then," he answered, setting by the spade and taking her arm instead, "you shall not go alone." So, arm in arm, they crossed to the wicket-gate, which George took care should click not, and away they went, Frail Age made wise by much experience of life, and Stalwart Youth eager and bold for aught that life might bring. Now since Age should never be hurried, they went at leisured pace, with a great moon to light them and give familiar objects a new, strange beauty.

"Grand!" said George, looking up and around. "What a glorious night! After all, it's a lovely old world, Hagah!"

"Ay, 'twould be, my dear, if only folk would let it be. God's handiwork is perfect; 'tis only us humans, his poor, misguided children, do mar it. The Good Lord made and meant all things in His earth to be beautiful."

"And yet, Hagah, Beauty can be—yes, and often is— evil, isn't it?"

"Ah, too often, my dear! And yet hid deep beneath the evil is something of good, the spark divine that one day, in this life or hereafter, will, by God's mercy, wake to a fire shall destroy all evil and flame to a glory ever-lasting. For though our poor bodies be ours to misuse, our souls are of God and in His almighty care."

"This is a wonderful thought, Hagah!"

"This, my dear one, is very truth of God—or so I do

believe." Here for a while they walked in silence, though
more than once her wise, keen old eyes scanned this face
she had known and loved all his days—the wrinkled brow,
musing gaze, and firm, set mouth, thus heeding all of
which, she nudged him with small, sharp elbow, saying in
the vernacular :

"Ay, Mast' Jarge, her do be a beauty sure-ly ! "

"Eh—her ? " repeated George, starting.   "Who . . .
whom do you mean ? "

"The Lady Clytie Moor, of course, my dear."

"Oh ! " he exclaimed.   "So you've met her——"

"No, George, she met me, and consequently I know
her far better than she is aware."

"How, pray tell me—how ? "

"Someone had told her of ' th' owd witch ', and she,
poor proud child, came to cross the old hag's clutching
palm with a whole crown-piece to have her fortune told."

"Well," said George, halting to ask the question, "did
you tell it ? "

"My dear, never did mumbling witch tell fortune or
forecast the future with more witchlike effect ! The poor
child flushed, then paled, breathed short, breathed deep,
and at last questioned that grim old sibyl in awful
whisper."

"Then, Hagah . . . may I ask . . . what you told
her ? "

"Oh yes, my dear, you may ask the lady herself."

"Good lord—no ! Not I ! I find her altogether too
infinitely detestable ; in fact, Hagah, she perfectly revolts
me."

"Aha ! " quoth Hagah in tone extremely witchlike and
with face hidden in her bonnet.   "Oh, well," and here
she gave his arm a tug, "let us go on or never shall I
reach home."

Mutely George obeyed, but, after a pace or so, turned
to enquire :

"Tell me, Hagah, what did you—what do you—think
of her ? "

" That she is a child of storm."

" Yes, by heavens, of wild and raging tempest ! Well, pray go on—what more of her ? "

" That, being so beautiful, she is the more apt for great evil or—greater good—and this, of course, depends."

" On what, Hagah ? "

" The man she marries."

" I pity the poor wretch ! Yes, by Jove I do ! He will certainly be the sorriest dog that ever howled, and serve him right, for——"

" Hush, my dear, listen ! Here comes my old, faithful Tom to greet me—yonder ! " Even as she spoke, towards them stalked a monstrous black cat, tail stiff in air, mewing hoarsely as he came.

" Folks say this is my familiar spirit, my demon—ah well, let them, for this faithful creature is all the years have left me to love and cherish. . . . Come, Tom ! " The great cat leapt to perch, somehow, on her shoulder and rub his black head against her furrowed cheek, purring in loud and raucous ecstasy ere he sprang to balance precariously upon the gate of her little cottage.

" Well, good night ! " said George. " And you are lonely simply because you are so proud ; there is a home for you at Sparklebrook, as Aunt has told you repeatedly, and you know I have loved you all my life, Hagah." So saying, he stooped and kissed the scant, white hair a-peep beneath her faded, old bonnet.

" My dear," she sighed, " I know this and 'tis my great and abiding comfort. . . . But now, George, this being th' owd witches' cottage, ay and the moon so bright, list ye to her words. Harkee, Mast' Jarge : him as is bold to front tempest shall find sure, sweet haven. Them as do hate now, do but hate for fear o' love as be so very gurt, it's strength do fright and shame 'em. Yet each shall to other and, 'spite themselves, find in each other life's glad fulfilment. Ah—you that be lover all unaware, flee where ye will, yet shall love find and claim ye for each other's own. When red mates wi' black, then shall be peace, j'y and the end o' hateful evil. So, lover as is so blind, think on this and know the truth at last! . . . And now, George, my dear, my love to Miss Isabel, and good night. . . . Come, Tom, my imp, my familiar demon, let us to bed."

"Wait! Hagah—wait!" cried George as she unlocked her cottage door. "For mercy's sake explain . . . tell me what you meant by all that—that rigmarole."

"Ay, maybe 'twas!" she nodded. "Howbeit, my dear, ' th' owd witch' has told your fortune—all for nothing, so maybe it nothing means. Think of it the best you can,—and so, God bless ee and good night!"

CHAPTER XIX

Tells of a beauty in distress

THE NIGHT was indeed so glorious that George, knowing sleep impossible, since he had so much to think about, took a walk, the better to meditate. Now as he went, slow of foot and bowed of head, the more he pondered old Hagah's amazing words and most disquieting suggestions the more shocked and dismayed he became; for as he wandered thus by shady lane and field-path his troubled thoughts ran on this wise:

"I a lover? What perfect nonsense! And with Lady Clytie! How utterly preposterous! I have always detested her and with a vehemence that amazes me. And she, of course, despises and hates me with an equal fervour. Very good! Then it is quite evident my poor old Hagah is losing her wits to suggest such absurd impossibility. Very good again." Here, glancing up, he found himself traversing a wood, its leafy gloom pierced here and there by radiant arrows of moonlight; and now as he went— almost it seemed the little, aged woman was beside him again, though now most truly witchlike, peering up at him from the shadows with her shrewd, bright eyes and saying again, though now in voice harshly unfamiliar:

"Ha, fool as loves without the wit to know it! Oho, lover, as is so blind, think on this and know the truth at last!"

"Well, but," thought George, "the truth is, she and I hate each other, now, as ever, and always shall, as a matter of course."

Here George imagined a very witchlike screech of mocking laughter, and then:

"Aha, 'tis love! And love so great its very strength frights and shames ee!"

" A horrid idea ! " thought George.

" Yet each shall to other, despite yourselves."

" A most ghastly suggestion ! " thought George.

" When red mates wi' black, then shall be peace."

" Too dearly bought ! " thought George. " If she is the black and I the red, as I suppose I am—and she loathes red hair, thank heaven ! Yet not so much as I detest her gipsy black. . . ." Thus thoughtful, George wandered on, careless of direction, until all at once he checked thought and step to stand motionless. And this for two reasons : first, the snort of a horse unexpectedly near ; and, second, the voice of a woman. But whereas the horse snorted with content, the woman's voice was raised in desperate supplication.

" Oh . . . please . . . no ! Oh, sir, I beg you leave me. Indeed I wish and need no escort——"

" And I repeat you are much too beautifully alluring to wander alone and at such hour. And so, my bewitching shy-sweet Dian, I must and will see you safely to your destination or, better much, remain and share your solitude."

" No—no ! I beseech you . . . go your way and suffer I go mine."

" Impossible, my beauty ; not to be thought of. Instead, I pray you, come—let us sit and gaze upon the moon and listen to our hearts that beat to tell us such night was made for love, for kisses——"

" Ah, don't . . . pray . . . let me go, or I . . . will scream."

" Save your sweet breath, loveliness ; be kind instead, for in this blessed solitude none may hear or see——"

" On the contrary, I can do both," said George, advancing, " and prove the sight and sound of you, Sir Humphrey, equally obnoxious, for I have long been honoured by this lady Mistress Tulliver's acquaintance and therefore I——"

" Oh . . . Mr. George ! " she gasped and leapt to clasp his arm.

Sir Humphrey Carr swept off his hat and bowed, saying pleasantly :

"It is Mr. Bell, I think ? Alas, sir, it seems I am trespassing on your preserves ; believe me, I had no idea ! Sir, my departure shall be instant. I had a horse somewhere about . . . ah, here he is ! And now, Mr. Bell, in taking my leave, permit me to congratulate you, happy man, and heartily commend your choice of womankind, and especially of a—womankind. Good night, happy ones. May Venus bless you—I leave you together and together wish you joy——"

"Sir," said George, freeing himself from the trembling girl, "I object to your damnable suggestions ! "

"Indeed, Mr. Bell, I thought and hoped you would ! " Laughing, Sir Humphrey swung lightly to saddle, saluted them with ironic flourish of hat and ambled away.

"Now, dammit," exclaimed George furiously, "the damn fellow leaves me looking the fool I feel I am. And you, Joan, what on earth——"

"Oh, George ! " she cried tearfully. "Thank God you came—in time."

"And quite by chance. By Jupiter you are far more a fool to run such shameful risks ! What in the world are you in such desolation at this time o' night ? "

"I'm on my way to Aunt Jemima in Lewes, for I——"

"But why, why in heaven's name at such confoundedly late hour ? Why aren't you safe home in bed ? "

"Because . . . Oh, George, I . . . I've run away."

"Have you, by Jove ? Then now you're going to run back again ! "

"No—no ! " she sobbed. "I won't—I won't—ever ! I can't abide Father, he be that cruel to me—I mean, he is so harsh and overbearing, George."

"Only because he loves you so greatly, Joan, you little fool."

"However, I won't go back home ! "

"Well then . . . " sighed George, very conscious of the silky tresses of yellow hair a-peep below the brim of

her small, coquettish bonnet.   There were also two eyes,
deeply blue, long-lashed and fearful, upraised to his
appealingly.   " Well," said he again, " what do you
propose to do ? "

" Stay with my aunt until I can k-keep myself.   I can
get a situation as teacher at my old school in Brighthelmston
—I think.   But now I must go to Aunt Jemima."

" What, all the way to Lewes at this time o' night ? "

" I can be there in time for breakfast, George, if we
start now."

" We ? " he repeated.   " Joan, d'you expect me to——"

" Yes, George, indeed I do.   I think you ought to
come and take care of me—considering ! "

" What pray ? "

" The gentleman—that horrid man, for one thing."

" And what beside ? "

" Because we were sweethearts—once ! "

" Years ago, when we were children, yes—merest
infants at our dame's school."

" But—you liked to kiss me then, George."

" Yes, I—I fancy I did—as a boy."

" Well, if you bring me safe to Lewes you shall kiss
me—although you're a man ! "   The lashes drooped, the
vivid lips quivered—George leaned forward, drew back
and muttered :

" Damme ! "

" Did you say ' yes ', George ? "

" No, I did not !   What I do say is—take my arm and
I'll walk you safely back home."

" Never ! " cried she resolutely.   " Not one step ! "

" Then I must carry you ! "

" Oh, but you wouldn't—you couldn't——"

" Oh, but I can and shall, over my shoulder like a—a
confounded sack of corn."

" Then, George, I shall scream ! "

" Then, Joan, if Sir Humphrey gallops back to the
rescue I shall do my best to grass him !   Come, Joan, for
your dear mother's sake and because I know in your heart

you know how your father loves you—more than his life, my dear, or anything in all the world.   He has always been so proud of you and so gentle with you when you were his ' little maid '.   Remember how he used to throne you high on the hay wagon, then take off his hat and salute you as his ' little Queen of the Hay ' and ' Sprite of the Harvest ', and all his men would bow and cheer their ' little Majesty '. Do you remember, Joan ?   Do you ? "

She did not speak, only her rebellious, lovely head drooped, and George continued :

" And when you were so ill we all feared you'd die. I saw your grieving father kneel by the kitchen settle and lift his face, wet with tears, to implore God to take him and spare his ' little maid.' "

The coquettish bonnet now hid her face.   But the great watchful moon saw, and made of her tears each one—a jewel ; though George, all unaware, went on :

" Joan, Oh, my dear, can you desert such a father and break his heart——? "

" Never ! " she sobbed.   " Oh, never !   So, George " —here she gave him both her hands—" take me back to him and, for his sake, kiss me and—take me back home."

So kiss her George did, though not those ruddy lips (wise fellow !) but upon that wayward, silky tress of hair. Then, catching up the valise that held her few possessions, he took her arm and away they went, striding apace like the vigorous young creatures they were : for now her only thought was to reach home before she was missed or her flight known.   But, despite their haste, this hope proved vain, for when they came in sight of the great farmhouse, its every casement seemed aglow, while many other lights bobbed and flickered far and wide across ploughland and fallow.

" Oh, George ! " she sighed a little breathlessly.   " All those lanterns !   Father must have roused the whole village to search for me, the darling !   And—listen ! " Upborn to them on the stilly air was sound of many voices ;

but one there was louder, hoarser, more insistent than any, a voice that broke oddly as it cried her name.

"Oh," she whispered, "'tis the voice of my father!"

"Yes," said George, "it is the voice of a man—who weeps——"

Uttering an inarticulate, sobbing cry, Joan fled towards this desolate voice.

"Father!" she gasped. "Oh, my dear——"

"Joan . . . my loved . . . my lost one . . . have ee come back to me? So the good Lord be praised!"

Now, seeing her thus safe in Abel Tulliver's arms, how she clung and how they kissed in fearful rapture, George set down the valise where it would be found and, leaving father and daughter thus reunited, strode away beneath the sinking moon, home and bedward.

CHAPTER XX

Tells how and why lordly sire became human father

THIS narrative here trends back a few hours to that precise moment when a shadow stole across the open page of the book my lord the Earl, seated in his tower garden, was reading, and, as usual, without aid of spectacles, a shadow this that, looming above him, remained motionless. Therefore he glanced up and thus beheld Sir Humphrey Carr smiling down at him; that is to say, his teeth gleamed.

"Ah, Humphrey," murmured his lordship, betraying no least sign of the shocked surprise so confidently expected, " it seems you are not in your adored Paris ; instead you crawl and creep upon my solitude, and consequently prove entirely unwelcome."

"As an—evil conscience, right noble lord and mine uncle, I—hope ! "

"Indeed you are my affliction, Humphrey."

"And son of your only sister—Uncle ! "

"Who married a scoundrel, Nephew ! "

"My lamented and more or less honoured sire ! An unfortunate gentleman, dear Uncle, used by you to— certain purpose, and thereafter by you cast aside and driven into exile. His son takes pleasure to remind you of this, and that sins come home to roost until they are paid off or, let us say, receive their customary fee."

"Is it money again, Humphrey ? "

"Again, sir, money it is. Thus by your gratitude for past services of my dead father, his son lives ! But, dear lord and uncle, I am not here solely to avail myself of your gratitude aforesaid—no indeed."

"Then why this infliction, Humphrey ? This sudden and most unexpected visitation ? "

" Alas, right noble lord and doting Uncle, I am most unhappily the bearer of—evil tidings, news indeed so—so sadly bad that I hesitate——"

" Humphrey, what devilish, teasing, wordy complexities ! Speak plain or be dumb and go."

" Oh, sir, I entreat your patience, for—dearest of Uncles—a cruel fate compels me ! Thus, sir, I must needs inform you, gently as I may, that your beloved son and my dear cousin, our Raymond, has met with—another grievous accident ! "

Now had Sir Humphrey smitten that silvery head with the heavy riding whip he handled so lightly the Earl could hardly have been more direly affected, for, uttering a strangled cry, he shrank ; he actually cowered, and, face hidden in clutching hands, pleaded brokenly :

" Don't . . . tell me . . . Raymond . . . is dead ! Hurt perhaps . . . badly injured, but . . . not dead——"

Sir Humphrey, seeing this proud head so abased, this once stately form now more pitifully bowed than ever, smiled, and remained thus in happy contemplation of this stricken father so long that at last from behind those clutching hands he pleaded again :

" Humphrey . . . tell me . . . he . . . is alive ! "

" My dear Uncle, I take joy to tell you that your dear boy is not dead . . . yet——"

" Ah, is he . . . injured so badly . . . dangerously ? "

" Sir, all I dare tell you or venture to affirm as fact is— that at least when I left him he was . . . still breathing."

" Ah, then . . . he is alive."

" He was, sir, when I left him——"

" Where did you leave him and why ? "

" I left him, Uncle mine, to the tender care of Beauty, ripely luscious, a lady whose name, I believe, is Standish."

" Standish ? " repeated the Earl, lifting woeful head at last. " Isabel Standish at Sparklebrook ? "

" The same, good my lord. Thither our poor, dear Raymond was conveyed . . . on a hurdle, by her nephew, a Mr. Bell."

" He ? " exclaimed the Earl.   " He—of all men ! "

" Oh, there were other men to aid him, Uncle."

" I must go, this instant ! I will go to my son ! " cried the Earl, grasping at his silver hand-bell—which was drawn gently beyond his reach by Sir Humphrey's riding whip as he murmured :

" Dear Uncle, rest content ! To save you needless fatigue I dispatched one of the carriages some while ago. Your darling son shall bless you with his presence very soon ! Meantime, by your gracious leave, I will seek our bewitching Clytie to pay her such passionate homage as respectful humility may allow."   Then smiling nephew bowed to haggard uncle and strolled gracefully away.

Close beside the Earl was a small table whereon, with divers other objects, lay an ivory paperknife shaped like a dagger which he now took up to gaze down at with a quite dreadful intensity : and never had the large, white hand which grasped it so purposely seemed more un-expectedly vigorous and powerful, while his very stillness was more ominous and terrible than any spoken word. . . . Motionless thus he crouched until upon the fragrant evening quiet was sound of hoofs, wheels and—a voice, at sound of which the Earl, sighing deeply, moved and most surprisingly—for, without an effort he rose and stood erect, proud head aloft, powerful shoulders squared, mighty arms outstretched yearning towards these sounds that told him his son was indeed alive and near.

" My lord . . . sir . . . Governor ! " cried this yet distant, most beloved voice.   " Oho, sir—I'm here ! Hi, you footman f'lo', where the dooce is his lordship ? "

Down and back into his cushioned elbow-chair sank the Earl, nor stirred—even when his eager eyes beheld his somewhat battered son and heir limping towards him, hat in hand ; nor even when this son halted to bow.   Then all he said was :

" Pray, Hurst, what is this I hear of yet another accident ? Inform me."

"Oh . . . well, sir," said the Viscount, awkward and abashed as he ever was in the austere parental presence, "it was merely a . . . a wheel off . . . so I naturally took a . . . a bit of a toss, no more.   I was, in fact . . . quite lucky really."

And now—a miracle happened, or so it seemed to the young Viscount, for this lordly sire of his, usually so ineffably stately and remote, suddenly became a father, with both hands outstretched to him, in whose voice was that he had never heard until now :

"Raymond, my son—come to me ! Come near ; yes, sit you by me—on the arm of my chair ! Now tell me of your accident, all that happened, every particular, and why, despite your very apparent bruises and abrasions, you consider yourself lucky, my dear boy ? " The Viscount, startled by this most un-sire-like endearment, glanced down almost apprehensively at his father, who, meeting this look, smiled ; whereat his son's astonishment grew.

"Raymond," said his father gently and with expression very like apology, "I have . . . very lately . . . suffered much, on your account. . . . . For, your infernally clever cousin Humphrey contrived that I should believe your accident fatal . . . yourself maimed and . . . dying.   So now, my son, tell me the truth of it while you speak ; pray give me your hand . . . that I may feel and know how truly alive you are."

Speechless with amazement, the Viscount obeyed ; but now, as hand clasped hand, each warm with vigorous life, the Viscount exclaimed impulsively :

"Sir . . . I say, what a grand fist you have . . . what a noble ' mauley ' for bang-up rib-roasters or knockdown levellers ! Pray, sir, did you ever ' put 'em up ' . . . use 'em, when you were young ? "

"Frequently, Raymond !   And to quite sufficiently ' levelling ' effect ! "

"Oh, sir, why—Governor, why have you never told me ? I knew, of course, you must have been dooced powerful once, eh, sir ? "

"Yes, my son, I was indeed. Muffles or raw 'uns, in the ring or out, wrestling, singlestick or the foils; few could match—yours most paternally, my son."

Now here the Viscount drew back the better to survey his father in a sort of ecstasy, saying disjointedly:

"Oh, the dooce! If I had only known . . . all these years! Sir . . . father . . . B'gad, I'm only just beginning to know you! At school other fellows used to boast no end—how their fathers did things . . . only I . . . all the while . . . was dumb because I didn't know my own father could have knocked the lot into cocked hats! Sir, did you ever meet a champion . . . fight him, I mean, of course, did you?"

"Yes, my son. Once I had the honour of a bout with 'Glorious John' Barty——"

"Sir . . . sir," gasped the Viscount. "Oh, Father, had I only known! Pray did you ever see Jessamy Todd in action?"

"I backed him more than once, fairly heavily and never lost, of course."

"Splendid, sir! And this reminds me, there's a f'lo' here in Ravenhurst that I met at Cambridge, a regular marvel foot and fist and no wonder, for he was Jessamy's pupil; and, Father, he is a fine, tip-top f'lo' named Bell, George Bell, whom I should like to introduce to you——"

"I have met the gentleman already. But, Raymond, come, let me hear of your latest accident and with every particular."

So Raymond told all he knew or could remember of his misadventure, while the Earl watched him and listened with such close attention that once again the Viscount was surprised, as he ended:

"And that's all, sir!"

"But why," the Earl demanded, "why should the wheel come off? The vehicle was new, I understand."

"Quite new, sir, but—off the wheel came."

"Could it have been tampered with?"

"Oh, gad sir, no! Quite impossible! Besides, who'd do such fool thing?"

"I am reminded of your other accidents, Raymond! Sir, did you travel alone? And if so—why? What of your groom and—that valet of yours, Tranter."

"I left them to follow with my other odds and ends, sir; goods and chattels and so on."

"Then how and where did you meet your cousin Humphrey?"

"I didn't, sir; 'twas Humphrey met me—I mean, he appeared quite unexpectedly, in fact, at the gate at Sparklebrook not long after they brought me to my dooced senses."

"How did he know you were at Sparklebrook?"

"He was told of my accident in the village and directed. . . . But, as I tell you, sir, the folk at Sparklebrook are grand people . . . of condition, too . . . especially Mistress Isabel. Egad, sir, I thought she was an angel! And so she is—almost! She's beautiful, sir, gracious and lovely, something between Venus and the Madonna. If you only knew her, sir——"

"Raymond, I do—or did, years ago, and——" It was now that my lady Clytie appeared to greet the Viscount and command them indoors, for evening had deepened to a night with a rising moon.

"Dearest, let me help you!" said she, giving the Earl her hand.

"And myself also, sir!" said the Viscount, giving his. So, with their aid, the Earl struggled to his feet; and thus, through the waxing moonlight, went they, arm in arm, though now father and son were knit each to each in a bond even closer and far stronger.

CHAPTER XXI

Shows the potency of a one-legged Dutch doll

SHE WAS very small, barefoot and ragged ; she was also weeping so bitterly that George halted his townward stride to look down at this little woeful person and ask the cause of her grief. The child peered up at him through tears and tangle of golden curls and, evidently reassured, checked her sobs to answer :

" P-please, sir, I falled down and hurted my poor Peggy so bad as her leg's comed off an' she only had one——"

" Show me ! " said George, with such look and tone that, after brief hesitation, the child scrambled to her little dusty feet and held up for his inspection a wooden Dutch doll whose once vividly scarlet cheeks were now somewhat haggard by stress of time and kisses.

" This be . . . my poor Peggy, sir," sobbed the child. " And here be . . . her poor . . . dear little . . . leg ! "

So, tucking his walking-stick beneath arm, George took the doll in one hand, leg in the other, whereat the child wept again, wailing louder than ever, until——

" Oh, Mr. Odious Bell," cried another voice, un-expectedly near, " how exactly detestably like you to make a child weep . . . to so torment a little helpless girl ! "

" And, oh, my Lady Random Clytie," he retorted, " how precisely like you to be so very perfectly idiotically mistaken."

" Beast, give the poor child her doll ! "

" Most gracious of ladies, give me, pray favour me with —a pin."

" Child," said her ladyship, reaching out shapely arms, " leave that very nasty man and come to me ! Come, little angel, come to me and be comforted." But the child, staring up at this grand lady in her plumed bonnet, her

silks and laces, whose voice, though soft, yet held a note
of command, shrank against George instead and even
ventured to grasp the skirt of his coat in her little grimy
hand.

"Wise little soul!" said George, with airy flourish of
the doll's leg. "This, my lady Clytie, proves how truly
marvellous is the instinct of an innocent child! And now,
gracious madam, if you have such common thing as a pin
about you anywhere among those coquettish flounces and
frills be good enough to produce it and you shall see me
perform on a lady's leg, a wooden one, alas, yet
feminine——" Here, to his no little surprise, Lady Clytie
laughed, and with such full-throated, joyous ring that the
child, peeping cautiously round George, smiled through
her tears—took one shy step—another, and then—was in
my lady's arms. And now, quite heedless of the silks and
laces aforesaid, down she sat on grassy bank beside the
road with the child beside her while George stood gazing
in ever-growing wonderment, doll in one hand, leg in the
other, and entirely unheeded now by child or women, and
therefore—

"Madam," said he, in tone of sharply virtuous rebuke,
"I sincerely trust, nay I beg and entreat, that you will not
teach this sweet innocent to curse and swear. Refrain, I
implore!"

My lady's only notice was to kick at him with foot shod
in silver-buckled walking-shoe, saying tenderly as she did so:

"Little angel, what is your name?"

"Please you, m'am, I be mother's Penelpee an' so that's
why I be only me and not a angel yet, like my father what
got killed at Wart-loo by old Boney."

"Oh, bless you, little Penelope! I must kiss you
because your brave father died for me as well as you and
our dear England and was such a gallant soldier."

"Yes, ma'm, an' in a red coat so fine an' he gived me
my Peggy what had bofe her legs then and now only one,
and now that's comed off, too, only the gentleman be going
to put it on again an' make her better again for me."

" Why are you so sure he can, my dear one ? "

" 'Cause he be so big like my daddy, an' so I like him, I do."

" How ever can you like him, child ?   Tell me why ? "

" 'Cause he talks so kind an' smiles at me wiv his eyes."

" No—surely not, little Pen ! "

" Yes ! " said George, drawing a pace nearer.   " Most certainly he does !   The child is perfectly right—look for yourself and see."

" Mr. Bell, I prefer looking at anything—except Mr. Obnoxious Bell ! "

" However," said he, advancing another pace, " if Lady Abhorrent Clytie will favour Mr. Abhorred Bell with the desired pin——" Here, and again to his surprise, my lady turned away, and, after brief space, proffered the article desired, saying :

" For this sweet child's sake ! "

" Then, my lady, for our child's sake, be thanked ! " said George, and, seating himself on the other side of little Penelope, laid by his stick, took out penknife and fell to work on the broken doll, saying as he did so :

" Thus, madam, with a nice decorum, we now bare poor Peg's injured—limb ; with gentle knife-point we reduce the fracture—so ! We now insert the pin, madam, bending the two ends—thus ; and lo—the leg of Peg is sound again and stronger than ever ! "

Penelope received her beloved Peggy with breathless delight, kissing and cuddling the poor, unlovely thing to her childish bosom with that innate spirit of motherhood which is surely one of the very loveliest things in life. Now glancing from this tender little mother to the woman who watched, George caught his breath—for in this moment the woman more than reflected the gentle loveliness of this lovely child, and when she spoke this beauty of tenderness was in her voice :

" Dear child, do you love that dreadful, old . . . Dear little Penelope, you love your poor Peggy lots and lots, don't you ? "

" Oh yes, ma'm ; yes I do."

" Then you shall have another, a bigger one, all dressed up in clothes you can take off and put on—yes, and a cradle for her to sleep in, a cradle with curtains.   Would you like that ? "

" Oh, I should . . . I should—if there'd be room in the cradle for my Peggy, too."

" Now bless your faithful little heart, there shall always be room for Peggy.   Where do you live, Pen ? "

" Over yon, ma'm, a long ways off, I do."

" At the extreme other end of the village," said George. " You see, I knew her father, boy and man—a fine fellow was Tom Lane."

" Perhaps you know her mother also ? "

" I did.   She was one of Aunt's maids before Tom married her, and from our cottage, too——"

" Do you know all the villagers ? "

" Of course !   We are a small community and pretty good folk—on the whole."

" But—do you mean all these—these common people are your friends ? "

" I hope so."

" You have a very—queer taste."

" A common taste, yes.   You see, noble lady, being a commoner myself I naturally like common, ordinary things and especially people."

" Then you certainly are not difficult to please ! "

" No, indeed !   Most people please me in some way or other, except one or two, here and there, now and then."

" So, of course, Mr. Superior, Superlative Bell, I am included in your exceptions, your ' one or two now and then, here and there's ', considering that, as I abominate Mr. Bell, Mr. Bell hates and detests me ? "

" He did certainly," George replied.   " Yes, madam, our Mr. Bell—commonly known as George, a name common as himself and therefore extremely apt—this common George Bell detested your most uncommon ladyship with a fervour that surprised himself. He did, I say, but——"

" Well ? " she enquired, with swift side-glance. "Why the past tense, and wherefore the ' but ' ? "

" Because today, here without the ' there ', and now without the ' then ', I regret to inform your ladyship in regard to your ladyship, I have made the shocking discovery that, for the present at least, George Bell, poor wretch, has mislaid his detestation, not to mention hate, loathing, and so on."

" How perfectly astonishing ! " said she, with another swift sideways glance.

" Yes," sighed George, " it amazes me, too ! "

" Then, for the present, you—no longer—hate me ? "

" No, I'm afraid I do not ! "

" Of what are you afraid ? "

" The future ! For instead of hate I dread to think what other wild emotion may fill its place."

" Yes, a truly dreadful thought, Mr. Bell ! Pray what are your present sentiments in regard to, for the moment, un-hated me ? "

" Bewilderment ! " he answered, watching the quiver of that lovely, sensitive mouth.

" Can it be," said these lips, upcurving to mocking smile, " that you are not well, or sickening for something, a fever or tertian ague, whatever that may be ? "

" Possibly," he answered gravely, " though I don't think so. The only explanation for this most stupendous change may be the certain fact that we, you and I, have one uncommonly common taste in common ! "

" Oh, never ! " she retorted. " We ourselves, our impulses and tastes, are as opposite and far removed as the poles ! "

" You are exactly right ! " said George decisively. " We are entirely opposed except for one small though quite incontrovertible fact."

" Oh ? " she murmured enquiringly, and now she turned to look at him. " And, pray, what is your fact ? "

"This!" answered George, and laid caressing hand on little Penelope's golden head. Lady Clytie glanced down at the child nestling between them, seemed about to speak, yet uttered no word and, speechless still, looked up at George, whereat, and once again, his breath caught in that odd, disturbing manner; and now, for a breathless space questing eyes of grey looked deep into eyes of velvety darkness that, questioning as keenly, widened slowly with a surprise changing to disbelief, changing again to—down swept black lashes; and, sighing deeply, she turned back to the child, saying and rather breathlessly but with that new and lovely gentleness in look and voice:

"Little Pen, isn't it time I took you safe home?"

"Please, yes, ma'm, else my gammer will shout 'Penny Oh Penny' for me like she do when she loses me."

"Then we had better go, my dear. Say goodbye to this gentleman and——" Here she started and glanced up as towards them, smiling, self-assured and immaculate as usual, strolled Sir Humphrey Carr.

"Well, well," he murmured, pausing before them to lean gracefully on betasselled cane, "upon my life and soul, what charming picture of rustical wooing or should one say rural felicity? And yet, my dear Clytie, one fears one must protest you entirely out of place, the conscious allure of that plumed bonnet, the delicious provocation of those daintiest of laces, for, oh, Clytie——"

"And, oh, Humphrey," she mocked, "how fatuous you are, how very tedious! Mr. Bell will agree with me in this, I think?"

"Heartily!" said George, whereupon Sir Humphrey, now smiling at him, retorted gently:

"Ah, Mr. Bell again, of course! Where Beauty is there one finds Mr. Bell. Again I commend his judgment of charms feminine. Last time it was the golden loveliness of dawn, now the profounder beauty of languorous night, apt season of allure and infinite possibilities—a gentleman of catholic taste."

George, scowling, reached instinctively for his stick; Lady Clytie, sitting up for adequate retort, remembered the child and laughed instead, yet with show of white teeth that snapped viciously on his name:

"Humphrey, run away! 'Tis you are out of place here and quite spoil the scenery! Get back to your Paris and its vile guillotine and howling mobs and grisettes and demi-monde and all the rest; be off where you belong."

"Brava!" he laughed. "Oho, Clytie, dearest of all Clyties, I find you even more ravishing than usual! Anger, my most lovely one, anger or passion of any kind so enhances your wild, dark beauty that, adoring you as I ever have done, so and ever shall, I protest from my heart that——"

"Sir," said George, looking up into the speaker's darkly handsome face, "I suggest your luscious, not to say fulsome periods are surprisingly ill-timed. Pray temper your fervour, restrain your passion, which I find quite nauseating; forbear until I am out of earshot."

"Mr. Bell, your departure is the consummation wished for and aimed at; your absence will be our joy——"

"No doubt, sir," said George rising.

"Speak for your odious self, Humphrey!" cried Lady Clytie, leaping afoot so furiously that the startled child cried again and sobbed until my lady caught her to the comfort of her arms.

"Saints preserve us!" exclaimed Sir Humphrey recoiling. "What have you there?"

"No fit company for you, Humphrey, so leave us to each other——"

"Together with—Mr. Bell—you, my adored one?"

"I am not your adored one! Go away before you make me swear and curse at you."

"Madam," George enquired, leaning on his stout ash stick, "is it your will to be all alone with—our little Penelope?"

"Yes—yes! How often must I tell you?"

"Then, sir," said George, fronting Sir Humphrey, stick in fist, "I am going to the town. May I now suggest you accompany me a little way?" Lady Clytie flashed a glance from now threatening ash stick to formidable tasselled cane, and, being quick-witted as beautiful, laughed again, saying lightly :

"What ridiculous fuss about nothing! I'm taking this dear little child home, and if you wish to join us, Humphrey, you may. Now, Penelope, wish good morning to Mr. Bell and thank him for mending your dear Peggy." The child obeyed, bobbing George a curtsy, small finger crooked beneath chin ; then, clasping my lady's hand, away they went towards the village, with Sir Humphrey in attendance, while George strode in the opposite direction; but when he had gone some little distance he paused to glance back and was oddly relieved to see how they walked with little, golden-haired Innocence between them.

CHAPTER XXII

In which is found a clue to the vanished heir

MR. JACKMAN stood motionless and dumb to stare at the square of flowing canvas outspread upon his desk, while Mr. Shrig, seated nearby, watched the hand of the clock creep the space of one minute . . . of two . . . of three, before the lawyer stirred, sighed and spoke :

" It's—incredible ! Shrig, it's—fantastic ! "

" But," said Mr. Shrig, his roving glance now upon the speaker's face, " 'tis a werry good likeness, sir."

" Good ? " snorted Mr. Jackman, his gaze still intent. " It is a miraculous likeness ! It might be—his very self ! "

" Ar ! " nodded Mr. Shrig. " Except for the armour, the fancy frills and that there pearl a-dangle in his listener ! And you re-mark his daddle, sir, his left famble on his sword ? "

" Certainly, certainly—even this is exact ! And done by Henry the Eighth's court painter Hans Holbein ; early work, too, and, as I believe, very rare and valuable ! And you found it in a dungeon of the old tower, eh ? "

" Ar ! In a place haunted by ghosts in the shape o' rats ! So, Mr. J., sir, I cut it out of its frame afore said rats could devour it, and brought it therefrom rolled up under my coat."

" Admirably right, Shrig, though a—hum—felony."

" Yet, sir, committed for the law, vich rules above all other rules, by a limb o' the law, who, so believing, acts according." Mr. Jackman chuckled, laughed, became solemn and sighed.

" This case becomes darker, more sinister, for the questions now confronting us are—how and why came such valuable thing in such place for rats to destroy ? By whom was it hidden there ? Who's the will and deed ? "

" Sir, all as I can tell you is as ekker responds in a visper
so werry faint that, sich being so, I must hark werry patient
till it grows louder and more distinct." Slowly, and with
infinite care, Mr. Jackman rolled up this precious thing,
saying :

" And yet, Shrig, this alone, though strongly presumptive,
is not evidence."

" No more it is, sir. But—the fact it does prove is—
that somebody, say a Mr. X, seeing this likeness, hides
same for fear it may become evidence later on."

" The supposition is reasonable, Shrig."

" And so, sir, my hopes is rose according."

" Ay, but the evidence we require, Shrig, is black and
white, the written word, marriage and birth certificates,
known personal effects, such as rings, jewels, lockets and
the like. Let us produce such direct evidence and this
age-old wrong shall be righted at last ! Meanwhile, I will
lock this amazement into safety."

This done, Mr. Jackman sat down at his desk, saying,
and with very troubled expression :

" And now, Shrig, a new anxiety presents itself—to me,
at least—this : whoever hid that portrait did so because
he has seen its family likeness to—the presumptive heir.
Hence I argue the identity of—our probable heir must
certainly be known. This being so, are we now to
apprehend . . . must we presume him to be . . . in
danger ? "

Once again, and very softly, Mr. Shrig murmured :

" Ar ! " Which monosyllable, and from such a man,
affected its hearer so greatly that he sank back in his chair,
whispering :

" Merciful God ! " And so for a space was silence
broken only by the deliberate ticking of the clock. Starting
up from his chair, Mr. Jackman paced to and fro, exclaiming
in the same hushed tone :

" Dreadful ! Outrageous ! Quite terrible ! " Then,
sitting down again, he leaned across his desk to whisper :

"Shrig, we must act and at once! We must get him away. We must remove him from all chance of harm!"

"Impossible, sir! Sich harm ain't to be elooded so."

"Nonsense, man! I repeat we must remove him as far as possible from this threat of danger."

"Con-trariwise, sir, the nearer the better?"

"Eh!—nearer? Shrig, what the devil d'you mean?"

"Sir, danger faced ain't so dangerous as danger as ain't, Mr. J., sir. Danger as is flew from is the danger as strikes, and—there y'are?"

The lawyer bowed troubled head upon clenched fist, but glanced up at sudden rap on the door, then leaned back in his chair as, receiving permission, George entered.

"Good morning, partner!" said Mr. Jackman, cheerily as usual. "Come in and sit down. You find us in conference, George."

"May I ask what about, sir? Is it concerning the vanished heir?"

"Why, as a matter of fact, George, the subject was mentioned."

"Then, sir, it is on this matter I wish to speak."

"Well, my dear fellow?"

"Well, sir, though Mr. Shrig here is my friend, I hope, yet in the quest for the heir, he is so evasive and mysterious, putting me off with merest trifles, holding me at arm's length, that I feel I am simply wasting my time—and his. How say you, Jasper?"

"Sir, and George, if my dee-duckshons concerning said vanished heir be correct, same is now in sich danger I shall need your help to pro-tect aforesaid young gent and may call on you therefore at any hour o' the day or night! And how says you to this?"

"As I said before, Jasper, that you can rely on me to any extent and at all times, and the sooner the better. But what of this confounded heir, Jasper, of whom you tell me nothing? Who is he? What and where is he? Does he know of this danger threatening him?"

"No more than a infant noo-born."

" Then he should be warned at once, surely ? And may I know who he is ? "

" Friend and sir, there's reasons as forbids."

" There, sir ! " exclaimed George, turning towards his partner. " You see now just how I am fobbed off with these evasions. And why—why all this confounded mystery as to this business you yourself engaged me upon : the discovery of this lost heir ; the, I suppose, rightful ninth Earl—why ? " Mr. Jackman, in the act of snuffing, paused to answer the more impressively :

" This reticence, partner, is and must be preserved owing to the fact that the person in question is, in the eyes of the law, altogether non-existent, a nebulosity, a mere figment without form, semblance or substance, since we can, as yet, adduce no direct evidence that he is himself existent— that is to say, the actual living embodiment of his grand- father Earl Philip's lineal descendant. In these simple words, unencumbered by any of our dog-latin or legal technicalities, I trust I make all perfectly clear, plain and evident."   Here Mr. Jackman inhaled his waiting pinch of snuff with subdued gasps of enjoyment, while Mr. Shrig's glance roved everywhere except in the direction of George, who glanced from one to other very dubiously as he enquired :

" Am I to understand, sir, from your needlessly plain though, permit me to say, somewhat involved statement that this rightful heir is indeed so, merely in your judgment, unsupported by any factual proof ? "

" Precisely, my dear George ! " said Mr. Jackman, dusting himself carefully with snowy handkerchief. " For the sad truth is that Truth itself, though plain and manifest, will and must be disbelieved and unregarded except Proof trumpet the fact."

" Ar ! " sighed Mr. Shrig. " For if Truth is, and Proof ain't, no more ain't Truth—in court o' law. And po-session being nine p'ints thereof, friend George, so it is and—there y'are ! "

" Which," retorted George, " is precisely nowhere."

" Eggs-actly ! " answered Mr. Shrig and with a beaming fervour.

" And now, sir," said George, rising, " since there is a great deal of routine business waiting my attention, I will, by your leave, get at it. Though first," he added, pausing with hand on the door latch, " may I prefer one last question ? "

" Certainly, my dear fellow, of course."

" Then, pray, do you suppose this heir to be Mr. Charles Mallory ? " Mr. Jackman seemed to ponder this query, then shook his head, saying :

" Well, no, George, no. Eh, Shrig ? "

" Since you ax me, sir, I should reether say—not hardly."

" Thanks ! " said George, and, with another very dubious glance at these two solemn faces, went out, closing the door behind him with extravagant and very evident care.

CHAPTER XXIII

Shows an uncle and a nephew

SIR HUMPHREY seated himself with an airy grace and smiled. The Earl, having viewed his immaculate person from head to foot, laid by the book he had been reading and sighed—noting which, Sir Humphrey smiled the more engagingly as he murmured :

" Dear Uncle, I fear my presence troubles your studious quietude ? "

" As usual, Nephew, of course ! Hence the radiance of your smile. Well, what new unpleasantness brings you upon me ? "

" How extremely—aware you are, my lord, despite your lordship's age ! "

" And decrepitude, Nephew."

" As you say, my lord. For indeed it grieves me to inform you there are certain very ugly rumours abroad concerning you and—a skeleton."

" Which does not surprise me."

" Rumours, sir, linking your most noble name quite damnably with these—osseous remains, suggesting these were once the—vital framework of your cousin Philip, seventh Earl."

" Remarkable ! " sighed his lordship.

" Sir," exclaimed Sir Humphrey, forgetting to smile, " I suggest the adjectives ' ghastly ', ' horrible ' and, under the circumstances, ' most dreadful '."

" I find it remarkable that for once rumour does not lie, Humphrey."

" Ah, you mean ? "

" That rumour and I are in complete agreement."

" As to the identity of these remains, sir ? "

" Precisely ! There is evidence which compels me to believe them those of my unfortunate cousin."

" So at last, dear Uncle, our family skeleton is free of his cupboard, that dark seclusion wherein he was thrust so suddenly and, shall we say, with a certain violence ? "

The Earl's white head drooped, and he sighed deeply, but beneath their black brows his bright glance was fixed musingly upon the silver-hilted small-sword that hung above the wide hearth. Sir Humphrey, beholding him thus bowed and mute, smiled happily and repeated :

" Suddenly, sir, and with violence—according to the unvoiced yet carefully written testimony of my late father, penned thus in full, and most convincingly, for the behoof of himself and family of which I, alas, am sole survivor, as you, of course, are perfectly aware."

Here again nephew paused to smile at uncle, this silent, aged gentleman who, once so proudly arrogant, now showed so humbled and powerless that he seemed to cower, or so thought masterful nephew as he continued :

" Consequently I am as eternally grateful to my father who, though dead, is still such potent factor to my present and future welfare—eh, most noble sir."

" Indeed," sighed the Earl, raising head at last, " your father proved such husband and parent that he is some excuse for his son, the egregrious offspring of unspeakable sire, personified depravity calling itself Humphrey Carr ! "

And now it was uncle who smiled while nephew scowled in a pallid fury so far beyond speech that his hands became white claws to rend and he crouched as if to leap. Then the Earl laughed, softly though with evident enjoyment, saying :

" Aha—I behold the real and absolute Humphrey, very son of dastard sire ! Well, is this enough, Nephew ? Come—if you will ! " And slowly he reached forth those once mighty arms of his. " Come, let us make an end— if you dare."

Sir Humphrey surveyed that bowed, so aged form and rose, glanced at these long arms, and hesitated, gazed into this calmly resolute, old-young face, and sat down again, saying lightly :

" Ah, dear Uncle, how perfectly we know and appreciate one another ! " And bitterly contemptuous, the Earl replied :

" So well, Nephew, that I am wondering how much longer you will resist the charms of your beloved Paris ? "

" I am here to inform your lordship. But first, I would know more concerning our skeleton, how he was discovered and where."

" By a fall of masonry, I believe."

" Ah, then it would of course be in that ghastly old tower."

" Thereabouts, Nephew."

" Then I shall trouble myself to look over it. Such place may possibly repay a search by one so aware of—past events, as myself."

" The tower is reported dangerous, Nephew."

" Nonetheless, sir, though grateful for your warning, I shall adventure it. Now as regards my return to France —when I tell you I abominate England, especially this part of it, and most particularly this grim desolation of mouldering stone, you will wonder why I thus delay my departure ; my answer is—Clytie ! "

" Mouldering desolation ! " repeated the Earl musingly. " I presume you mean the Castle——? "

" Certainly, sir ! This is no place for youth and beauty, such sweet flower of glorious young womanhood as our Clytie——"

" To be sure there are certain parts of the fabric needing repair, especially the tower——"

" Sir, I speak of Clytie. I demand to know why you doom her to be prisoned thus, her glowing beauty unseen and unenjoyed until—ah, dear Uncle—until dawns that happiest of days when she, and by your expressed will, shall bless me with——"

" Nay, but, Humphrey, did I not hear her, and of her own expressed will, curse you very heartily the other day ? "

" Which, my dear Uncle, in such passionate beauty, as she, is akin and next best to kissing ! However, sir, you are now informed and are to know it is my fixed determination to own her as my wife, soon or late and by——"

" Though much later than soon, Humphrey, I think."

" And yet, dearest of lordly Uncles, I venture to think that presently you shall think of this as I desire ; yes, that you by will and word shall urge bewitching Clytie to my arms. Indeed, Uncle, I even dare to prophesy that in the future you shall——"

" The future ! " exclaimed the Earl, with gesture so sudden and unexpected that Sir Humphrey started. " The future ? This most terrible unknown, so relentless in its approach . . . to bring upon us chances good and ill . . . wherein evil may evil do that good may endure ! Who speaks of the future speaks of death, since in the future the Death's Angel awaits us one and all ! Are you ready to die, Humphrey ? "

Leaping afoot, Sir Humphrey recoiled a pace, to stare down into the bright eyes that gazed so serenely up at him.

" Sir . . . sir . . . Uncle," he stammered.   " What . . . the devil do you mean ? "

" Not devil, Humphrey ; ah no ! Death surely is the kindly angel shall free us from this painful clog we call ' body '. Are you as ready and willing to meet this angel as, most certainly, I am ? Are you ? I wonder."

" Then, sir, I leave you wondering. Ponder you on death while I seek bewitching Clytie to woo and perchance win her to my close embrace—as I shall to wifehood—by your gracious aid, dear Uncle, and with your blessing. Of this I am perfectly assured, eh, sir ? " Receiving no reply, Sir Humphrey laughed gently, bowed gracefully and departed, humming a gay little French song.

And now once again the Earl stared up at weapon above the hearth, this deadly small-sword whose bright steel had been dimmed years ago with a man's life blood ; and presently, as if drawn and compelled by this, he rose and, crossing the room with quick, firm step, raised his hand to press upon a certain part of the intricate carving beside the mantel, and, with no sound of movement, a wide panel slid aside, opening upon a darkness into which he stepped. Back slid this noiseless, stealthy panel and the spacious chamber was empty.

It was some half-hour later that in the drowsy afternoon stillness of the tower garden Clytie screamed and beckoned frantically, crying:

"Humphrey!" Instantly he leapt towards her, in which moment death missed him by a hair, thudding to earth dreadfully close behind him; and, turning in affright, he beheld a jagged piece of masonry half-buried in the turf. Pale of cheek and wild of eye, he glared from this up at the old tower immediately above, whose lofty battlements seemed to scowl down upon him so malevolently that he shrank backward on stumbling feet while his horrified gaze scanned every crenelle, loop-hole and crevice. Then he drew a shuddering breath, licked dry lips, and enquired brokenly:

"Clytie . . . what . . . tell me . . . what was it? What did you . . . see?" And breathlessly she replied:

"A stone, Humphrey . . . a great stone . . . falling——"

"Yes . . . yes," said he wildly, "but why . . . why should it fall, why . . . why?"

"Because of time and neglect, of course! Another stone fell last week. See where it lies yonder!"

"Ah, but why . . . why should this one fall so horribly near me? Had you not called, I . . . should be dead now . . . most frightfully dead! Yes, very unpleasantly dead."

"Well, I did call, Humphrey, and so you are as unpleasantly alive as ever! And only the other day I warned you of the tower——"

"The cursed thing should be pulled down, and certainly shall be—someday!"

"But certainly not by you, Humphrey!"

"Who knows?" he retorted. "Who can guess what the future—ha, the future!" he repeated, and, leaping to a run, vanished into the tower; still running, he mounted the narrow, winding turret stairs, nor paused until, sweating and breathless, he reached the battlements, and stood panting to gaze wildly around, but saw only that grim and ponderous flagstaff that seemed in turn to threaten him; nevertheless, being spent and breathless with his fury of haste and dreadful suspicion, he leaned against this—only to start away, for the massive beam seemed to shudder at his touch as if imbued with dreadful life. . . . Thus presently he ventured near the battlements and, peering down from this height, saw Clytie gazing up at him in amazement. . . . And then into this sunny garden came the Earl. Now seeing how painfully he hobbled on his crutch-stick, so feeble and stricken by more than age, Sir Humphrey's fearful suspicions were lulled. . . . Now to my lord's aid sped Clytie, talking excitedly, so that presently the Earl also gazed upward and, hobbling near, cried solicitously:

"Humphrey, come down! Come down, I say! There's death for you in the tower! So come down and live if you will. Up there the Angel of Death awaits you, biding his time!"

Sir Humphrey shuddered so violently that he wondered, for, as he began to descend that steep and narrow stair, and very heedful now of his every step, fear crept beside him. Thus when at last he stepped from gloom into sunshine, despite this genial warmth he was trembling still.

CHAPTER XXIV

Tells how love smote the Viscount

OF ALL the many stiles in and around Ravenhurst village, there was one that daily compelled George's notice, since this was associated in his mind with dainty feet and ankles— and the unforgettable memory of a leg, glimpsed rather than seen, and yet—an abiding memory.

So this afternoon, glancing thitherward as usual, George halted on his way homewards and teawards, for, seated disconsolate upon this stile, was the Viscount, hatless head bowed, slim figure drooping, slender legs in gleaming boots and snowy buckskins dangling forlornly. Noting all of which, George hailed him the more cheerily :

" Hallo, Corks ! Why the woe, and wherefore the dejection ? "

The Viscount started, glanced up, shook his head and sighed : " Old f'lo', it's happened."

" What has ? "

" The most dooced of all things most dooced ! I've met my fate ! In the coppice yonder, and I shall never get over it, never be the same ! I'm grassed, George, completely floored and done for."

" Good lord ! Old fellow, are you hurt ? "

" Doocedly ! You can't see it, but I am——"

" Oh damme, Raymond, not another accident ? "

" Worse, old f'lo' ! I'm winged—internally, yes, b'gad, and e-ternally . . . Cupid's arrow . . . a dooced bull's-eye ! Never thought it possible, but it is—all in one confounded moment, quick as a dooced flash ; one glance and I was confounded, absolutely, for this is serious, the real thing at last ! That's why I'm perching here like a confounded crow . . . to think and muse and wonder at the wonder of her like the fool I look——"

" And without your hat ? "

" Yes, I left it in the wood! A golden beauty, George . . . dazzled me like a beam of blinding sunshine."

" Well, but who is she, Corks ? "

" No idea, and that's the dooce and devil of it! There she was, and Humphrey grasping her horse's rein and her hat on the ground and her hair down, a golden splendour; And she looked at me, George, a look that pleaded my help, so naturally I went for Humphrey on the instant and he knocked my hat off and rode away laughing like a dem hyena. Then she thanked me, old f'lo', in a voice lovely as herself; then while she did up her glorious hair—did I tell you it was golden as——"

" You did, Corks, you did."

" Well, while she was crowning her beautiful head with it, I dismounted to pick up her hat, and my horse bolted! However, I picked up her hat, gave it to her, and trod on my own like a dem fool, and, being such a fool, let her ride away without even begging to know who she was. And, ah, George, I'm afraid she was laughing at me——"

" But dear old Corks, who wouldn't laugh at a fellow standing on his own hat ? And I can't believe you're serious—this short, chance meeting—a woman you have never seen or heard of."

" George, I'm so serious that she is the one and only woman for me in all the world! And I shall never rest until I find her again and tell her so."

" Which seems perfectly incredible to me."

" How often have you been in love, George ? "

" Never! I mean, not really. And I don't ever wish or expect to be."

" And when you are you'll feel just as dooced as I do. Love is a disease, George, that seizes a f'lo' before he knows it and plays the very dooce with him. I know! I've had it frequently and more or less badly, but never like this— all pain, no joy, and a frightful feeling of dem'd un- worthiness——"

" My poor old Corks, you need the firm, strong hand of a friend to pour tea into you! In weal or woe, grief or gladness, day or night, there's nothing like tea. Beer is good, ale better, so is wine, but best of all is tea! So stop dangling your legs on that stile and let us eftsoons and forthwith to Sparklebrook, Aunt Isabel and tea."

"Thanks! sighed the Viscount, quitting his perch. "I never drink the stuff as a rule, old f'lo', but just at present, and poured by your lovely aunt, there's nothing I should like better—of course except——"

"I know, I know!" said George as they linked arms. "The sooner I get tea into you and plenty of it, the—— "

Horsehoofs behind them, approaching at leisured amble ; together they turned and beheld beauty throned on beauty— that is to say, Joan Tulliver seated gracefully upon one of her father's splendid horses.

"Oh, George," breathed the Viscount in awed tone and with look of ecstasy, "there is perfection . . . both of them !" As he spoke, four-legged perfection was reined to a walk while two-legged Perfection raised whip in smiling salute, murmuring demurely :

"Good afternoon."

George bared his head, saying after brief hesitation :

"Joan, I present Raymond, Viscount Hurst. My lord, Mistress Joan Tulliver."

The Viscount bowed, saying rather breathlessly :

"Madam, I . . . I am honoured ! "

Joan inclined her beautiful head, answering gently :

"My lord, so am I." And, thought George, no high-born lady could have looked more graciously dignified as she sat her spirited animal, swaying so easily to its every impatient movement, and so conscious of the Viscount's dumb adoration that she turned from him to enquire:

"George, what do you think of my mare ? "

"Splendid ! " he answered, stepping back the better to survey this magnificent creature.

"Beautiful ! " sighed the Viscount, stepping forward to gaze up at this lovely rider.

"Yes," she murmured, so very aware of the Viscount that she looked over him at George. "Father gave her to me."

" Then he's splendid, too, Joan, though you know this even better than I do, of course."

" Of course ! " she repeated fervently.

" The Viscount and I," said George, " are on our way to Aunt, Joan, and tea, and there is always a welcome for you at Sparklebrook, Joan, so will you go with us ? "

" Oh, I should love to ! " she sighed. " But there are cows to milk and butter to make . . . for, you see, my lord, I am a farmer's daughter and a very busy person, and I'm late already because that. . . . Oh, that Sir Humphrey stayed me—this is why I was so glad of you, my lord, and am so very grateful to your lordship though, I'm sorry for your poor hat."

" Pray, do you often—ride to town ? "

" Sometimes, my lord."

" Then perhaps—sometime—I may hope for the pleasure of escorting you ? "

" Perhaps, my lord."

" And perhaps, considering you and old George are such friends and we are friends also, you will favour me, for friendship's sake, by calling me Corks as all my real friends do—just Corks."

" Oh, my lord, I couldn't and will not, because it is such a most—unsuitable name and so ridiculous ! "

" Raymond then, please, or Ray. Will you ? "

" Perhaps, my lord. And now I must go at a gallop ! Goodbye, George. Please give my fond love to Miss Isabel ! " And away she went ; but in that moment turned to wave gauntleted hand, saying : " Goodbye— Raymond ! " Then her mare reared coquettishly and set off at a gallop that all too soon bore her out of sight.

" She said it, old f'lo', she said it ! " exclaimed the Viscount in murmurous ecstasy, gazing at the dust of her speedy departure as if it were a glory. " And, George, she can ride."

" Of course ! None better, Corks. Cross country, fair or foul, none can match her. She has ridden since she was a baby——"

"Oh!" exclaimed the Viscount in a rapture. "What a woman! And to think you knew her and I never knew or guessed."

"I've known her all her life——"

"Marvellous! But, b'gad—are you in love with her, too?"

"Of course not!"

"Astounding! But if not why the dooce not? Seems inevitable! How can any f'lo' help being up to his confounded ears in——"

"Arternoon, gen'lemen!" Together they started and turned, to see Mr. Shrig beaming at them across the stile.

"Well met!" said George. "If you feel inclined for a cup or so of tea, Jasper, go with us to the cottage."

"Thankee kindly, sir, but dooty forbids. Hows'ever, I'll toddle along o' ye till Dan'l meets me wi' the gig." Speaking, he crossed the stile with surprising agility, and along the winding, tree-shaded road they went at leisured pace, for though old Sol was trending westwards he still blessed them and the peaceful countryside with his kindly warmth. Thus presently George, stifling a yawn, enquired :

"Well, Jasper, old fellow, my man of mystery, how goes our heir, to you now apparent it seems, by whom, it as surely seems, I am never to see or know? Is he still safe and sound?"

"Ar," replied Mr. Shrig with throaty chuckle. "Safe as the Bank o' England and sound as—a bell! The young gent is all a-blowing and a-growing at this here i-denticle moment like vun o' your lady aunt's bee-oo-tiful roses."

"Are you keeping him safe—under lock and key, Jasper, night and day?"

"Not eggs-actly, friend and sir, hardly lock nor yet key, and yet, if need be, so it might. And talking o' keys, m'lud Vi-count, happening in the Raven Inn I there met y'lordship's gen'leman walet, Mr. Joseph Tranter, and a werry affable, nice-bespoke person he is."

"Yes, he came to me with the highest references," said the Viscount sleepily. "But what was he doing at the Raven?"

"Taking a sociable glass along of himself and later, along o' y' ludship's noble cousin, Sir Humphrey Carr."

"Oh, but, I say, you never mean Humphrey was drinking with my f'lo' Tranter, in public?"

"Not in public, m'lord, no. But in the public stable-yard they took werry par-ticklar notice o' y' ludship's ruinated gig. And talking o' gigs, have you brought any o' your guns along o' you from London?"

"Oh yes, several——"

"And oo is a-looking arter 'em?"

"My groom, O'Brian, trusty careful man and pretty good shot."

"Now talking o' guns, m'lud, how long has Mr. Tranter been in your service?"

"A year, more or less."

"And intro-dooced to y' ludship by your cousin, Sir Humphrey?"

"No, I had him from old Popples—Lord Barham. And he suits me well enough—on the whole—so why bother?" Here the Viscount yawned, Mr. Shrig pursed his lips in soundless whistle, and George wondered, more especially when meeting Mr. Shrig's roving glance the lid of that nearest bright eye flickered, warning George's closest attention as he said:

"Talking o' walets in general, gen'lemen——"

"Oh, but we're not, you know," sighed the Viscount.

"No more am I, m'lud, no not even o' vun in par-ticklar, for," said Mr. Shrig, working a large, boldfaced silver watch from his fob, "by the sound o' they veels yonder should be my gig a-coming." And, sure enough, round a curve of this shady road came that fleet-seeming horse and lofty vehicle driven by the ever woeful person in drooping whiskers.

"To the minute, pal!" quoth Mr. Shrig as the gig came to a stand. "How's things, Dan'l?"

"Bowmon, Jarsper. They birds has flew to roost and by different ways."

"Did they sing—so as you could enj'y same?"

" Ay, Jarsper—but only a note or so."

" Even a note is oceans better than none, Dan'l ! Vich being so, gen'lemen, I bid ye good day ; and, friend George, sir, please conway my best respex to your lady aunt. Sirs, your werry obedient ! " So saying, Mr. Shrig ascended the high vehicle very nimbly, Dan'l cracked the whip, whereat the speedy horse instantly proceeded to whirl them out of sight.

" What the dooce were they talking about, d'you suppose ? " enquired the Viscount, as they went on again.

" Corks, I've no idea ! Jasper Shrig is the most confoundingly secretive, devilish mysterious of fellows."

" And eyes, old f'lo' ! I have never looked into such eyes——"

" Yes, sharp as infernal needles——"

" Eh—needles ? What the dooce—I said ' eyes '——"

" Yes, Shrig's eyes, and I agree with you, they——"

" No no, hers, old f'lo', hers."

" Oh, you mean hers ? said George. " Yes, I believe they are blue, or violet, or——"

" Blue ! " exclaimed the Viscount indignantly. " Of course they're blue ! Blue as heaven and make a f'lo' dream of paradise and—what the dooce ! " he exclaimed as over the hedge nearby leapt a horseman astride a powerful creature that pranced, snorted and reared until compelling to unwilling submission, and Charles Mallory was smiling down at them.

" Lord love me ! " said George, admiringly. " That was well done—and yet another horse, Charles ? "

" Yes," he answered, caressing the animal's proudly arched neck with gently masterful hand. " I can't use another man's property, George—so when are you coming to claim him, that horse of yours ? "

" Never, Charles . . . I don't know . . . by Jupiter, you overwhelm me ! However, it's teatime, so along with you and toss off a cup or so."

" Gladly ! But what of my horse ? "

" We'll stable him in the barn."

" But, George, how can I—inflict myself—uninvited ? "

" Damme, Charles, I'm inviting you ! "

" Thanks—but your—Miss Isabel——"

" She will welcome you for my sake and your own."

" My own sake ?   Do you think she will ? "

" I'm certain of it !   She thinks no end of you."

" Does she, George ?   Does she indeed ?   Then I'm with you——" But in the act of dismounting Charles paused to enquire :

" But, my dear fellow, how do you know she ever troubles to—to think of me ? "

" Oh . . . well," said George, somewhat at loss, " by this and that—a word here and there, a look now and then, and so on."

" Nothing more, George ? "

" Not that I recall, except she admired you, of course, the skilful way you doctored Corks here."

" Hear !   hear ! " murmured the Viscount.   " You certainly did, b'gad, Charles ! "

" And anything else ? " he enquired wistfully.

" Yes, that you were gentle as a woman——" Charles Mallory sighed and seemed to droop.   " Though last night, old fellow, as we lit our bedroom candles, she said —and this was odd because we'd just been talking of pickled onions which I'm no end fond of—but she said, and don't take it amiss, old fellow, because——"

" What, George, what did she say ?   What ? "

" Well, what she remarked was, and mind you, Charles, I'm pretty sure she meant it kindly."

" George, in heaven's name, what said she ? "

" That she felt sure you could be terribly stern, dreadfully masterful and frightfully compelling if—what, are you off ? "

" Yes ! " said Charles Mallory, his eyes shining as he urged his eager horse forward.   " Yes, to tea, George, to tea !   Why dally ?   Company, forward—march ! "

F

CHAPTER XXV

Describes a visit of gratitude

WITH her hand upon the large silver teapot, Miss Isabel paused to glance towards the tall yew hedge which, shutting out the dusty highway, made this corner of the garden a bowery seclusion.

" What now, Aunt ? "

" Hoofs and wheels, my dear, and they are stopping ! "

" They have stopped ! " said George and also glanced up expectantly. Then as the gate clicked he started afoot, gazing speechlessly from bowed and stricken age to vigorous youth proudly erect in glowing beauty. So was a moment of stillness wherein George saw only Lady Clytie, while she gazed as steadfastly at Miss Isabel, whose bright eyes returned this wistful regard with a scrutiny that appraised every feature from low-arching brows to rounded chin and every visible garment from bonnet-plumes to sandalled foot. . . . Then, baring his silvery head, the Earl spoke in that pleasing voice of his :

" Madam, Mistress Isabel—dear lady, I am here to attempt the impossible, which is to express my deep obligation to you, my eternal gratitude for your tender care of my son in his recent accident. By your gracious mercy he is alive——"

" Oh, but, my lord," said she, advancing to greet him, " your thanks are more justly due to . . . our friend here, Mr. Mallory . . . his skilful surgery."

" Then, Mr. Mallory, pray know me infinitely your debtor."

" Oh, well said, sir ! " exlaimed the Viscount. " I tried to say as much but couldn't. A bit shaken at the time, but couldn't express myself, never can ; you have me beat at this as all else. . . . But, sir, do you wonder that when I opened my eyes and saw Miss Isabel I thought her an angel ? I did actually, Father."

" And no wonder, Raymond. For indeed Miss Isabel, the lovely child, as I remember you, has blossomed into such lovely woman as might be the good angel to bless any man ! And today, thanks to your care and Mr. Mallory's skill, my son, instead of being—only a memory, is here alive and well, to enjoy your gracious hospitality. So heaven bless you both and may you know such happiness as that with which you have blessed me. And now . . ." he sighed.

" Now," she repeated, and, taking his hand, led him to the well-laden table, " I was just about to pour out tea. Pray join us. Sit down here by me ; I have not forgotten how you enjoyed a cup of tea so many years ago."

" I do still and shall like nothing better. But first I present my loved ward, Lady Clytie Moor." And now once again eyes, blue and dark, beamed in shrewdly critical appraisal as only eyes feminine might, lips smiled in murmurous greeting, graceful bodies swayed and sank in stately curtsies.

And so, presently, was the subdued tinkle of delicate china, with murmur of happy voices and laughter, and (to George's vast surprise) none gayer than the Earl ; yet after some while, despite his ease and charm of manner, he became silent and under cover of the general conversation leaned towards his hostess, murmuring sadly :

" With the passing years all earthly things must change for better or worse . . . but no thing and no one so much as I ! You see me now the poor, mere ghost of what I was. This is the never-ending tragedy, that we and all our world must suffer age and decay—the mortal and inevitable change——"

" Except our beloved downland yonder, my lord ; they never change, and I pray God they never will. Look at them now sweeping away in glory to the sea ! "

" Yes ! " he murmured. " Yes, there is immortality, the everlasting sanctity of silence. They show now precisely as they did in those happier days, when you, your father and I galloped over them so joyously! Do you remember those days?"

"I shall never forget them."

"Your father was my honoured friend and you and your sister Helen my companions."

"And when Helen was from home I used to play hostess to you and Father and pour tea for you after a gallop."

"You were a fearless horsewoman even then."

"And you, my lord, you could ride and gentle anything on four legs!"

"Yes, I was not the shadow I seem today."

"Indeed no! Helen and I used to think you quite glorious, so tall and immensely strong! And, oh, I shall never forget how easily you twisted that poker round Sir John Carr's neck because he tried to kiss me."

"So I did!" sighed the Earl, smiling though rather sadly. "We neither of us cared for Sir John, I remember."

"I detested him! A hatefully evil wretch! When you made him a cravat with that poker I wanted to kiss you."

"I should have been the happier and richer——"

"I heard Sir John had to sleep in that poker that night at least."

"He had to go to bed in it. . . ."

So they talked, these two, of other days like the old friends they had been, until, this meal over, my lord demanded to be shown round the garden. So Miss Isabel gave him her arm, proud to show him not only her roses abloom in fragrant glory, but the vegetable garden also, where the aged one, plying a very leisured spade, paused to goggle and mop unperspiring brow. . . .

Meanwhile Charles, talking horse with the Viscount, led him away to the barn for my lord's opinion on his new purchase, thus leaving George alone with the tea-things, and Lady Clytie, who instantly leaned graciously towards him to say, in gentle, cooing accents:

" Damned wretch—why did you set your aunt against me ? "

" Eh . . . why . . . what . . . good lord—— ! " stammered George.

" I suppose you told her I swear ! Did you ? "

" Well, no . . . I . . . not exactly. What I mean is——"

" You did ! So now I detest you for a tell-tale ! Oh, beast, devil take you, curse you ! "

" Hush—she may hear you and——"

" Let her ! The sooner the better——"

" But she—she does not dislike you——"

" She does worse ; she scorns and—pities me ! "

" But—great heavens—how do you know she does ? How can you be so sure——? "

" Because I do and I am—thanks to Mr. Abominable Bell ! Why did you tell of me ? "

" Because you had shocked me——"

" I meant to ! "

" Besides, I hardly knew you then, and——"

" Do you think you know me now ? "

" Better than I did. However, I am perfectly certain you are wrong——"

" If you mean I'm wrong to swear, I——"

" I do not ! Oh no, your swearing is mere silliness ! No, I mean about Aunt Isabel——"

" She despises me——"

" Impossible ! She would never be so damnably unjust ! "

" Now you are swearing——"

" Then pray forgive me ! But I cannot allow you to impute such injustice to my aunt——"

" Merely because she is Mr. Hateful Bell's aunt——"

" No, because she is her kind and gentle self and too wise to prejudice anyone——"

" Oh—indeed ! Yet with her first glance she said to me : ' Ah, so you are the young person who dares to swear at my perfect and wonderful nephew ! ' "

" Now, damme, she never uttered a single word ! "

" With her eyes, Mr. Idiot Bell ! With her very first glance she looked all this at me—and more ! "

" I think you are absurdly fanciful——"

" And I know you are a dense, insensitive, oafish clod. . . . But, oh, I did so want her to love me—even a little. . . . I never had a woman friend."

" But plenty of friends masculine, of course ! "

" Of course."

" In London, I suppose ? "

" Yes, the Earl kept open house and we saw a great deal of company, this is why I love the country."

" Do you ? Really ? "

" Is it so incredible that I should ? "

" Yes ! With your feathers, frills and flounces you are quite out of place in our simple rusticity—like your too-splendid Sir Humphrey——"

" He's not mine ! And don't ever dare class me with Humphrey, curse him ! "

" No, forgive me, I should not, indeed I do not, so pray your forgiveness."

" Odious man, you pray in vain ! And here comes your splendid aunt to glare down her stately nose at me——"

But instead, Miss Isabel reached out both hands, saying in her gentlest tones :

" Dear child, the Earl has been telling me of all your devotion to him and what a blessing you are and have been. And because he was my dear friend years ago, I should like to kiss you—if I may."

" Oh," said Clytie, with a sound very like a sob, " if you—only will——" Then she was in Miss Isabel's embrace, kissed and kissing ; thereafter, with arms entwined, they paced cottagewards in murmurous, suddenly familiar converse. . . .

George was gazing after them in no little surprise when he felt a hand upon his arm, a gentle hand, yet in its light contact he sensed a latent power, a physical strength which, thus hidden, seemed to him the more terrible; then in voice gentle as his touch the Earl spoke:

"Mr. Bell, my son has spoken much of you lately and I am heartily glad to make your better acquaintance! Pray let us walk—at stricken age's hobbling amble. . . . Today I have renewed my friendship with this noble lady, your Aunt Isabel, she and your mother, then little more than children, were very dear to me, years ago."

"Then, sir, did you ever meet my father, Captain Philip Bell?"

"Never, alas! A very gallant gentleman. Today I heard from Isabel of him and your valiant mother, the splendour of their death! The next best thing to knowing how to live is to know how . . . and when . . . to die."

"But my lord, who can know ' when ' to die?"

"Only such as die for and to sufficing purpose. Now talking of Raymond, the son whose gentle mother died to give him life—he, like myself, is by nature solitary, blessed—or cursed—with hosts of acquaintances but no real friend. Today I am hoping he has found one in you at last. Yes, I am hoping he will be a frequent visitor here, this remote and lovely haven, and that you and he will consort together—very often."

"My lord," said George, somewhat bewildered, "I . . . indeed you honour me!"

"I do more!" said the Earl, halting suddenly. "I welcome you as my son's most trusted friend and my own! So, George, give me your hand!" George did so—and the question he would have asked concerning the Viscount, the warning he meant to utter, faltered on his lip and were never spoken, for just then the Viscount hailed them cheerily, the others rejoined them and conversation became general.

For some while after the guests had departed aunt and nephew were profoundly thoughtful; Miss Isabel's stately head was bowed above the stocking she had sat down to darn, but her needle-hand was still; while George, who had taken off his coat, minded to work on the arbour he was constructing, did no more than gaze absently towards his toolshed :

"Anyhow," said he, on sudden impulse, "I can never believe or even think of him as a murderer."

"Gracious goodness!" exclaimed his aunt, starting. "A murderer? Where, what—who——?"

"The Earl!" said George in tone of conviction. "He might kill in fair fight, but murder, no—never!"

"Of course not!" said Miss Isabel indignantly. "What gave you such a wickedly unjust idea?"

"That skeleton, Aunt! Rumours! For how did Philip, the seventh Earl, die in such place and such manner? I was pretty sure I knew the answer, until today—but now I'm all at sea again, for the Earl is more of a contradiction than ever and utterly confounds me. The oftener I see and hear him the more I am bewildered; he seems to positively radiate such power of mind, yes by heaven—and body, strength in weakness governed by indomitable will—a man to be feared and hated, or honoured, and—yes —loved, in heaven's name, which, and what is he?"

"Both, perhaps, my dear."

"Well now, Aunt Belle, you who knew him years ago, what think you of him now?"

"That he is to be—greatly pitied."

"Aunt, you astound me! He is a spirit that soars above pity and would scorn it! I sense in his apparent feebleness a hidden strength, a latent power that might be very terrible."

"Ah, but my dear, the strongest of us is, and must be, the helpless victim of destiny."

"Oh?" murmured George, pondering this.

"Yes, my dear! And don't ask me what I mean because I have no idea! And now for your other question?"

"Which question, Aunt?"

"The one you wished to ask, meant to ask, and have not—yet."

"I suppose you mean . . . her . . . your opinion?"

"Of course."

" Well, what do you think of—her ? "

" So much that I pity you also."

" Good heavens !   Why ?   What have I done to be pitied ? "

" Fallen so pitifully in love, George."

" Not I, my dear !   Oh no !   Certainly not !   Nothing of the kind——"

" Everything of the kind, my poor boy !   She knows it, of course !   I knew it at once, and she, knowing I know, does not know what I am thinking about it or how I shall take it, and is wondering how and what, at this moment, I'll be bound."

" But, Aunt Belle, I assure you most solemnly——"

" George," she retorted, rising, " don't be silly !   Bring in the cushions when you come, there will be a heavy dew tonight.   I'm going to help Betty prepare supper, so come in when I ring."

Then away she went, leaving George gazing at those particular cushions which had propped Clytie's lithe shapeliness with eyes extremely thoughtful and not a little troubled.

CHAPTER XXVI

Gives some description of a gentleman's gentleman.
And a kiss

MR. JOSEPH TRANTER, sleek of person, well bespoken, deft of hand and soft of foot, was all that a gentleman's gentleman could possibly hope to be. Just at present he was " turning out " his gentleman ; that is to say, preparing my lord Viscount for the afternoon ride which had become so usual of late.

" Ha, the dooce ! " exclaimed the Viscount pettishly, surveying his reflection in the long mirror. " Dooce take it, Tranter, I believe this coat wrinkles across the shoulders ! "

" Oh no, my lord ! " cooed his gentleman in dulcet tone. " Your lordship's pardon, but no, the garment sits your lordship to admiration ! "

" Well, is this the best hat I have ? "

" Your lordship owns so many hats it is most difficult to differentiate, but indeed this, my lord, is in the very latest mode, perfectly *comme il faut*—suffer me, my lord ! " So saying, Tranter poised the hat, placed and fitted it gently upon his young master's fair head at the exactly proper angle, then stood back to survey the effect with sternly critical eye.

" Well ? " enquired the Viscount a little anxiously.

" Ad-mirable, my lord ! " sighed his gentleman in a sort of ecstasy. " Your lordship is the absolute quintessence to woo and capture the regard feminine—— "

" Eh ? Whose regard feminine ? Tranter, what the dooce are you driving at ? "

" My lord, I spoke but in generalities."

" Oh well, give me my whip ! No, not that, my heaviest crop ; I'm riding Thunderbolt."

"A wicked creature, my lord! A vicious animal! I beg you will take every care, your lordship's life being so extreme precious!"

"Precious," repeated the Viscount, with a last glance in the mirror. "Yes, I begin to think it is and hope it may—become more so." Then, spurs jingling in eager, youthful haste, down sped he to the spacious courtyard where Thunderbolt, his favourite horse, was being held, more or less, by two struggling stable men, advised and encouraged by my lord's head groom, Tim O'Brian, who, thus regardant, chewed placidly upon a straw, and, who, as his young master appeared, instantly removed this straw to touch eyebrow and say:

"'Tis a throifle fresh loike he is, y'r anner———"

"So much the better, Tim!" laughed the Viscount as, watching the opportunity, he mounted, steadied the eager animal like the horse-master he was, then, at his word, back sprang the stableman, and he was off and away at a gallop.

"Ah!" growled one of the stablemen, shaking his head knowingly. "Yon brute'll be the death o' somebody yet———"

"And, my good fellow," said Tranter, who had followed his gentleman into the afternoon sunshine, "I'm inclined to agree with you———"

"Are ye now, me foine buckeroo?" demanded O'Brian. Teeth champed viciously on the straw he was chewing again. "And phwat moight ye mane be that same?"

"No more than I say—and no less, my very good O'Brian!" Having said which, my lord's gentleman smiled, nodded and strolled away, leaving Tim O'Brian to scowl and chew his straw more viciously than ever.

Meanwhile the Viscount rode apace in glad and eager expectancy of one who, he hoped, would soon bless his sight with her radiant loveliness; thus his slender brows knit in quick frown as, turning a bend in this pleasant, winding road, instead of this hoped-for vision he beheld George; and, masking disappointment in a smile, he reined up, soothed his rampageous animal to partial quiescence and enquired :

" Whereaway, old f'lo' ? "

" Home," George replied, " though I lingered, hoping to meet you."

" Did you though ?   What for ? "

" To ask you a question."

" Well, ask away."

" Right !   Now tell me, are we friends ? "

" A fool of a question, George, demme !   Of course we are, now and ever.   David and Jonathan, Damon and Pythias, what's-a-name and you-know-who—we beat the lot of 'em for true friendship and dooced devotion, as you ought to know."

" Then, Corks, old fellow, because your friendship so truly honours me, I dare to ask you—what of—her ? "

" Her ? " enquired the Viscount.   " Who ?   Oh . . . I see. . . .   Of course. . . .   You mean—her ? "

" Raymond, I've known her family all my life and they're grand folk.   But . . . after all . . . she is only a farmer's daughter, but you are a great gentleman, a nobleman who must some day be the Earl and . . . well . . . what of her ? "

" Ah," sighed the Viscount, shaking his head, " that's the dooced question !   She will make a most beautiful countess if she only will, but will she ?   My—my wife, George, I hope !   This is my dearest wish !   She has become the most sacred thing in life to me !   How could you think otherwise or that I——"

" Forgive me, Raymond.   I was a clumsy fool ! "

" True enough, George !   But then you were also her good friend, and as her friends are mine, of course, so you and I are twice friends, and in her name I thank you for doubting me—I mean for protecting her against me or what you suspected I might possibly be—which was quite impossible, considering she is she and I feel so dooced unworthy that I've never dared so much as to kiss her hand, as yet. So d'ye see, as for you, George, all I can say is, thanks."

"And all I can say is—good luck, Corks, old fellow."

"I shall need it, George, for I haven't said a word to her yet of—— Oh, dooce take everything, there's Clytie!"

"Oh? Where?"

"Riding across the meadow yonder. If she expects—— Tell you what, old f'lo', she's making for that gate. Meet her there and keep her talking till I'm well away. You see, I'm hoping to meet—her! Goodbye!" And off galloped the Viscount at such furious speed that he had very soon vanished round a bend in this pleasant, tree-shaded road.

Thus when my lady Clytie reined up her mare to open the gate, there was George to do this for her.

"Goodness—me!" she exclaimed. "What amazing courtesy!"

"Madam," said he, bowing and wafting her forward with flourish of hat, "your humble servant ventures to bid your ladyship good afternoon!"

"And sir," she responded, smiling down on him, "my ladyship, touched by your most unexpected but very proper humility, begs to thank you. And now, pray tell me was it poor Ray who fled at sight of me?"

"He had an appointment, I believe."

"Oh yes, with his newest flame. I wonder if you know her or of her, since you are acquainted with everyone hereabout? I hear Raymond is philandering with some rustic Venus, some farm girl or——"

"On the contrary," said George, frowning, "Raymond is paying his addresses to a lady who honours me with her friendship, Mistress Joan Tulliver, of Burnt Ash——"

"Oh? And a friend of Mr. Bell! Happy, happy—lady!"

"A life-long friend, madam, as are her father and mother. May I know how you happen to be aware of her?"

"Merely by servant's gossip, sir."

"I am amazed your haughty ladyship should stoop to heed such vulgar tattle! Was it by chance, at a keyhole?"

"Oh," she cried furiously, "how dare you make such—such odious suggestion! Hateful man! I overheard quite by accident—Raymond's furtive, slinking valet talking with detestable Humphrey—two beasts!"

"I see. But how should they know?"

"The valet-beast spied Raymond with this—this lady in the Home Wood. . . . And to dare suggest I listen at keyholes—you are a third and most damned beast!"

"But, gracious lady, a truly contrite beast who most humbly craves your pardon."

"Which I refuse, of course!"

"As I, of course, expected! Indeed you are, at times, surprisingly childish for a person so well grown and so fully—developed."

"And you are disgustingly coarse! Fully developed indeed!"

"Graciously so, my lady, especially on horseback!" At this, her riding-whip became a menace, George's raised stick a defence; then her ruddy lips quivered, parted to flashing smile and she laughed, saying:

"How ridiculous we must appear!" Then she rode through the gateway, which George closed and fastened, like the true countryman he was.

"Well?" she demanded, looking down on him.

"Exceeding well!" he answered, gazing up at her. "Who wouldn't be, in such countryside on such glorious day?" Here, as she prepared to ride on, he enquired: "Pray, are you going far?"

"Only to the town, sir, for sake of the little common taste we have in common, to buy her promised doll and cradle."

"Then, if you are in no hurry, I should like to accompany you a little way."

"Oh—Mr. Bell!" she exclaimed, regarding him beneath lifted brows. "Can it be possible you begin to enjoy my hated company?"

" Surprisingly ! " he answered.

" Mr. Bell, you become my astonishment ! "

" And my own ! However—may I ? "

" If you so desire—but on condition you tell me all about this lady of the farm."

" With pleasure ! " said George, as they went on together.

" Then first—is she very pretty ? "

" No, she is radiantly beautiful."

" Radiantly ? Meaning, I suppose, golden hair and blue eyes ? "

" Yes, but such eyes and hair as are rarely seen."

" She must indeed be very lovely ! "

" She is both lovely and beautiful, and that is also all too rare."

" Pray, what is the difference ? "

" Beauty can be evil ; loveliness—never."

" And alas," she exclaimed mockingly, " I am dark as moonless midnight and swear most shockingly ! Alack a-day, poor me ! How can such as I ever hope to be lovely, Mr. All-knowing, Easily-shocked Bell ? " George merely scowled—wherefore she enquired plaintively : " Are you weary of my company so very soon ? Then, before you leave me, please tell me this : do you believe poor Raymond loves this most beautiful loveliness, or is it merely another affair ? "

Now at this George turned to frown up at his questioner and was dumbstruck to see her dark beauty gentled to such tender loveliness that he took three or four strides before he could reply, and rather unsteadily :

" Moonless midnight . . . can be beautiful and lovely as the day, if . . . you only will ! And as regards the Viscount, I believe he loves deeply, truly, and, yes, unselfishly, with all that is best in him."

" Oh ! " she murmured. " Is there such love ? "

" Yes ! " said George, with the utmost fervour. And in the same gentle voice she enquired :

" Do you speak from experience ? "

" Well—no.   That's to say, I . . . what I mean is——"

" You don't know anything about it ! " she retorted, with look anything but gentle.

" Do you ? " he demanded sharply.

" Yes indeed, Mr. Bell ! "

" By . . . actual . . . experience ? "

" By much and long experience ! " she nodded.

" Meaning you . . . are truly . . . in love ? "

" Meaning that I love the dearest, noblest, grandest man in the world ! "

" So ? " murmured George, his step losing much of its spring.

" Yes ! " said she, reining back her mare beside him. And after he had trudged thus some while he enquired :

" May I know . . . who . . . ? "

" Yes, Mr. Densely Dull-witted Bell, you ought to have guessed the only one answering such description is my dearest, the Earl of Ravenhurst."

" Ah ! " sighed George, striding on again.   " I see ! But is he truly such marvellous being ? "

" He is more !   He is so generous, wise and just, so perfectly fearless and brave as a lion, as a hundred lions !   And but for him I should have been killed or—worse ! "

" Then God bless him ! " said George impulsively. " Tell me how and what happened."

" It was on our last visit to France—the Earl has property there—and we were driving to Calais on our way home when we were surrounded by horrid men on horses flourishing guns and swords—I mean the men were.   They compelled our coachman to turn, and as he did so—a miracle happened !   And you will never guess what that was !   The carriage had half-turned so that our horses and the robbers' horses were all crowded close together when —the miracle befell—the Earl who had been crouched beside me half asleep suddenly rose up, threw open the coach door, leapt at the nearest man, wrenched his gun away and beat him from the saddle !   Then he raged among the others—like a giant, terrible in his strength. Oh, but glorious, too—beating them down with that gun, men and horses, too! And when there were none left for him to fight, he tossed away the gun and came hobbling to clamber back into the carriage, like the invalid he is."

"Good—great Jove and Jupiter!" exclaimed George, halting in amazement. "What a tremendous exploit!"

"Yes," said she, halting also. "I told you it was a miracle!"

"But what did he say? How did he explain——?"

"By terror! Yes, he did, for as I settled him among his cushions again he said: ' Clytie, dear child, no wonder you are pale and trembling, for those poor rogues so terrified me that I forgot I was a stricken, feeble, old man!'"

"I—wonder!" said George musingly.

"What about, pray?"

"Many things."

"Tell me one."

"I'm wondering if you had seen Sir Humphrey in Paris or anywhere else?"

"No! But, oddly enough, he met us quite by accident on the road just before we reached Calais."

"How did the Earl greet him? I mean—did he mention the robbers?"

"Yes, but only casually."

"Can you remember his exact words?"

"Something about French cut-throats being poor material. But why are you so very curious?"

"Because the whole business was curious!"

"It was very wonderful, but—extremely hateful!"

"Yes," said George, pondering, "I'm afraid so."

"What are you afraid of, pray?"

"I—don't know, and that's why!"

"Whatever do you mean?"

"That, not knowing, I cannot tell you; would to heaven I could!"

"You are hatefully mysterious."

" Yes, I'm afraid so."

" Then to change the subject, your aunt has invited me to visit her."

" She was always a wonderful person."

" Are you aware she asked me to tea this afternoon."

" No ; did she though ! "

" Yes, she did ! And I shall join her for tea whether Mr. Bell likes it or not."

" Madam, our humble Mr. Bell will be happy to wait upon your ladyship hand and foot, or, rather, cup and plate, to keep each constantly replete ; his care shall be to watch your eating and drinking with a regardful constancy and anxious solicitude——" Clytie laughed.

" Good gracious ! Must I be constantly eating and drinking ? "

" With an occasional pause for breath and speech. But your chief concern must be to eat and drink, for Aunt Belle's tea is nectar, and her homemade cake, ambrosia, food for gods and goddesses ; so for a while, by Aunt Isabel's magic, I pray you—be a goddess."

" You are fond of your aunt ? "

" Well, yes," answered George, his voice deepening, " I am fonder of her than fond. She is everything to me, my family in one. Oh yes, I'm fond of her."

" And, I suppose, she is as fond of you."

" I hope and venture to believe so."

" And I suppose she believes you the most wonderful nephew that ever happened ? "

" Well, hardly ! Aunt Isabel is too wise——"

" And regards you as a creature apart—extremely preciously precious ? "

" Lord love your pretty limbs, lady—no ! Having mothered and fathered me all my life, she knows me inside and out—for precisely what I am—a fairly ordinary, well-meaning fellow and a great deal better than your petulant ladyship troubles to imagine him in your cold and prideful aloofness."

" Cold ? " she repeated. " Yes, Mr. Obnoxious Bell

can transform me to an icicle or fire me with justifiable anger, and——"

"Good!" quoth George. "Our Mr. Bell is far more potent than poor George can ever hope to be——"

"Oh? And pray what has poor George to hope for? Did he not detest me? Did we not detest each other the instant we met?"

"He and we certainly did," said George, confused.

"Don't we now, and—more than ever?"

"Do we?" he enquired wistfully, as he turned to stroke her gentle mare's glossy neck. "In this world all things are prone to change."

"Let them!" she retorted. "But I do not change and never shall. . . ." Hardly were the words uttered than— it happened! For her and for him life and the whole universe changed completely. And the first cause of this tremendous event—a small cur-dog. Out from the hedge sprang this creature of destiny to snarl and snap. Up reared the terrified mare. George leapt, and once again Clytie was in his arms—but—this time he kissed her, suddenly, forcefully and—upon her lovely mouth . . . lips that in this deathless moment quivered responsive in sweet surrender. . . . Then, very fool-like, he set her down, stepped back, and exclaimed idiotically:

"Heavens and earth! What now?" And with the utmost composure she replied:

"The mare! Don't let her run away."

"It was," said George, grasping the bridle just in time, "it was that confounded dog."

"Oh no," she replied, with justifiable scorn, "it was this presumptive, odious Bell person!"

"Yes!" sighed George. "The fool kissed you."

"I am too well aware of it, sir."

"He acted," said George, "like a—a confounded ass——"

"No, like an objectionably amorous man!"

"Highly deplorable," said George, "and most regrettable!"

" Do you think so ? "

" No, I don't ! "

" Then you do not regret your abominable act ? "

" Not for a moment."

" I never expected to be subjected to the horror of Mr. Bell's kisses ! "

" Of course not ! The mere idea (speaking for Mr. Bell) was and is just as abhorrent to poor Mr. Bell. But (speaking as George) it was so very much the reverse that I am perplexed and utterly confounded."

" Was it to insult me that you—did it ? "

" No ! No indeed ! "

" Then was it a—kiss of hate, to shame me ? "

" A thousand times no—it was not ! How could you think so ? How can you believe me such a contemptible, dastardly villain——"

" Very easily ! " she retorted, with snap of white teeth.

" Yes," he sighed, " I asked for that——"

" And, Mr. Amorous, Odious Bell, what I ask you is this : if I visit your aunt am I to become the victim of your kisses, behind her back ? " Finding no adequate retort to this, George said nothing, but acted instead ; that is to say, he took her in his arms again and drew her, unresisting to his breast. Thus, for a space, they stood mute and still, then—Clytie closed her eyes. . . . Whether or not George would have kissed her again cannot be told, for at this precise moment he was startled (and so was she) by a cough, unexpectedly near.

CHAPTER XXVII

In which Jasper Shrig enlists an able assistant

THIS might very well be a chapter of The Cough, since coughing, besides being a nuisance to both cough-er and cough-ee, may be (and often is) an artful mode of expression and of varying degrees, from the politely modulated A-hem, to the brassy, or thunderous Cough Explosive. Thus a cough, properly coughed, may express scorn, anger, warning, reprobation, and very many other passions and emotions. . . . However, the cough that startled George (and Clytie) was of that placid, gentle nature best described as the Cough Discreet; together therefore they glanced up and thus beheld Mr. Shrig beaming down on them through a gap in the hedge above.

"Lady and sir," quoth he, touching hat-brim with knobbed and bludgeon-like stick, "axing your pardons both, but things being so, I'm bold to beg your ass-istance, my lady, and likewise adwice and ditto, sir, ag'in win-dictiveness in the shape of a certain party."

"Right!" said George. "You know I'm with you anywhere and at any time, Jasper."

"Thankee, sir and friend! But how says you, my lady?"

"I don't know," she replied, surveying him with her bright, direct gaze. "You must tell me more. Besides, you terrified me in the tower and I hate being frightened, so, all things considered, I don't think I like you, Mr. Shrig."

"My lady," he sighed, "those lovely eyes o' yourn, though so werry bee-ootiful, are most on-common sharp and, being femmy-nine, can reckon up a man the good and bad of same, dewide him and subtract him and know if he be true or false, vorthy or no. So—look me over, my

lady, and judge according." Steadfastly she gazed at Mr.
Shrig, whose keen eyes looked as steadily into hers while
his round, usually stolid face was slowly transfigured by
the smile that, dawning upon his firm-lipped mouth, quite
banished its customary grimness.

Very deliberately Clytie drew off her gauntlet and
reached out her hand, saying :

" Jasper Shrig, I find I can like you so much better than
I deemed possible that I give you my hand and with it my
confidence—on the condition that you trust and confide
in me." Off came Mr. Shrig's famous hat ; then, taking
this proffered hand, he stooped and touched it with his
lips, and no courtly gentleman could have done it better,
and none with more sincerity ; and Clytie, instantly aware
of this, enquired, with look and tone so sweetly altered
that George wondered :

" Now, pray how can I help you ? "

" My lady bright," replied Mr. Shrig, " favour us by
seating your lovesomeness on this here grassy bank and
you shall hear, adwise and act—I hope ! "

So, when George had tethered the mare, down they sat,
with Mr. Shrig between them, who continued thus :

" First, m'lady, I'd like your opinion of my lord
Wicount's gentleman, Mr. Joseph Tranter."

" I think he's a beast ! " she replied instantly. " A
sly, slinking, furtive beast——"

" Eggs-ackly ! My lady, you have him—in a nutshell ! "

" But surely you are not interested in this low creature,
a mere servant ? "

" Sich is so, my lady. For ' servant ' sounds werry like
' serpent ', and a serpent's a snake, and snakes bite and
sting and all unbeknown—if hidden in the grass ! And
this here snake is a-crawling in grass as is on-common
thick and long—at present ! "

" What have you against the wretch ? "

" First, his record and the fact as he's up to no
good."

" Do you mean he's a thief ? "

" I know as how he's stood trial for same and got off for lack of evidence."

" Then he shall be dismissed at once——"

" To vich, my lady fair, I responds and with all doo respect—perish the thought! Leave windictiveness alone——"

" Good gracious—why ? "

" Because, for the present, windictiveness is safer at the Castle. Lady, snake aforesaid, finding the grass so werry nice and thick, 'll lie snug and so can be kept under obserwation."

" Mr. Shrig," she exclaimed indignantly, " do—not ask me to peep and pry upon a servant, or anyone else ! Because if you do——"

" I don't, marm—no ! Here's another thought as can perish. No ; all as I ask of you, lady o' loveliness, is as you'll help me and the law, by engaging a werry small, sharp person to live along o' the folks up at the Castle."

" Oh ? But what kind of person ? "

" Werry small, werry sharp and answers to the name o' Gimblet—a b'y, m'lady."

" Mr. Shrig, whatever do you mean ? "

" A lad o' mine, marm, a orphan urchin as I've took under my ving and am learning to grow into a limb o' the law ! Vich, though small, a right promising young limb he is, ar—sharp as a packet o' needles, as razors and stilettos, vich therefore I've named him Gimblet."

Clytie laughed again, then said dubiously :

" And you wish me to find your Gimblet boy a situation at the Castle ? "

" Pre-cisely, my lady—if you can."

" Of course I can."

" But the Earl's butler, Mr. Hook, seems a extryordinary high-nosed forbidding sort o' gen'leman ? "

" So he may be—in the servants' hall, but——"

" And likevise Mrs. Jarman, the housekeeper, is a lady not to be sneezed at——"

" But how on earth can you know about them ? "

" Obserwation, my lady. Now if they should object to you engaging my Gimblet——"

" Mr. Shrig, they wouldn't dare. Gracious me—I should think not indeed! When can I see your boy ? "

" This i-denticle moment, my lady ! " So saying, Mr. Shrig whistled the opening bars of " Come lassies and lads ", very pleasant to hear, whereat ensued a rustling and down from the adjacent hedge slithered a diminutive person clad resplendently at each extremity in the smart, cockaded hat and little top-boots of a very small groom or " tiger ", while his midward section was adorned by the many-buttoned jacket of a page ; a rosy, undersized boy, with short, pugnacious nose and eyes blue as cloudless sky, even brighter than his glittering buttons and far wiser-seeming than his years. Standing before them, upright as a soldier, this boy now raised hand to hat in smart salute and said in voice sweet as choiring cherub :

" Y'r servant, m'leddy—I hope ! "

" Marm," quoth Mr. Shrig, " my lady beautiful, there y' are ! This is my Gimblet ! Take off his hat and boots and he's a page ; put 'em on again and he's either a tiger or a werry small groom ! And your lovesome ladyship'll find him werry knowing and handy wi' hosses. Also he can read, write and cypher or cook you an egg, grizzle a rasher, brew coffee or tea, vash a plate or cup and sarcer and never a break nor crack ! "

" Mr.—Shrig ! " she exclaimed, smiling at the boy, who, grinning responsively, was instantly solemn again as a page-tiger-groom in such boots buttons and hat ought to be. " Oh, Mr. Shrig, I am overwhelmed by your Gimblet and his so many accomplishments ; he is truly *multum in parvo*, so many in one ! Of course I'll engage him. He shall be my three-in-one—page, tiger and groom, and general factotum besides. Tell me, boy, would you like to stay with me ? "

To which he answered in voice sweet as throstle's pipe :

" Yes, m'leddy, and no bleed'n' error ! "

"Gimblet!" cried Mr. Shrig hoarsely. "Ha' done! No swearing; you'll shock the lady, and then——"

"Oh no!" she sighed, glancing at silent George. "I also swear at times, quite dreadfully, and have shocked poor Mr. Bell more than once. So, Mr. Shrig, I will have your boy, though for the time being he must have another name, something more suitable. Wilfred or Oswin are pretty names, and yet perhaps one more ordinary and quite common like Tom—or—George——"

"Excellent!" laughed George. "Pray name him George so that when you call 'George' you'll remember another George. A George who may banish all memory of our Mr. Bell. Then besides, George is old England's patron saint. George is also England's King, and George is, moreover, your very humble servant to command. Indeed there is much to be said for George——"

"So much," she laughed, "that I shall probably call him Tom, Dick or Harry. Though he's such a dear little anomaly that I ought to find him a suitable name. Mr. Shrig, how long may I keep him?"

"Vich depends, my lady, on snakes and sich like crawly creepers."

"You will wish to see him frequently to—report progress, I suppose?"

"Thankee, my gracious lady bright, I shall, though not at the Castle! So if you allow him an hour's leave of absence of a Monday, Wednesday and Saturday, if that'll not illconwenice you, I shall be werry dooly grateful. Is it so agreed?"

"Of course!" said my lady, rising. "May I take him with me now?" Mr. Shrig heartily agreeing, she took his ready arm, led him to her mare and with his assistance mounted, saying to George as she settled herself and took the reins:

"Mr. Bell, I go to prepare for my visit to a certain gracious lady—although she possesses a nephew! Yet for her sake I shall adventure him and any possibly dread contingency that his mere presence implies. So, sir, and to you, Mr. Shrig, I bid a very good afternoon ! Come, boy ! I think I shall call you Parvo—what do you think of that as a name ? "

" Sounds blee—furrin' t'me, m'leddy, but you says it so pretty I don't mind. So it'll do."

" Now bless your bright eyes and dear little top-boots. So will you ! " She laughed and reached down to touch his rosy cheek with caressing hand, whereupon he stood at attention with another soldierly salute. Then, smiling down on him, " Come, my Parvo," she said in her gentlest tone, " and don't let me ride too quickly for those very smart, little legs." Then, reining her mare to leisured amble, away she went, her small, triune servitor striding beside her and making the very utmost of his gleaming top-boots.

" A grand little fellow ! " said George, gazing after them.

" Ar ! " quoth Mr. Shrig, also thus intent.   " And a werry grand and noble lady, bee-oo-tiful, lovesome, sharp as a set o' razors and extryordinary lovely ! "

" Lovely ? " George repeated as if demanding this question of himself. " By Jupiter, Jasper, I believe . . . you are . . . perfectly right ! "

CHAPTER XXVIII

How the " Sagamore " (and another) came home

MEANWHILE on this same warm and sunny afternoon Mistress Isabel was busied, as usual, in her garden, but, which was most unusual, today, instead of working-gown, she wore a robe, a vesture, a " creation " which, though flounced here and there, was so artfully contrived that, with her every gesture, it evidenced the lovely shape of her.

To be sure this afternoon Lady Clytie Moor was to visit her, yet this could scarcely be the reason why she paused so often in the delicate clipping of certain trim hedge to glance expectantly towards the wicket-gate or hearken for its warning click ; thus the shears she wielded were frequently idle and no sound to break the drowsy stillness except the sleepy twitter of birds. It was during one of these silences that she heard at last the sound of horse-hoofs approaching at a speed which suggested impatience, slowing to deliberate pace that told of eagerness suddenly restrained. . . . Then she began snipping and snapping with her shears quite randomly—for these horse-hoofs had stopped. Snipping, she listened until the gate clicked, then, graciously deliberate, she turned, but opened her beautiful eyes wider than usual at sight of a very handsome head out-thrust towards her with large, gentle eyes, beautiful almost as her own, pink nostrils a-twitch, and silky ears pointed towards her, for this head was equine. But beyond this stately head was another with face and form as handsome. . . .

" Pray, Mistress Isabel, may we come in ? " enquired Charles Mallory wistfully.

" Of course ! Yes ! " she replied. " But—both of you ? "

" Please ! You see, I have taken the liberty to bring George his horse, since he wouldn't fetch him."

" Oh, but . . . Mr. Mallory ! " she exclaimed, laying by the shears and advancing to greet him. " Did you say— George's horse ? "

" Yes, this animal belongs to George. And I believe he knows he has come home."

" Home ? " she repeated, caressing the animal's velvety muzzle with knowing hand. " But George never owned a horse."

" George became possessed of this one on that for me most fortunate and happy day we met."

" Oh, but—but—what can I say ? Such magnificent creature—and a present ! It is quite too much ! Besides, we have no stable."

" The barn yonder will do admirably."

" Oh . . . well," she murmured, still caressing and looking at the animal. " Pray what is the name of this noble gentleman ? "

" Yes," sighed Charles, looking only at her, " he is indeed a gentleman, so I called him the ' Sagamore ' in memory of another gentleman, an Indian chief, who was a friend of mine in America, and who, incidentally, saved my life."

" Then no horse could have a better name ! " said she, still gazing only at the animal.

" And my name, Miss Isabel, is—Charles ! Now may I lead the Sagamore—home ? "

" Yes," she answered, still fondling the horse, but with swift, brief up-glance at the man. " I . . . of course, if . . . if you must . . . Charles ! "

Amazing fact ! Mistress Isabel of all created beings had actually stammered, was flushing, and, of course, aware of this, gave all her attention to the animal again.

Lightly, joyously, Charles swung to earth, the wicket-gate clicked wide, and he with Sagamore entered the garden, this, to him, the loveliest place in all this lovely England—or anywhere on earth.

They walked with the noble horse between them, though now each was conscious only of the other. . . . And thus it was they brought the Sagamore home.

"Mr. Mallory," said she, taking up the shears again which looked too heavy for those slender, sunkissed, shapely hands, "I must leave George to thank you for such noble gift, for I . . . indeed I cannot."

"I beg you won't!" said he, as with hands of gentle mastery he relieved her of the shears and laid them by. "Instead I wish you to advise me regarding my future, if you will be so very kind."

"I will do my best," she promised, glancing from her idle hands to the shears, while he, gazing only at her half-averted face, continued :

"I returned to this Old England of ours where I had the honour to be born, forty-five years ago, intending to restore the old home of my ancestors at Mallory in Kent and there end my days. But now my great desire is to remain in Sussex, to buy a house and settle down hereabout. Would you advise me to do so ? "

"Sussex," she answered, taking up the shears again, " is one of our loveliest counties—at least, I think so."

"Then here is one bond between us, for so do I. Next, do you think I should make a good neighbour ? "

"Yes. Oh yes."

"I'm glad you think so, because, subject to your approval, I intend to buy Felstead Manor, a grand old house situated neither too far off nor too near."

"Felstead ? " she repeated, glancing up at him in glad-eyed surprise. "How strange that you should choose Felstead. I was born there and passed some of my happiest years there ! And you have decided to buy it ? "

"Only if you think it suitable ! Do you ? "

Now, becoming aware of the shears, she began snipping and snapping at the yew hedge quite wildly until once again his strong though gentle hands compelled them from her, and, laying them out of her reach, he enquired :

"Do you advise my buying . . . your old home . . . Isabel ?"

"No!" she answered, frowning to see how she had mutilated the hedge. "Oh no, most certainly not!"

"Will you please tell me why?"

"Mr. Mallory, it stands to reason—such a . . . a desolate old place as Felstead would be too large and . . . dreary for you . . . a solitary person."

"But, Isabel, my dream is to make Felstead a home once more. I am hoping, very humbly, yet with all my heart and my every breath, that I shall not be lonely if ever I make—your old home mine. So . . . may I, shall I buy it, Isabel ?"

She glanced desperately towards the shears, saw them beyond her reach, and so, because for once the situation was also beyond her power to cope with, Mistress Isabel turned to run away ; forgetting pride, dignity and all save the look in his eyes and the wild leaping of her heart so long immune from such terrific, soul-shaking emotion. Mistress Isabel Standish turned to speed away, but found this impossible because of the arms that stayed her.

"Isabel," he pleaded, "can you . . . will you make Felstead, or any other place, a home for me . . . my home . . . our home ? Will you?"

"No!" she replied, quick-breathing. "Oh, never——" His arms relaxed. "Never . . . unless you——" His arms tightened.

"What? Isabel, for mercy's sake, what must I . . . what will you have me do?"

"Say . . . you . . . love me!" His arms became all possessive.

"Love you?" he repeated. "But, oh, my dear, this you know already! I worship you, I always have done . . . from the first moment I saw you, surely you know this?"

"Yes," she sighed, turning to face him despite the fervour of his clasp. "I knew this, but . . . oh, why don't you tell me so?" Uttering this question, she

looked up at him, a very eloquent, most revealing look. . . .
Then he told her, and so convincingly that, after some
while :

" Oh ! " she murmured. " My hair . . . it's all coming
down—look at it ! "

" Yes," he said and kissed it.

" Oh, but," she sighed, " you—will find silver among it
if you look ! A wife whose hair is turning white ! "

" But, Isabel, a husband who is grey as a badger ! "

Softly mellowed by distance, Saint Mark's church clock
chimed the hour.

" Four ! " gasped Isabel. " Four o'clock already !
And Lady Clytie coming for tea . . . at any moment !
And my hair. . . . Charles, pray let me go ! " After a
brief interval he did.

Now when she had vanished indoors, Charles Mallory
glanced up and around like one who walked in a new and
glorious world ; then, coming beneath that ancient pear
tree called " Tom ", he clapped hand upon its rugged bark
as if greeting a friend.

" Old thing," said he, " you small part of Old England—
I'm home. Yes, I'm home indeed at last, and part of
England, too ! " But now came George, who, espying
his lonely figure, vaulted the wicket-gate, crying joyfully :

" Well met, Charles, old fellow ! What a perfectly
glorious afternoon ! "

" Oddly enough," said Charles, as they shook hands,
" I was thinking precisely the same ! What is your
reason for knowing this day to be so particularly glorious ? "

" B'gad, Charles, I hardly know—except perhaps—oh
well, this and that. What's your reason ? "

" George, I have decided to remain and—make my
home—here in Ravenhurst."

" Hurrah ! " exclaimed George, tossing up his hat and
catching it. " Have you decided exactly where ? "

" Yes, I'm going to buy Felstead."

" Are you though, by Jupiter ! But, my dear old
fellow, it will cost you no end to make habitable and

more to keep up !   It's a fairly large property—and a big house for a solitary bachelor."

" But I—shall not be solitary or a bachelor ! "

" Eh ? Not a bachel—— You never mean—oh Lord—do you mean—marriage, Charles, a—wife ? "

" I do indeed ! "

" Oh ! " exclaimed George, in shocked surprise.   " This is come in the wind, a leveller for me, Charles, and a confoundedly serious business for you !   Marriage so often blows friendship sky-high and clean out of time, floors friendship completely, and, well—my friends are very few !   Have you well considered this—this move ?   From every angle ? "

" Yes, George, I have."

" And quite determined on it ? "

" Yes !   Quite ! "

" Oh well," sighed George, " though married and done for, you'll still be a neighbour."

" And friend, George."

" Good !   But, Charles, a wife usually demands so much of a man's time and attention !   Where is he going ? When will he return ?   And so on.   Wedlock, old fellow, is a fetterlock that chains a fellow to his spouse's apron-strings, indoors and out—— And you needn't laugh, my poor Charles, for I tell you marriage is freedom's ending."

" No, George—a beginning to something far better than such freedom——"

" But, Charles, I tell you——"

" And, George, I'm telling you that bachelor freedom is mere selfish waste of life leading to ultimate loneliness."

" Oh well," sighed George again, " do you think we can still be close friends, in spite of your wife ? "

" Because of her, George ! "

" Ha !   Then may I ask . . . do I know her ? "

" Certainly !   Can't you guess ? "

" I haven't the vaguest idea."

" She will bless our sight at tea today——"

" Tea ? " gasped George, starting. " Of course . . . so she will ! Charles, you don't . . . oh, damme, do you mean Clytie . . . Lady Moor ? "

" Damme—no ! " Charles laughed.

" Then who in the world—— Oh, my dear old Charles, is it . . . can it be—Aunt Isabel ? "

" It is—and will be ! Such is my dearest hope."

" Is it all agreed and finally settled, Charles ? "

" Well, not in so many words, but——"

" Let there be no ' but ' about it, old fellow. Don't let her shilly-shally, as I'm afraid she may do. Keep after her and win, and God bless you both ! "

" Then, George, you will . . . can you so welcome me as your . . . as . . . her husband ? "

" Yes, and with all my heart, Charles, and three times three ! Though, by Jupiter Olympus, this will put Jackman's pipe out . . . and dear old Aeneas——"

" Do you mean they both—love her ? "

" They have for years, old fellow. And there were others. Aunt might have married at any time and any one, almost and no wonder, for she was a beauty and——"

" She is, George ! "

" Of course ! And I used to wonder why she never did until it dawned upon my crass stupidity that it was for my confounded sake ! "

" Then," said Charles fervently, " thank God ! "

" Well, for God's sake, Charles, and hers and yours, don't allow any more of this too-angelic self-sacrificing nonsense ! If, though it's hard to believe she would ever marry anyone, yet if she really loves you and will—which, mind you, I think is highly possible—then be devilish downright and compelling, don't let her back out at the last moment, or——" At this moment from the barn, hard by, issued a most unexpected sound.

" Good lord ! " George exclaimed. " A horse whin-nied——"

" Your horse, the Sagamore."

" My horse ? "

G

"In the barn yonder!"

"You mean—— Oh, Charles——?"

"Go and look!" To the barn forthwith sped George,
there to gaze entranced upon this four-legged splendour,
while Charles turned to gaze cottagewards with an equal
fervour; and then his eyes were blessed by the sight of
her as from the road came the heavy rumbling of a carriage
slowing to a standstill, thereafter the wicket-gate clicked
and into this sunny garden stepped Clytie to be greeted by
her stately hostess. . . . For a moment they stood at gaze,
then, reaching forth her two hands, Mistress Isabel said,
voice warmly caressing as her look:

"Yes, my dear, indeed you are very welcome!"

"And, oh," sighed Clytie with an almost tearful eagerness, "how glad I am to know it . . . that you can like
me . . . a little. . . ."

Then Miss Isabel kissed her.

CHAPTER XXIX

In which the Gimblet operates

THOUGH Joseph Tranter was soft of foot, and just at present rather more so than usual, the little feet of my lady's page-tiger-groom were perfectly soundless as, small top-boots tucked securely beneath one arm, he stole after the almost noiseless Joseph. Thus unheard, unseen, he followed—down narrow-winding stair, to the gloomy old guardroom of the tower, down more steps to a stone-flagged passage, an echoing dimness shut in by a green wall of dense leafage. Through and beyond this rustling screen Tranter vanished. Thither crept his little follower, first to peep cautiously, then to crawl with scarcely a rustle, out into a shadowy wood where trees grew high and so close that their great, widespreading boughs interlaced to shut out the sunlight. . . .

And after some while into this solitude, on slow-pacing horse, rode Sir Humphrey Carr, a frowning, thoughtful gentleman. Reining up beneath a tree greater and taller than most, he beckoned fiercely with that heavy, gold-mounted whip he always carried, at which summons Tranter came to stand beside his stirrup—and both, of course, completely unaware of the bright eyes and sharp little ears that watched and listened, heeding their every word and gesture.

" Tranter, did you—try my bedroom door last night— did you ? "

" No, sir ; certainly not ! "

" Well, someone did, and it must have been you. Come now, Tranter—it was you with some item of news, some fresh discovery ? Say it was you."

" Sir, I can only repeat—it was not ! "

" Are you lying—I wonder ? "

"Alas, sir, I cannot help your wondering." Sir Humphrey sat mute a while, to scowl down at the whip grasped so lightly, then demanded suddenly as though impelled to speech :

"Do you ever hear footsteps at night . . . in dead of night . . . in the cursed hush and stillness—slow, soft footsteps, Tranter ? "

"Never, sir ! "

"Again I wonder—are you lying ? "

"Sir, you must wonder and judge for yourself. But I never hear any footsteps in the night."

"Well, I do ! This accursed place is haunted—not by the dead but—the living ! A vital soft-breathing presence . . . a purposeful stealthiness, a creeping, furtive menace ! And you, damn you, have heard nothing ? "

"Nothing whatsoever, sir."

"Do you know—Death struck at me—in the tower garden and—in broad daylight ? "

"With a great stone, sir ! Oh yes, most distressing——"

"How should you know it was a stone ? I never told you ! "

"I heard such mention in the servants' hall, sir."

"How did they know ? "

"Sir, my lady Clytie's maid is——"

"Ha, yes, Clytie, of course ! Devil take these women's tongues ! Yes . . . a stone ! So close I felt the wind of it . . . the very wind of Death ! "

"A truly shocking experience, sir. No wonder you are so terribly shaken and unnerved."

"Who the devil dares to say I am ? "

"Sir, I merely ventured to express——"

"Then don't ! Instead give me your report."

"At once, sir ! First, I have observed my lady Clytie in more familiar company, a much warmer association with the young lawyer, Mr. Bell ; she becomes, let us say, ever kinder, and they consort more frequently——"

"Ha ! Do they so ? "

"They do indeed, sir ! This very day a happy chance so

placed me that I beheld them in each other's arms, close
locked in—well—most passionate embrace."

"Tranter, is—this true?"

"So true, sir, that I grieve to tell of it—knowing your
own warm regard for her ladyship."

"Hold your cursed tongue!"

"As you will, sir. I'll be dumb. Though alas——"

"What? Why 'alas'?—damn you!"

"Sir, there is—yet more."

"Then tell it, man, tell it!"

"Ah, sir, they . . . while locked thus . . . breast to
breast, ah, then—sir, pray command yourself and be
prepared—they kissed! Kissed, sir, as only lovers dare
and do, they—— Oh, they dwelt upon each other's lips
for quite appreciable time! Now as regards my lord
Viscount——"

"Kissed—did they?" repeated Sir Humphrey, hissing
the word through hard-shut teeth. "The proud, two-faced
liar, the deceiving wanton!"

"Alas again, sir, that it should be so! And she such
most beautiful young lady, sir, the embodiment of
feminine perfection and delicious womanhood! And he,
this happy man——"

"Ha yes! With such fellow! This Bell! This damned
lawyer fellow! He must be—taken care of, Tranter!
Yes—he shall be well attended to, his looks completely
altered and himself in no condition for any further love-
making! And this, soon as possible, though not by us,
ah no! The means to this desired end, must be imported!
So you will obtain leave of absence, speed to London and
—import them."

"Meaning your Inseparables, sir, your three bruisers
who——"

"You know where to find them, Tranter?"

"Oh yes, sir, unless they are in gaol——"

"Why the devil should they be?"

"Their last service, sir—the young French gentleman
who followed you from Paris in quest of his——"

" Silence !   You've a cursed loose tongue ! "

" Only when we are completely private as at present
——"

" Well, you're for London and speedily ! Now what of
my dear cousin and this farm wench of his ? "

" They meet very frequently of late, sir, and their love-
nest the little ruined temple in the wood, not half a mile
hence, and——"

" Wait ! Those footsteps in the night, Tranter, those
stealthy movements so deathly ominous ! I'm still wondering how—and why—you, who are so extraordinarily
acute, have neither seen, heard nor sensed this—this
furtive menace ? Why, Tranter, why ? "

" Simply because, sir, I'm happy to say I sleep much too
well to be troubled by such phantasies."

" Phantasies, Tranter ? "

" So I dare pronounce them, sir."

" And you—sleep too well—ha ? " With the word he
stooped so suddenly that Tranter recoiled as from a blow.
" Now—hear this ! " said Sir Humphrey with a smile
which his cowering hearer thought terrible because quite
merciless. " Except you do—better than you sleep—
sleep you shall and never wake—in a hempen cravat—
noose, gallows and gibbet, Tranter ! "

" No, sir—no ! " he wailed, clasped hands raised
imploringly. " I have tried my utmost, done my best for
you, but——"

" Your best has been repeated failure ; that boat,
the——"

" There is still the future, sir——"

" And the future is death, Tranter, death for all of us
soon or late ! But ha—mark this ! Should I die untimely,
by accident—a stone, for instance, a shot from the dark
or knife in the back—in such eventuality, my lawyer will
open a sealed packet wherein are certain papers ! Are you
warned, Tranter ? "

" Needlessly, Sir Humphrey ! For on my knees I
protest before God——"

"Enough, enough! Only remember! And now of your future activities, your next—let us hope successful and quite final achievement. I have evolved a plan whereby you may serve me triumphantly and thus rid yourself for ever of your compelling incubus—myself. It is a subtle plan, Tranter, shall afford you a means to—act, and—yourself entirely unsuspect—leave another to bear the onus. In other words, a stalking-horse. And talking of horses, take and tether mine, then sit you beside me on this fallen tree and hear all particulars."

And presently seated in this remoteness, this leafy seclusion—yet with small sharp ears and quick bright eyes to hear and see their every word and gesture—Sir Humphrey detailed his scheme :

" You have seen this Joan Tulliver ? "

" Frequently, sir."

" And—her father ? "

" No, sir, not as yet.   Must I ? "

" Listen, Tranter.   I made the man's acquaintance days ago at the King's Head.   Farmer Tulliver, though mere farmer, is extremely proud—of himself, his family, and especially his daughter.   He is also wealthy, a large land-owner and power among his own class.   Moreover, and I repeat this, he is passionately devoted to his womenfolk, especially his beautiful daughter—a proud, passionate man ! "

" Is he our stalking-horse, sir ? "

" Yours, Tranter !   Yours only, since you are the agent principal, and to make him your agent unaware will be absurdly simple ! "

" But how, sir ?   Pray instruct me."

" Your Farmer Tulliver is a jovial soul of easy approach, especially on a market day.   Upon such day, therefore, you will approach him, drink and talk with him and at the right instant make brief mention of his daughter. Becoming more familiar, speak of her beauty, her innocence and, by degrees and your usual tact, hint at her association with the Viscount, a young man so immensely her social superior, the pity of it, the danger of it, she so young and he so old and experienced in seduction, so shockingly notorious for his profligacy. . . . And so on, Tranter, until devoted father, maddened and heedless of bystanders, raves and rages for the young villain's blood and declares, and in the hearing of as many as possible, that he will, to save or avenge the tarnished honour of beloved daughter, shoot the young villain as any devoted father should ! "

" And then, sir, I suppose——? "

" The young villain is found, extremely dead, Tranter, vengeful father is apprehended, tried, found guilty, public sympathy enlisted, and devoted father receives nominal sentence or goes forth a free man to cheering multitude and lives out his days, honoured by all. . . . *Quod erat demonstrandum*.   Well, Tranter ? "

" Indeed, sir, you are such a master of strategy that all I can say is——"

" Say nothing ! Listen ! Horses—and coming this way ! My horse, I'll meet them. Now, off with you, be zealous and—remember."

Now when Sir Humphrey had ridden away and Joseph Tranter vanished whence he had emerged, the very small page-groom proceeded to get into the top-boots ; this achieved, he pulled down his smart, bright-buttoned jacket, smoothed his brown curls and went bold-striding to seek, first his cockaded hat, this badge of his devoted service, and, thus properly arrayed, present himself before his lady to beg instant leave of absence.

CHAPTER XXX

Of woodland magic

TEA HAD been over long ago, hostess and visitor had kissed " Farewell awhile ", and my lady Clytie was upon her homeward way, but not in the carriage ; for, the sunset being so unusually glorious, as if indeed old Sol, thus setting, had set himself the difficult task of making this most beautiful countryside yet more lovely—owing to this circumstance my lady Clytie Moor had suffered George to send away the carriage.

Thus just at present she, and George, of course, are walking along the more or less dusty turf that borders each side of this familiar, winding, tree-shaded road, but they have not gone thus very far ere she demands ruefully :

" Now why, considering this dress was never intended to be walked in, should I be tramping and trudging in the dust ? "

" Quite impossible ! " said George.

" What is ? "

" You don't tramp and you couldn't trudge—with those feet ! "

" My feet ? And what is wrong with them, pray ? "

" Nothing ! And we are not wallowing in the dust, either."

" Oh, Mr. Bell, how insufferably correct you are."

" And it will be a most glorious night ! Which is another reason you are walking."

" Glorious night indeed ; whatever do you mean——"

" The moon will be full, or very nearly ! "

" Good gracious ! The moon won't rise for hours and hours yet ! "

" Of course not. This is why I desire you won't hurry me, or yourself."

"Do you suppose it is likely I shall rove and ramble about the country with Mr. Preposterous Bell, waiting for the moon to rise?"

"Not with your Mr. Obnoxious Bell, but with humble George, George dares to hope."

"Then Master Humility George hopes vainly!"

"Yes, I feared so. However, will you allow meekly modest George to conduct you by the field path?"

"And the woods, so frightfully dark and solitary? I thank too modest George, no, most certainly not!"

"Madam, our Mr. Bell demands why you refuse and wherefore you dare not trust yourself with George in woods or out, dark or light—or anywhere else. Wherefore and why?"

"I did not say I didn't! The word 'trust' never passed my lips."

"Tush, my lady, you quibble! But let it pass. Ignoring your base insinuation, indignant George merely repeats—tush and bah!"

"And so very like a sheep!" she laughed, while George chuckled saying:

"Please tell me what you think of my horse, Sagamore?"

"He looks everything a horse should be."

"Yes!" sighed George rapturously. "And the gift of Charles, bless his generous heart! And—what a gift! Charles must be pretty well-to-do."

"Yes, indeed. The Earl says he is fabulously wealthy."

"Charles? Is he, by Jupiter! It seems hard to credit, for Charles is such an unpretentious fellow—sometimes almost humble. Fabulously rich! Amazing! But how should the Earl know, pray?"

"How should he not? He and Mr. Mallory are distantly related, and, besides, my dearest knows something about everything and everybody."

"Yes," said George, with conviction, "I can well believe it!"

"And rich Mr. Mallory, poor man, is quite hopelessly in love with your splendid aunt!"

" Well now," exclaimed George, halting to say it. " How in the world could you possibly guess ? "

" Because, Mr. Purblind, Unobservant Bell, it is so perfectly obvious to any fairly intelligent person with only one eye, and that half shut ! The question is—does she return his devotion ? And, oh, it must be glorious to be so loved, so worshipped and adored, and by such man ! "

" Yes, Charles is a truly grand man, one in ten thousand ! But how do you like Aunt Isabel ? " he enquired as they walked on again.

" I admire her, of course, and love her—I think. I shall if only she will let me. She positively terrified me at first."

" As-tounding ! " exclaimed George, halting again. " Perfectly amazing ! "

" Oh ? Why the profound astonishment, sir ? "

" Because I can scarcely believe you would ever fear anyone or anything."

" Well, I do. I'm afraid of two people, and one—was your aunt."

" May I know the other ? "

" Devilish Humphrey ! For he is a devil through and through ! Most human beasts have some redeeming quality, but—not Humphrey. Oh no, Humphrey has none, not a single one, damn him ! "

" This is the first time I have heard you swear tonight."

" Yes, but of course I always swear at, or about, Humphrey. So let us change the hateful subject or I must swear again. For instance, why did you want me to walk and why are you with me now in this solitude—and night coming on ? Does Mr. Superior Bell know ? Of course not ! Can addle-pated George reply ? No, and again of course not ! So don't try ! "

" No," sighed he, " I—I'd better not."

" Much better ! " she retorted.

" For one thing," he continued, " you'd never believe me, not possibly, it's all too confoundedly impossible and absolutely unreasonable and beyond human understanding."

" Yes ! " said Clytie.

By this time they had reached a certain gate, and here she paused, saying :

"Last time I was here you opened it for me. Please do so again."

"But," said George, surprised and hesitant, "this leads to the field path and—the woods."

"Yes, the dark and lonely woods, so please open the gate." Speechlessly he obeyed. When he had closed and secured the gate, they went on together through a glimmering dusk, towards those dense woodlands where already night gloomed.

"Lady . . . Clytie," said he at last and in that deep, soft voice of his when profoundly stirred, "you . . . honour me, and I . . . am most truly grateful." To this she made no response, and they went on, and at very leisured pace, in a silence George had no desire to break, for, thus speechless, he sensed a communion more intimate and all unknown until this moment. In this all-pervading hush, in the shadows deepening about them, was a magic spell that enthralled him. Thus it was Clytie who at last broke this enchantment.

"I suppose now that you own such a splendid horse, you will often ride this way—to and from town ? "

"Yes," he replied, troubled now by a strange new diffidence, "yes . . . and I hope . . . perhaps I . . . that is . . . sometimes——"

"Yes, Mr. Bell, I think it quite possible."

"Possible ? " he repeated, enquiringly.

"That we, by chance, of course, may—happen to meet."

"Extraordinary ! " he murmured in awed tone. "You seem to be able to read my very thoughts."

"Sometimes they are so very evident, sir."

"Good—great Jove ! " he gasped, in sudden dismay. "Are they ? Can you——? "

"I can ! Though only—now and then."

"For instance," said he, glancing and almost apprehensively towards these sombre woodlands, "can you—now ? "

" Yes," she answered, gazing also at this dark immensity, " now, most certainly."

" Oh ! " murmured George, his step faltering.

" Yes ! " sighed she.

" Then perhaps you'll . . . wish to . . . keep to the open fields ? "

" I should, of course, were I alone, but not now."

" Ah ! " sighed George, and on they went in a silence that was very eloquent. And thus, as night closed round them, they reached the edge of the forest. And here she paused to enquire :

" Do you know these woods ? "

" All my life ! " he answered. " Every glade and path, and, yes, every tree, almost. This was my boyish playground, and I loved it . . . it's glorious in the daytime."

" But perfectly awful now ! " she sighed. " More dreadful than I thought."

" However, you needn't go this way."

" Of course not, and this is why I must and will."

" Because you are afraid ? "

" No, because this hateful darkness wants to terrify me —and shall not ! "

" Mag-nificent ! " said he fervently.

" If you mean these detestable woods——"

" I don't ! I mean you—your grand spirit ! "

" Oh ! Then please let us go on."

So into this leafy darkness he led the way—until she cried, in voice of panic :

" Wait—wait for me ! Where are you ? "

" Here, close by," he answered, pausing. " Hadn't your ladyship better take firm hold of Mr. O. Bell's coattails ? "

" My ladyship will most gladly—if only she can find the things ! Yes—she has them, one in each hand. Now forward, Mr. O. Bell—' O ' standing for ' obnoxious ', of course ? "

" Yes, of course. But why is the poor fellow so stigmatised ? "

" Because he is always so odiously right, so contemptibly correct and obnoxious generally."

" And what of your humble servant, George ? "

" So long as he remains truly humble he will be—merely George."

" Ah well, mere George will never forget this walk—shall you ? "

" Never ! It will be a haunting nightmare. Oh, isn't there a glade somewhere about ? "

" Yes, on our left, this way. It is called the Abbot's Ride."

" Why abbot ? "

" There used to be an abbey hereabout and it must have been beautiful ages ago. I can show you the ruins, if you wish."

" Not in this horrid darkness."

" Of course not. In the daylight—sometime."

" Yes, in the blessed daylight. I feel now, in this dreadful gloom, as if the sun would never rise again."

" It never can—until after the moon——"

" Ah, the dear moon ! When will she come to light us ? "

" Pretty soon now. . . . And here we are in the Abbot's Ride," said George, as they stepped out into a more spacious darkness.

" How fearfully hushed and still it all is ! "

" Oh no ; the woods are full of sound, all kinds of strange rustlings and odd, unaccountable noises."

" Well, I don't wish to hear any of them. Why are we standing here ? What are we waiting for ? "

" Gracious, though impatient lady, humble George in his ghastly, slavish meekness is deliberating whether or not he dare offer you his arm. Shall he so venture ? "

" No, I thank him ! Pray let us go ! "

And now they went side by side and so near to each other that ever and anon their shoulders met, their arms and hands touched, at which times George's thoughts rioted : " Her loveliness so very near . . . a form soft

and yielding to be embraced . . . a mouth sweet with
life . . . lips that might, again and even now, quiver
responsive to his kiss. . . ."   Here, suddenly remembering
how she might be aware of his thoughts, he flushed
shamefully in the darkness and, not knowing what to say,
spoke at random :

" Talking of horses——"

" But we're not ! "

" No—well—do you remember once saying you would
trample me underfoot ? "

" No—yes !   But for mercy's sake don't bring that up
against me now and—in this desolation."

" Very well !   Only I——"

" Wait ! " she pleaded.   " At least wait until the moon
comes to light us."

" I merely wish to enquire——"

" Well, don't—oh, not yet."

" Poor slavish George meekly obeys your ladyship."

" I hope, considering this horrible wood, George is
more slavishly meek than he sounds ! "

" Lady, no man in any wood was ever meeker, especially
in such wood as this."

" Why this particularly ? "

" Because this wood of ours is full of potent enchantment, reeking with it !   Can't you feel it ? "

" How—what kind of enchantment ? "

" A spell of witchery !   A subtle magic ! "

" White magic or black ? "

" Well, considering this darkness, it should be black—
and would be but for humbly deferential George, a poor
meek wretch for your ladyship's scorn."

" But I don't . . . at present."

" Aha—and there is another and far gentler, kinder
lady—yonder comes Her Gracious Majesty the Moon !
Hail, fair Luna !   Queen of the Night, all hail ! "

And, sweeping off his hat, George bowed towards the
ever-brightening effulgence glimpsed, low as yet, beyond
trees and thickets, saying :

" My lady Clytie, stoop that proud head, bend that dimpled knee and salute Her Serene Majesty."

Laughing, she did so, sinking in profound curtsy—in which moment the rising moon, as if in requital for this homage, sent a level beam to make a glory all about them, in which radiance they stood to gaze—not up at Luna's serene majesty, but on one another ; and at this moment, by moon-magic (or some secret enchantment of her own) Clytie's dark beauty was perfected by loveliness.

" So this," said she, turning to glance round about them as the radiance brightened, " this is the Abbot's Ride, yes and mine also. . . . I often ride here and I love it, but even more tonight ; it looks so delightfully— mysterious."

" It does," said George as they moved on again.   " It is indeed mysterious because close by is what old Hyden the woodsman used to call the ' Shirker Creep '."

" What an odd name."

" But very apt because it's a very odd place, an ancient, underground passage leading from the very heart of the Castle, that old tower, out into this part of the woods, a secret way and still difficult to find unless you know exactly where to look."

" Do you ? "

" Naturally ! I used to play there as a boy ; it was my outlaw's cave."

" Then there is something else you shall show me—in the daylight, if you will.   But now," said she, stopping to front him in the moonlight, " I will answer the question you demanded of me in the dark—about my trampling on you—as if I were an elephant ! "

" Dear lady, not an elephant, but that which might be more unjust and pitiless—a fierce and furious female— human, of course.   You did once threaten to stamp on me, I believe."

" Not upon Mr. Bell's odious person but his quite detestable heart."

" I see," said George gravely.   " This would be rather

worse for unfortunate Mr. Bell ; but, pray, what of the heart of meek and lowly George ? "

"Never 'wear it on your sleeve for daws to peck at '."

"Ah, indeed, poor old Will ! " sighed George. "Our Shakespeare knew all about it ; the poor old boy's heart must have been jumped on frequently—Anne Hathaway, I guess."

"Oh no, far more likely by the Dark Lady of the Sonnets."

"Yes ! Yes, of course ! " George exclaimed. "The Dark Lady, beyond all doubt ! The Dark Lady, cold, cruel and capricious ! Could she, I wonder, ever have been as dark or—anything like my lady Clytie Moor ? Yes, I wonder ! "

To this she retorted, and with unseen smile :

"Then, of course, Mr. Bell must always remain a wonderful man ! And any man merely filled with wonder must be the dreariest of men and simply made to be trodden upon by any—— Oh ! " Uttering this " Oh " of surprised delight, she stopped : for, and quite suddenly, they were out of the forest at last.

"How . . . perfectly . . . wonderful ! " she sighed.

And indeed the moon, now high above them, by her gentle enchantment, was giving to all familiar objects a new, strange beauty, more especially one ; for there rising above the shadowy village soared the aged tower of Ravenhurst as it had done through so many centuries, but tonight, no longer grim and threatening, it showed magically transformed to thing of Faerie.

"Oh ! " murmured Clytie again. "I never thought . . . I never dreamed it could ever seem . . . so beautiful ! "

"Nor I ! " sighed George. "Though on such a night as this . . . anything might happen ! "

"But," said she, sighing also, as she glanced back at the sombre woodland they were leaving, "nothing has ! And . . . because of this, I could almost——" Here she paused to sigh again.

" What ? " murmured George, leaning towards her
loveliness.   " Oh, pray . . . what could you . . . do
almost ? "

" Love Mr. Bell."

" Then . . . what of George ? You don't mention his
name, you never do.   Oh . . . Clytie, what of George ? "
And turning now to look at him, she answered in tone
gentle as his look :

" The George who so protected me against the . . .
magic of this dear, enchanted forest, will take me safely
home."

" Of course ! " said George, though he sighed deeper
than ever as they ascended the grassy slope towards the
Castle, nor did they speak until the ancient tower loomed
above them, grim now and more threatening than ever, or
so it seemed to George.   But in this shadow, two white
hands came out to him, a voice sweetly hushed, spoke :

" Because George is stronger than I deemed any George
could be, I give back to George what George stole from
me the other day. . . . So, George stoop George's head ! "
Mutely he did so, and felt on his the close, soft pressure of
these lips sweet with life, this mouth he had so yearned for
in the wood. . . . Ensued a moment never to be forgotten
and all too brief, for as he stood thralled by the unexpected
wonder of it, she was away with tempestuous flutter of
petticoats that told of haste almost panic.

Motionless a while stood George, blissfully unaware of
the prying eyes that, having seen too much, glared such
deadly menace from the stealthy dark.   Thus when at last
he stepped from the shadow of the tower, it was into an
enchanted world more radiantly glorious than he had ever
known or dreamed possible.

CHAPTER XXXI

In which his aunt advises George

BESIDE the open lattice Miss Isabel sat writing and, thus busied, seemed younger and, if possible, rather more beautiful than usual as her eyes, aglow with a new light, followed these lines her pen was tracing so swiftly :

" Most unexpected and ever dearest Charles,
  " When least expected you have brought a joy into my life—the one I had denied myself until you made me know that without this I, who have been so well-content, should be poor indeed. And all this after so brief a courtship ! But, dear Charles, I am old enough to recognise truth and know sincerity at a glance, and in your dear eyes is truth and with this a love that makes me very humble. Yet it is not for this alone I love you, and, oh, Charles, with a quite terrifying fervour (Oh what shameless confession !), but for what you are, have been and will ever be. And now, my dearest of men, I must tell you how, ever since yesterday, that most wonderful day of my life, I have been troubled about my poor George, because this chance of the happiness you offer me must leave him desolate ; our union will be his loneliness. Thus today, yes and half the night, I have been wondering and scheming how best to break the news of our soon marriage which fills me with alternate . . . "

Here suddenly her busy quill was arrested by a sound, a muted, persistent buzzing that greatly puzzled her because it seemed above, below and all about her, now in the house, now in the garden, indeed the summer air seemed vibrant with it ; so bewildering was this vague disturbance that she called to Betty in the kitchen nearby :

"Betty, do you hear that very peculiar noise?"

"Ay, mam, that I do, and I be a-wondering what it doo be."

"So am I! It seems to be everywhere at once and yet nowhere exactly! Whatever can it be?"

"Mebbe bees, mam, bees be a-swarming p'r'aps somewheres about like."

"Bees, Betty? A swarm! Goodness gracious! And we have that empty hive; how very fortunate."

"Ay, mam, and it be a good skep, sure-ly!" Miss Isabel laid down her quill and rose, instant for action, saying:

"If it is bees, Betty, bring a tray, bring two, and we'll rattle and bang them down. I'll call Jabez, but wait until I summon you!" So forth sped Miss Isabel, light-footed and nimble as any dryad, and, following this extraordinary sound, paused suddenly to laugh sweetly clear as a girl, laughed until she was compelled to lean against the aged pear tree to wipe her ever-beautiful eyes, for—George was grooming his Sagamore, doing it as such splendid creature deserved and so perfectly oblivious to all lesser things that he was quite unaware of his aunt until she spoke:

"George, dear, if you can moderate the extreme sibilance and power of your hissing, I should like a word with you; several, in fact."

George, busied with the Sagamore's off-fore, ceased hissing to smile and say:

"Aunt Belle, our ears attend you! But first may I tell you—Sagamore is as splendid as he looks—a mouth like velvet, and such action! Today, as you know, I rode him to town for the first time, took him through the thickest traffic, High Street and Market Square, sheep and cattle all over the place and he behaved like the gentleman he is! Several of our sporting farmers wanted to buy him. Briggs and Haydon especially! Aha, but best of all Abel Tulliver couldn't find a fault in him anywhere, and you know what a judge he is! And all because of Charles—his generosity! Dear, good old Charles!"

" Yes, my dear, and when you've finished adoring his gift, come and sit with me on the lawn. I . . . have something to tell you."

" Ay, ay, Commander, I'm finishing now."

Thus presently seated together beneath the pear tree, Mistress Isabel, glancing up from the needlework that apparently engaged her, said and in the most casual tone :

" My dear, I have been thinking lately that it is time you got married."

George was afoot at a single bound.

" Married ? " he gasped. " Good . . . great Jupiter ! Why ? When ? Who ? "

" Sit down again, George. Now, to answer your absurdly astonished questions one by one and in their proper order : Because you are of age. Whenever your loving womenfolk elect. And I can think of no lovelier wife for you than Clytie Moor."

" Cly——" George gasped again, then stammered : " But she . . . she is a lady born . . . blue blood . . . an aristocrat and I . . . I'm only a commoner——"

" And yet, my dear, I venture to say a most uncommon commoner. Besides, George, love levels all such petty distinctions."

" But . . . oh, Aunt Belle, she is so proudly, infernally, damnably aloof, and——"

" Do not swear, George ! And of course she is—as any self-respecting, young and beautiful woman should be."

" Yes, she is quite . . . quite dreadfully beautiful ! "

" Why dreadfully ? "

" Because she . . . affects me so . . . powerfully."

" Dear George," murmured his aunt, bending over her needlework to hide her sudden smile. " There is an adage saying ' Beauty is power ' and it always will be, of course— and Clytie is supremely beautiful ! "

" Yes, but is she—lovely also ? "

" So lovely, my dear, that she won me despite my former prejudice against her."

"Oh well," sighed George despondently, "what am I to do about it?"

"The natural and proper thing, marry her."

Up started George again to demand of his aunt and the universe in general:

"How can I? How dare I, when she is her scornful, arrogant self while I am only poor, hopeless, confounded me?"

"Quite easily, my poor silly boy, considering she is more wildly in love with you than you with her——"

"Impossible!" he sighed. "For . . . oh, Aunt Belle, I love her—more than my life! You are right as you always are, for I . . . have loved her from the very first. I know it at last, for, like the fool I am, I mistook it for hate! And now . . . oh, my dear . . . help me now as you have always done . . . advise me, tell me what I should do . . . and how . . . for it all seems so hopeless and . . . I'm lost. . . ."

Down went her needlework, and, drawing him to the bosom, his secure haven in infant woes and childish griefs, she kissed his red hair, saying very tenderly:

"George, my dear one, because your love is so truly sincere, trust to it, have faith in yourself . . . and though Clytie hides her love because its depth and passion frightens her, bless her—be only the more patient."

"Aunt Belle, you teach me to love her even more—if that is possible."

"Because I am so sure and certain she will prove your abiding happiness. And, George . . . my dear, if, as I believe you are to be blest, we might be . . . married on the same day . . . a double wedding."

"Yes—oh, grand!" he exclaimed. "She and I . . . you and Charles! Ha—splendid!"

Mistress Isabel was so startled and surprised that she pricked her finger; and now it was she who gasped:

"Oh—you—knew? George, you—guessed?"

"Dearest of all and every aunt," he replied complacently, "any person of ordinary intelligence with only one eye, and that fast shut, would have known all about it instantly."

" Goodness gracious, I hope not ! " said she, over and round the wounded finger she was sucking.

" However," said George, rising, " if he doesn't turn up pretty soon, I shall gallop the country till I find him ! "

" Who, my dear ? " she enquired, serenely innocent.

" Charles, of course ! I wonder what's keeping him ? "

" Probably—Felstead Manor—no, he is coming now— I hear his horse."

" Can you, by Jupiter ! I can't—yes I can though—but how d'you know it is Charles ? "

" Because I do ! " she answered, starting afoot as nimbly as George himself.

" Aunt," laughed George, " my beloved Belle, being in love suits you. I vow the mere thought of Charles makes you younger and more lovely——"

" George, don't be so ridiculous—stand out of my way. I must go indoors to——"

But even then Charles leapt from his horse, clicked through the wicket-gate and came hasting joyously to say :

" Isabel, Felstead is ours ! Tomorrow an army of workmen begin on it—for, George, my dear fellow, last night she—my Isabel, promised to make it—our home."

" Hur-rah ! " cried George, tossing up his hat and catching it. " God bless you both ! " Then, having kissed his aunt and grasped the hand Charles proffered, he went and saddled the Sagamore and rode blithely away in the hope of meeting the woman he so truly loved.

CHAPTER XXXII

Describes a family scene

SEATED in the tower garden Clytie was attempting the hitherto unwonted performance with needle and cotton, but doing it so badly that often she stamped slim foot at her clumsiness, and once—parted her lips to swear, checked the impulse and instantly demanded of her silver thimble : " Now, why didn't I ? " And, well knowing the reason, sighed, frowned and went on plying her wayward needle until, hearing a gladly familiar step, and tossing needle, etc., aside, sped light-footed to meet the Earl, to give her arm, aid him to his great elbow chair and settle among the cushions placed there for his comfort, and, this done, back to her needlework, which unprecedented spectacle seemed for the moment to smite him speechless ; then :

" Clytie—my dear child—what, in the name of all that is marvellous, are you doing ? "

" Dearest heart," she replied demurely, " I am doing my very awkward best to make for myself a—an intimate garment."

" But, my love, why—when you can buy them by the dozen ? "

" Because I am taking old Father Time by the forelock, dearest."

" May I know why ? "

" Because someday some man may wed me."

" Fortunate fellow ! "

" Of course, sir ! But then, again of course, he may happen to be a—very poor man."

" Would you marry a poor man, Clytie."

" Dearest, for the third time—of course, if I loved him."

" Alas ! " sighed the Earl, watching her beautiful, intent

210

face. "How utterly foolish and recklessly improvident love may be."

"Only—some love, my dear one, for other love may inspire life with a new purpose, laziness to determined effort, and——"

"And my Clytie to try her hand at stitching! Who is he, my dear?"

"Who is who, sir, pray?"

"Do I know or have I ever seen him—your beloved pauper? Is he, as I suspect, Isabel's nephew, young George Bell? I see—your eyes have answered me. I ventured to ask because you are so inexpressibly dear to me. . . . I have loved you so truly all your life that my hope was you and Raymond would mate. But now, since this wish, like so many others, is not to be fulfilled, let me assure you, beloved child, you may wed whom you will, yes—no matter whom, if you truly love and respect each other. And you shall never have to sew or work your fingers to the bone—or prick them till they bleed as I fear you will if not more careful."

"How can I . . . help it," she sobbed, "when you make me blind . . . oh, my dearest . . . blind with tears because of your . . . unfailing goodness and love?"

"Goodness?" he repeated sadly. "Ah, but your tears, Clytie, are my most precious jewels—a glory shall light me—yes, a glory that shall be mine though all else fail and I be doomed to—darkness everlasting." Now at this she leapt afoot, with tender mother-cry, to clasp him in the warm comfort and protection of her arms, saying:

"Oh, my lord, my dearest one, what dreadful words are these?"

"Folly!" he laughed. "An old man's nonsensical babble. There, there! Sit down, get on with your stitching, beware of your needle, and tell me who and what is the sprite in buttons, the top-booted atomy of whom I have caught a brief and fugitive glimpses, lately?"

And, smiling through her tears which she hastened to dry, Clytie answered:

" Dearest, he is a trinity, my page-tiger-groom, who, if need be, can boil an egg, fry bacon, brew tea and perform many other wonders, a tiny *multum in parvo*, Parvo for short. And besides his other accomplishments, he talks like what he describes as a chick-a-leery cove, whatever that may be, speaks like a London street arab in voice sweet as throstle's pipe, talks like a man of the world and deports himself like a very small grenadier. Shall I find him for you ? "

" Yes, indeed, pray do—no, yonder he comes to find you."

" Gracious ! What sharp eyes you have, dearest ! Parvo ! " she called. " Come here to me ! " The boy obeyed so speedily that his little gleaming top-boots seemed to twinkle.

" Parvo, you must remember this gentleman is—my lord—the Earl—of Ravenhurst." The boy saluted smartly, then piped :

" That's for the lord, my lady ! " He took off the cockaded hat with a flourish, clapped it to his small chest and bobbed curly head, saying, " and that's for th' Hearl, my lady ! "

" Now, Parvo, tell my lord who and what you are."

" Gimblet, m'lud, as m'leddy d' call Parvo as sounds furrin but I don't mind seein' as 'ow she's her, and I'm her page 'n' tiger 'n' groom hi am, m'lud."

" So many in one," said the Earl smiling, " and that one so very small ! "

" Yus, m'lud, but I'm gettin' bigger, I ham. Since Jarsper, my Guv'nor, took me I've growed hinches, hi 'ave."

" Excellent ! And how old are you ? "

" Nobody don't seem to know, sir—m'lud, 'cos I never 'ad no farver nor muvver to say, but our Dan'l he says as 'ow I'm fifteen. Corp'ral Dick reckons as I'm lots holder, but my Jarsper he says I'm as hold as Mister Meethoosalem, a gent wot lives in the Bible an' is a werry hold party——"

" Indeed ? " laughed the Earl. " But why that sudden frown, my boy ? "

" 'Cos I don't like 'im, m'lud, the Long Un, the tall, dark gen'leman a-peeping at us from that hold place as looks summat like the Tower o' London——" As he spoke, forth from the Tower strolled Sir Humphrey, whereat the Earl frowned also, saying :

" Parvo, you are not only a smart page, but a very sharp, intelligent boy——"

" Charming ! " sighed Sir Humphrey, sinking languidly upon the rustic seat beside Clytie. " Such homely vision of simple domesticity ! Dear Clytie, I never dreamed those most beauteous hands could—shall we say—stoop to the vulgar employ of needle and thimble, which I believe was originally called a thumb bell. A bell, Clytie, a bell, but—only for the thumb ! "

" Thimbles, idiot, don't go on thumbs ! "

" They must have done so originally. But, talking of bells, my bewitching enchantress, the word ' bell ' is also enchanting, a lovely word as I'm sure you must agree, though its bewitching sound may enchant the more irresistibly, of course, in the sweetly seductive hush and tempting seclusion of a wood—at night. Tell me, dearly loved Clytie, is this——"

" Pah ! " exclaimed the Earl. " Humphrey, what the devil is this nauseating scent, the atrocious perfume you seem drenched with ? Its cloying sweetness stifles me."

" Indeed, sir ? " said Sir Humphrey, with contemptuous laugh. " I take leave to inform you how this most recherché preparation is entirely *à la mode*, the very latest Parisian——"

" Precisely, nephew ! A Parisian abomination ! Pray remove it as far as possible ; I suggest—back to Paris."

With leisured grace Sir Humphrey rose and, thus towering in his strength above the Earl who showed so pitifully weak and helpless amid his cushions, nephew smiled down upon uncle, who did not trouble to move or even glance up, and so ensued a quite dreadful stillness (or so Clytie imagined), a silence so charged with hate and menace that Clytie held her breath (and also her needle poised for swift, offensive action), while her little page, screened and forgotten behind the Earl's great chair, crouched as purposefully; the Earl spoke at last and in tone almost pleading :

" Stand away !   You come 'twixt me and the sun ! "

" Do I, Uncle ? " laughed nephew, bending a little nearer.   " However, I enjoy the prospect of you—for, believe me, sir, you present such pathetic—shall we say epitome ?   No, I choose picture—a picture, my lord, of aged nobility proud in decay and so very much at ease. Ah, well the good God forbid I should ever—ha, should I say—put out your sun."

Here, uncle, troubling to move, glanced up at nephew and enquired casually :

" Pray, Humphrey, why do you so persistently tempt me to kill you ? "   Sir Humphrey's dominating figure quailed and, recoiling, he threw out both arms as if warding off an unseen assailant, and when he spoke—in gasping voice, in look and gesture were the swift alternations of terror, defiance, and entreaty that rose to wail of supplication :

" So—now . . . do I know . . . at last ?   Am I sure . . . at last ?   That stone !   Those footsteps . . . in the night. . . .   You ?   Is it possible ?   Ha, death of my life !   Can it be——"

" Humphrey," said the Earl contemptuously, " you babble ! "

" Uncle . . . let me know !   Admit it or deny !   Make me sure . . . yes or no, I beg you . . . pray you . . . let me be done with this . . . this torment of uncertainty, this haunting——"

" Humphrey, command yourself !   This shameful exhibition of hysterical poltroonery evokes only contempt and disgust !   You prove craven as your egregious father——"

" My father—ha !   By God he knew how to whip you to heel . . . to make you cower and cringe !   Ha, yes, and so will I . . . for hear this and be——"

"No!" cried Clytie, leaping between them. "Humphrey, go! For dear God's sake go, or . . . here is death! Oh, begone!"

"Death," repeated the Earl and in that same dreadfully hushed tone; "quite true, Humphrey—shall it be now?" And he made to rise.

"Don't!" panted Clytie. "Oh, my dearest, don't!" Then, with wild, compelling gesture, she fronted Sir Humphrey crying and in voice of breathless horror: "He will . . . he will unless . . . you go . . . for your own sake . . . for all our sakes I beseech you . . . leave him to me . . . go!"

Sir Humphrey's tense form relaxed, he sighed deeply, then contrived to smile as he said:

"Who could resist such plea so sweetly humble and uttered by such bewitching lips—and tongue? Beloved Clytie, I go to dream upon your too-luscious beauty and, between whiles, to take such, shall we say—natural precautions as I deem adequate. Tonight, sir, do not hope to see me at your board. I sup with a certain Farmer Tulliver who, though a farmer, is, for want of better, fairly goodish company. So, dear Uncle, for the present, adieu! Alas, I could wish you a little kinder, but—as it is, so must and indeed—so shall it be! Ah, and Clytie, I shall return by the Abbot's Ride—you may know it—and there, in that discreet and leafy seclusion, you may bless me with —your presence, if you desire, and there make me—more your own impassioned Humphrey than ever. Nay, right noble Uncle, do not stir; your dutifully obedient nephew departs even now."

So saying, Sir Humphrey bowed profoundly and sauntered away.

Scarcely had he gone that Clytie, covering her face, burst into a passion of weeping; but presently a long arm forthreaching encircled and lifted her with strength of a giant, to clasp and comfort her with the tenderness of a mother; and thus cradled in the mighty comfort of these arms, she pillowed her lovely head on the breast that had so often been her childish haven and sure defence against everything and everybody.

"Fie, now!" murmured the Earl, as if she had indeed been a child again. "Fie upon my little Clytie! You I have taught to fear nothing! To permit such poor thing as Humphrey to so affright you——"

"Not that . . . that beast!" she sobbed, nestling closer. "Not that . . . evil wretch. No—it was—you! Oh, my dear one, it was you I feared and for your own beloved sake! You looked so fierce, so terrible, so very——" She choked the word in a sob, wherefore he kissed her and spoke it for her :

"Murderous! And I must now reproach myself for such regrettably vulgar lack of self-control, and, my Clytie, beg you will forgive and forget the lapse."

"Of course!" she sighed, looking up into the face now so ineffably gentle. "But, dearest, when I remembered how glorious . . . but terrible you were against those French robbers in spite of their swords and guns——"

"His agents, my child."

"Oh! Are you sure?"

"I made perfectly sure later on. For I have agents also."

"What a monster of evil he is!"

"Poor Humphrey has the misfortune to be the only son of an evil sire."

"Then knowing him for what he is, why—oh, why do you allow him here, or anywhere near us?"

"Why does a rat scamper in the wainscot? But enough of him. Choose we a better, indeed a lovelier theme."

"Yes, dearest, yes! What shall it be?"

"May I suggest the Abbot's Ride?"

"Oh, my surprising, wonderful dear!" she exclaimed, and kissed him gratefully. "I'm longing to tell you about —everything, as I used to do as a child, do you remember? And how gravely you would listen and how gently and wisely you would advise, but never command—merely suggest what I should do! Oh, do you remember?"

" Dear child, those are some of my brightest memories. But now—the years have sped and——"

" Now," she repeated, nestling to him again, " you are still my beloved wise-counsellor ! And, oh, what infinite comfort to still confide in you as implicitly now that I am a woman and—find myself—quite surprisingly—shy."

" Clytie, your childish confidences were the joy of my then loneliness. Now that you are indeed a woman, they honour me, and to advise you is my old man's privilege."

" Oh," said she, in tearful voice, " my great, strong, weak, meek, proud, gentle, wise and wonderful dearest of dears ! Only God knows what a blessing you are to me or how much I love you . . . as I always have and ever shall—— ! "

Here, having kissed him repeatedly (a kiss with each and every adjective), she nestled close again, saying :

" I suppose you know the Abbot's Ride ? "

" Oh yes ; I galloped it repeatedly long ago."

" Well it was there Humphrey, judging by his odious talk of ' thumb bells ' until you checked him so adroitly with his hateful perfume, it was there, deep in the woods, the Humphrey beast must have spied us."

" My dear, of course ! Spying is inherent with him, so be warned ! Your pauper must take greater care of you— in the future."

" The future ? " she repeated, sitting up and speaking in a kind of hushed ecstasy. " Then you don't . . . you won't . . . mind——? "

" Indeed I do, and so much that I shall demand he take far greater care of you and——"

" Oh, he does ! He will ! He—did ! In the forest ! In all that dark solitude ! This is why I used the woods, to—try him, to . . . tempt him . . . just a little——"

" Oh, eternal, everlasting Spirit of Eve ! " sighed the Earl, though his shapely lips were smiling. " Alas for poor Adam ! What of him, my Clytie—Eve ? "

" Adam, beloved my lord, was merely Mr. Always-discreet, Ever-irreproachable Bell—at first ! Then, by degrees, he became merely George, then merely sighful George, then ironically humble George, and lastly—almost angelic George. Almost, because, in spite of George, George cannot help being a foolishly adoring, adorably human George."

"And most truly a man, dear child, if he has won my Clytie at last—when so many other mere humans have failed !"

"Oh, then, my dearest of all earthly lords, you will not forbid me ?"

"No, my dear !"

"And you will not mind—giving me to him ?"

"Dear child, nature ordains that I must part from you —sooner perhaps than later, and—when the Angel of Death summons and leads me—whithersoever he will, I shall front my destiny with mind more content because I shall leave you in the care of such strong-armed, clean-souled man as your George. For I have added him up and am content. And now——" At this moment they were startled by hearing in their immediate vicinity a sound best described as a strangled falsetto sneeze.

"My gracious !" exclaimed Clytie. "Parvo ! We have forgotten all about him ! Page, where are you ?"

"Hat y'r service, m'lady !" he replied, uprising like a gnome from behind the Earl's great chair.

"Have you been listening, Parvo ?"

"Ar, m'lady, I have—wi bofe me y-ears."

"Then you are to forget everything you heard."

"Yes, m'lady—in at me one hear-'ole and aht at t'other, so don't ye worrit."

"On the contrary !" said the Earl, smiling. "Boy, come you to me."

"Hat your service, too, m'lud."

"Then tell me, did I not hear you mention the name of Jasper Shrig ?"

"No, m'lud ; I honley says Jarsper cos Jarsper don't like names spoke aht lahd."

"Cautious Jasper ! Well, my boy, you will do your

very best to remember and to tell Jasper Shrig all you heard and everything you saw—especially one tall, dark thing on two legs.   Can you guess whom——"

" The long un, m'lud, Srumfree ! "

" Precisely !   Have you any pockets ? "

" Pockets, sir ?   Yessir, I got free as I can get at and two as I can't."

" Well, put this guinea in the safest one and tell Mr. Shrig I gave it you because you are quite ' up to snuff ' ! Off with you ! "

" Wot—nah, m'lud ?   To Jarsper ? "

" To your Jasper certainly and at once ! "

The boy turned to begone, turned back to salute, dropped his guinea, picked it up, put it into his cherub's mouth for safety and twinkled away.

" Is he not a perfect little wonder ? " said Clytie, looking after him with a smile.

" Yes," sighed the Earl, " he is a child aged by early neglect and sharpened by privation and suffering.   Such as he neglected still may grow to achieve individuality on the gallows, or loved and cared for, achieve far better than most.   And now, my Clytie, pray order my carriage, the lighter one."

" At once, dear one.   Are you going to town ? "

" I am."

" Oh, but—what of poor me ? "

" I suggest you take a ride—to the Abbot's Ride or thereabouts."

" Oh, my beloved lord, for this I shall kiss you again."

CHAPTER XXXIII

Of no particular interest except to Clytie

" BY George, George," said Mr. Jackman, glancing through open window into that retired thoroughfare which is still neither street, road, lane nor alley, " that really is a most remarkably fine horse of yours ! "

" Yes, sir," answered George, reaching for hat and gloves, for the day's business was done, " he is, indeed, and the princely gift of Charles—Mr. Mallory ! "

" As you have already informed me, and several times."

" Because I can hardly believe it—even yet."

" Ah ! " sighed the little lawyer, and very plaintively turning from the bright prospect without to the somewhat dingy one within. " Your Mr. Mallory ! As you are aware, he has completed the purchase of Felstead Manor, and so . . . I presume . . . it will go back to the family . . . by marriage . . . with . . . Is it true, George, he . . . and Isabel ? "

" Yes, sir ! "

" Ah well, well—with me it has always been a case of . . . hope deferred, and so long that at last . . . today . . . hope dies and must be buried for ever beneath these dusty tomes and parchments ! And yet . . . maybe poor hope's pale ghost may haunt even a lawyer's. . . ." Here Mr. Jackman, seeking comfort in snuff, choked and wiped tears shed for lovelier reason than mere snuff—at which awkward moment Mr. Beeby tapped to announce :

" My lord the Earl of Ravenhurst, gentlemen ! "

The Earl, bowed upon his ebony stick and with quick, bright up-glance, took the arm George ventured to proffer and, with murmur of thanks, sank into the nearest chair, glanced up and around with those apparently all-seeing eyes of his and said :

" Sirs, pray forgive this somewhat late visit, but I feel the matter is urgent—life being so uncertain. In a word, then, I desire you to draw up a codicil to my will leaving a third of all properties of which I die possessed to my beloved ward, Clytie Moor, but should my son Raymond, Viscount Hurst, pre-decease her, then in this event all properties, excepting those entailed, shall, I devise and command, be hers also, in most grateful acknowledgment of her unfailing devotion to me and the incalculable joy she has brought into my life . . . a happiness which has been my solace and blessing. . . . This, gentlemen, is my last will and testament, inadequately expressed—yet sufficient to my purpose. I desire this shall be ready for my signature tomorrow. You will have it ready ? "

" Certainly, my lord, without fail."

" Then, sirs," said the Earl, rising to shake hands, " I will delay you no longer . . . but I shall expect you at the Castle tomorrow. . . . George, have the goodness to lend me that arm of yours so far as my carriage ? " George obeyed and, thus linked, was again instantly aware of the vital power and dominance of this man despite bowed head and silvery hair.

" Yes," said my lord, pausing to survey the Sagamore with expert eye, " a noble creature, grandly formed and instinct with glorious life. . . . And life is action, George, the will to do and achieve some great purpose, good or evil ! Yes, yours is a knightly steed, George. Ride him like a knight for the good of some one or some worthy end. Life, this pitifully brief space of physical awareness, should be so used that when we are at point of losing it we should do so with little regret as may be. . . . And here am I sermonising by reason of your horse ! Pray help this garrulous old person into his carriage and be done with him." But, being seated in this luxurious vehicle, the Earl leaned forth to glance from Sagamore to George and enquire :

" I presume you are about to ride homeward ? "

" Yes, my lord——"

"Then I suggest you go by the Abbot's Ride."

"The Ab——" George gasped. "My lord . . . oh, sir . . . do you . . . can you mean——"

"Precisely, happy youth! Good luck, George, and—ride, Sir knight—ride!"

Now when he had watched my lord's carriage out of sight, George, bright of eye and flushed of cheek, swung blithely to saddle and, with cheery word of thanks to shock-head, galloped away to—that which awaited him in the Abbot's Ride.

CHAPTER XXXIV

Which is singularly short

THE CASTLE'S youngest boot-and-knife boy, feeling and seeing his own blood, clasped wounded nose, leaned head to door, and wailed so loudly that my lady Clytie, habited for riding and on her way to the stables, turned hitherward to know the wherefore of this dolorous outcry, and thus beheld her little cherubic page jeering the sufferer while putting a finer polish on those diminutive top-boots.

"Parvo," she demanded, "whatever is the matter?"

"Hif you please, m'lady, 'snothink! I honly give 'im one on the beezer, 'cos he was agoin' to black the tops o' me tops! And top-boot tops should ought to be brahn tops, so brahn they're a goin' to be, m'lady."

"But you should not have made his poor little nose bleed."

"Hif you please, m'lady, a bleedin' snitch don't matter, a drop o' the claret ain't no cause for young Jim t' pipe 'is heye s'lahd, an' he's bigger'n me an' I fout him fair, I did."

"And b' the powers," chuckled Tim O'Brian, appearing from nearby stall, "that's as thrue as y'rsilf is beautiful, me lady! B'ded, mam, y'r little tiger is that same b' nature and a two-fisted little wonder besides——"

"But, Tim, I don't want him to be that kind of tiger."

"There's worser beasts, mam, and, 'n the curse o' Cromwell, I know o' two, bad cess to 'em! And your mare's ready and waiting, my lady. Will I put ye up now?"

"Please, Tim." So the well-groomed, glossy creature was led out, then with slim, booted foot in Tim's ready hand, my lady mounted lightly to saddle, there to settle herself gracefully and say:

"Tim, I bid you take care of my fierce little tiger for me."

"My lady, I will that! A pleasant ride, mam." Then, and with that unusually-gentle smile that makes mere beauty lovely also, Clytie rode away to that which was to cause her dread, anxiety, and fullness of joy—in the Abbot's Ride.

CHAPTER XXXV

How George, eluding death, found joy

FAST rode George, glorying in the smoothly supple power of the splendid creature that bore him so lightly, whose four rhythmic-beating hoofs, almost soundless on the wayside turf, were throbbing little faster than his eager though troubled heart; for, though the memory of a certain deathless moment had blest him ever since, he was still uncertain and humbly doubtful if such happiness as he now yearned for could ever be his. So now, to make sure of this once and for all, he urged Sagamore to even greater speed, and nobly that proud-spirited gentleman responded, plying mighty hoofs faster between back-whirling hedges and trees until before them to the left was a gate with dense woodland beyond; a gate—but at such time and on such errand no thought had George of halting to open it, nor had the Sagamore, for at touch of knee he swerved, at spoken word, set himself, and, rising with gracious ease, was up and over and galloping on speedily as ever. And thus, too late, George beheld the death that threatened him—a thin, stout cord there was no avoiding; and so, rising in the stirrups, he took it across breast instead of throat, and was swept from the saddle into a black nothingness. . . .

The cord vanished, voices muttered, but even then, before lurking villainy could steal forth and bludgeon prone helplessness to certain death, the thud of rapidly approaching horsehoofs checked and scattered them in panic, stealthy flight. And so came Clytie.

Reining up her mare in full career, she leapt to aid him. Crying his name, she knelt to raise him, and, seeing how his head drooped unresponsive in a pallid helplessness so dreadfully like death, she clasped this poor thing to her bosom, bedewing it with her tears, sobbing, praying, pleading :

"God . . . Oh merciful God, don't let him die ! Oh George, my own . . . my dearest, speak . . . speak to me . . . look at me . . . open your eyes. . . . Oh, dear God, have mercy . . . on him . . . and me. . . ."

Thus she wept and supplicated, until :

. . . To George, in painful darkness, stole a gleam of light . . . growing stronger, brighter—until it hurt his eyes and added to the dizzying throb of his head ; and presently with this light a troublesome voice babbling nonsense, a voice becoming louder to recognition, uttering words of nonsense—amazing, unbelievable, adorable :

"George, my love . . . my darling ! Oh, dearest love . . . don't die ! George, I want you. . . . Oh, look at me . . . speak to me . . . love me. . . ."

"Clytie," he gasped feebly, "I am . . . I do . . . I will . . . because . . . Oh, Clytie, I . . . worship you ! Be merciful and . . . kiss me at last . . . properly. . . ."

And after being thus merciful, said she, breathless and suddenly dubious :

"Oh, but I . . . thought you . . . were nearly dead ! "

"So did I ! " he sighed, gazing up at her with eyes aglow with joy of life. "I suppose I ought to be——"

"Are you in pain ? "

"Only my head ; but what matter, what does anything matter except that we——"

"How did it happen ? "

"Happen ? Oh, it was a rope——"

"No, I mean your accident. Did the Sagamore throw you ? "

"Certainly not. By the way, has he bolted ? "

"No, he is close by, grazing with my mare."

"Wise old fellow ! Like master, like——"

"And you say he did not throw you ? "

"No. As I tell you, it was a thin rope——"

"Your head," said she with anxiety renewed, "is it troubling you—very much ? " And down came her cool, soft hand to feel his brow and smooth his red hair.   " This poor, dear head, does it feel so painful and—strange ? "

" Not with your beloved hand to bless it."

" Then, oh, George, can you think clearly and tell me exactly what happened ? "

" Yes, of course ; it was a rope——"

" Oh, my dear, my dear ! " sighed she distressfully. " How. . . . Oh, my poor darling, what do you mean ? "

" A twisted thing, usually made of hemp ! "

" There ! There ! " she murmured in growing apprehension. " I roused you too soon ! Close your dear eyes until you feel better."

" I am better, thanks to you, and——"

" Can you move, even a little ? "   George did so, but with such evident and painful effort that her arms came to help, to lift him until his head lay blissfully pillowed in her soft lap ; and now, beholding the light in these eyes gazing up at her, Clytie flushed with sudden adorable shyness, or so thought George as he murmured rapturously:

" How beautiful you are ! "

" Only beautiful ? " she enquired wistfully.

" Beautifully lovely ! And, Clytie, it was a rope. I saw it quite plainly, and felt it, too——"

" But there are no ropes in woods, George——"

" Oh, but, confound it all, I tell you——"

" Very well, there was a rope ! Only please do not excite this dear head ! Close your eyes and rest perfectly still a little longer."

" Darling Clytie, stoop that lovely head, use those pretty ears that I'm going to kiss as soon as possible——"

" No, George ! "

" Yes ! But now, listen hard and heed my every word. There was a rope—a thin, murderous cord stretched across the glade from tree to tree impossible to elude, too low to duck under, so I managed it should catch me across the chest instead of throat. This is the ugly fact wherefrom I surmise or presume that somebody desired or desires somebody's death. The question is—am I the somebody so doomed, and, if so, who is the somebody who so desires and dooms ? Was this death-trap set for me or——"

" It must have been ! Oh, George—it was ! Yes, it was—— Oh, how frightful——"

" Clytie, why are you so sure ? "

" Because I had just ridden the whole length of the glade and there was no rope then ! It was your death someone planned ! "

" Yes, I think this is fairly evident. But who and why ? How can my death benefit anyone, and hence—what the motive ? Here are questions to which our Jasper Shrig would certainly retort ' Echo alone responds '. However, pretty soon—why, Clytie, why are you shivering so dreadfully, and why hide your dear, lovely face ? "

" Oh, George," she whispered, " it is all so—dreadful ! So ghastly ! Murder so nearly succeeded. You would be lying dead but for a miracle. . . . God was merciful ! "

" Amen ! " said George fervently. " Yes, I am alive, somewhat ' grassed ' for the present, but I shall soon be right again, getting stronger every minute, and then—oh, Clytie—what then ? "

" Well—what, George ? "

" I love the way you say ' George ' ! "

" I love the way you say ' Clytie ' ! "

" I believe we informed each other of the stupendous and amazing fact that we love each other—or was I still dazed and dreaming ? "

" It was no dream, George."

" Then again I thank God ! Clytie, say ' Amen '."

" Amen ! " she murmured obediently.

" And to think," sighed he blissfully, gazing up into the dark eyes that, looking as steadfastly down into his, were telling him so very much that, for the moment, rapture held him mute.

" Oh ! " he exclaimed at last. " However could we have mistaken—such love as this, for—hate ? How blind we were ! "

" Yes, George."

" What a perfect fool was I ! What a crass, abtuse, dense and absolute confounded numbskull ! "

" Yes, George ! "

" What a perfect fool. But, Clytie—what of you ? "

" Oh, I was only just a little stupid—at first, because I knew long ago, of course."

" What, pray ? Dear heart, tell me ! "

" That I loved you, George ! I do and always must."

" Ah, my dear, and I can only repeat I adore you over and over again until it sickens you and——"

" George, you really are a—Mr. Absolute, Confounded Numbskull Bell ! To dare imagine George's Clytie could ever be sickened by hearing George telling her such —oh, such heavenly truth—if it is the truth ; is it, George ? "

" Yes, by heaven, it is ! And that is the frightful part of it."

" Oh ? What part is so frightful ? "

" That because I love you so truly, heart and soul and body, I am—afraid to marry you."

" Afraid ? Whatever for, I mean—why ? "

" Because I fear that someday in the future you may regret, for I shall never be able to give you all those luxuries you've been used to all your life—jewels, dresses and—and other whatnots and so on——"

" George, my darling, I love you more than all the luxuries and whatnots in the world ! So, George, dear— do not be a fool of a George, because your adored Clytie insists on being your wife whenever your lordship will take and make her so."

" My lord ! " he repeated, contriving to sit up at last, though with her ready aid. " My own Clytie. Since you will give up so much for my sake, I can now tell you yet another marvel. The last time I saw the Earl he grasped my hand in that vital clasp of his, bade me come this way— and said ' Good luck, George ! ' But . . . he suggested I . . . should——" George, suddenly dumb, bowed his head ; but she had glimpsed the sudden horror in his eyes and cried with passion as sudden :

"What are you saying? What are you thinking?" And miserably George replied:

"He suggested . . . the Abbot's Ride——"

"And you dare to think such vile evil of such as he . . . to imagine he would stoop to such hateful wickedness?"

"Oh, Clytie, what am I to think?"

"The truth! And this is the very truth! It was by his direction, his will and spoken work that I am here! He sent me to you because I told him I loved you and because he is so—so splendidly grand, a truly noble nobleman, and now—oh, now you——" Here, sobs choked her.

"Now," repeated George and very fervently, "I love him also and honour him above all men—and humbly crave your pardon for so misjudging him. Will you, can you—forgive me?"

But before she might answer was sound of happy voices with jingle and creak of harness, then towards them, and at very leisured pace, rode the Viscount and Joan Tulliver. . . .

"Eh—what's wrong there?" cried the Viscount and came galloping to leap from saddle and enquire:

"George . . . what the dooce? Are you hurt? Can I do anything——"

"Thanks, it's nothing much, Corks. I took a bit of a toss . . . be all right soon. Aha, Joan, bless your lovely eyes! I believe you have met Lady Clytie Moor?"

"Yes, yes I have," she answered, bending over him. "But, George, you look dreadfully pale! Oh, Lady Clytie, is he badly hurt?"

"Certainly not!" said George.

"Yes, he is," sighed Clytie. "So much worse than he admits, that I have been nearly distracted, wondering how I could get him home——"

"On the Sagamore, of course!" said George, and setting his teeth, struggled up to his feet, took a stride— and would have fallen but for Clytie's ready arms.

"Help me, Ray!" she panted. "Raymond . . . help me to . . . lay him down. I . . . believe he's going to faint!"

"Oh no, I'm not such a poor fool," he retorted and fainted as he spoke.

"Water!" cried Joan. "And there's a brook nearby . . . if I only had something to carry it in!"

"My hat!" said the Viscount. "Show me this dooced brook and we——"

"Not you, Raymond—you must ride home for a carriage," said Clytie; "one of the largest—and, for mercy's sake, ride fast, Ray."

"Trust me!" he cried, and, leaping to saddle, was off and away at stretching gallop. And presently back sped Joan with his hat dripping water, with which blessedness and George's neckerchief Clytie bathed his head and face until he sighed, opened his eyes and, gazing up into the anxious loveliness bent over him, said ruefully:

"It seems . . . I am a . . . poor fool!"

And, after surprisingly short while, back galloped the Viscount, hatless still, with news the carriage was coming —and a flask of brandy with which he insisted on dosing their invalid until he choked—whereafter the carriage duly appeared, a great, cushioned chariot half filled with pillows. . . .

So thus, as evening deepened to night, they brought George home to Mistress Isabel's instant and efficient care, aided by Charles Mallory's oft-tried skill in the treatment of wounds and the hurts this frail body may have to suffer by man's despite or chance of cruel circumstance.

CHAPTER XXXVI

Tells how love banished anger and thwarted evil

" so—that, my dearest," said Clytie, frowning at the recollection, " that is the hateful story, the tale of attempted murder so very nearly successful! And you can guess, as I do, the——"

" Hush, child! Guesswork is worse than useless! Does anyone know of this beside your two selves ? "

" Not a soul! It is all so—so sordidly evil that George has substituted the branch of a tree for that murderous rope. . . . The mystery is, how did it get there, how did it vanish, how was it done ? Can it . . . oh, will it happen again ? This is what terrifies me! Oh, my dear one, if we could only find some evidence, some clue to give proof manifest."

" Expert Villainy leaves none, dear child! However, I suggest you seek Mr. Shrig, the law officer, and inform him of every particular—but make no mention of your personal suspicions. How did you find your invalid today ? Better, I hope ? "

" Better than merely better, my dearest ; he is so well recovered that Isabel allowed him down for tea in the garden, and—— Oh, there's Humphrey, damn him! If only the earth would open and swallow him! "

" It will, my Clytie, soon or late—it will! "

Sir Humphrey approached with his usual languid grace, supremely elegant from glossy boots to no less glossy black curls, for his hat was in his whip-hand, a gentleman entirely *à la mode*, faint-smiling with air of masterful self-assurance. Said he, bowing graciously :

" Most noble of uncles, your dutifully obedient nephew presents himself to express his most grateful thanks. Indeed, sir, your kindly forethought touches me very sensibly."

" You are possibly alluding to the disappearance of your baggage, Humphrey ? "

" That was in my mind, sir."

" I ordered its removal, Nephew, that with it I might also be rid of—temptation, for my own sake and, incidentally, yours."

" And, sir, I am profoundly grateful. For, by odd coincidence, I had already decided on a change of habitat."

" You will find your belongings at the Raven."

" And no better place, Uncle ! Again—my thanks."

" When do you return to France, Humphrey ? "

" Soon as may be, sir. There are but two reasons for my delay, the one a—small matter of business which has engaged my attention some time . . . this I am now determined shall be settled with complete finality ; my other and most delightful delaying cause is my wife-to-be."

" Who is the favoured lady, Humphrey ? "

" My dear lord—need you ask ? Who but this armful of warm loveliness, our Clytie ? "

" Insufferable beast ! " she exclaimed.

" My beautiful termagant," he sighed, " I wait your pleasure——"

" Go to the devil and be damned."

" Joyfully—with you, my Clytie ! " he retorted, seating himself beside her, whereat she leapt away from him so wildly that she tripped in the long skirt of her riding-habit, recovered and cried passionately :

" I am not your Clytie."

" You will be ! " he nodded. " Oh yes, you shall be glad to wed me yet, for your own precious self, for my joy and—the sake of—let us say—others ! "

" Never ! " she cried. " The mere thought is as abhorrent and almost as abominable as your wicked, hateful, accursed self ! "

" Humphrey," enquired the Earl, " did you hear, by any chance, of poor Mr. Bell's accident ? "

" No, sir—and yet, now you mention it, I did——"

" What ? "

" I hardly remember . . . some tattling trifle . . . thrown from his horse, or some such——"

" Where ? "

" In the Abbot's Ride . . . at least . . . so I heard."

" From whom ? "

" Noble sir, you appear strangely interested in this young fellow. I wonder why ? "

" And I am wondering how you know where this accident took place."

" By hearsay, dear Uncle, merely by hearsay ! " he answered, smiling happily from one intent face to the other.

" And who," Clytie demanded, " who told you ? "

" Ah, to be sure," he murmured, " this unfortunately fortunate young man is, I remember, honoured by your— friendship, Clytie mine ! "

" Yes ! Who told you where it happened ? "

" My informant, dear persistent Beauty, was a very worthy person, a farmer, Tulliver by name, and his mention compels me to inform you that I fear, yes, indeed, I consider—alas, dear Uncle—that our poor Raymond's life is directly threatened, that death may strike him— suddenly."

" And you," said the Earl, " you have entertained this hope so many years ! Do you expect its fulfilment at last, and if so——"

" Uncle ! My lord, I protest——"

" And I presume you have some feasible explanation, some reason why and by whom my heir is to be— removed ? "

" Dalliance, sir, and a—devoted father ! Our farmer has a daughter of surpassing beauty, and Raymond is— Raymond. Wherefore and therefore, Beauty's so very devoted father has made public avowal that he will protect daughter's honour—with a gun ! So, my dear Uncle, I now implore you, for poor Raymond's sake, to use your influence to restrain and guide him, for, sir, should anything terrible befall 'twill be due to his own—let us say—too amative nature——"

"Beast!" exclaimed Clytie. "Loathsome hypocrite, you make it all sound as evil as your wicked self!" Wafting her a smiling kiss, Sir Humphrey continued:

"And, Uncle mine, I must prepare you for the further unwelcome fact that I have cause to apprehend this same fond father intends to—actually—dare your noble presence, a positive incursion! And at any moment now. But," said Sir Humphrey, glancing expectantly up and around and fondling that ornate whip of his, "should there be the least show of bodily violence, I shall intervene at once, by word or even act; you may depend on me, sir."

"Talking of death," sighed the Earl, "I become ever more convinced, Humphrey, that you, as the saying goes, will never make old bones."

Sir Humphrey seemed about to rise, but did not, made an effort to speak, yet was dumb—and then from echoing stableyard was sudden clatter of horsehoofs, hubbub of voices dominated by one louder, harsher than all others, whereat Sir Humphrey's tense form relaxed and he drew a deep breath as into the quiet of this tower garden strode a wild, menacing figure; on he came, a scowling, desperate man, fierce of eye, dusty with hard riding but flushed with more than fury of haste, who now halting before the Earl with ring and stamp of spurred heels and, with no word or gesture of salutation, burst into passionate speech:

"My lord, I'm Tulliver, Abel Tulliver of Burnt Ash! Take heed to your son, take heed, I say! . . . I love my daughter better than my life and I be ready and willing to lose it for her sake . . . shed my blood to save her from the shame and degradation of your damned son! She be no game for the likes of he. So warn him . . . beg him leave her alone or, by the God as made us, I'll be the death of him! I'll shoot him down, or, better, I'll choke his cursed life out wi' these two hands! So take heed, my lord, and warn him off! Lords don't wed wi' farmers' daughters and she shan't go t'other road! To save her from that— I'll kill him joyful and go to the hangman more joyful! So, for the last time, be warned and——"

"Hush—listen!" said the Earl imperiously.

"No!" roared Abel ferociously. "'Tis for you to listen to me——"

"Hush!" said the Earl again. "I think my son is here to answer for himself, as he shall to you and to me. Listen!" Horsehoofs again in the stableyard—young, glad voices, laughter. Then into the garden came the Viscount, radiant-eyed, for with him, very shy and therefore rather more beautiful than ever, was Joan, who, at sight of her scowling father, uttered a faint cry and shrank to the shelter of the Viscount's ready arm.

So, thus embraced, they advanced.

"My lord, sir—oh, Father," cried the Viscount, "congratulate me, for I have found—for you a lovely daughter and for myself a most beautiful Viscountess! For, sir, she—Joan, at last, has promised to marry me! And the very dooce of a time I've had persuading her to—to be my wife. But she has, and so—Mr. Tulliver sir, oblige me with your dooced fin—I mean shake hands, sir, and congratulate me too!"

In a dazed sort of way Abel Tulliver took this proffered hand, but before he could find speech Sir Humphrey laughed and rose, saying:

"Tulliver, my worthy friend, here was cruel waste of heroic paternal sentiment! Such piteous exhibition of a devoted father's lacerated heart, I confess my own bled for you. But all's well, it seems, so pray accept my congratulations among others!"

Then Sir Humphrey strolled away quite unheeded by the others; for just then Joan, blushing and shyer than ever, was looking down at the Earl, who, smiling up at her, said to the Viscount:

"Indeed, Raymond, you have chosen well! Stoop, my daughter-to-be, bow your loveliness that I may greet and make you welcome. . . ."

And presently, butler and footmen, having brought the wherewithal, glasses were brimmed and emptied, whereafter Abel, still somewhat bewildered, finding himself alone with the Earl, rose to go.

"My lord," said he ponderously, "I be all of a maze . . . never thinking such could be, but seeing 'tis—all I can say is . . . thankee, my lord, and goodbye. Also, sir, if I were a bit rough like at first, I'm now bold to say I regret it——"

"Mr. Tulliver," said the Earl, beckoning him to be seated again, "in like case I should have been just as rough, perhaps even a little more so. Now I understand you breed horses. I did so once, and should be glad to compare notes. . . ." And so they did, with such enthusiasm for this most engrossing subject that when Clytie sought them in the glimmering dusk they were at it still.

CHAPTER XXXVII

In which Mr. Shrig proposes how

IN a part of the road where nobody could possibly overhear Mr. Shrig stopped his gig, sighed gustily and spoke :

"This here case, Dan'l, ain't a case, it's two . . . it's three . . . 'tis half a dozen ! The Earl, the wi-count, the wanished heir, Sir Humph, Jos Tranter ! And atop o' them, three attempts at murder as didn't come off and another as mustn't ! Vich, I o-pine, should keep us pretty busy."

"Ay ! " murmured Dan'l, caressing the whiskers thoughtfully. "A bit in-volved like and a fairish orkard handful, 'specially these two, Sir H. and Jos. According to Gimblet's report—true capital coves both, eh, Jarsper ? "

"Dan'l, you and me has tackled willainy of all sorts, afore now, male and fee-male, but none more slimily artful than these same two capitals, vich therefore shall be allooded to henceforth as Mr. A. and Jos B."

"And, Jarsper, I reckon Mr. A's the worser."

"Ar ! He's slimy as a slug and slippery as a eel, and therefore likely—to wriggle off, dodging the law for lack o' evidence—unless took red-handed in the werry act."

"Which, Jarsper, can't be, seeing as how according to Gimblet's report, when the deed is doing, he'll be miles away on the London road."

"Eggs-ackly, Dan'l ! But you'll be there afore him."

"Oh ? Shall I, Jarsper ? "

"Ar. On a hoss, in a mask, and a barker in each fist, Dan'l."

"Eh ? " he exclaimed, sitting up, keen-eyed and eager. "Am I for the High Toby lay, then—a highwayman ? "

"That same, Dan'l, a genty cove o' the Toby consarn, and the most fee-rocious robber as ever robbed!"

"Noble!" exclaimed Dan'l, smiling at the prospect. "Rob him, do I? And with violence, Jarsper?"

"No more than befits the o-casion, Dan'l, say a tap on the tibby vith the barrel o' your barker, just sufficient to topple his tattler dicer, no more. But you take his bung, and tattler nobble hes blunt every farden and, most expecial, take his hoss, leaving him afoot and penniless."

"Prime!" said Dan'l and actually chuckled, in which rare moment his haylike whiskers, forgetting to droop, seemed positively to bristle until he clutched, restrained and cherished them and, so doing, enquired:

"But wot o' these here, Jarsper?"

"You must lop 'em, Dan'l; cut 'em a bit shorter."

"Jarsper," he demurred, reproachfully, "for dooty's sake and your sake I've shed my blood afore now, but—to ask this o' me is coming it too strong!"

"Ar, mebbe so, Dan'l, and you'd never be the same without 'em. So, 'stead o' lopping, tuck—tuck 'em up under your mask—that should do."

"It shall; he'll never twig my identity. And when I've robbed him, how then?"

"Then you'll off vith his hoss and the mask and gallop to the Castle bearing a letter I shall write for the Earl telling as how Mr. A, then on his road to wisit him is not only Jos B's accomplice in murderous attempt, the fourth, on his son's life, but prime contriver of and mover therein."

"But, Jarsper, that don't prove him so. Your letter ain't evidence against Mr. A; we still can't take him, no— nor so much as accuse him legally. So how then?"

"Then," repeated Mr. Shrig, his gaze on the distance, "then, Dan'l, the Earl may act—I hope!"

"Act? How? Lor lumme, Jarsper, you mean——?"

"Dan'l, if the law can't act for lack o' proof, wengeance can. So I'm agoing to give wengeance a chance to choke off murder afore it can—strike and do—the deed! And," sighed Mr. Shrig, taking up the reins, " never nothing could be fairer! Now let's take a peep at this here little tample as my Gimblet tells of, and then, leaving you to keep an ogle on you know 'oo, I'll to the heir, a wisit, friendly and onofficiel."

CHAPTER XXXVIII

In which Clytie hears a dreadful truth

" HIF YOU please, m'lady, can I h-ave leave o' h-absence for a h-our ? "

" Not to fight again, I hope ? "

" Ho no, m'lady—business ! "

" Oh indeed ; what kind of business, Parvo ? "

Laying chubby finger beside cherubic nose, he winked one bright eye and whispered the one word:

" Jarsper ! "

" Oh ! " said Clytie, whispering also. " Then of course you may, but take care of my little Parvo. "

" Yes, m'lady, and thankee ! " Then, with smiling salute, he twinkled top-bootedly away. Clytie, thus alone in the tower garden, bowed stately head resignedly again, plying her needle so much worse than usual that she frowned at it and, wishing to curse it, sighed instead—in which moment she glanced up and—beheld Sir Humphrey watching her from the dimness of the old tower, and swore instantly, saying :

" Damn you, Humphrey, why do you prowl and peep ? I thought we were rid of you, curse you ! "

Slowly he approached and stood to smile down at her, that is—he showed two rows of very white, sharp-looking teeth ; so much that, frowning up at him, she demanded :

" Why bare your fangs at me like a vicious famished beast ? "

" Because, Enticement, " he murmured, " I am famished, hungering for you ; for you I am here. And I come and I go how, when and where I will. Today I am here to offer you marriage—no, don't speak yet ! I am here to offer and give you my name, to make you my lady,

241

bestowing on you the title you never had, to make the false real and transform lie to truth, for——"

"Humphrey," she broke in, bitterly scornful, "I have no idea what you mean, nor do I care . . . though the mere thought of marriage with you shocks and shames me."

"Listen to me!" he said, smiling, but with gesture fiercely compelling. "My meaning is this : I will marry you notwithstanding the fact that you are a nameless nobody! I will stoop to lift you to an honourable position in society despite the shameful fact that you are, and were, a miserable waif, some poor wretch's byeblow—found in a ditch and——"

"Humphrey!" she gasped, appalled by his dreadful words, but even more by his convincing look and manner. "What—oh, what are you saying?"

"The shameful truth, my poor, deceived Clytie, the sordid, horrible truth—you are child of shame, offspring of direst poverty or guilt. You were found a tiny child in filthy rags left to perish in a ditch—Uncle Roland's horse shied at you and nearly threw him. But my lord, for a whim, took you up, brought you home, gave out you were child of a dead friend and lady in your own right. I say it was his whim to father and mother you, call you his 'little lady Clytie' with servants, nurses and governesses to wait upon your ladyship and a host of friends to pay you homage—and thus he has trained and bred you into the absurdly arrogant, gloriously beautiful sham you are——"

"Liar!" she panted. "O beast. . . . Oh foul beast and wicked liar——"

"Silly child!" he retorted. "I speak truth and you know it, yes—I see it in your eyes! This is the sordid truth of you, my wretched darling. . . . Your clod-hopping lover, your rustical George quite naturally believes you a proud lady of high degree and reaches up from his dunghill to clutch and possess you in that belief; ah, but—suppose he is given proof of what you really are, a sham, a living lie, a damnably seducing counterfeit, a mere——"

Voiceless, she leapt, wrenched that ornate whip from his startled grasp and, speechless still, beset him with such fury of blows that he, warding his face with up-flung arms, stumbled backward . . . back until he reached the shelter of the old tower; therein he retreated, and there she paused to regain her breath, then, hurling the heavy whip at him, she turned and fled to the one whose strength had been her defence and whose patient tenderness her comfort since childhood. . . . The Earl was at his desk writing busily, but at her sudden entrance he glanced up and, beholding her wild, distressful look, laid down his quill to reach forth those long arms of his, saying :

" Clytie ! My beloved child, what is it ? " And, falling to her knees beside his chair, she told him, ending with the agonized plea :

" Oh, tell me he lied ! Dearest, tell me it is not true ! " For a moment he was silent and utterly still, then he laid both hands upon the dark head as if in blessing and answered gently :

" It is all quite true, Clytie ; you were indeed a foundling——"

" Oh then," she gasped, with sudden passion of tears, " I am truly a . . . nobody . . . a nameless creature from the unknown . . . a child of shame——"

" No," he answered very tenderly, " you are truly the beloved child of my adoption, daughter of my love, and woman of my respect ! Clytie, my ever dear one, it is not that which we were, but what we are—this only matters and is of any account." Here, with effortless strength, he lifted her to his breast and cradled her there until in the cherishing comfort of his embrace her sobs were hushed, and, drying her eyes, she said :

" Knowing this, I ought to love you more than ever and shall . . . and do . . . if this is possible. But . . . oh, my dear, this knowledge has changed me and all my world ! It has . . . shocked me, shamed me so bitterly

that it hurts now, but will be an agony later on.   For . . .
oh, my dearest, however can I tell—him, as tell him I
must—but how ? ”

" Soon, Clytie, and in few words as possible.”

" But it will shock him also, it must, and—perhaps hurt
him dreadfully ! ”

" Now as to this,” said the Earl with one of his too-rare
smiles, " I will venture to prophesy, if you will sit up
and give me your complete attention.   Now are you
listening ? ”

" Yes,” she answered, smiling through her tears, " yes,
of course I am, you know I am.”

" Very well.   This is my prognostication : he, your
George, will rejoice and be glad, yes, and honour you the
more for the valorous truth and honesty of you——”

" Oh, my beloved dearest,” she sighed, kissing his
silvery hair, " if you think so, I must and shall believe so ! ”

" Then, my child, go and prove this !   Away now, into
your habit and ride to meet your chosen man and let him
prove indeed what true prophet I am.”

" Oh,” cried she, tearfully, " how wise you are . . .
how gentle with me and . . . what a blessing you have
always been to your poor Clytie !   And all I can do is to
kiss you—like this !   And pray God's eternal blessing on
you—as I have done ever since I was old enough to know
how deep and truly I loved you.”

CHAPTER XXXIX

Tells how they had tea with a witch

" GEORGE," enquired Miss Isabel as he pulled on his riding-boots, a recent purchase, " are you sure you feel able to ride so soon ? Are you perfectly sure ? "

" Lord bless your lovely eyes, I'm fit as a fiddle, right as a trivet."

" Doctor Dale ordered you complete rest, so don't ride far ; and dear John Jackman said he will manage without you——"

" True enough, he will," laughed George, a little ruefully. " I'm not exactly a necessity ! " So saying, he stamped his boots easy, embraced his aunt, kissed her and strode out to the Sagamore. Thus presently away he rode seeking her who at that precise moment was riding to meet him, with the natural result that very soon they espied each other and instinctively urged their horses to speedier gait, gazing upon one another as they approached; so they met, they stopped—and now, beholding the adoration in his eyes, she forgot all else for the moment and enquired demurely :

" George, whatever are you staring at ? "

" The lovely shape of you."

" Mr. Bell, you are extremely—personal ! "

" My lady, I am indeed, and glorying in it. Oh, yes, because all that I behold of you is mine and soon will be—more so ! "

" Fie, Mr. Bell, fie ! Are you trying to make me self-conscious ? "

" Yes, dear lady of loveliness—so if you can oblige devoted George with a blush—ah yes, very, very beautiful ! "

" Oh, George," she laughed, " instead of being so idiotically Bell-ish, tell me where you are taking me."

"Anywhere my lady will, though I thought we might pay our respects to my dear old Hagah ; we can go by the Abbot's Ride, and——"

"No ! Not that way ; it is too soon after——! No. Besides, I . . . I have something to tell you, so let us take the lane yonder."

"As you will, sweetheart ; it will bring us to Burnt Ash Farm. Abel Tulliver's place. We might call there instead."

So down this lane they rode, between blooming hedge-rows and shady trees until in a place where trees reached forth leafy bows as if to embrace one another, Clytie checked her mare, saying, and in tone troubled as her look :

"This will do ! "

"Yes, but," enquired George in sudden anxiety, quick to heed her altered expression, "what is it ? You've gone so pale. . . . Oh, my dear, you . . . you aren't going to faint or . . . anything of that sort . . . because if so——" Here he dismounted. "Oh, Clytie, let me help you."

"Yes," she sighed, "please help me down——" Even as she spoke, he had her in his arms : and now, standing in his embrace, she gazed up at him with a wistfully questioning look that was almost fearful, yet contrived to smile and enquire, lightly :

"Who is it you have in your embrace, Mr. Bell ? " And as lightly he replied :

"That most beautiful of women, Lady Clytie Moor."

"No such person, Mr. Bell ! "

"Oh, indeed, madam ! Who then, pray ? "

"Sir, the creature you are clasping so fervently, the woman you were about to kiss believing her Clytie Moor, is—a nameless sham, a living lie, a miserable counterfeit." George's arms relaxed, fell from her and he recoiled in amazed and speechless bewilderment, wherefore she threw back that proud, stately head of hers to view him with wide, dark eyes that seemed to flare, then close to gleaming slits, and when she spoke it was with lips that curled in bitter scorn :

"Indeed, sir, I am no lady ! Twenty-three years ago I was found, a miserable atom in filthy rags—left to die in a ditch. My lord's horse shied at me . . . would to God it had trampled the wretched life out of me ! But the Earl, being the noble gentleman he is, took me up . . . to his tender care . . . had me educated . . . called me ' his lady Clytie,' so ' my lady ' everyone imagined me. But in reality I am—a no one, nameless, penniless, with nothing —nothing in all the world I can call my own——" Here she paused, and so for a space was silence ; then :

"Oh, my lady," said George, in that deep, soft voice of his, " how utterly mistaken you are ! For now and always you have—poor, Mr. Obnoxious Bell . . . he's not such a bad sort of fellow—when you get used to him. So now, dear my lady and most beloved of women, here he is upon his knees, begging you to take him and—make the best of him, if only you——" With sobbing, inarticulate cry, she stooped to clasp him, then sank down to his embrace, clinging to him, saying brokenly :

"Forgive me . . . forgive me ! For, oh, I doubted you and wished to die ! But now . . . oh, George . . . my beloved, how gloriously wonderful that you can love me so truly ! "

"Ah, but," said he, almost as brokenly, " how wonderfully glorious that you . . . can stoop to love . . . Mr. O. Bell, poor, old . . . Obnoxious——" But here she silenced him with the sweet passion of her lips. . . .

And, after some while, they left this narrow, leafy lane that was to be so dearly remembered hereafter by both.

They rode slowly and in a silent communion too rapturously intimate for words, through a radiant world towards a yet more glorious future in a speechless content, until at last, and very tenderly, Clytie said :

"He was right, and he always is ! "

"The Earl ? "

"Of course! He told me you would be glad and—love me only the more, God bless him!"

"Amen!" said George with fervour. "And yet only yesterday I was perfectly sure I could never love you more, and now I'm just as certain I can and do, which is pretty marvellous! But then—you have grown and changed from beauty to loveliness and so are more beautiful, and, beside, you are so adorably, nobly, bravely, truly honest and—oh, by Jupiter, if you soar any higher you will rise beyond the reach of our poor, old Obnoxious——"

"Oh, then," she sighed, "let George remember I am merest woman, his only and—forever."

"Then, woman of George, by George's behest, pause instantly and kiss Mr. Adoring Bell."

They checked their horses; they leaned towards each other, were arrested by sound of wheels, and, glancing round, beheld Mr. Shrig bowling towards them behind his speedy animal. Reining up smartly beside them, he beamed at George and lifted his hat to Clytie, saying:

"My lady, you are a blessing to the uniwersal eye, or as you might say ogle or peeper!"

"Oh, Mr. Shrig," she laughed, "what gallant compliment!"

"And it ain't quite finished, my lady, for in all this here wale o' sorrer, tears, grief and general wiciousness, said peeper never see anything so blooming as your leddyship's lovely self! And talking of yourself, how does my Gimblet soot?"

"I love him! He is the very dearest little tiger who ever twinkled in top-boots—when he isn't a tigerish little tiger and—two-fisted terror."

"Ar, he can use 'em, m'lady, I've took particular care to larn him the straight left and right swing, pivoting on left toe——"

"Aha, Jessamy Todd's finisher, Jasper."

"That same, sir and George! Ay, Gimblet's a goodish b'y, though he gets hisself werry tangled up vith his h-aitches, vich is the reason as I'm so precious careful wi' mine. So, my lady, if you'll trouble to correct him I'll take it werry kind."

" Then of course I will. Pray has my dear little page been of use to you, Mr. Shrig ? "

" Ar ! Life and death, my lady ! Through him Willainy shall be took in the act, and Wiciousness choked——"

He stopped suddenly as through a gap in the hedge, and with scarcely a rustle, stepped old Hagah, bearing a large basket on her small, thin arm. And never since those now happily distant times when she had made awesome dread her shield against brutish Ignorance, had she appeared more truly witch-like as, bowed upon her staff, she peered up at them each in turn, mumbling sounds that might have been magical spells, blasting curses or merely words of greeting. Mr. Shrig, however, and to George's pleased surprise, saluted her with greatest courtesy ; he even removed his hat again, saying :

" Good morning, marm ! You see me on my road to pay you a wisit."

" Ha ! " she cried bitterly. " You and y'r red weskit ! Whenever did the law trouble for a witch except to torture, burn, drown or hang her ? So hold y'r tongue and be off—wi y'r red weskit—afore I curse ee ! "

Mr. Shrig blinked and was dumb, Clytie reined nearer to George, who, strangling laugh to cough, contrived to say :

" Hagah, dear, please don't be too hard on poor Mr. Shrig ; he means well, and is my friend."

" Aho ! " she exclaimed, turning to glance up at George with merry twinkle in her shrewd eyes. " Then let him ketch them as needs ketching . . . ah, hang and jibbet 'em 'stead o' troubling the likes o' poor old me. Don't ee let him try none o' his Bow Street tricks on me, wi' his red weskit ! "

" Dear old Hagah, of course not ! And now what greeting have you for Lady Clytie ? You remember her, of course."

" Ay, for sure, Mast' Jarge, I mind her a sight better than her knowed herself—eh, my pretty ? "

"Yes," answered Clytie, smiling. "Yes you did—when you told my fortune; but—what now?"

"Now," said George, "we also intended paying you a visit, Hagah."

"Then, m' dears, come y'r ways and I'll brew tay and mebbe tell ee a thing or two."

"Marm," said Mr. Shrig very wistfully, "am I inclooded in this there inwitation? And spite o' my red weskit?"

"D'ye drink tay—you?"

"By the pot, marm, hot or cold, vith sugar or no ditto milk. I have drank enough tea t' float a ship o' the line, ar—a whole fleet o' seventy-fours!" During this speech old Hagah peered up at him again, scanning his every feature, blunt nose, square jaw, wide humorous mouth and eyes keen as her own, and which, like her own, twinkled, though his tone was more wistful than ever, as he enquired:

"Mrs. Hagah, how about me?"

"Ay," she replied, with quick nod, "you'll do!"

"Then," said he, beaming, "by your leave!" Almost as he spoke he was down in the road, had lifted her into the gig and was seated beside her, all in as many moments.

"Well, I never!" she exclaimed breathlessly. "And my owd basket, too! Well . . . I never did!"

"But you have, marm, for here y'are. Now, this rug about ye agin the dust—so! Now, ketch hold o' Jarsper's arm and off us goes!"

Away they went indeed, and at such pace that Hagah, like the spirited old soul she was, laughed and breathed deep to the rush of air sweet with the tang of earth and sea, gazing around her glad-eyed. Thus all too soon the journey ended at her little lonely cottage bowered amid the green. Here, when they had tethered their horses and eased girths, she made them welcome, laying by her broad, country idiom with her faded old shawl and bonnet, and speaking now like the strange, graciously dignified old person she was; then she set each to work, Mr. Shrig to bellows the smouldering fire, George to bring water from the well while she and Clytie prepared and laid the meal.

And presently fire blazed, kettle boiled, tea was brewed, and down they sat. And after some while George said :

" Did you ever taste such jam as this, Jasper ? "

" Never in all my nat'ral, friend George, though you have, I'll lay—man an' b'y."

" Yes, indeed ! Hagah and her jam and cakes are some of my earliest recollections."

" And werry nice, too ! " said Mr. Shrig, turning to beam on their aged hostess. " And, marm, seeing as how you knowed friend George as a infant, you mebbe knowed his dad also ? " Old Hagah, instead of answering, hunched above her cup, glared at her questioner with expression so very witch-like, that George laughed and set his arm about her, saying :

" Anyhow, my dear, your prophecy about—us—has come true, thank heaven ! "

" Yes ! " said Clytie. " But this was only the good part of my fortune, because you warned me also of—of evil, sorrow, hatred and—blood ! So, please, dear Mrs. Hagah, will you tell me just what you meant ? "

" Murder, p'r'aps ? " Mr. Shrig suggested brightly.

" Ay," she retorted. " Like enough unless you can prevent it—wi' y'r red weskit ! And so," said she, turning to Clytie, " 'stead of evil, m' dear, think o' the good, of your love, that blessed hour when ye shall be man and wife——"

" Ar ! " quoth Mr. Shrig heartily. " And talking of infants ! "

" Jasper, hold hard ! " exclaimed George in startled tone. " You're too confoundedly previous——"

" Oh no, friend and sir, for, d'ye see, this here most particklar infant happened fifty-odd years ago, precise date dooly wrote down in my little reader, but no need referring thereto, for you'll remember, eh, Mrs. Hagah, marm ? "

Old Hagah merely looked at him and sipped her tea ; wherefore he continued :

I

"A man child, marm, naming no names, aged about twelve months, brought to your care here about the midnight hour by, mentioning never a name, a dewoted father 'oo, having left said infant safe here along o' you, and no care could be safer, departed herefrom and never returned. Cor-rect, I hope and wentur' to think, marm?"

"Your nose," she replied, between sips of tea, "is sharper than it looks."

"Mrs. Hagah," he beamed, "you do me proud! Vich therefore I am bold to beg as you'll answer a question or so, mentioning never a single name. F'rinstance, can you remember if——"

"Ay, Master Jasper, there's times as I remember to forget and others when I forget to remember! However, ax y'r question, though I know it afore you speak!"

"Do you, marm? Now I vonder if you can and do!"

"Ay, 'twill be about papers, trinkets and sich."

"Eggs-ackly! And, marm, your vits are a sight sharper than my nose, ay, by goles they are! My question was and is, did this same dewoted father, still mentioning no name, give——"

"No!" said George emphatically. "Hang me if I'll endure any more of your confounded mysteries, Jasper. What you mean is—when Philip, the seventh Earl, gave his baby son and heir to your safe keeping, Hagah, did he also give you his personal effects, money, jewellery, marriage and birth certificates of his son?"

Then Hagah set down her cup, straightened her old back and answered:

"Yes, George my dear, he did."

"And, Hagah, when he left here on that fateful night, did he tell you where he was going?"

"No, my dear, he did not."

"Was he armed?"

"He wore a sword as all gentlemen did in those days."

"Had he pistols also?"

"I saw none."

"And—what of the baby?"

" I carried him to safety as I had promised on the Book."

" Where to, Hagah, where ? "

" George my dear, this is one of the times that I remember to forget."

" Then, if you please, marm," sighed Mr. Shrig, " can you tell us all as happened, 'twixt you and him, on that night—in your own vords ? "

Old Hagah refilled her cup, sipped, glanced at each keenly intent face and nodded.

" Ay, I'll tell ee, brief as I can. You must know I helped to bring Lord Philip into this world and I loved him like my own. . . . That night when he came knocking at the door yonder to bring me the young life in his arms, I saw death in his face. ' Hagah,' said he, ' take my little son who should soon be the earl, for my heart lies dead with my beloved wife and all that was best in me I buried in her lonely grave and yearn for the hour that shall reunite us . . . though first I have a last duty to perform ! ' I asked him what duty, but 'stead of answer he brought my old Bible—there 'tis—and set the Holy Book 'neath my hands that clasped his sleeping child, and now says he : ' Swear before God on your hope of salvation that, should I not return, you will protect my son from the blasting curse that is Vane-Wynter—the " Black Winter." Let my son bear another name, no matter how humble ; give him the hope of life and such chance of happiness as may be ; keep him from all knowledge of his birth that, 'stead of a lord foredoomed by accursed name, he may enjoy life as a man should. Swear me this, Hagah, or better he die now by hand of his dying father than suffer as I have done ! ' So what could I do but take this fearsome oath. Then my lord kissed the child and me and went away, as I knew, to his death, for return he never did. So there's my tale, m' dears," said she, reverting to the vernacular and making the most of her nose and chin, very witch-like. " I've told ee in m' dear lord's own words purty nigh, for they be words from a heart-broke man as died too young ! And now who's for more tay ? There be more in pot."

" Oh," sighed Clytie, " what a pitiful, tragic story ! "

" Ar ! " nodded Mr. Shrig, thrusting finger and thumb into pocket of the red waistcoat. " And, Mrs. Hagah, you'll have noticed this afore now, or summat like it, p'r'aps ? " And on the table before her he placed a shining silver button.

And when she had gazed at and sighed over it, she returned it, saying :

" Yes, Mr. Jasper, my dear young lord designed this himself and had them made by the dozen. . . . You found this . . . at the Castle ? "

" I did, marm. So here's final proof of his i-dentity, at last ! And, now, if you please, I'll ax you for proof of his son's identity—naming no names——"

" Eh, proof ? " she exclaimed. " Of . . . Lord Philip's son ? Why ? "

" Because, never mentioning no names at all, not even in a visper, I know oo he is and eggs-ackly vhere he is at this here i-dentical moment ! " Here, his nearest eye, seen only by her, flickered in lightning wink as he continued :

" This being so, marm, lemme have trinkets and docky-ments aforementioned, and he shall be Earl of Ravenhurst in the twinkle of a bedpost ! "

" Yes," she nodded. " Yes, he would, of course ! But what I say is—no ! So long as things be as they be, ' no ' it is and shall be ! The oath I swore to my dear young lord shall bind me—till the ' black winter ' be past ! So now, if nobody wunt have no more tay, come ee, m' dears, and help old Hagah to wash up and put away."

CHAPTER XL

A short though pregnant chapter

AFTERNOON, very hushed, very airless and so warm that Sir Humphrey, seated upon that same fallen tree which had served him thus before, removes his hat to dab moist brow with dainty perfumed handkerchief, then cherish his left cheek with particular tenderness because of the ugly line that flames upon its somewhat ill-shaven pallor, and, wincing to the smart of it, scowls the blacker upon the man who gazes on him so blankly from face so very set and therefore quite expressionless ; and both of them quite unaware of the small feet that have crept so stealthily and the bright eyes that watch from nearby thicket.

" Well, Tranter, can't you answer ? I ask you—when ? What the devil are you staring at ? Speak and answer—when ? "

" On Friday, sir, at——"

" Four days hence ? But why keep me waiting ? Why defer it until then—why not today or tomorrow ? "

" Sir, you forget. Friday is . . . his lordship's birthday."

" Ah, but yes, so it is ! Dear Raymond will be twenty-four. He is fortunate to be so old ; a charmed life hitherto, eh, Tranter ? So on Friday he will be so unexpectedly aged ! Yet why wait till then ? Birthdays, as you know, are never celebrated by the Earl, and wisely, I think, for each is but another milestone on the road to death, that hideous finality ! So damn all birthdays, say I ! Why must you select this one ? "

" Because his lady desires to receive her engagement ring from him in the one spot hallowed by their love—the phrase is her own, sir—and she has named the hour of sunset, at the little temple."

"But, Tranter, you cannot—perform—in her presence —unless——"

"I trust not, sir. My hope and belief is that my lord, urged by a lover's impatience, may arrive there much before the time appointed, as indeed he usually does."

"You have witnessed many of their—let us say— amorous dallyings, eh ? "

"No, sir. I have merely taken note of the place and time of their meetings, only because compelled by an extremely unpleasant duty."

"Sometimes, Tranter, I perceive in you some faint graces of a gentleman."

"I was—once ! "

"And this makes you the more dangerous—a tool deadly and double-edged ! I must beware ! "

"You are, sir, and you do—constantly."

"Ha, devil—what do you mean ? "

"Merely that I hope you are no longer troubled by— footsteps in the night, or——"

"No, I am not ! And I sleep with my pistols in reach."

"I commend your caution, sir ! Oh, but—your pardon, that mark, sir, that dreadful weal upon your cheek—it looks most painful——"

"And is nothing ! A branch caught me. But have you any news for me, any items of interest ? "

"I fear none worthy of your notice, sir—except, perhaps, my lady Clytie's engagement to——"

"Pah ! You mean liaison——"

"Oh no, sir, her engagement to Mr. Bell, sanctioned and acknowledged by my lord the Earl and by him proclaimed and made public——"

"How the devil—when he never stirs abroad ? "

"Because the county stirs to him lately. All the gentry call nowadays to pay their respects ! The Earl has become extremely popular and——"

"He always was—when he troubled to be so."

Sir Humphrey yawned, flinched to the pain of his

smitten cheek, and, thus reminded of Clytie, rose to scowl at the pallid Tranter.

"So then you will—perform—on Friday at sunset, positively?"

"Yes, sir."

"May I know—how—this time?"

"One of my lord Viscount's duelling pistols bearing his crest and initials."

"Excellent, Tranter! Most admirable! Failing the devoted father, we have suicide for a love that despairs, an amorous quarrel—or some such youthful nonsense! Tranter, I congratulate you! On Friday, then, an hour before sunset, I shall take the road and await news or sight of you at the King's Head in Horsham. Thenceforth, Tranter, the Sword of Damocles will threaten you no longer—that ponderous weapon suspended by a single hair, or—shall we say—a hempen noose adangle from a massy beam? Ah well, Friday at sunset shall decide!"

CHAPTER XLI

Relates the last talk of father and son

" THIS thing," said the Viscount, frowning at his reflection in the looking-glass, " is the very dooce of a cravat you've tied me into ! Demme, Tranter, it looks more like a confounded hangman's knot ! " Tranter's usually deft hands faltered and fumbled very oddly—like his voice when he replied :

" Indeed, my . . . my lord, it . . . it is the very latest mode, quite——"

" Well, I don't like it—no, demme if I do ! Whip it off and tie me a ' butterfly ' or ' loves-throne '."

" As you will, my lord."

" You probably know it's my dooced birthday—you do know it, don't you ? "

" Yes, my lord."

" Then why the dooce don't you act up to it and make the best of me, everything as tip-top as possible—what the devil's the matter with you, Tranter, eh ? "

" Nothing, my lord."

" Well, you look dev'lish queer about the gills— haven't been boozing, have you ? "

" Certainly not, my lord."

" Then I suggest you do ; might make you a trifle less like a walking dooced corpse."

And presently, the cravat being tied to his near satisfaction, the Viscount went in quest of his father and found him, as usual, in the tower garden.

" Sir," said he, as they saluted each other, " I beg to inform you this is my birthday."

" I am sufficingly aware of it, Raymond."

" But, sir, what you are not aware of is the fact that this is, and ever will be, the best of all my twenty-four ! "

" Because it will bring you a young and beautiful wife ? "

" Yes, sir, though I was not thinking of her for the moment—— "

" Remarkable, my son ! "

" Yes, sir, so remarkable that, well—I'm remarking on it, because it is only lately you have allowed me to become really aware of my father, to—appreciate you as such and have permitted me the honour to become almost intimate at last . . . to feel I am truly your son and that you . . . I mean we, of course . . . find it possible to . . . that is, sir, that I discover that I—well—like you far better than I ever thought possible . . . indeed quite surprisingly doocedly well, sir—if you gather my meaning."

" You are telling me that you love your father ? "

These awful words struck the Viscount dumb, and caused him to exhibit such acute discomfort that the Earl laughed, then reached out his hand, saying :

" Why that look of shame, my son, that expression of conscious guilt ? I accuse you of nothing more heinous than love for your father—or am I mistaken ? "

" No, sir, certainly not—no indeed ! Only, as a matter of fact, I have always respected you so—so very doocedly and from such a distance that I never thought the—the other thing—could be possible."

" The ' other thing ' being love for me, Raymond ? "

" Well, sir, to be quite frightfully frank, I—what I mean is—yes ! "

" Indeed," said the Earl, smiling, " we English are a strange contrary race ; ashamed of our best impulses, we hide our noblest virtues and parade the worst of ourselves ! A queer people, my son, but individual and perfectly original, thank heaven ! Thus now upon this your twenty-fourth birthday we, forgetting all save that we are father and son, dare to avow our love for each other."

" And respect, sir ! " added the Viscount, rising to say it. " Love and respect, Father ! "

" Respect and love ! " the Earl repeated. " And of the two, I choose love."

"But, Father, can there be one without the other?"

"Certainly. For love that is real is and must be all-forgiving, and which of us humans but must have something to forgive one another at some time or other? However, my dear Raymond, I wish you the old hope that you have many happy returns of this day."

"Thank you, Father!" said the Viscount, as they clasped hands again. "And now, sir, I should like to show you the—the ring, if I may, and greatly desire your opinion of it—though Clytie helped and really chose it."

And when the Earl had examined and commended this splendid thing, the Viscount replaced it in its box, flushing self-consciously, thrust it back into waistcoat-pocket, grasped his father's hand again, more self-consciously, and strode away on feet light (almost) as his heart—while his father gazed after him, listening to the jingle of spurs until they died away; then he sighed, and shivered violently as with some foreboding of what was to be so very dreadfully soon. . . .

In the stableyard the Viscount called for Tim O'Brian, who peered instantly over one of the many half-doors, saying cheerily:

"Ah now, me lord, shure and it's mesilf is afther wishin' ye arl the luck in the world and many happy returns o' this blissed day."

"Thankee, Tim, old boy! I'm a little before my time, but——"

"Indade and y' are that! Two hours and a half afore th' hour ye named and more. Y' order was for six o'clock and 'tis long afore four!"

"Oh, well, no matter. It's a grand day for a gallop."

"'Tis that indade! Will ye have Thunderbolt?"

"Not today; he needs too much dooced attention, Tim. No, tell 'em to saddle Tristram."

"Ay! And 'tis wise y'are, my lord. I'm f'ever expecting that wild devil to be the dith o' ye."

"Nonsense, Tim! Thunderbolt's a grand mount. All he needs is riding. He's the best horse in the stables."

"Hows'ever, me lord, if he b'longed to me, b'jabers, ay, b'arl the powers, I'd have him shot ! "   Almost as he spoke, one of the many doors nearby creaked.

"Eh ? " cried Tim, glancing thitherward, " which o' ye lads is there in Tristram's stall ? "

A moment's pause, then this door creaked again and out stepped Joseph Tranter, sleek and immaculate as ever, though in the afternoon sunshine his face showed ghastly pale as he advanced to bow and say in his softly modulated voice :

"I am here, my lord, in quest of my lady Clytie's page."

"Are ye now ? " demanded O'Brian suspiciously. " Then ye should be knowing mighty well as he's out in attindance on m'lady at this moment ! "

"Thank you, O'Brian ; I was not aware of it."

"By the way, Tranter," said his happy young master, " since you are not in attendance for the next few hours, you may perhaps stroll as far as the Raven. If so, take this, to quaff a dooced flagon or so to my present and future happiness."   Tranter received the coin with murmurous thanks, bent his supple back in obeisance lower than usual, and went his way with his almost noiseless step. Even as he vanished, Tim spat after him, saying :

"Tare an' ages ! Ah, 'tis him turns me stomach ! I can't abide him at arl, at arl ! "

"Well, Tim, you don't have to ! Instead, go order the lads to saddle Tristram—hold hard ! First, seeing you are my old Tim, take these five guineas, in case you also find your way to the Raven——"

"Ah, my lord," said he, glancing from the money in his palm to the Viscount's happy, smiling face, " 'tis no call y' have to remind me ! Haven't I been afther drinking y'r health and the saints' blessings on ye since ye straddled y'r first pony ? So now I says it again—long life, me lord, and may the sweet saints o' God have ye in hes care, wi' y'r lady wi' arl happiness and in good time the joy o' children."

"Thanks, Tim, my old f'lo'. I suppose . . . in time
. . . we may. I hope so, demme! And now—dooce
take you, go order Tristram."

Thus very soon the Viscount was mounted and smiling
down on O'Brian, who smiled up at him, saying:

"A son, m'lord! An heir, to carry on the name!
Holy Mary, phwat a day that'll be!"

"Yes," said the Viscount very solemnly, "the grandest
day of my life, Tim, a day to live for!"

Then, turning Tristram's lofty head, the Viscount set
off at a graceful canter; thus eager for life and the joy of
it, he rode, foredoomed, to meet that never-suspected,
stealthy evil that even then was speeding to meet him.

CHAPTER XLII

In which Tranter performs

" TRISTRAM, my old Ironlegs," said his rider, halting him at a shady part of the high-road, " we're ages before our time and that's the dooce of it ! Question is : shall we go and meet her ? No, we think not. Better obey her instructions, eh ? Agreed ? Very good ! Instead I'll read you what she commands. So listen ! "

Thrusting hand into the breast of his coat, a garment of supreme artistry moulding his lithe, young shapeliness, the Viscount drew thence a letter, already somewhat crumpled by frequent perusal, and, unfolding it very tenderly for the precious thing it was, he again addressed his horse :

" Tristram, old lad, this is the first love-letter she has written me as yet, so cock your ears, both of 'em, and listen ! " Then, in voice hushed and gentle, the Viscount read :

" ' Dearest, beloved Raymond ; darling '—that's how she begins, and b'gad, Tristram, it's almost as marvellous to read as to hear her say it !

" ' Dearest, beloved Raymond ; darling, when Saint Mark chimes six, be waiting at our sanctuary for—your own—happy—ever-loving Joan. PS. I beg you will not be late. '

" Dooced touching, eh, Tristram ; plaintive ! As if I ever should or even possibly could keep the sweet soul waiting or fail her in any way ! I can't bear to think of it."

So saying, the Viscount refolded this most precious missive and set it back upon his heart, repeating : " Keep her waiting ? Not I ; demme, not while I live ! For, Tristram old boy, only death could keep me from her now, and perhaps—not even that ! So, oh, boy, get on, Tristram.

Come now, a gallop. Instead of being a moment late, will be dooced early! To it now!"

True, much before the time appointed youthful Impatience rode blithely into this leafy solitude where, instead of Love, Death already awaited him.

Before the little temple he dismounted and tethered his horse, but then instead of entering its shady coolness, for the afternoon sun was very hot, he strolled beneath the shadow of the great tree, there, to pass the time, took out his penknife and began carving upon its mighty bole and had completed a somewhat wobbly heart embracing the magic letters J O A when his blade snapped. So he tossed the useless thing away and stood a while to listen and gaze about him in this hushed seclusion where no leaf stirred in the drowsy, windless air, and no soul broke the silence except the sleepy twitter of birds and sweetly plaintive notes of a blackbird. And now, once again, he drew forth that cherished letter, unfolded it and, with his eyes down-bent to this, slowly approached and, at last, entered the little temple—to be met by flame, smoke, and sudden sharp agony that struck him down to lie outstretched and very dreadfully still. . . . Ensued a furtive rustle of leafage, dying swiftly away to an ominous stillness wherein no bird twittered and the blackbird's mournful song was hushed.

Thus for some while was no sound of life to break this awful silence until, sweetly mellowed by distance, the clock of Saint Mark chimed and told the hour of six; then, even as the last stroke quivered upon the air, was muffled thud of horsehoofs drawing nearer . . . nearer yet . . . checked to a trampling halt. . . . Silence again, but now more terrible than ever . . . a fearful hush broken all at once by a woman's heart-broken cry, rising, shrilling to a scream of wild despair.

CHAPTER XLIII

The High Toby concern

SAINT MARK was yet tolling this most fateful hour of six as Sir Humphrey, having topped one of the many hills, spurred his foam-spattered animal to a full gallop that he might put as many miles as possible between himself, a certain little ruinous temple and the pallid, desperate man who was to make him heir to one of the richest earldoms in the country.

This thought was so inspiring, the day so fair, and every prospect so pleasing, that Sir Humphrey began to hum, and then to sing, softly melodious, a gay little French chanson until—song and steed were checked suddenly by a masked horseman who seemed to leap out upon him from the hedge, a violent ruffian this, who flourished a pistol in each fist, one of which he thrust into Sir Humphrey's astonished face while with the other he sent Sir Humphrey's hat flying and rapped him smartly on his shining, perfumed hair :

" Y' bung, y' prese, damn ye ! " growled this masked ferocity as Sir Humphrey, clapping hand to smitten crown, reeled in the saddle. "Come on now—y' purse, y' watch, y' rings—hand over afore I blast y' liver—hand over ! "

Sir Humphrey's obedience was instant.

"Now, geddown and pick up y' dicer, y'r hat—in the ditch there, curse ye, and sharp's the word ! " Again Sir Humphrey obeyed speedily as possible ; but as he stooped to recover the now miry and crumpled thing that had been his hat, was sudden clatter, and, starting up, he saw his brutal assailant make off with his horse at furious gallop.

Then indeed Sir Humphrey gave tongue, cursing loud and bitterly in English and French until, seeing there was no one to hear his so eloquent futility, he sighed instead, hurled his ruined hat back into the ditch and began to walk with strides very different to his usual leisured amble. But he had not gone far when round a bend in the road came succour in the shape of a man driving a gig mounted on extremely high wheels who at Sir Humphrey's urgent summons, pulled up to enquire :

" Vot now, sir ? Has your hoss ditched you and bolted ? "

" No—no ! I've just been robbed ! A masked villain has left me afoot and penniless———"

" Eh, robbed, says you ? Robbed, eh ? Burn my neck, says I, you don't say ! "

" But I do say ! The murderous rogue assaulted me also—actually dared to strike me, damn him ! "

" Strike you, sir ? Think o' that now ! Though I don't ob-sarve no blood on you, no gaping vound nor yet even a bleed'n' scrat, Sir Humphrey, so———"

" Ha, you know me, do you ? And I seem to have seen you before—somewhere or other, have I not ? "

" Werry likely sir, me being Jarsper Shrig o' Bow Street, at your service, sir, now and hereafter—I hope ! "

" Then you can serve me now by taking me———"

" Vith J O Y, j'y, Sir Humphrey ! But, sir, con-carning this here masked willain, this despret High-Tobyman, did you happen to notice if same carried veapons ? "

" Happen to notice ? Of course I did ! The fellow threatened me with a pistol in each hand—he would never have dared me else———"

" Two pistols, sir ! Then, dog bite me, he must ha' been him as is called the ' Galloping Death '. I reckon you're werry fort'nate indeed———"

" Fortunate ? " repeated Sir Humphrey furiously. " Don't I tell you he stripped me penniless, assaulted me most brutally———"

" A bit onfort'nate, p'r'aps, sir, but there's others far more so ! Ar, there's others oceans more misfort'nate than yourself, at this here i-denticle moment, Sir Humphrey ! "

" Oh ? Indeed ? Who, pray ? "

" Your dewoted and noble uncle, f'rinstance ! "

" The Earl ? Ah—what of him ? "

Now here, in accordance with that carefully timed plan which, owing to youthful impatience, had already failed so disastrously, Mr. Shrig began drawing upon his imagination, saying :

" Sir, your uncle has had—a stroke ! "

" What kind of a stroke ? "

" A—deathly stroke and is a-calling for you werry pitiful—at death's door ! "

" Do you mean he is—actually—dying ? "

" Ar, he is so, pore gen'leman ! Dying he is, sir, by the minute, with every tick o' the clock and a-calling for his nevvy Humphrey as frequent, though werry feeble ! "

" But why—why call for me when his son is there ? The Viscount is with him, of course—I suppose ? "

" The Wi-count, sir——! " Mr. Shrig sighed deeply and shook his head so ominously that Sir Humphrey made a quick pace nearer to demand and in quite altered tone :

" What of him . . . cousin Raymond ? Is he . . . has he been . . . another accident ? Ha, death of my life— can't you speak ? What's amiss ? Has anything . . . happened ? Answer me ! "

Mr. Shrig, gazing down upon his eager questioner with expression of the deepest gloom, sighed again, shook his head more ominously and replied in voice awed to dreadful whisper :

" Sir, all as I can say is—least said soonest mended, vich can't be nohow and therefore, not being possible—ain't ! "

Even as the words were uttered, Sir Humphrey leapt, swung himself lightly to the seat beside Mr. Shrig, and, gesturing to the road before them, said commandingly :

" Drive ! "

K

CHAPTER XLIV

In which Dan'l, despite his whiskers, is neither mild nor meek

MEANWHILE Joseph Tranter, clad for travel and bearing a valise neat and trim as himself, was on his unhurried way to the village ; but though checking the folly of haste, his every sense was so painfully alert that he became suddenly and dreadfully aware of stealthy movement nearby, a faint rustling, the snap of a dry stick—his guilty heart leapt, half-choking him ; panic urged him to instant flight. Instead, he halted to change the valise from one hand to the other while he glanced furtively in the direction of these soft and therefore terrifying sounds, and thus beheld a small face peering down at him through a gap in the hedge.

"Ah !" he exclaimed with gasping sigh. "So it's . . . only you !"

"Yes, 's me."

"But what are you doing there, little Parvo ?"

"Takin' a bit of a walk, I am."

"Where to, my boy ?"

"Village."

"Well then, come here and walk with me."

"Whaffor ?"

"Bullseyes, as many as you can eat."

"Sixpenn'orth ?"

"Yes, all you want."

"Cor strike me blind !" exclaimed the cherub, and down the bank he slithered, looking smaller than ever in mere shoes and cap. "Sixpenn'orth you says ?"

"Yes. Come along."

"Well, I am a-comin' !"

"But not so far off—you must walk beside me or no bullseyes !" Warily the boy approached, taking care to keep just beyond reach of this pale-faced man who contrived to smile despite the fear that stiffened his lips and furrowed his brow so deeply as he said in soft, wheedling tone :

"Why, Parvo my boy, I believe you're afraid of me."

"No, I ain't afeard, I ain't ! "

"Then why do you keep at such a distance ? "

"Nuffink, only 'cos you sounds kinder than you looks."

They were approaching a narrow by-lane, a winding, shadowy solitude.   With his haggard gaze on this, Tranter instinctively quickened his step and, glancing furtively at the boy, saw how those bright eyes watched his every motion, and fear grew to terror as, with laugh like a croak, he said :

"Little Parvo, my dear boy, I really do believe you are afraid of me—are you ? "

"No, I ain't afeard o' you nor nuffink."

"I wonder why you fear me, Parvo ? I've never done anything to hurt you, have I, my boy ? "

"No, you ain't an' you'd better not try neither ! "

"How can you think I ever would harm you ? "

"Easy !   I think o' lots o' things, I do."

"What sort of things, my boy ? "

"Ain't a-goin' to say ! And I ain't your boy."

By this time they were very near that shadowy lane, and Tranter's step became slower as he said very gently and with another smile :

"Parvo, my dear, sometimes lately I've thought you were watching me . . . following me about. Were you, my boy ?   And if so, why ? "

"'Cos I likes the way you walks, so nice and soft."

"Do I, Parvo ? "

"Yes.   So I tries to do the same."

It was now that far on the road before them was a swirl of dust where two horses galloped though only one bore a rider ; but, despite distance, Parvo recognised this rider and became bold.

"So you did follow me, eh, my little man ? " enquired

Tranter, smiling wider than ever as he halted, for they had reached the narrow by-lane at last. " You did follow your friend Tranter, didn't you, my dear ? "

" Yes, I did."

" Where ? "

" Lots o' places."

" Clever boy ! Where did you follow Tranter most often ? "

" Froo the tunnel into the wood."

" Ah, what a smart little man ! And what did you see ? "

" You an' S'Umfree."

" Did you though ! And could you hear what was said ? "

" Yes, I could."

" Brave boy ! And what did you hear ? "

" Lots, and—'bout the Viscount's dooling pistol and 'ow you——" Dropping his valise, Tranter sprang with hands that clutched, that lifted and bore their struggling, choking captive into the shadowy lane, hands of panic and therefore utterly merciless. . . . The boy uttered a strangling scream lost in the thudding of hoofs ; and then a voice spoke :

" Easy there, easy ! "

Tranter loosed his helpless victim and, turning, beheld a man surprisingly near, a meek-seeming man whose mild features were rendered even more so by a pair of hay-like whiskers mournfully adroop, and in voice mild as his looks, the man spoke again :

" I want you, Joseph Tranter, and you know why and wherefore, but if you want me to tell ye I'll say——" Again Tranter leapt, this time to fight for life and freedom like the desperate wretch he was ; but, despite whiskers and seeming meekness, this man proved so extremely otherwise, that Tranter very soon lay dazed, breathless and bleeding with this man seated firmly upon his help-lessness, who now enquired :

" Did he hurt ye, Gimblet ? "

" No, Dan'l, honly me froat a bit."

"Then go and bring the hosses."

"Ay ay! But, oh, Dan'l, I b'leeve he done it! I hears a shot and I see him run——"

"Not him, Gimblet, 'tis too soon, 'tis only just gone six! Go you and bring the hosses. "

And so after some while, with Tranter bound securely upon one horse and the boy perched before him on the saddle of the other, Dan'l rode forth of that narrow, shadowy lane.

CHAPTER XLV

Tells how Mr. Shrig persuaded Tranter to speak

IN A certain corner stall of the spacious stableyard behind the Raven Inn Joseph Tranter sat huddled, chin on breast, as if gazing down at his two hands shackled helplessly before him, while Dan'l, seated upon an upturned wooden bucket nearby, puffed serenely at short clay pipe and gazed thoughtfully out into the wide stableyard just now radiant with the glow of early sunset; thus they remained, captor and captive, scarce moving, never speaking in a drowsy stillness with nothing to hear except twitter of sparrows, cooing of doves, distant lowing of cows and, at last—footsteps.

Dan'l sat up with a jerk and removed his pipe, for these footsteps, unwontedly slow and heavy, were so eloquent that his whiskers (those sensitive adornments) drooped more despondently than usual, as he rose, for towards him trudged Jasper Shrig, a haggard figure of dejection, who, pausing, leaned upon his knobbly stick, bowed his head abjectly and said in voice like a groan, these two most tragic and grievous words human lips may utter :

" Too late ! "

" So ? " enquired Dan'l, tapping out his pipe with due care. " Dead is he, Jarsper ? "

" Ar ! Or as good—meaning the rewerse. . . . Oh, Dan'l, I acted ten, say fifteen, say half an hour—too late ! "

" No, Jarsper, 'twas him, as now ain't, as come there hours too soon ! "

" Hows'ever, I've—failed, Dan'l ! And failure is a pill so werry hard to swaller—it pretty nigh chokes me."

" Shall I fetch ye a pint o' comfort in a pot, Jarsper, to help it down like ? "

"Thankee, no! Comfort ain't for me, in a pot or out; I'm past it, Dan'l."

"Wot o' number one, Jarsper? You picked him up afoot as expected, eh?"

"I did, to the minute. You played your part like the Dan'l you are; 'tis only Jarsper as fails! Me, your humbel servant, J. Failure Shrig——"

"Lord, Jarsper, don't take it so hard, nor yet abuse yourself for wot you couldn't help. For, though Jarsper Shrig, you're only human, arter all."

"True enough, Dan'l! But never—never so perishing human as now."

"And how about number one, wot did you do with him?"

"I dooly delivered him at the Castle; he should be safe along o' the Earl by now."

"Safe, Jarsper?"

"Ar! Safe for good and all—I hope! Now let's take a peep at number two. . . . He looks a bit bloody, Dan'l!"

"Resisted arrest, Jarsper, also attempted to scrag the Gimblet."

"Did he so? The wiper! Can he talk?"

"I dunno. He give a groan or so, not so long ago." Entering the stall, Mr. Shrig gazed down at their wretched prisoner and enquired:

"Joseph Tranter, can you hear me?"

The shape of misery remained motionless and dumb, therefore Mr. Shrig poked and stirred it gently with his stick, then demanded:

"Are you listening now?"

The drooping head nodded feebly.

"Werry good! Then, Joseph Tranter, you are apprehended for the murder of Raymond, Vi-count Hurst, by into the body of same shooting a lead ball whereof he dooly languished and died—or soon must—and this against the peace of our Sovereign lord the King. Have you anything to say?"

The drooping head swayed from side to side.

" No ? Then listen again.   Joseph Tranter, you sure as death'll dooly hang ! You are for the nubbing-cheat, the gallers, Joseph, the Tyburn Jig, dangling in a noose to kick and jump your windictive life out—except—you turn King's Evidence, naming your accomplice him as set you on aided and abetted you to commit this heenious fact, name him and save your life.   Do you speak ? "

The helpless prisoner drew a shuddering breath, but remained dumb.

" Joseph Tranter, you'll be stood in a cart, your arms bound and a rope about your wicious neck. The cart'll then be drove from you and you'll be left to choke, jerk and jump till you're dead—except you testify and name oo set you to the act, this crime as you have tried afore in manners warious—a boat as sank, a gun, a veel as come off, linchpin o' same having been removed. Do you testify ? "

The shape of misery writhed, groaned but uttered no word.

" Joseph Tranter, arter you're dead—vich may take you, say five minutes, say ten or, mebbe fifteen, you'll be took down, stripped, tarred, clamped into iron cage and hung on a jibbet as a public varning, or—give to the surgeons to be cut up, Joseph, bit by bit—unless you turn evidence, thereby saving your miserable life and precious carkiss. So, for the last time—is it ' yes ' or ' no ' ? "

" Yes . . . yes ! " gasped Abject Misery at last.   " I'll speak . . . I'll tell . . . everything . . . how he tortured me . . . drove me . . . drove and compelled me . . . I'll speak . . . or write——"

" Werry good, Joseph Tranter. Up now, and toddle along o' me. Dan'l—the gig ! "

CHAPTER XLVI

Giveth brief description of vengeance

IN THE Castle was awed and dreadful tumult : hurrying feet were hushed, voices spoke in fearful whispers, especially when passing the door of that chamber where Dr. Dale, with Clytie to aid him, was doing his utmost to hold Death at bay, until, fast as speeding hoofs and wheels could travel, further help might arrive. . . .

Meanwhile, the Earl sat alone, gazing down at the letter which had compelled him from the bedside of his dying son ; this :

> " MY LORD,
> " I have the actual murderer, viz. Joseph Tranter. But his accomplice and employer as planned the Deed, I cannot touch for lack of proof and therefore don't name him though your lordship knows him as well as I do and better, being related. I therefore beg to warn your lordship as he (this same party unnamed) will call to condole with your lordship some half-hour after receipt of this from your lordship's obedient servant in all due respectful sympathy,
>
> " J. SHRIG."

Having read this letter again, the Earl rose and, crossing to the great carved mantel, set wide the secret panel, tested the lock of the one door and, sitting down at his desk, placed his watch before him, took quill and began to write :

> " To the Ninth Earl of Ravenhurst.
> " MY LORD,
> Since I die tonight by the hand of my son's murderer or my own, I deem it proper to set forth in few words as possible how my cousin Philip, George, seventh earl and your lordship's grandfather, died. Briefly,

then—upon the night of 30th June, fifty-nine years ago, I was seated with my unworthy brother-in-law, Sir John Carr, in this same room, when the panel, of which few had the secret, was dashed violently open and in upon me leapt one reported and believed dead and buried in America, my cousin Philip. In the moment of his wild and sudden intrusion, he drew his sword, and crying, ' Dastard and murderer ', bade me arm and defend myself, nor would he allow me speech or afford me any word of explanation. Compelled thus with his point at my throat, I reached from the rack the nearest small-sword and stood on my defence and, deaf to my entreaties, he instantly assailed me, an attack so furious and wild that it seemed he sought his own death rather than mine. Thus scarcely had out blades crossed than, crying a woman's name, he closed with me and sank impaled upon my steel. Thus died my unfortunate and unhappy cousin. And then I committed the great folly of my life, for I took this twice dead man in my arms, bore him into the secret Priest's Chamber, and there hid the body to avoid all chance of scandal. And this is why my only sister's husband, Sir John Carr, and his equally unworthy son, have blackmailed me ever since. Lastly, I here most solemnly declare I had no knowledge that cousin Philip was married, much less had been blessed with a son and heir. And this I avow as truth in the name of that God I denied when my devoted wife died twenty-four years ago.

" Upstairs my only son is dying, or is already dead, and my own time is near, for as I pen these the last words I shall ever write I hear the step of his murderer. Thus, as his guilty hand opens the door, I subscribe myself for the last time

" Roland, John Vane-Wynter,
" RAVENHURST."

" Come in ! " said the Earl, as he sanded and folded this letter. " Come in, Humphrey, and hear me say with deepest sincerity you are most heartily welcome—at last ! "

Standing upon the threshold, nephew gazed speechlessly at uncle, who proceeded to wafer and seal his letter, saying casually as he did so :

" You may enter and close the door, Humphrey ! You may also be seated—for a little while. But, pray why do you stare on me as I were a ghost ? "

" On the contrary, Uncle, it is with surprise and—joy, naturally ! For I was under no little apprehension on your account, sir."

" Indeed ? May I know why ? "

" That fellow Shrig or Grigg, informed me you were dying."

" And he was perfectly correct, Humphrey. I am dying. So are you ! With every breath we draw and move we make, the Angel of Death steals nearer ! Oh yes, we are both dying, though you, Humphrey, will die— a day too late, alas ! "

" Too . . . late ? Uncle, what . . . what the devil do you mean ? "

" That I ought to have killed you before today, nephew ; better still—years ago——"

" Killed me ? " repeated nephew, starting forward in his chair to gaze at uncle between eyelids viciously narrowed. " So then here's an end to the damned mystery at last ! It was you attempted my life here . . . that stone . . . the footsteps in the night . . . the soft fumbling at my door . . . it was you ! "

" Oh no, Humphrey, no ! I should never have bungled your dying. No, I suspect it was that poor wretch you drove to murder for you—to do that you dared not—he to run the hazard and you, immune and beyond reach of the law, to profit and enjoy."

Sir Humphrey sat rigid, grasping that ornate whip of his in both hands and so tightly that his knuckles gleamed white; then he relaxed, lolled back in his chair and shook his head.

" Dear Uncle," he sighed, " you talk so very wildly and look so devilish odd that I fear you are indeed ill physically, mentally or both, and——"

" On the contrary, Nephew, I was never better. Watch
now ! " Then, to Sir Humphrey's fearful amazement, the
Earl's bowed form straightened, the mighty shoulders
expanded, and with lithe, effortless movement he rose and
stood erect, dominant, relentless and terribly serene ; and
when he spoke it was with a smile :

" Lo, for you, my Humphrey, like Samson, my strength
is renewed within me for a little while, nor shall your
secret weapon avail you——" Up started Sir Humphrey,
and as he did so his whip, wrenched asunder, left him
armed with a foot of glittering steel.

" Stand . . . away ! " he panted. " Away . . . you're
. . . mad ! "

" No, Humphrey, I am sane Justice ! I am Vengeance !
I am Death—come and embrace me."

And speaking, he took a slow pace nearer, reaching
forth his long arms. . . . Sir Humphrey, recoiling, glanced
wildly around, then, desperate with fear, leapt and smote
—vainly, it seemed, for that oncoming figure of doom
never faltered ; therefore he turned and, taking the only
course of possible escape, sprang and vanished within that
square of dimness beside the mantel. But with hand
spread upon pulsing wound, Vengeance followed. . . .
Up narrow stairs and along dim passageways in the thick-
ness of these old walls, up more steps, and so, at last, to
the battlements of the grim old tower. . . . Here Des-
peration fronted Vengeance to smite again, but that
murderous dagger-hand was seized, twisted. . . . From
gasping mouth issued an agonised cry choked to a thin
wheeze and presently to silence ; then Vengeance became
dreadfully busied. . . .

And, after some while, the Earl, glancing upward, sank
to his knees, then slowly to his face, and with silvery head
pillowed upon the time-worn stones where soared the
great flagstaff, he said brokenly :

" Now . . . Lord God . . . I come . . . to thy judgment. . . ."

CHAPTER XLVII

Concerning a certain flagstaff

THE MOON was rising in splendour when Mr. Shrig, having seen their prisoner securely bestowed in Horsham jail, reined in his horse to descend that steep hill into Ravenhurst village, at which moment Saint Mark began to chime and strike the hour.

" Nine ! " said Mr. Shrig, counting the strokes. " Nine o'clock, Dan'l ! "

" Well, wot o' that, Jarsper ? "

" I reckon as 'tis about time."

" Time for wot ? "

" For us to pay a wisit at the Castle. Now ax me the reason for same."

" Well then—why ? "

" To see if things has took place as I hoped and expected. ' Wot things ? ' you axes me, to vich I reply : I give him an hour for it and he's had two, and two being more than vun, my hopes is rose according."

" But who have you give an hour to and wot for ? "

" To him as, if he acts as by me expected, sarves the law and saves us oceans o' trouble."

" Jarsper, I still don't twig."

" Vich, Dan'l, I didn't hardly think as you could."

By this time they had passed through the silent village, and now, rounding a bend, Mr. Shrig suddenly pulled his horse to a walk, for someone in a smock-frock that gleamed ghostly in the moonlight was gesticulating at them very strangely from the middle of the road.

" Wot now ? " sighed Dan'l mournfully. " Who's that a-jigging and flourishing at us so wild-like ? "

" Looks like a werry aged party, name o' Jabez," said Mr. Shrig, reining to a stop ; for indeed old Jabez it was who capered on tottery legs, flourishing his stick in a dreadful kind of triumph.

"Oho!" he cried. "Aha! Look at I, will ee! I've see it—I've see it! Another ghost—up yon at Castle— agin' the moon—'igh up, sky-'igh. A rare ghos'ly sight it be, same like arl ghostesses should ought for to be! I see un wi' me owd eyes, plain as plain!"

"Eh, a ghost, d'ye say, Gaffer?"

"Ay, don't I tell ee! 'Tes ghost out o' the past—the bad owd days, evil, evil! Yonder it be—up agin' the moon! This be two ghostesses as I've found! Go ee and see if I be liar or no, go and see."

"I will that, Gaffer, and thankee! At the Castle, you say?"

"Ay, the owd tower. Gashly! Oh, gashly!"

"Old codger's pretty drunk!" said Dan'l, as they drove on again.

"No, Dan'l, not him, not old Jabez."

"Eh, not? And him a babbling o' ghosts and sich-like!"

"Ar! But he said more. 'The tower,' says he, and 'high up, sky-high—agin' the moon'."

"But, Jarsper, wot's it all mean?"

"Dan'l, in about seven, say ten, say fifteen minutes us'll find out and larn if old Jabez be drunk or no. This road'll bring up pretty nigh the Castle."

"But it's on-common late to visit the Earl, Jarsper— past nine o'clock!"

"This here has been a on-common day—vun murder already, and 'oo knows how many more?"

"Egad, Jarsper, ain't you content with one?"

"Dan'l, I'm never content till justice has been done and the law dooly satisfi——" He checked speech and gig together—for they had topped the hill with the Castle thus in full view; and now ensued a moment of breathless silence. When at last Dan'l spoke it was in awed astonishment.

"Look . . . look, Jarsper, up yon! Lord love me

eyes—look up there . . . a-danglin' from the flag-pole——! "

" Ar ! " murmured Mr. Shrig. " Sky-high, agin' the moon—like old Gaffer said."

" But—it's him, Jarsper ! 'Tis number one and dead as mutton ! "

" As I expected and—hoped, Dan'l. Nobody could be deader ! "

" But how ? And who ? And wot d'ye mean by ' expected ' ? "

" I expected a hour might be long enough for justice to act, Dan'l, and the gen'lemanly wiciousness a-dangling up yonder agin' the moon proves how right I am ! For justice has been done, the law windicated, willainy has his doos and our case happily con-clooded ! Now 'tis for us to take him down afore the whole willage is up. So, Dan'l, sharp's the vord ! " So saying, Mr. Shrig touched whip to horse and away they bowled towards that grimly old tower above whose hoary battlements, once again, was a pendant ghastliness, this the last victim of lordly justice, high hung for all to see.

CHAPTER XLVIII

Tells how George met the heir

" WHY . . . surely," said George, staring at the object displayed so prominently in the middle of Mr. Jackman's littered desk, " surely that is old Hagah's box ? "

" That i-dentical ! " quoth Mr. Shrig.

" But I buried it—weeks ago ! "

" But self and Dan'l dooly dug same up, days ago, by Mrs. Hagah's instructions, spoke, wrote and signed ! "

" And in it," said Mr. Jackman, laying his hands upon the box almost caressingly, " in it, George, such documents as prove to us, and will later establish to the authorities, the quite unimpeachable identity of—the long-lost heir ! "

" Then, sir, I congratulate you—and him, whoever he is. But my present worry and harrowing anxiety is for Lady Clytie Moor. I think you know we are to be married, but—— Oh, damme—since that ghastly business at the Castle I've neither seen nor heard from her, though I—— Oh, I've written so often and haunted the place—nor has Aunt Isabel ! Consequently I'm in the very devil of a state. Why this silence ? Why shut herself away— why ? "

" My dear George, surely this is not so very surprising if you consider the, as you say, so recent ghastly business— the Earl's death—her shock at finding him, her grief at losing him ? "

" Yes, yes indeed ! " sighed George.   " She loved him very dearly, and no wonder ! Yet why must she refuse to see me—or my letters ? For she sends them back with the seals unbroken ! "

" Some natures, George, when deeply hurt, must hide their wounds and suffer in solitude. Give her time, my dear boy ; have patience until the first agony of her grief is abated.   Wait, my poor fellow, and all will be well. Meanwhile, referring to these documents which you have not yet troubled to even glance at, these, George, and the personal trinkets that wait your inspection, empower me here and now to pronounce and salute you as George, Philip Vane-Wynter, ninth Earl of Ravenhurst——"

"Me?" exclaimed George, regardless of grammar. "I—the Earl? Good, great Jupiter, what incredible nonsense!"

"Nevertheless, George—my lord, it is a fact evidential, actual and quite incontrovertible! You are indeed the ninth Earl."

"Vich," quoth Mr. Shrig, "and furthermore, m'lud, I have here summat as, though dumb, speaks werry plain, summat as carries conwiction per the ogle or, as you might say, the eye or blinker, so, my lord, have a look at this!" Very carefully he unrolled and held up an aged canvas, saying:

"There, my lord, take a peep at—yourself!"

George looked—and sank into the nearest chair, to gaze in speechless wonder, for there, in splendid gilded armour, left hand poised gracefully on gold-hilted sword, stood the very image of himself.

"So here y'are, friend George, my lord—hair same, face same, features eggs-act, everything i-denticle, even to the crooked little finger o' your left daddle! This is the portrait o' Philip, John, fourth Earl, as I found in the dungeons of the old tower. I showed same t'other day to Mrs. Hagah, the Earl being dead, poor gen'leman, and she give me further information, tells me o' the box yonder, and so—there y'are!"

"However," said George, rising, "I don't want this earldom and won't have it!"

"Pooh, George!" exclaimed Mr. Jackman in shocked tone. "Nonsense, my lord! This is your natural heritage——"

"Which I refuse to accept!"

"But, my dear George——"

"More especially while old Corks, the Viscount, is alive!"

"But they give no hope of his recovery; he may die at any moment——"

"God forbid, sir! But if he does, then we will talk of this again," said George, sinking down into his chair despondently. "But now, no more of it, I beg. And if you are my friends don't call me 'my lord'! And since I am glad to believe you are truly my friends, then in friendship's name—oh, I beseech you—tell me all that happened, everything you know about my lady Clytie and her strange illness."

"Not an illness, my dear George—though I suppose such grief may be a sort of illness—but so far as I can learn she is shocked beyond the natural solace of tears, eh, Shrig?"

"Eggs-ackly, sir! Vich is only to be expected, seeing as how I found her clasping the dead Earl to her tender buzzum and that same all stained in his blood, like her pretty hands—and never so much as a tear! And seeing as how she cradled said bleeding corpse nor moved though self and Dan'l hauled down his murderer alongside of her as she knelt. So, arter hauling carkiss o' same out of her sight, 'Lady,' I says werry gentle, 'if you could let fall a tear or so 'twill do you a power of good.' She looks up at me most piteous, and, 'Oh, Mr. Shrig,' says she, 'if only I could.' 'Then, my dear lady,' says I, 'if you can say a vord or so o' prayer 'twill do him a power o' good.' And so she did, in a visper, stooping close above him. By now Dan'l had routed out some o' the footmen to carry the Earl to bed, and she rose to follow, and, all a-drip with his blood and looking down at it, says she, 'Oh, Mr. Shrig, if only this could be mine 'stead o' his'n.' Then she follers the dead, leaving a red trail behind her, poor lady!"

"And was this dreadful sight the last you saw of her, Jasper?"

"No, sir; my last glimp' was her dressed all in vite, like an angel, nothing black about her except her hair, and a-holding of my lord's dead hand, but still—never a tear! And she ain't shed none yet, according to my little Gimblet."

"Ah, yes—yes, the boy! Is he still with her?"

"Ar, he's the only living creeter as she allows in sight or sound of her——"

"Then I must see him, Jasper! But when and where?"

"He reports to me at the Raven every arternoon 'twixt three and four o'clock—if possible, vich——" Now at this precise moment Mr. Beeby tapped upon and opened the door to announce:

"A person named Daniel, gentlemen, with the boy Gimblet——"

"Then pray admit them, Beeby!" Almost as the words were uttered, Dan'l appeared, hat in one fist, his other hand upon the drooping shoulder of my lady's little tiger-page, who, despite top-boots and smart hat, showed woefully forlorn and lamb-like.

"Gov'nor and gentlemen," said Dan'l, "we beg to report as lady has departed suddenly to parts unknown. Tell 'em, Gimblet!"

The boy dropped his hat and let this cockaded glory lie unheeded, saying in voice that trembled on the verge of tears:

"She's bolted, Guv'nor! Oh, Jarsper . . . she's run and . . . left me!"

"Left you . . . ?" gasped George. "But why . . . when . . . where has she gone?"

"Oh, sir, I dunno! All as I can tell ye is as she's gone and left me! She comes to me in her bonnet an' ' Goodbye, little Comforter,' she says; ' tell dear Mister Shrig as I'm grateful to him for lending me you '—meaning me. Then she kisses me and I didn't mind 'cos I liked it, ' and,' says she, ' if you see Mister Bell wots now the Earl,' she says, ' give him my love,' says she, ' and tell him 'tis best to forget for the Earl's sake,' she says and how I'm to give you this here, sir."

And from the breast of his smart jacket he drew a folded paper.   Taking this in hands that trembled, George opened it and read :

"This is goodbye to the Earl, but it nearly breaks my poor heart to leave my Mr. Bell.   Yet it is best for your lordship.   I pray God you may love and wed a really noble lady someday instead of this nameless woman who grieves for her beloved dead and will do her best to be worthy of him and his unfailing love."

"Yes," said George grimly, as he refolded this note, "she is gone !   Which means, of course, that I must seek till I find her.   Yes, by God, I will not rest until I find her or——"   He choked—then strode out and away to begin his quest.

CHAPTER XLIX

Which tells of a breaking heart

TEN DAYS have dragged their weary length, and beneath the old pear tree a haggard George sits inert, gazing down dull-eyed at the toes of his riding-boots which, like his rumpled garments, are thick with the dust of long and hard riding.

He heard the quick, light tread of feet, but never stirred until Mistress Isabel stood beside him, then he glanced up at her, but with look of such despair that she stooped to touch his drooping, disconsolate head and enquire very tenderly :

" Still no news, my dear ? "

" Nothing ! " he answered, with a sigh like a groan. " Not a word, never a sign . . . and so I'm afraid, my dear, very . . . dreadfully afraid there never will be ! I've ridden all over Sussex and beyond . . . and all in vain. She's lying dead somewhere . . . in some lonely wood or silent pool ; she must be . . . or I should have found her or had some news. So I think she is surely dead ! The blow that killed the Earl, killed her, too, and now . . . I think is . . . killing me——"

" George, don't ! Oh, don't ! " cried Miss Isabel, falling on her knees the better to comfort him. " Oh, my poor, dear boy, don't say or even think such dreadful things ! Your Clytie lives—I know, I feel it——"

" Why—why did she leave me ? " he muttered brokenly. " All these days . . . and nights . . . of torture ! "

" I know, my dear, I know."

" If I could only sleep properly, but . . . every time I dream I see her dead and wake sick with horror. And this ghastly fear is with me in the daytime now ! So day is haunted like the night, and I . . . can't bear it much longer——"

"George, dear—dear George, don't break your heart—never lose ho᠊e! She will come back, I know she will! Then besides Jasper Shrig . . . Charles is searching with all his many agents——"

"Yes, dear; good old Charles! Yet this makes me the more hopeless—for with so many searching we should have had some news of her long ago—had she been alive!"

"Has our old Hagah returned yet?"

"No, her cottage is still deserted.

"Well, I feel convinced—if there is anyone in this world who can best help to find your lost one it is Hagah! So watch for her return."

"Ah, my dear," he replied hopelessly, "I never pass the place without stopping and always find it empty and desolate . . . . The whole world has become a desolation! You have Charles now, thank God, for should Clytie be dead, then—if heart can break, mine will, and so much the better because without her I can't live! Not that I wish to die, but merely because I must. Every day I feel this more and know it more certainly. It is as if she were dead and her spirit calling mine . . . and so I'm hoping this call won't be in vain. So——"

"George, have done! Such preposterous fiddle-faddle! Such wicked nonsense! Stop it this moment! Cease, I command you!" said Miss Isabel with all her old imperiousness—but dropping a tear on his haggard brow; whereat he kissed her and contrived a laugh more dismal than a moan, as he said:

"Dear Madam Tyrant, beware! Hither cometh one shall order and command thee anon, to wit—thy soon-to-be lord and master! Greeting, Charles. Another day of failure for us, it seems."

"The day is not done yet, George."

"No, there are some hours before sunset, thank God! I shall be off again so soon as the Sagamore has had a feed. Lord knows he's earned it! How does our invalid today Charles? How is poor old Corks?"

"Better and better, George! There is now no longer any

danger of a relapse ; he should mend apace. I left him sitting up trying to write to Joan, but, hearing your voice, he desired me to say he 'begged a dooced word' with you."

"Charles, you and my belle aunt have saved his life, which merely proves what a marvellous pair you are—though, mark you, she's a tyrant, old fellow ! She has been bullying me without mercy. She needs a strong man's hand, Charles, and kisses thereafter ! However, I leave you to cope with her, and God bless you both ! " With a visible effort, George rose and plodded wearily indoors. Scarcely had he gone than Mistress Isabel sobbed :

"Oh, Charles, my dear . . . my dear ! " and clung to him like the terrified woman she was—shaken by a fear unknown till lately, a dread that had been growing and now found utterance in these arms that were to become her refuge. "Oh, Charles, he is . . . dying ! Yes, dying upon his feet ! He seldom eats and . . . when I wake in the night, as I do so often lately, I hear him stirring. And sometimes he goes stealing into the darkness . . . to Sagamore, and rides away on his never-ending quest. If Clytie is not found soon . . . soon . . . Oh, Charles, comfort me . . . ! "

Meanwhile George trudged indoors and, mounting the stairs, paused at a certain door to square his shoulders, knocked and entered the invalid's room, saying cheerily as possible :

"How goes it, Corks, old hearty ? "

"Dooced splendidly marvellous, old f'lo' ! " answered the pale shadow of my lord Viscount, smiling brightly amid his many pillows. "But what of you, George ? B'gad, y' look as dusty as a confounded miller ! Any news of Clytie ? dooce take her ! "

"Not yet, Corks. After all, it's only been . . . ten days or so . . . And you are really better, Charles says."

"Yes, strong as a horse, almost ! I began to mend the moment your beloved aunt had me carted here, bless her ! What with her care, Charles's doctoring, and my Joan's devotion, I shall be straddling Thunderbolt pretty soon.

And, by the way, George, what I wanted to say is—I'm no end glad you've turned out to be the Earl; amazing fact——"

"But I'm not and don't intend to be. This very confounded heritage is yours and shall be. You were born and bred up to it and so——"

"George, my dear old ass, if the law says you're a dooced earl, a dooced earl you are and must be; there's no jibbing or balking the fact. Besides, I could never fill adequately the place of my . . . my splendid father, but you might, almost. Don't shake your confounded noddle at me, George, for the law is the law, and, such being so —so it is and must be——"

"I'm wondering how the devil you know about it, Corks. I thought I had pledged Shrig and Jackman to keep it dark. How did you?"

"Mum, George, mum! A little bird and so on——"

"Ah, Shrig's young imp, I guess! Oh, well, what matter, for as I say——"

"Hark, old f'lo'! Who's down there in the garden?"

"Aunt Isabel and Charles."

"Ah yes, but—she's there, too, my Joan! Can't you hear her? I do! Give her a hail for me out of the window."

"I'll do better. I'll send her up to you, Corks." So down went George to greet a radiant Joan, who, at his word, sped lightly up the stairs. . . .

"Oh, my dear," cried Miss Isabel, "you are not going out again?"

"Yes, yes, of course, I must."

"But supper will be ready soon! I'll hurry it."

"Thanks," said George, his haggard gaze turned stablewards, "I couldn't."

"And you were away at teatime! Did you have anything to eat?"

"I don't remember."

"Then let me make you a sandwich, just one——"

"Isabel, my blessed Aunt, I should choke. I'll eat like

an alderman when I'm hungry, but now," said he, kissing her anxious face, " wish me luck."

" Ah, my dear, I'll pray for you."

So George came to the stable, tightened the Sagamore's saddle-girth and was about to mount when Charles called on him to wait, saying :

" George, your aunt believes you are dying."

" So do I, old fellow, and the sooner the better."

" Have you no least consideration for her feelings, George ? "

" Yes, God knows I have ! "

" Then, in His name, show it for her sake."

" How so ? Tell me—how ? "

" By eating whether you want to or no. By seeming less doleful than you are, hiding your pain lest she suffer with you—as she is doing ! By acting the part of——"

" Charles, I have never acted or made pretence with Aunt Isabel ; I should scorn to ! Besides, she'd know it at once ! "

" However, George, it is a man who hides his grief ; it is a boy who parades it ! "

" Do I parade it, Charles ? Yes . . . perhaps I do—though quite unwittingly. I answer her questions and tell her my troubles as I have always done, though never such blasting trouble as this. Yes, you are right, the time for my boyish confidences has passed, I must be dumb hereafter, for her beloved sake and, by Jupiter, I will ! And, dear Charles, God only knows how infinitely glad I am that she has you to go beside her all the way, a long, happy way, I hope. And now, old fellow, I am heartily grateful for your advice, henceforth she shall hear no more repining and I'll eat when she will—even though it nauseates me."

Then George mounted, rather clumsily, like the weary fellow he was, but reached down to grasp the hand Charles proffered, with the words :

" God bless and give her back to you, George ! "

" Amen ! " he sighed, and rode away on that quest which he knew would end only with his life.

CHAPTER L

Which ends this narration, and, it is hoped, satisfactorily

TO SEARCH until he found her, which it seemed was never to be. Therefore George despaired, and, having no idea whither now to ride on such hopeless quest, dropped the reins and left choice of direction to the Sagamore, who, perfectly aware of this, tossed his noble crest and set off at a brisk though easy canter.

And as George rode thus chin on breast, heedless of how, when or where, he pondered—not his grief and dreary future, but the words Charles had uttered so gently yet so very forcefully, thus :

" A man hides his grief ; a boy parades it."

This led him to the thought which had haunted him so persistently of late : if death had indeed claimed his beloved, as he now believed, why wait for the same dark Angel to summon him ? Why not seek him out, with the hope and faith that this Angel would lead and guide him to wheresoever—she—awaited him ? Even as his grandsire, the seventh Earl, had done upon his cousin's sword-point. Suicide, then, was in the family with many other sins ! But was suicide a sin . . . ? "

Thus George rode in earnest debate with himself until the Sagamore halted at last and whinnied softly to draw attention to the fact. Then George lifted heavy head, glanced up and espied a wisp of blue smoke uprising from a weather-beaten old chimney . . . above a thatched roof bowered amid trees. For a moment or so he gazed at this, scarce heeding, then drew a deep breath . . . for this was the chimney of old Hagah's cottage, and that wisp of smoke might mean . . . anything . . . depth of abiding sorrow or fullness of life and infinite joy . . . which ?

So, fearful, George hesitated. Not so the Sagamore, for with smooth, long stride he advanced until the cottage was in full view. He drew nearer until George, stooping, could peer through the lattice—and thus beheld a face peering out at him. Then the casement was flung wide and old Hagah exclaimed :

"George! Now for the dear Lord's sake what ails ye? So thin, so pale as a poor ghost! And the agony as looks on me from y'r eyes! George—what is it?"

"Death, Hagah—I hope!"

"Stuff and nonsense, m' dear! What talk be this o' death and you so young and strong wi' life?"

"An empty life, Hagah dear, a desolation, for I've lost Clytie and I'm dying for her! I've been seeking her day and night . . . ever since she left me . . . and now, at last, I believe she is . . . dead, and if she is . . . I shall be glad to die, for . . . oh, Hagah, I can never live without her and so——"

From dim interior of the cottage rose an inarticulate cry, a rush of passionate movement, and to him, with arms outstretched, leapt Clytie, no longer inarticulate but talking, laughing, weeping :

"Oh, then, my George . . . my beloved one, take me . . . love me . . . never let me go, for . . . I am dying, too. . . ."

Somehow George was off his horse—they were in each other's arms, gazing at one another in an ecstasy far beyond speech. Thus for a while they were mute, so rapt in the bliss of their reunion that they did not even kiss ; for the present they were content with each other's nearness and awed by the wonder of their joy. Clytie it was who spoke at last :

"George, this strange love of ours must be quite terrible that it could kill us as it was doing!"

"No, the lack of it!" he said as, thus embraced, they drew fresh life and strength one from the other. "Without love we should certainly die! And this is the only kind of love for such as we."

"Such as we!" she repeated, as they gazed entranced eye to eye. "We who first mistook our love for hate! We who are sure it could be our death! We who know at last that it is our very life!"

Beside the cottage door was a time-worn bench, and here they sat to gaze upon each other in the sunset glow, conscious only of one another and in a silent beatitude.

"Why did you leave me?" he enquired at last.

"Oh, George, when I found—him—lying beneath the dead—and himself so terribly dead, the whole world seemed a desolation! And when I heard you were the Earl and I the poor, nameless creature I still am—ah, then I was utterly lost, hopeless, and it was then Hagah found me . . . just in time."

"So God bless her!" murmured George fervently. "But, oh, Clytie, Clytie, how foolish, how wicked of you to run away, allowing your cruel pride to afflict us both with such anguish, such frightful dread and anxiety! By heavens, woman, your damned pride might have killed us both, was killing us, slowly torturing us to death! Wasn't it?"

"Yes," she answered, "with every breath."

"Well now for this, my Lady Prideful Folly, you deserve to be spanked——"

"Yes, but—not now!" she sighed meekly. "Kiss me instead, and comfort your poor, nameless woman."

"Firstly, she is not nameless because she is my lady Clytie and always will be. Secondly, she is not poor but an extremely rich person, thanks to a provision in the Earl's will. And thirdly, the only thing that matters to me in all this world, is the fact that—you are—you!" Now at this, nestling close, she kissed him as she thought he deserved. . . .

Down went the sun—but they never noticed; forth stole the shadows—but they never heeded, and both so still and silent in their profound happiness that they might have been asleep, until:

George sniffed! He lifted his head from where it had lain so sweetly pillowed and—sniffed, not because he

wept or had taken cold, either, for, borne to him in this
dewy twilight came a fragrance sweeter and more alluring,
just then, than breath of flowers or all the vaunted spices
of the Orient.

" Clytie," he murmured, " I smell ham—frying ! "

" No, George, only bacon ; all we can offer you."

" Only !   Bacon ! " he repeated in awed tone.

" There will be eggs—I think ; and tea, of course."

" Eggs ! " quoth he in a muted ecstasy.   " Oh, Clytie,
I haven't been hungry for weeks ! "

" Nor I, George ! "

" Yet the marvel is, my Clytie, I'm perfectly ravenous
all of a sudden."

" And I'm famishing, George."   Out from the casement
nearby came Hagah's small head to say :

" Then, my silly children, come and eat."

" Eat it is ! " laughed George, lifting Clytie afoot with
sudden joyous strength.   Then indoors they went, to find
the table laid with snowy cloth and thereon a great dish of
fragrant ham bedecked with golden-yoked eggs.   George
gazed at this yearningly, then, picking up their little aged
hostess, kissed her repeatedly, saying :

" Oh, Hagah, my dear, where should I be now—and
where my beloved Clytie but for you ? "

" Ha' done, George ! " she laughed.   " Where I would
be is on my feet and where you should be is sitting to the
good food.   You two children as love each other so
foolish fond to die of it ! Love be a disease wi' the pair o'
ye—but marriage shall cure ye—mebbe ! "

" Never in this life ! said George, gazing at Clytie.

" Nor in any other ! " said Clytie, returning his adoring
look as fervently.

" Ah well, let's hope so ! " quoth old Hagah.   " But
now, m'dears, set ee down and eat and the kind Lord o'
love and life bless ye ! "

So down they sat, all three, and eat George did, in a
blissful silence, yet even so, glancing up very often from
the delicious food on his plate to the delicious loveliness

seated opposite, who, meeting his glance, forgot to eat until urged thereto by Hagah.

"And now," said George, when at last his hunger was satisfied, "pray tell me how you met each other and why I find Clytie here with you, my dear?"

"Well," answered Hagah, with quick, warning glance at Clytie, "she came to me here one night, a woeful, lost creature, afraid o' the dark——"

"But far more afraid of—myself!" said Clytie.

"Nay, now, m' dear, why talk o' that?"

"Because George shall know exactly what kind of woman he will marry. Oh, George, I meant to die! Having lost all I loved and not knowing where to go, I should have killed myself had not Hagah found me in time and comforted me—like the dear angel of goodness she is!"

"Yes," said George, reverently, "she has always been my good angel." Here he took Hagah's small, bony hand and raised it to his lips. "Yes, ever since you saved my infant life! And now you have saved my Clytie for me——"

"From the dreadful sin of self-murder, George! Are you ashamed of your wicked, craven woman?"

"Clytie, are you ashamed of your wicked, cowardly man who thought of doing the very same?"

"And 'tis ashamed ye should be, ay—both o' ye!" exclaimed Hagah. "So now, 'stead o' talking o' such past evil, have some more o' my precious tay; pass your cups, both o' ye!"

"Thanks, my blessed dear——"

"And since ye must talk, talk o' something better."

"Very well, I'll talk of you and Clytie. Tell me where you have been hiding all this grievous time, Hagah?"

"Eh?" she demanded, suddenly crouched and witch-like. "Hiding is it? Aha! 'Twas in a fair place, a good place, a safe place! But where 'tis—I forgets to remember, and 'tis place as my lady Clytie shall remember to forget, 'cording to her promise! Eh, m' dearie-sweeting, eh?"

" According to promise, Hagah dear. So there is no need to play witch, though indeed I love you however you are, and always shall ! " said Clytie, kissing her.

" But, George, this I can tell you," nodded Hagah. " That Shrig man came very nigh finding us, drat him ! Ah well—how do you like being the Earl ? "

" So little, my dear, that I don't intend to be——"

" Ah, fool George ! " she cried fiercely. " You are, you must and shall be ! You, the Red, shall make an end o' the Black Wynter, at last—for good and all ! "

" But suppose," said George, glancing at Clytie's night-black tresses, " I should . . . someday . . . have a . . . black-haired son ? How then ? "

" Ye be a counting y'r chicks afore they'm hatched, Mast' Jarge, m'lord ! And if so be—can evil come out o' good ? Hows'ever 'tis as the kind God wills ! And now, Mast' Jarge, 'tis time ye carried your lady home and left th' owd witch to her tom-cat, her fire and her dreams. Hearkee—yonder—theer be Saint Mark telling the hour ! "

To them through the open lattice, borne upon the warm, still air of this midsummer night came that long familiar chime :

" Half-past nine ! " sighed George. " Aunt Isabel will be growing anxious ! Clytie, we must go—and, by Jove and Jupiter, what a welcome she will give you ! "

" Will she, George ? Oh, but Hagah dear, I hate leaving you all alone——"

" Tush, child, I'm used to it——"

" But you must promise to visit us at Sparklebrook."

" Not merely visit," said George, " but stay and soon or I'll ride over and carry you there, I swear it by George —the George who loves you, Hagah ! "

" Ay, I'll come, m' dears, and bide a while and be glad to, till the day as Parson Aeneas says you into one, man and wife. So for a while, goodbye, and the kind Lord have ye in His love and care."

And presently, as the moon rose to light them, George,

having tightened the Sagamore's girth, swung blithely to saddle, thence reaching down both eager arms murmured :

" Clytie, your pretty foot on mine—so, your dear hands in mine—now . . . beloved, up with you to my heart ! "

Lightly she mounted, and, lying thus in his close embrace, sighed happily :

" Oh, dearest of all men, surely there never was, there never can be such love as ours ! "

" Never ! " quoth George fervently as the Sagamore, aware of his precious burden, moved forward at sedate pace. " Never ! " said George again. " Never in all this glorious world was such love as this of ours ! "

And, bless them, they believed it !

So thus with Clytie upon his heart, they took that road which was to bring them to love's fulfilment and the inevitable joys, sorrows and tribulations of that stern reality called Life.

*　　*　　*　　*　　*

Now might be told how and why Ravenhurst village decked itself in garlands, why old Jabez donned his best (and only) beaver hat, how gaily Saint Mark pealed his bells, and how the Reverend Aeneas, doleful of visage though merry of eye, spoke the words that made two— one.

But your author is uneasily aware how much too long and possibly how prolix this narrative has become. Therefore here, with glad-eyed George, his beautiful Countess, and all other characters he has brought together, hoping for your interest and sympathy, he bids each and every kindly patient reader a hearty and sincere

Farewell.